MALTESE ATTACK

BOOK 1 OF THE ONE HUNDRED YEARS OF WAR SERIES

JAY PERIN

For permission requests and any other info, please email: ***books@EastRiverBooks.com***

Publisher's Cataloging-In-Publication Data
(Prepared by The Donohue Group, Inc.)
Names: Perin, Jay, author.
Title: The Maltese attack / Jay Perin.
Description: [New York, New York] : [East River Books], [2021] | Series: [One hundred years of war]
Identifiers: ISBN 9781736468012 (paperback) | ISBN 9781736468005 (ebook)
Subjects: LCSH: United States--History--1969---Fiction. | Middle East--History--20th century--Fiction. | Petroleum industry and trade--Middle East--History--20th century--Fiction. | Families--Fiction. | Mahābhārata--Adaptations. | LCGFT: Political fiction. | Thrillers (Fiction)
Classification: LCC PS3616.E7443 M35 2021 (print) | LCC PS3616.E7443 (ebook) | DDC 813/.6--dc23

Editors:
Chase Nottingham
Elizabeth Roderick *http://talesfrompurgatory.com/*

Cover: *www.ebookorprint.com*
Maps and illustrations: Murat Bayazit
Video (book trailer): Nauman Gandhi
Special Mention: Marcus Jordan *https://www.marcusjordanart.com/*
Ashley Redbird *http://www.redbird-designs.net/*

www.EastRiverBooks.com

To Bards, to Minstrels, to the Poets of Old;

To Vyasa, to Homer, to Scheherazade;

To Every Storyteller Who Has Gone Before.

Table of Contents

Cast of Characters

Temple – the senior senator from New Jersey, friend to the Sheppards and the Barronses

Delilah "Lilah" Sheppard – daughter of the former U.S. Special Envoy to the Middle East

Harry Sheppard – son of a small-time oil driller in Libya, American expat

Daniel Sheppard – Lilah's twin

Andrew Barrons – Lilah and Daniel's brother-in-law, billionaire oilman from New York

Ryan Sheppard – father to Harry (and his brother and sister), owns a small oil company in Libya called Genesis

Caroline Barrons – half-sister to Lilah and Daniel, married to Andrew

Sophia Sheppard – mother to Harry and his two siblings

Saeed al-Obeidi – Harry's friend and part-time rig worker at Genesis

Dante Maro – secretary to Harry's father

Colonel Sheffield Parker – American expat

The al-Obeidi tribe and Khadeeja – Saeed al-Obeidi's family

Jared Sanders – owner of Sanders, Incorporated, political enemy to Senator Temple

Chapter 1

January 1974

Egypt-Libya border

The blades of the search-and-rescue helicopter thwacked the salty air above the Mediterranean coast, creating a staccato rhythm. The choppy engine was also whirring loud enough to drown out thoughts. Hot wind gusted into Temple's eyes as he leaned out from the open cabin, squinting at the steep, sparsely vegetated cliff marking the border between the two countries.

Trucks, vans, and cars, bound for Alexandria, idled along Halfaya Pass. Inspecting the vehicles, Libyan soldiers swarmed their side of the border and paid no attention to the American chopper hovering one thousand feet above.

"Aren't they supposed to ask us for identification?" Temple hollered into the mouthpiece, swatting at his billowing shirt.

His headset sputtered. "No one cares as long as we stay in Egyptian airspace," said the pilot. "They've gotten used to us." The operation to find the two abducted teenagers had been in effect for months.

Temple grimaced and withdrew his head into the cabin, not looking forward to the conversation he was expecting to have with the teens' families when he landed. As a U.S. senator, he'd known the political situation was unstable. Dammit, he'd warned the families, told them to get out. He'd alerted them enemies were hiding amid the chaos, waiting for a chance to exact revenge. They'd stayed in the country, anyway. Men with the power to stop the criminals were indifferent to the potential for trouble and refused to act. No one—not a single soul—had been willing to sacrifice profit or safety to battle evil. Two young people paid the price for the stubborn stupidity of their guardians. Innocent blood was shed because of the greed and cowardly apathy of those who should've known better.

Gaddafi—the Libyan dictator—denied responsibility for the kidnapping of the former ambassador's sixteen-year-old daughter and her friend. But his government refused to let American personnel conduct a search within the country's borders. Instead, they presented to the U.S. government several mercenaries involved in the crime, claiming to have apprehended them after an exhaustive hunt. The criminals insisted the hostages escaped, the boy having killed one of the guards.

Since then, there was one phone call from the boy, suggesting they were on their way to the Egyptian city of Alexandria. In the weeks after, the United States military kept reconnaissance flights going along Halfaya Pass, the closest border crossing to the city, and intelligence sources in the Middle East were alerted to look out for the kids, but no one spotted them. Chances were they were dead. It was time to call off the search. Senator Temple—as a friend of the families—was asked to fly to Egypt and persuade them to quietly accept reality.

Before he could say anything, he ran into the girl's twin brother. Apparently, it was the twins' seventeenth birthday that day. The silent desperation in the boy's eyes compelled Temple into volunteering to join this flight. Not to mention the splinter of guilt in his own heart at the knowledge he, too, played an inadvertent role in the tragedy. The pilot was surprised, to say the least. He never expected to have a U.S. senator for his partner even if the cargo they were trying to retrieve included the child of a diplomat.

This would be the last such flight, Temple promised himself. Enough time and money were wasted on this futile operation. The kids were surely dead. After all, there were many ways for a young person to die in the North African country... the unforgiving Sahara Desert, its animals, the warlords who ruled the villages, and very often, the brutal government. All anyone could do now was pray their deaths had been painless.

"Senator." The pilot's shout interrupted Temple's train of morbid thoughts. "I think that's Lilah."

"*What?*" Temple grabbed the military-issue binoculars by his side. One hand clenched around the doorframe, he leaned out to check. The sandy wind whipped around him and pulled taut the safety line securing him to the chopper. Blinking away the grit, Temple peered through the lenses.

Gaddafi's border patrol was still detaining all vehicles on the hilly pass. Soldiers separated men from women, holding all of them away from the caravan. There were quite a few camels and donkeys, the owners gripping their leashes as the patrol conducted the inspection. "Where?" Temple asked.

"Not with the crowd, sir. Check the port side. Look for yellow clothes. She's dressed local."

There. A figure ran between boulders, her robes flying behind. The girl was a couple of hundred feet from the group under inspection, concealing herself behind the limestone formations. She looked up at the chopper before plastering herself to the side of a rock.

The brief glimpse was enough. The young girl in the photograph... a picture taken at some school dance... *Oh, my God! It's her. Lilah.* "What about the boy?" Temple asked urgently. "There were two kids."

"Could be with the caravan. Let me—" The pilot stopped to curse. "We have a problem, Senator."

"I see it." One of the Libyan soldiers had detached himself from his team to follow Lilah. If she got caught, there was little a single search-and-rescue chopper could do to help. Temple grabbed the rifle from the other seat. "Hold position and inform the ground team."

"You're not likely to get that fellow with an AK-47," warned the pilot, twisting around in his seat. "Not the best weapon to use against a moving target from a chopper. *And* they'll shoot back."

Plus, the U.S. government would have a hell of a time explaining why the senior senator from New Jersey shot a member of the Libyan armed forces. "I'm not trying to kill him," Temple said. "All we need to do is distract the border patrol for a couple of minutes. We'll buy the girl some time to hide. Get us out of here the second I fire."

His fingers trembled when he took aim. Temple's stint in the army between world wars never involved active combat. The helicopter shuddered. With a gasp, he tumbled back into the seat. Sweat trickled down his neck, a sour stench saturating the muggy air inside the cabin.

When Temple scrambled to recheck the terrain, Lilah was not where she'd been, but her yellow robes made her easy to spot even behind the rocks at the far border of an open space. The soldier in pursuit sprinted across the clearing toward Lilah. Temple swore and again took aim.

Before he could press the trigger, red-orange fire mushroomed on the ground. A blast reverberated its way up to the chopper. The soldier's body disintegrated, ripped into pieces and scattered across the terrain. Temple's mouth fell open. Sounds struggled to escape.

The headset sputtered again. "Minefield," said the pilot, voice terse. "Lucky girl."

Lucky? Lilah was retracing her steps, keeping herself hidden by the boulders, out of sight of the officers running to the scene. There was no hesitation in her gait. Temple watched, his heart thundering. What the devil had just happened? Did the man accidentally walk to his death, or was he led to the landmines? How could she have known there were explosives buried in the clearing? Why would the young lady even be aware of the existence of such dirty weapons?

The girl was born to a diplomat, raised in an intellectual environment. Sweet and loving and bright from what her twin brother said but stubborn as a mule according to the rest of her family. Lilah had never been exposed to the rougher elements of society, much less to violent death. Yet she didn't pause in shock at the grisly end to the soldier hunting her.

The border patrol gathered at the edge of the open space, their attention on the remains of their comrade. No one ventured close. Behind their backs, Lilah rejoined the convoy and climbed into a pickup truck, her movements quick and sure.

"The Libyans claim we're encroaching their airspace," said the pilot. "They're trying to stop us from us seeing any more than we already have."

Probably, but it didn't matter. There was nothing more Temple could do at the moment. Lilah was back with the convoy. On her way to safety, hopefully. "Land us before they shoot," ordered Temple.

The pilot set the chopper down on the Egyptian side, a few feet from the exit point where the families of the kidnapped teenagers waited. Temple jogged out from under the blades to join them. Craggy rocks blocked their view of the events behind the border gate, but vans and cars packed with traders and their wares were inching past. It appeared the loss of a soldier in the mine explosion shifted the border patrol's focus, and the weary travelers were finally allowed to leave. The pickup truck Lilah climbed into lagged at the tail end of the caravan and was still waiting to make it through.

"Did you see Harry?" asked one of the men, voice eager.

"Only Lilah," Temple admitted to Harry's father. "We didn't have a chance—" Another chopper appeared in the cloudless sky with no insignia to suggest American or Egyptian military. It didn't look Libyan, either. "Who the hell—"

A boulder exploded on the pass, raining large, sharp pieces of rock all around them. Fire shot into the sky, and flames engulfed the vehicles. The ground shook with a loud boom. "Bomb," someone shouted.

Screaming men and women stampeded, carrying crying children. A short, plump figure covered entirely in a black *burka* emerged from the blaze, screeching nonstop. Temple tried to leap out of the way, but she careened straight into him and knocked him to his knees. Still shrieking, the woman continued to run. Repeated explosions drowned out the roar of the chopper overhead. The air reeked of molten metal and burning plastic.

Temple spotted Lilah behind the gate. Even with the monstrous flames, there was still room for her to run to safety. "Hurry," he tried to yell, his throat closing in panic. But she pivoted as though preparing to return to the Libyan side.

"Harry," bellowed the boy's father.

Bodies—human and animal—rushed past, impeding Temple's vision, and he had to strain to see. On top of a twenty-foot drop partly obscured by the blaze and the grimy air, there was a dark form. Harry Sheppard, the second kid.

"Lilah!" Harry screamed. Behind the boy, Libyan soldiers scaled the rocks, cornering him on the cliff that marked the border with Egypt.

Lilah looked up at the sound of her name. Flames engulfed the gate in front of her. Temple clambered to his feet, his attention on the girl trapped on the Libyan side by the burning gate. Wind slammed into the rocks; flames spiraled to the sky. Lilah disappeared from Temple's view.

Chapter 2

Two years earlier, March 1972

Paris, France

"Cherry blossoms." Lilah sniffed, loving the sweet scent of the blooms mixed with the smell of fresh-cut grass. The pink flowers were everywhere... on the trees, drifting through the air in the gentle wind, carpeting the ground. A few feet from her, the Eiffel Tower loomed against blue sky, tufts of white clouds floating around its tip.

Before her father's retirement from the state department, Lilah traveled a lot—more than most other fifteen-year-olds. But she'd never been to France before. How cool was it that her first trip to the country was with her best friend, Harry? Well, his family, too. But today, it would be just the two of them. Without even waiting for breakfast, they'd left a note and snuck out of the hotel before anyone noticed they were gone. Dan, her brother, knew, but they were twins, and twins were *obligated* to cover for each other.

Her morning just couldn't get any better. Or more French. There was a couple by a hedge, shoving their tongues into each other's mouths. A man in a black beret and striped tee sat on one of the park benches, playing a few tentative notes on his accordion. The song sounded familiar. Tilting her head, Lilah tried to place it.

Harry followed her gaze to the musician. "Stairway to Heaven," he crooned, his voice rich and deep as he sang Led

Zeppelin's hit.

For the millionth time, Lilah wished she could sing like Harry. Whenever she attempted even the simplest tune, her vocal cords went to war with each other. Dan once bluntly said people would pay her money to stop. The only one who ever put up with it was Harry, but she didn't want to start the day with an assault on his eardrums.

Still singing, Harry did a quick whirl and a shuffle. "Wanna dance?"

Lilah swayed in time with the accordion music and flapped her elbows.

An eyebrow raised in challenge, he asked, "It's all you have, Princess?"

"*Don't* call me—" The nickname was a favorite taunt with some of the kids in her class, and Harry *knew* she hated it. He was simply needling her into—

"Prin... cess," he chanted.

Clapping her hands twice, she executed neat kicks to the side and came to a stop in what she hoped was an elegant pose. She threw in a bit of twist. The chunky heel of one of her brand-new ankle boots sank into the wet grass. She stumbled, barely stopping herself from going nose down on the ground. When she sneaked a glance at Harry, his arms were outstretched to catch her.

Stuffing his hands into his pant pockets, he chortled.

Lilah made a face at him before kicking off the boots and pirouetting on one foot. Cold wetness squished between her toes. The dew on the grass seeped through her tights. "*Eek.*" She lurched to a stop. "You always talk me into doing ridiculous things... and now, look!"

Mischief lit up his coffee-colored eyes. "It takes real talent to be successfully ridiculous."

The cool breeze gusted, ruffling the dark hair brushing his collar and sneaking under the neckline of Lilah's dress. She shivered.

"Here." Harry shrugged off his bomber jacket. "I told you Paris is still cold in March. You should've bundled up instead of wearing that silly outfit."

What? She'd packed the peasant dress in her favorite red only to impress Harry. Her slightly wavy hair—so black it was almost blue as a classmate once said—was brushed until the tresses shone. A narrow headband was tied hippie-fashion. She even used her new kohl pencil. Thanks to her Indian mother and Irish-American father, Lilah would never need to spend a penny on tans, and most people seemed to find the contrast between her light-brown skin and hazel eyes appealing. Wasn't Harry in the least tempted?

But then, Harry wasn't *most people.* He'd known her since they were in diapers. Their parents had been friends since when Harry's father approached Lilah's papa for assistance with his flailing oil business in the Middle East. The men shared the same last name and an ancestor who immigrated to America back in the sixteen-hundreds, but their friendship transcended the tenuous connections. Papa might have retired from the state department and taken his family back to Brooklyn, but the families vacationed together at least once a year, usually on the long winter break

Harry got at the American school in Libya.

Over the last couple of visits, though... Lilah ended up smacking herself in the head a few dozen times to stop the bizarre impulse to run her fingers through his hair. Whenever he sauntered by, she had to grit her teeth to overcome the itch in her chest to breathe in his scent.

The idiot boy seemed content arguing about the Beatles and debating the war in Vietnam and discussing life after high school. Harry already knew Lilah's eyes were set on Harvard Law, and she was now familiar with all the ways to get into the SEAL program. He decided Maritime College in New York and the navy ROTC—reserve officers' training corps—was his best route to his dream career. Besides all this, Harry had plans to take Genesis Oil from the few wells in Libya to "the biggest, most badass" drilling company in the world.

Plus, Harry went out of his way to... *Argh.* Lilah's fingers still twitched with the urge to box his ears at the thought of the snake he gifted her on her fourteenth birthday. He'd actually imagined the prank was funny! Oh, she made him pay. She owed it to her future self as a lawyer. He apologized a *million* times before Lilah deigned to utter a friendly word. Still, she had to accept reality. A gallon of chocolate ice cream and a sobbing spell into her pillow later, Lilah resigned herself to the fact that the stupid, *stupid* boy would never see her as anything other than his buddy.

Then, Harry and the rest of the Sheppards unexpectedly arrived in the States on spring break. They'd planned a detour to Paris before returning to Libya and asked Lilah's family to join them. Her parents agreed but needed to go to India first to visit an ailing relative. Lilah and Dan would fly straight to France with

Harry and his family, and the twins' parents would reach the city in a couple of days.

The afternoon before they flew out, Harry made a confession. He liked her... *like*-liked her, not *only*-liked her as he did all these years. When he threw a nervous "Well?" in Lilah's direction, something in her chest took flight. Her lips curved up in joy, and the familiar grin lit up his face. Neither of them said a word, but they didn't have to.

Or so Lilah thought. She should've made things clear right away. If she did, Harry wouldn't have been acting as though the mumbled conversation never happened.

He hadn't taken much trouble with his appearance on this morning's trek to the Eiffel Tower. His flared jeans were frayed at the hem and stained with oil. The long-sleeved, yellow shirt fit him well, but Lilah remembered seeing him in it the year before. The dark-blue bomber he was holding out to Lilah as protection against the chill was a varsity jacket with a wrestling patch on its sleeve.

No, he didn't seem to care how he looked. More to the point, he apparently didn't give two bits how *Lilah* looked. With an inner hmph, Lilah yanked the jacket from his hand and pushed her arms through the sleeves. Her legs were long, but Harry was several inches taller with build to match. His jacket hung on her shoulders, concealing the figure her mid-thigh dress so lovingly clung to. Not that it mattered... not when the view never impressed him. "Did you change your mind?" she asked. "About liking me?"

"Huh?"

Tucking her chilly hands into the pockets of the jacket, she shrugged. “If you’d rather stay friends, just tell me, okay?” She braced herself for the worst. *Don’t you dare,* she threatened silently. *Or I’ll... I’ll...*

With a ferocious glare, Harry asked, “Why? Did you find someone else?”

Lilah gaped. “In *two* days?”

“You said you want to be just friends.”

“I didn’t say—never mind.” She flounced off in the direction of an empty bench. With each of her steps, water squished out of the bottom of the sodden tights. *Darn it.* She should’ve put her shoes back on.

“Where are you—” A huff, a scuffle.

When Lilah turned, Harry was skirting a couple of blondes in floral pants and matching headbands. Both wore shirts knotted right under their breasts, revealing their entire midriffs. *“Bonjour,”* cooed the blondes, wiggling their fingers.

Harry flashed them his usual charming grin and cooed the same in response.

Wet tights and all, Lilah wheeled around and stomped to the park bench, plunking herself down.

In another couple of seconds, he was standing in front of her. “Your shoes,” he said, thrusting them under her nose.

As she was shoving her feet into the boots, she muttered to herself, “Give *them* your jacket.”

“What?”

Yikes. "Nothing."

"Why should I give them anything? Let them ask their own boyfriends."

Boyfriend? Keeping her eyes on the grass, she asked, "So you haven't changed your mind about us?"

"No!" He collapsed next to her on the bench. "It took me a year to work up enough nerve to tell you. I'm not about to let you go. Not unless you *want* me to."

"*Me?*" Lilah twisted around to face him. "*You* haven't—" She darted a glance at his scuffed sneakers. "Oh, forget it." She didn't really care what he wore, but after his confession, she'd thought... some move, some attempt at lip contact... nothing, nada, not even a longing look. He was driving her crazy.

"You're driving me nuts," Harry complained, leaning forward with his hands gripping the edge of the seat. "I wanted to come to the park so we could..." He flushed. "...uhh... kiss or something, but you'd rather fight."

He continued grumbling, worrying out loud if she said yes only because she didn't want to hurt his feelings. Lilah barely heard the words. Swallowing hard, she said, "I thought *you* didn't want to... you know... kiss."

Harry stared at her in silence for a second or two, then he guffawed. "Are you kidding me? I haven't thought about anything else this last week. Not even the problems with Genesis."

He hadn't? She bit back a grin. Then, his words registered. "What problems with Genesis?"

His eyes clouded over with worry. "Your papa didn't tell

you?"

"No," Lilah said, alarm creeping into her mind. Her parents' savings were tied up in the company. They met when Papa had been the American ambassador to India. A few months after their wedding, they moved to New York, and Harry's father approached, asking for help with Genesis. Having worked his way up the ranks in the state department, Papa wasn't rich like the political appointees, but he invested every spare penny he possessed in the floundering business.

Harry was a newborn at the time, and the ambassador's wife was pregnant with the twins, Lilah and Dan. Even with the injection of cash, the Sheppards' financial situation continued to be precarious, and they dropped Harry off with Lilah's parents. When Lilah's papa was appointed Special Envoy to the Middle East, Harry moved with the family to Tel Aviv and lived there until he turned six. A few years after Harry's parents took him to Libya, Lilah's elderly father retired from the state department, and now, they lived in Brooklyn. Except for Papa's pension and the small salary Lilah's mother got from her job at the United Nations, all their money was in Genesis.

"Gaddafi's goons have been cooking up issue after issue," Harry continued. "New licensing regulations, lightning inspections, demands to sell half the shares to native Libyans... we know what he's after. He wants us to give up and leave so he can take over the wells *we* built with our sweat and blood. He's already driven out some of the other drillers with his antics. Then there's a second dumbass who's trying to buy Genesis Oil for cheap—anyway, Father's hoping your papa can do something."

"Gaddafi won't listen to the U.S. government," Lilah said

instantly.

She kept up with news from the Middle East. Relations between Libya and the United States had soured in recent years. Her papa said there were rumors the American ambassador might soon be recalled. Also, a few weeks ago, Lilah had asked if they could take one of their trips to Libya to meet friends, but Papa and Mama vetoed the idea. They surely didn't think there was any physical risk, or he'd have urged everyone he knew to get out. No, he wasn't worried about their safety in the country, but a vacation there wouldn't be fun this year. He never breathed a word about problems specific to Genesis Oil, though, probably because he didn't want his kids worrying about it.

"That's why my father wanted your papa to come to Paris," said Harry. "They're going to see if they can get the French to talk to the Libyan ambassador. Gaddafi's at least on talking terms with the government here."

"Papa will do everything he can," she soothed. Not simply to protect his investment. Her father always went the extra mile to help people. There had been relatives who commented in Lilah's hearing what her mother—young, exotic, and a lawyer for the United Nations—might have seen in a widower twenty years her senior. The man had a teenaged daughter, to boot—Lilah's half-sister. The Indian lawyer had simply tumbled into love with the kindhearted diplomat at first sight. Lilah's father would give it his all, trying to help Harry's family.

"I know he will," Harry agreed. Another of his mischievous grins lit up his face. "Which is why we should talk about other things. About kissing, for instance."

Heat rushed into her cheeks, and she bit her lower lip, trying not to make any awkward squeaks.

Harry's eyes snapped wide open. "Let's go," he said hoarsely.

"Where?"

"To the tower."

Hand in hand, they ran through the park, managing to avoid colliding with the tourists taking pictures. Someone yelled, but neither Harry nor Lilah paid any heed. Laughing in joy, they got to the street where the shrill sound of bicycle bells mingled with the honking of cars. The aroma of buttery croissants clung to the air.

"Mademoiselle," shouted someone. Something metallic jangled right in front of her nose. With a yelp, Lilah skidded to a stop. Harry stumbled, managing to catch himself before he fell.

"Collier?" asked a skinny black man.

Lilah shook her head in incomprehension. "Wha—"

"Necklace," Harry translated. He knew an *insane* number of languages. Just like Lilah, he'd grown up with English and Arabic and Hebrew, along with the Hindi cuss words he learned from her Indian cousins. He actually *enjoyed* learning new ways to talk to people, taking French lessons and picking up smatterings of Italian and Greek from the European kids who lived in Tripoli.

The peddler rattled what looked like a giant key ring crammed with replicas of the Eiffel Tower. Thin chains hung off each tiny tower.

Lilah was about to decline when Harry said, "Lemme buy you one. A souvenir." Handing the peddler a fistful of coins, Harry took the silver locket and matching chain Lilah pointed out. Words tripping over each other, he recited, "...one thousand and sixty-three feet tall..."

Sweeping her hair aside, she invited him to adorn her neck with the trinket. His lecture faltered to a stop. When he fastened the chain at her nape, his fingers trembled against her skin.

"Are you nervous?" she asked.

"Hell, yeah," he said. "Once we kiss, you won't be just Lilah. You'll be my... uhh... *habibti*."

The Arabic word for "beloved." A shiver went up her spine.

Harry stopped one more time by a garbage can to spit something out. At her questioning look, he flushed. "Gum."

"When did you—"

Eyes filled with yearning, he said, "I can't wait."

Neither could she. They raced up the stairs all the way to the observation deck, where there were already groups of tourists exclaiming over the beauty of Paris.

The city was *gorgeous*. It spread out in front, splotches of green and pink telling them spring was here. Boats sailed lazily on the Seine. The wind *was* nippy as Harry warned. Even with his jacket protecting her, Lilah's teeth chattered.

"Hold on," he said, moving in front of her to block the wind. "Better?"

Not yet. She wanted the kiss he promised. Lilah took a step back, leaning against one of the iron pillars. Harry's hands came up, palms flat on the pillar on either side of her face, holding her there without touching her. Around them, visitors continued laughing, chatting, snapping pictures. No one even glanced in their direction.

"Got to ask," Harry murmured, both his voice and breathing unsteady. "Are you sure?" The sharp longing, the uncertainty over what lay ahead... everything currently churning her insides was reflected in his eyes. At her tentative smile, his eyes zeroed in on her mouth. With a small cough, he bent his head.

Coughing? Why was he coughing? Was she wearing too much perfume? He always said he liked the lotus oil scent, but— "Wait."

Harry jerked back, his hands still on the iron pillar. "What?"

Frantically, Lilah scoured her brain for words. *Do I stink?* No, that would totally kill the moment. Besides, he wasn't coughing anymore. "Which way?"

"Huh?"

"Do we go right or left?"

Confusion on his face, Harry said, "Straight ahead until our lips bump."

Lilah rolled her eyes. "Do we tilt our heads right or left? So our *noses* don't bump, I mean. We have to breathe, right?"

"Uhh... left, I guess."

"Okay," she said and pouted her lips, tilting her head left by about forty-five degrees.

His face descended toward her. His cheeks looked so smooth he had to have shaved in the morning. The sandalwood scent of his cologne filled her nostrils... the perfect amount of fragrance...

not too little, not too much. God, he smelled *good*. How could she have believed he hadn't been thinking of kissing her? He'd even chewed gum.

She never chewed any gum. The mouthwash commercial said the effect lasted for hours, but did it really? What if Harry recoiled in disgust?

"One more thing," Lilah said quickly. Once again, Harry jerked back. "What if I bite you?" she blurted. Harry's mouth dropped open. "Accidentally," she assured him.

"Why don't we do this?" he asked, tone even. "You write out a list of instructions. We can both study it and decide how to proceed."

Lilah stuck out her tongue. How was she supposed to explain all the crazy thoughts suddenly running through her mind? "I'm just trying to make sure I don't do anything stup... that nothing goes..."

"Are *you* nervous?" he asked.

"*Yes.* I've never done it before, and I don't want you thinking I'm horrible at it, *okay?*"

"It's *my* first time, too."

Taken aback, she asked, "Really?" Whenever he visited New York, the girls in Lilah's neighborhood hung all over him.

"I live in Tripoli," Harry pointed out. "They'd chop my head off if I tried to kiss a girl. Also, you..." His gaze drifted down to her mouth. "Can we figure this out together?"

There was no tilting their heads at precisely the right angle, no worry about biting, not even any thought of breathing. The first soft brush of his lips landed on hers. There was a minty taste in her mouth, the smell of him in her breath.

When he lifted his head, she was grateful she was leaning against the pillar. A pulse pounded in her ears.

He was staring bemusedly at her. What was he waiting for? Didn't he realize she wanted him to keep doing it? Her arms came up to circle his neck. With a sigh, she yanked his head back to hers.

He didn't need more persuasion. "Habibti," he murmured, right before claiming her lips a second time. Again and again, they devoured each other.

If any of the other visitors on the deck laughed, Lilah didn't hear them. She couldn't see them. All around her was Harry. His face, his warmth, his whispers. He kept his hands on the pillar, shudders racking his body.

Lilah didn't have a clue how long they stayed on the deck, heading back down only because of the need to eat. From the bakery a few blocks farther, they bought baguette sandwiches. Harry refused to let go of her hand even as they wandered along the sidewalk, munching on the food.

Their chatter would've seemed absurd to those who overheard. Their spurts of happy laughter would've made no sense to anyone except themselves. Every so often, they stopped to kiss... at street corners, on the bridges, waiting for the pedestrian lights to turn on. She didn't have a clue where they were going, and Harry didn't seem to, either.

Sunset brought a drastic drop in temperature, forcing them to return to Hôtel Marceau Champs Elysées, where their families had rooms. The woman at the reception desk looked up as they walked in. Eyes widening, she exclaimed in French.

Harry frowned. "She's saying we finally got home. Guess we got all of them worried."

"We left a note," Lilah said. "Also, *you've* been to Paris before. It's not like we would've gotten lost."

"Doesn't matter. We're still going to be in trouble for sneaking out."

"Papa and Mama are supposed to get here tonight," Lilah said, feeling mildly anxious. "They're going to ground me, for sure."

"Me, too." Stoutly, Harry added, "Well, I'm not sorry."

"Neither am I." They grinned at each other. "Do I look all right?" Lilah asked. She might not regret playing hooky, but she didn't want their families finding out what they'd been up to, either.

Harry assured her there was no untidiness on her person she couldn't blame on the hours spent trekking city streets. "Ready?" he asked, his knuckles poised to knock on the door of room twenty-four.

Before she could respond, the door opened. Harry's older brother, Hector, poked his blond head out. He'd moved out of the family home in Libya many years ago but still opted to come along on this vacation. It *was* a business trip, masquerading as a vacation, so Hector's presence made sense. "Where were you two?" he asked, tone irate.

"Out," Harry said firmly. Hector was twenty-two and a trained boxer, but Harry never let either factor stand in the way of pushing back hard. "Like we usually—"

"Get inside," snapped Hector. "You can stay with Sabrina while I go to the airport." Sabrina was Hector and Harry's eight-year-old sister.

"Heh?" Harry frowned. "What happened to everyone else?" If Hector was on his way to pick up Lilah's parents, any of the rest of the group should've been able to babysit—Harry's father or mother or Lilah's brother, Dan. "Everything okay?" asked Harry.

Hector ptchaaed. "If everything were okay, would I—" He broke off, his blue eyes flicking to Lilah.

"What's going on?" she asked, the trepidation on Hector's face finally registering.

Swallowing visibly, Hector said, "There was something in the news. We don't know for sure if it was your parents' flight, but there was a plane coming from Bombay which crashed into a mountain in Dubai."

Chapter 3

An invisible fist slammed into Lilah's chest, making her stagger. Shock... disbelief... it was a misunderstanding. Her mama and papa were fine. They *had* to be fine, but they always called when they were going to be late. Why hadn't they called? It was almost dinnertime.

When the reporter on the evening news announced there were no survivors, Lilah shook her head. *No.* It couldn't be true. She wept in fear in Harry's arms until a knock came at the door. Gasping and sobbing, Lilah scrambled up and ran to open it. Her parents would be outside, their faces exhausted.

One look at her twin's stark pallor... at the trembling hand he held over his mouth... Lilah knew. His body racked by sobs, Dan called her name. Terror—stomach-churning terror—gripped Lilah. "No," she said, shaking her head. She begged God to let it all be a horrible, horrible nightmare.

The morgue in Dubai... she screamed over and over until she threw up. Adult voices echoed all around, telling Lilah what to do, where to go. Telling her to be strong. Like a puppet, she followed instructions. The faces around her should've been familiar, but except for Harry and Dan, she didn't recognize anyone.

Stumbling out of the airport in New York... the city was so big and scary. At her side, Dan whimpered. When Lilah turned to check, she saw that his eyes were just as lost as hers, his fingers as frozen.

A flash came from across the street. Someone was taking

pictures. A journalist? The untimely end of a former ambassador in a plane crash would've been news back in the States. Her papa and mama's deaths were not for sale. Lilah squared her shoulders and stared unblinkingly at the reporter, refusing to let the vulture capture her devastation on film. Her shoulders shook in agony. She hurt everywhere. In her head, in her heart, in all her body. Harry drew her against his chest, concealing her pain from the rest of the world. His shirt soaked up her silent tears.

A few days later

Green-Wood Cemetery

Brooklyn, New York

Struggling to hold back sobs, Lilah kissed the bronze casket resting majestically under the tree. Morning rain showers left the metal cold and wet against her lips. "Papa," she whispered. She wrapped her arms around the second coffin. *I love you*, she silently told her mama. The void within her chest throbbing painfully, Lilah staggered back under the big, black umbrella she shared with Dan. More light rain suddenly pattered on the nylon, creating a strange song.

Through the fog clouding her mind, she heard one of the mourners murmur, "Death is terrifying enough even under the best of circumstances."

A hushed voice responded, "Poor things... to lose both parents at fifteen... what are they going to do?"

Lilah rubbed a fist over the blazer she wore, trying to ease the deep ache. Wind whistled across the nearby pond and rustled through the trees, shaking loose the yellow flowers from the branches and blowing goosebumps under her thin stockings.

Shivering in the chill, she barely heard the words of the minister as he said the final prayers committing the remains of her parents to the ground.

The string quartet played "Nearer, My God, to Thee" while the caskets were readied to be placed in the graves. One of the pallbearers glanced back at Lilah as though requesting permission... Harry. The drizzle plastered his dark hair to his scalp, and his face was red and blotchy from weeping for the couple who'd been his parents until he turned six. The fellow next to Harry murmured something to him, and the men lowered the boxes carrying Lilah's papa and mama into their final resting place. Shoulders shaking with silent grief under his rain-spattered black jacket, Harry returned to one side and stared straight ahead into the trees.

The minister summoned the twins to the graveside. Dan tossed mud in and returned to the spot next to his sister, his weeping loud and harsh. Cold fingers took the umbrella from Lilah and guided her hand to the mound of earth next to where she stood. Tears. Hot, unstoppable tears. Lilah couldn't see. She didn't *want* to see.

"My dear, everyone's waiting," someone whispered. Gentle hands nudged her forward.

She stumbled to the graves, wet dirt leaking between her fingers. A raw, animal sound reverberated in her head. Someone was crying. Was it her? The fog in her mind got thicker. Her knees buckled.

Harry broke off from the ranks of the pallbearers, his arm catching her around the shoulders. "I'm here," he whispered into her ear.

The mourners didn't stay long after the funeral, and only a few accompanied the orphaned twins back to the Brooklyn brownstone, which was just as well because neither could work up enough energy to talk to anyone. Dan was in the armchair next to the electric fireplace in the living room, staring with puffy eyes at the fake logs.

Lilah sat on the carpet, resting her head on the couch. She scratched at a smudge on the rose-colored rug. Dan spilled spaghetti sauce on it last month, and they'd moved the floral settee an inch to the side to avoid discovery when Papa and Mama got back from dinner. Now, she'd give anything to hear Papa's scolding.

Next to her, collapsed on the rug, Harry stayed quiet. Rain had cleared up, and afternoon sunlight poured in through the shuttered window, throwing slatted shadows on his face. He was probably super tired with all the errands he ran the last couple of days, but there was no mention of taking a nap. "You need something?" he whispered.

Lilah shook her head, the movement causing a pulse to throb above her right eyebrow.

A man thundered from the other end of the room, and the hammering behind her brow became acutely painful. Andrew Barrons, the oil driller married to the twins' half-sister, never bothered to lower his voice. "You're dealing with a lunatic, Ryan," he said. "Get out of Libya. The situation is unstable."

Ryan Sheppard, Harry's father, mumbled an answer.

What? Oh, the problems with Gaddafi. Lilah desperately

wished Andrew would stop. How could he bring up business with Papa and Mama barely in the ground? Yes, Genesis Oil was in trouble, but Ryan needed to grieve, too. He'd been Papa's closest friend.

In the large hall past the living room doors, muted voices offered condolences to Lilah's half-sister, Caroline. Or Mrs. Andrew Barrons, as Caroline preferred to be called. Andrew owned one of the biggest oil companies in the world. With Caroline arranging the entire funeral, everything had been tasteful, including the monochromatic mix of white carnations and mums and lilies decorating the brownstone. Lilah would hate the blooms forever, their sweet fragrance a constant reminder of death.

"We both know about him," Andrew boomed, "rivals disappearing, convenient deaths. Don't risk another confrontation. Just sell it."

Startled out of her mental fog, Lilah threw a questioning glance at Harry. He sat up with a frown and peered at his father. Ryan was murmuring in response to Andrew's alarming advice.

"Who're they talking about?" she whispered. "Gaddafi?"

"Dunno," Harry whispered back. "There's another dumbass... he wants Father to sell the business."

Someone who resorted to killing his rivals? "Andrew's talking crazy, right?" she asked.

"You know how he is," Harry said, watching his father placate the rich and powerful driller.

Andrew did a lot more things in the oil sector other than exploration, but drilling was what the company started with more than a century ago, so the chief executives were stuck with the label of driller. For Andrew, anything to do with business was an emergency. He didn't care the rest of the family was still reeling from the unexpected deaths. He didn't care that the company would be the last thing on Ryan's mind right now. In a week or two, the Sheppards would have to put aside the pain of loss and figure out another way of dealing with the unstable situation in Libya. But not today.

"All right," Andrew huffed. "I'll see what I can do. And don't forget about—" He shot a quick look at Dan.

Ryan nodded, murmuring again.

"We'll talk when you get back to Tripoli," Andrew said.

Something knotted hard in Lilah's chest. What would happen to Dan and her when the Sheppards left? Money, school... Lilah remembered Papa's old lawyer talking to her at the wake, but she never heard a word.

The men stopped by her twin on their way out. Andrew always treated Dan like family. In contrast, Lilah was invisible to both Andrew and Caroline. Andrew leaned down to Dan and muttered, "Think about my suggestion, son. We have decisions to make." Dan nodded, not looking up. The men left, closing the door behind them.

"What suggestion?" Lilah asked.

Her brother kept his eyes firmly fixed on the hearth. "Something about adoption."

Pressure receded from behind her brow. Shame attacked. She'd misjudged Andrew. "That's kind of him." Talking about adoption this soon after the funeral was insensitive. Still, it *was* nice of him to be concerned.

"Forget it," Dan muttered. "We'll stay here."

Lilah stared. "By ourselves?"

"We don't need Andrew," Dan argued, eyes strangely desperate. "Papa's lawyer says there's a little cash in the bank. Also, we'll get survivor benefits from both Mama and Papa. Then there's the stock in Genesis. The house is ours, too... well, ours and Caroline's, but she's not going to care."

Lilah's shoulders slumped in relief. It was good to know they wouldn't be entirely dependent on Andrew's charity, but Dan's suggestion was crazy. "No one's going to let us live on our own, Danny," she said, somehow finding comfort in the name her twin hadn't used since they turned ten. "We're minors."

"We'll find a way," he insisted.

"Why're you acting so weird?" Granted, Caroline never wanted much to do with them, but Andrew loved Dan like a— "Andrew didn't offer to adopt *me*, did he?" Lilah asked, sitting up. "Only you."

"Delilah, Daniel," someone called from the hall.

The armchair scraped the rug. Dan stood with haste and hurried out the door, leaving guilty silence in his wake.

#

Next morning

Brooklyn, New York

Harry shoveled scrambled eggs into his mouth and struggled

with the intense urge to toss the contents of his plate onto the faces of the Barronses. The unfeeling couple was at the kitchen table, talking to Harry's father. The twins were also present, but they were silent. Harry, on the other hand, had quite a lot to say. He wished like hell he could tell the Barronses where to go.

The twins needed time to... *Harry* needed... dammit, he hated this raw feeling in his heart. He simply wanted to be alone with the people who loved the couple he carried to their graves yesterday. Lilah's papa and his kind humor... her mother who'd tugged Harry into her embrace along with her children... they were gone, creating a cold void in the warm and loving memories of his past.

When his own parents tore him away at the age of six from the only home he'd known—from his best friend, Lilah—Harry didn't sleep for weeks. He cried into his pillow every night, begging God to somehow send him back to Tel Aviv. Even when he finally accepted he'd never get to return, Harry knew they were merely one phone call away. He knew his own family loved him. They'd only been looking out for his safety by having him live with Lilah's parents until then. Now... Lilah... Harry couldn't even imagine how she and Dan were feeling, left with the Barronses as their closest relatives.

The thermostat was set to a warm seventy-four, but Lilah shivered, pushing food around her plate. Tears trickled down her cheeks, and she leaned forward, letting her hair curtain her face. Lilah hated it when someone caught her crying.

She wouldn't care about her best friend seeing. As their mothers told it, from the time baby Harry glowered at the screeching infant through the rails of her crib, they'd been partners-in-crime. He knew her every mood, including her hurt and her fury and the stubborn pride which melted away at his teasing. Other than him, only her brother and her parents knew what a warm, loving girl Lilah really was. Her half-sister, Caroline, might as well have been a stranger to the twins.

Within months of the wedding of Caroline's widowed papa to the Indian lawyer he met in Bombay, his seventeen-year-old daughter from his first marriage announced her engagement. She married the wealthy oil driller, Andrew Barrons, then a single father some fifteen years her senior. Unfortunately for her, she couldn't hide the fact the twins were related. Caroline strongly resembled Dan with the same dark eyes and hair, but as far back as Harry could remember, she acted as though her two siblings didn't exist. Andrew at least showed some concern for Dan, if not for Lilah.

The oilman's current focus was on business, though. Andrew continued droning on about the political situation in Libya. "Genesis is not worth the risk, Ryan."

Suuure. For a billionaire like Andrew, an outfit like Genesis Oil was not worth it, but for the Sheppards, it was all they had. What a privileged ass Andrew was. He always looked the part, too. Caroline once informed them Andrew's patrician features—including the brown hair and blue eyes—came from his Norman ancestors. She was very proud of the Barrons lineage. What she thought of Andrew's idea of adopting part Indian, part Irish-American Dan, Harry couldn't begin to guess.

Right on cue, Andrew turned to Dan. "What did you decide, son?"

Harry speared a slice of bacon and scowled at the driller. *Jerk.*

Lilah's hand shook when she reached for her glass of OJ.

Eyes fixed on his plate, Dan said, "I don't think it's a good idea."

Andrew's eyebrows rose. "Why not?"

"What will happen to Lilah?" Dan asked.

It wasn't as if Lilah needed the Barronses for financial support, and the relief in her eyes when she heard about the money had shocked Harry. He never realized she was worrying about it. There was no reason to. The Sheppards would never abandon her.

"The adoption is only a formality to make you my legal heir," Andrew coaxed Dan. "Delilah can also live with us."

Some of the stiffness left Dan's shoulders, but he still said, "It's not the same, sir. She's my *twin.*"

"Why's this such a big deal?" Andrew asked, frowning.

Dan stayed mute, refusing to look up from his plate.

Andrew huffed. "All right. If it makes you feel better, we'll adopt her, too. It's only paperwork."

Buy one, get one free? Harry fumed. *Is she a pet fish or something?*

Sophia Sheppard, Harry's mother, walked in, holding his eight-year-old sister by the hand. She threw a questioning glance at Ryan. He explained, "Andrew's planning to adopt both of them."

Sophia said, "Good thought. This will give them *both* some stability. Let's get started right away. I'd rather have it all done before we return to Tripoli."

"I'll call my lawyer and get things straightened out," boomed Andrew, rubbing his hands together.

The fork clattered as Lilah set it on her plate. In a subdued tone, she said, "Excuse me, Andrew. I'd rather not."

Andrew swiveled toward Lilah. Eyes narrowed, he took one long look, studying her expression. Unblinkingly, she stared back. Ryan and Sophia Sheppard exchanged glances.

Go, Lilah! Harry cheered.

Andrew Barrons nodded once. Twisting in the chair, he refocused on Dan. "See? You were worrying about nothing. She doesn't mind."

Idiot, Harry spat silently, glaring at the oil driller. Ghabi, coglione... insults of increasing vulgarity in Arabic and Italian and every language Harry knew crowded his tongue, begging to be let loose... only to be discarded with great regret when he caught his mother's squelching eye. Neither they nor the twins could afford to antagonize a powerful man like Andrew Barrons.

Andrew continued talking to Dan. "And why would she? This is a big opportunity for you. You're never going to get another offer like this."

Harry bit back curses. Andrew Barrons was a jerk, but he was a shrewd jerk, trying to manipulate the twins like this.

Lilah flushed. "I swear I don't," she assured Dan. "Andrew's right. You should take his offer. He said we'd *both* be living with him, anyway."

Liar, Harry muttered. She minded all right. He eyed Dan, having a very good idea of what was about to transpire. *One... two...*

With a low growl, Dan dragged his chair next to his twin's. "Listen to me; I *know* how you feel. It ain't gonna happen."

Way to go, Danny! Harry applauded.

Andrew rubbed the back of his neck. "I don't understand you, Daniel."

In his mind, Harry snorted. The entitled jerk assumed the siblings would simply fall in line.

The driller continued arguing, but none of it worked. In the end, the Barronses had to be satisfied with the twins' acceptance of the offer to live with them, minus the adoption. *What's wrong with the son he already has?* Harry wondered. Caroline didn't have children, but Andrew had one with his deceased first wife. Vaguely, Harry remembered his brother talking to Andrew's son at the wake—a blond guy who looked like he was at least twenty.

Lilah pleaded fatigue when the family gathered in her father's home office to iron out details, and she went to the roof, seeking quiet. Metal steps clanged as Harry followed her up the spiral staircase.

The narrow brownstone houses in this part of Brooklyn tended to be packed in tight rows, and the backyard next door was easily visible from the rooftop of Lilah's home. Flowerbeds were dug up in preparation for planting. The smell of damp earth clung to the air, reminding Harry of the fresh graves at the cemetery. He shoved away the hard grief within his rib cage. His sorrow would have to wait its turn. Lilah was hurting much, much more than him... her parents' passing, the worry about money, her idiot relatives... the goddamned universe was piling problem after problem on the poor girl, but she was determined to face everything *her* way.

They huddled together for warmth on the concrete floor, and the unique lotus scent she wore filled his nostrils. He played idly with her long, dark hair, vaguely wondering how locks so black could glint deep blue under sunlight. Lilah resembled her mama while Dan and Caroline took after their father in appearance. "You *knew* Dan would refuse once you did," Harry accused.

Lilah shifted away, her face tight and hazel eyes flashing. "Why should I let them adopt me? They want only Dan."

Harry warned, "Dan's gonna lose out. Andrew's right about one thing. It *is* a big opportunity."

"You really think my brother's going to choose Andrew's money over me?"

"No. All I'm saying is—look, Danny's your twin, so he won't let Andrew use money as wedge. But why would you even leave the possibility open? Talk to Dan. Ask what he wants."

She bit her lip, confusion replacing the anger in her eyes. "I could, but I don't want Andrew adopting me, and Dan's never going to agree to let anyone adopt just him."

"I get it. Still, it will be better if he knows he's not going to lose you even if he does agree." Meditatively, Harry added, "You took a chance there, habibti. What if Andrew told you both to get lost?"

"We wouldn't have starved," she snapped, temper sparking once again. "And Naani would've taken us."

Naani... Lilah's Indian grandmother. The seventy-some-year-old lady was severely arthritic and confined to a wheelchair. Not to mention the fact she forgot her own name half the time. There were a few cousins in the extended family, but who knew if the government allowed orphaned American kids to be taken out of the country. Still, no matter what the circumstances, Lilah would refuse to bend. "You're too damned stubborn," Harry said with the usual mix of awe and exasperation.

She frowned.

"Even your father used to say so." Obviously, Harry's recollection of their first day of kindergarten was vague, but Lilah's papa had been fond of relating the time he picked up his ward and the twins from the principal's office. The staff at the school in Tel Aviv hadn't known what to make of the little girl who wouldn't let the class move on, insisting the biblical Delilah betrayed Samson because she was a patriotic Philistine.

"Papa loves to embarrass me." Her eyes brimmed. "...loved."

Harry dug into his pockets, and his fingers closed around something solid. Drawing out the object, he frowned at the chess piece, the black king from Lilah's set. She'd destroyed him the last couple of times they played chess. Poker was more his game. Not wanting to be humiliated again, he hid a couple of her pieces, but he had no idea how one got into the only suit he owned. "Here," he said, handing it over, ignoring her puzzled look.

After a few seconds of watching him poke back around in his pockets, she asked, "What are you doing?"

"My handkerchief... must've dropped it someplace." His mom had tucked a neatly folded square into the pocket of his blazer.

"I'm okay." Lilah wiped away tears with the back of her hand.

"I don't like to see you cry, all right?"

"Yeah, that's why you got me a snake."

Harry groaned dramatically, making her giggle through her tears. "It was a *lizard*," he objected, savoring the sound of her soft laughter. "A glass lizard. It just looks like a snake. And it's been a *year*. How many times do I have to apologize?" He let her swat him, holding his arms up in mock surrender.

The heel of her hand landed hard on his thigh, and she fell against his shoulder before straightening. "Sorry," Lilah mumbled.

Wild heat spread through Harry. Gritting his teeth against a whimper, he nodded. *What the hell, man? She just buried her father and mother.* Yeah, and if they could hear what Harry was thinking now... they were never coming back. He'd never get the chance to tell them how he felt about their daughter.

The twins' mama had been a mother to Harry, too. She'd taught all of them their letters, refereed quarrels, nursed them through childhood illnesses. If Harry looked carefully, he could probably spot the pale marks on his hands and feet... faded scars from some kind of viral rash he caught as a toddler. When the hardhearted doctor they saw at the time said scarring happened only because Harry picked at the scabs, Lilah's mama took the then-four-year-old into her lap and made up heroic stories about each mark. One was a star captured by little Harry, one an elephant he tamed, one a thunderbolt he shot from his hands. Together, they counted thirty-two magical shapes. And she never forgot which scar was what.

His heart squeezed painfully hard. Lilah... *her* agony... Harry couldn't begin to imagine. She'd adored her parents, and they'd blanketed her in love. Now, once Harry returned to Libya... "I'm glad Andrew's letting you and Dan live with him," Harry said. "It's better to have family around."

"Andrew's letting us live there only because he wants to try and change our minds. I'm sure of it. But adoption means lots of things, right? Taking the name, his money, and all? I don't want it. Dan wouldn't, either."

"Not if he has to sell you out for it," Harry agreed. "But wanting and needing are two different things. Lilah, you know very well your naani's not gonna be able to help. What if the government puts you and Dan in foster care or something? Face it; you *need* Andrew. Don't piss him off too much."

"We only need him until we turn eighteen," Lilah said, tone unyielding. "After that, Dan and I will be legally allowed to live on our own, *and* we'll have full control of survivor benefits."

"In the meantime, Andrew's going to keep pushing for adoption."

"He can push all he wants, but I'm not going to agree. Once we turn eighteen, he'll have to stop pushing. We'll be adults. It's not even three years until then. I can hang on for that long. Then, I—*we*—will be in college."

"Gotta give it to you, habibti. You're something else." Harry had a great deal of respect for Lilah's capacity to stare down an adversary, be it a grade school bully or a billionaire oil driller. Hell, he was downright proud of her. "If I were you guys, I'd let the Barronses adopt me and spend every penny they have in the bank." He waggled his eyebrows.

"*You* wouldn't even need Andrew," she grumbled. "There would be *hundreds* lining up, begging to take you home. The whole world likes you."

"All you gotta do is look into their eyes and let them know you like *them.*" Most responded favorably to attention. Friends *and* foes. The only time he didn't do it was when he was with Lilah. Even if they weren't already friends, she'd have seen through it.

"What if you *don't* like them?" Lilah asked stubbornly.

"Princess, is it beyond you to be nice?" At the reproach flickering across her face, Harry chuckled. "Try it."

"No matter how hard I try, Caroline's not going to change her mind about me. I look too much like Mama." Lilah averted her eyes. "I can hold on for three years."

His heart heavy, Harry said, "I wish you could come home with us to Tripoli, but New York is probably safer."

She glanced back at him. "What's going on, Harry? What was Andrew talking about?"

"This—" Harry broke off, swallowing a curse. "—driller who wants to buy Genesis for a quarter of its worth."

"Who?" Lilah shivered. The breeze from the Atlantic was mild, but the spring day was already chilly.

Without answering, Harry wrapped his arms around her, gathering her body close. So much was going on back in Libya. Harry was aware of the struggles his parents faced, building up Genesis. The business finally started to take off, but with success came corporate raiders. The crazy bastard Andrew was talking about was one. Then there was Gaddafi, determined to drive all foreign drillers out and take over. It seemed to Harry they were surrounded by enemies. They'd been hoping Lilah's papa could do something, but now... wetness stung Harry's eyes.

Everything, *everything*, was happening all at once. His parents couldn't afford the luxury of grief at the loss of their friends. Putting aside their pain, they needed to hang on, somehow. There was no choice. The oil company was not just *their* source of livelihood. Like Lilah's parents, many of the Sheppards had invested in it. If Harry's father let Gaddafi win, all the investors would lose their savings. Many would be left bankrupt.

The one hope remaining was the presence of the bigger oil companies. Andrew Barrons might have moved out, but other businesses like Standard Oil and Shell and Mobil still maintained subsidiaries in the North African country. Gaddafi was after them, too. If the oil companies let him have his way, it would set a bad precedent for dictators around the world. The Sheppards were desperately hoping the big corporations would compel the Americans and the Europeans to take action, forcing the Libyan dictator to back down. If the governments refused... the big companies could afford to cut their losses; Genesis couldn't.

Harry wished he could talk to Lilah about it. He could rage and rant to her about everything under the sun, but not today. There was already enough for her to worry about.

Grief clearly made her more fatigued than he realized, or she'd have prodded him for answers. "When are we going to meet again?" she asked. "I don't think Andrew will bring us over."

"And Father can't spare me from the wells." Harry worked at

the family's rigs on weekends. It was a tightly run ship, and every hand counted. They'd already lost Harry's older brother when he returned to live in the States.

Lilah could visit Tripoli on her own, perhaps. But if Andrew Barrons had it right, Libya was not safe for the Sheppards. How could it be all right for Lilah? Still, her papa—the ambassador—would've urged his friend and family to get out if he believed safety to be an issue. Then again, *he'd* been more concerned about Gaddafi while Andrew was likely talking about the crazy guy who wanted to buy the business. Harry suppressed another curse, his mind ready to explode from all the conflicting thoughts. In a mild voice, he said, "Gotta figure something out."

She laid her head on his shoulder. In a few minutes, her even breathing and slack weight told him she'd fallen asleep. The chess piece he'd returned, the black king, was still in her grip. Trustingly dozing in his arms, Lilah cuddled closer. Her breast brushed against his chest. A jolt ran through Harry.

The idea they couldn't see each other... no, he couldn't stand it. Mad dictator or greedy businessmen, she would visit.

Feverishly wondering if it were possible to die from frustrated lust, Harry sat there until late, letting her rest. Occasionally he glanced at his watch. The Rolex had been a gift from his brother. A couple of hours slipped by, but Lilah continued sleeping.

The sun was on its way down when she finally stirred. He dropped a kiss on her head and murmured, "We'll find a way." She would be safe. After all, he'd be with her.

Chapter 4

Three months later

Upper East Side, New York City

Swatting away the hands dabbing powder on his nose, Temple settled deeper into his chair and refocused attention on the papers he was holding. It wasn't easy. His stepbrother's Gilded Age mansion had six stories—not including the basement—and the office room next to the conference hall was reasonably large, but there were at least a dozen people currently stomping through it.

"Senator," the chief of staff exclaimed on a long-suffering sigh. "You're going to be on television. We need to make sure you look good."

Temple chuckled. "You mean I need to look young." The challenger in the New Jersey race was thirty-eight to Temple's sixty-five and at six-foot-three, several inches taller than the current senator. "The trick is not to pretend to be someone else. It is to present what I am as better than what my opponent is." He turned to the makeup woman. "Don't cover all my gray. Just make sure it looks..."

"Distinguished," completed the woman, studying Temple's visage. "You already have nice blue eyes. Add a little salt-and-pepper hair, and we'll have the ladies swooning."

"I just want them voting," Temple said dryly. Or he wouldn't have agreed to this press conference. Media organizations had been clamoring for answers from Senator Temple, the chairman of the Committee on Interstate and Foreign Commerce, on the situation in Libya. Answers were what he didn't have. However, this was an election year, and Temple had no choice but to face the press.

When he finally seated himself at the conference table, the hall was packed with journalists. Every chair was occupied. There were quite a few men standing. Television cameras lined the back wall. The attendees started with a little chitchat about the latest gossip in DC, and Temple shot a few personal questions to the reporters, asking after their families.

The first real question came from the *Wall Street Journal.* "Senator, what exactly is our plan for Gaddafi? He doesn't even bother with negotiation. He announced on radio they were nationalizing the local assets of British Petroleum. What happens when he goes after American businesses?"

With one finger, Temple scratched the side of his nose and gathered his thoughts. The U.S. support of Israel in the 1967 Arab-Israeli War already resulted in a short-lived oil embargo. At the time, the Americans were saved by the more moderate governments in Kuwait, Saudi Arabia, and Libya, which circumvented rules to supply oil. Now, Libya was under the control of a madman. If he weren't kept happy, there could be another blockade. Even the ever-reliable Saudis had signaled they might not be able to rescue the Americans from the blockade or the economic downturn sure to follow. Coming on top of the protests against the war in Vietnam, a recession would most certainly lead to political unrest.

The commerce committee even conferred with the secretaries of state and defense on the possibility of assassinating Gaddafi or toppling him from power. Both options were ruled out. Gaddafi was supported by the Soviet Union, and the West could not afford to open another front in its war with the communist state.

If and when Gaddafi went after American businesses, there was nothing the U.S. government could do without risking total chaos. Temple knew it; every member of the commerce committee knew it. If he admitted any of it on camera, the stock market would crash. The unrest they were desperately trying to avoid would be at their doorstep in the morning.

"Negotiation," Temple said, keeping his expression confident. "Gaddafi might have oil, but he needs markets to sell it to. We're not completely weaponless." Except, they were. The American businesses in Libya would have to fight their own battles.

Another reporter raised a hand.

"Yes, sir?" called Temple. "The *New York Times*, right?"

"Right," said the reporter, adjusting his glasses. "Let's talk about Vietnam."

With an inward sigh, Temple nodded.

"The North Vietnamese Army caught us by surprise," continued the reporter. "President Nixon has withdrawn his preconditions for a peace agreement, but enemy forces are still..." The reporter recited numbers—of lives lost, of money wasted, of days spent in armed conflict. "How are we planning to win this?"

The latest military campaign was designed by North Vietnam to give itself more negotiating power at the peace talks. It could not have come at a worse time for the United States. The American president went on television to announce to the nation he'd have to escalate the war efforts. The public long ago soured on anything to do with Vietnam, but with the economy as shaky as it was, President Nixon could ill afford failure on the foreign policy front.

"There is no military on earth as capable as ours," Temple responded, maintaining a firm tone. "No soldier more willing to sacrifice in the service of..." He took questions for another hour, dancing around dangerous truths without ever acknowledging or refuting them. His press secretary was bustling toward the conference table to end the session when a hand rose at the back of the hall.

"What's new with your family, Senator?" asked a man Temple didn't recognize. "Your son is getting married soon?"

Temple riffled through the papers on the table in front of him. The press secretary bent down, whispering, "*National Enquirer.*"

Ahh. The tabloids could make or break a political career. Some of them boasted of better circulation than the respected broadsheets. With a friendly grin, Temple said, "Yes, to one of his colleagues. A lovely young lady. My son *is* pushing forty, so I'm thankful she agreed to take him on."

Temple's only child was a classics professor at Harvard. He and his fiancée dropped by the campaign office on their way to Greece. They did extend an invitation to the wedding. Temple supposed he should thank the young woman for the kindness. Indeed, it wouldn't have occurred to her betrothed to invite the father who'd been too busy for him when he was growing up.

After the death of Temple's wife, father and son maintained little contact.

"What about your stepbrother's grandsons?" asked the reporter. "Seven of them, right? Our readers would like to know what's going on in their lives."

Of course, the tabloids were interested in the young men. They were heirs to this large mansion and the rest of the family holdings. Temple smiled. "College is the only thing going on. My brother wants to give them a few years to mature before turning them loose on society."

"Any of them home now?" persisted the tabloid reporter. "It's summer."

"Afraid not," Temple said cheerfully. The lads would be working their butts off for the family company until the military academy in West Point opened for the new school year. "They all have jobs with Kingsley Corp."

"Mr. Temple," called a bespectacled young man from the front row. "That brings us to *my* question. As the chairman of the Committee on Interstate and Foreign Commerce, you're privy to confidential information coming out of the Middle East. You're related to the Kingsleys who own one of the world's largest oil services businesses. How can the voters be sure there won't be any conflict of interest?"

The secretary bent forward. Without glancing back, Temple held up a hand. He knew who the young reporter was. "You've been covering New Jersey politics for how many years?" Temple asked, maintaining his pleasant expression.

"Five," said the young man.

"Your publisher." Temple sat back, casually crossing his legs. "If I'm not mistaken, he's closely allied with one of the main contributors to my opponent's campaign."

The young man flushed. "The publisher's politics don't influence my work, Senator."

"In other words," Temple said, tone soft. "You've learned how not to let outside pressures impact your job. In just five years. Do you know how long *I've* been in politics?"

Titters rose in the hall.

Temple allowed himself another small smile. "A couple of decades. I've been a member of the same committee during the time. We've survived multiple conflicts in the region, including the problems between the Palestinians and the Israelis. Through it all, my stepbrother's company—Kingsley Corp—provided services to the drillers operating in the Middle East. The people of New Jersey have not seen me showing them any favoritism."

Doggedly, the young man asked, "Can you deny that the Kingsleys benefited from the friendliness shown by the U.S. government to some of the rulers in the region? So how can we be sure your family's well-being won't be on your mind when you talk to Gaddafi?"

"Whatever policies I promoted were for the well-being of the nation as a whole. The Kingsleys might have benefited, but I cannot ask them to cease operations while I'm in active politics. What you need to find out is if I've put my thumb on the scale for them at any point. I urge you to ask around. I want you—and every voter in New Jersey—to be satisfied with my job performance."

The young man agreed, "Rest assured, I will."

"While you're at it," Temple continued, "check into your publisher's favored candidate. I'm sure your readers would like to know why an oilman from Oklahoma, the son of an Austrian immigrant who used to live in Malta until the First World War, is supporting my opponent. This supporter has no connections to my home state, but he does plenty of business in the Middle East. Also, unlike the other American drillers in the region, he's quite friendly with Gaddafi and every other tin-pot dictator. Why is such a man bankrolling my opponent? What has my opponent promised?"

"Senator," called out a female voice. The reporter from Associated Press was gray-haired, her eyes shrewd and spine slightly bent. "Why not be blunt? We all know who you're talking about."

Temple nodded. "Jared Sanders."

The same evening

New Castle, New York

The name carried the impact of a gunshot. In the home office of Andrew Barrons, Temple stayed in the leather chair and watched the drama from the morning being replayed on television. With a muttered curse, Andrew muted the sound and tossed the remote to one side of his vast desk. He rocked back in his own chair, eyes on the TV encased in the wooden cabinet lining the wall. On the opposite wall were large windows overlooking perfectly manicured lawns. Except for the chirping of birds, all was silent. For Temple, the roominess and the tranquility of the limestone mansion with its neoclassical architecture were usually a welcome change from the clutter and clamor of the Kingsley mansion set smack in the heart of New York City. Today, even the creamy cold coffee in the frosted glass in his hand couldn't soothe the feeling of impending doom.

"We should've taken care of Sanders when we had the chance," Andrew said. "You, me, and Ryan Sheppard. Because of your stepbrother, everything fell apart."

Temple took a deep breath and reminded himself Andrew was a major campaign contributor. He was a mere twenty-one when he inherited the Barrons holdings from his father in 1946. Andrew immediately financed Temple's first campaign to replace *his* departed father as the U.S. senator from New Jersey. Forty-one-year-old Temple was unsurprised by young Andrew's shrewd move. An up-and-coming politician connected to the wealthy Kingsleys? Oh, yes. Definitely someone Andrew would want to have on his side. The Kingsleys *were* American aristocracy with egos to match their family money. Unfortunately for Andrew, the Kingsley patriarch—Temple's stepbrother—prized his public image and how the family was viewed more than any political pact. The attempt at an alliance against the ruthless upstart—Sanders—collapsed because of the arrogance of the people involved, and Temple swore never to try it again. The resulting coldness between the Kingsleys and the Barronses didn't stop Andrew from continuing to fund Temple.

Ryan Sheppard had not fared as well. He lost all the money he inherited and nearly went into bankruptcy before somehow getting the recently departed diplomat to invest in the failing company.

Andrew brooded, "Sanders isn't stupid... his father came from

Malta to the States with no more than a few dollars and managed to start the company, but Jared's the one who built it into what it is today. I'm sure he figured out what we were planning to do. Now, he's bigger and stronger than before, and we're all going to pay the price. One by one, he's going to pick us off. He's already after Ryan. With you and the Kingsleys, Sanders is first going to squeeze *you* out of power. Who knows how he's going to attack me?"

Not a mention of how Sanders was on good terms with authoritarian regimes around the world. Not a word about the national security threat he clearly was. But that was Andrew Barrons for you.

"You'll be fine," Temple soothed. "Barrons O & G is too big a fish for even Sanders to swallow. As for me... I'm going to win this round. At some point, Sanders might find a candidate who can bring me down. Afterward, my brother will have to either go down fighting or accept Sanders as lord and master. Ryan is the one who's in trouble now. Andrew, I came here to ask you to call him. Help him get out of there before things go south."

"Ryan claims he cannot afford to leave."

"Andrew," exclaimed Temple. Softening his tone, he continued, "Ryan has a family to feed. Not to mention the rest of the Sheppards with money in the company. Telling him to chuck everything and leave is not enough. Your father-in-law was one of the biggest investors in Genesis. For the sake of your own relatives, help Ryan. Give him a loan to start something back home."

Andrew sat up. "Are you kidding me? Ryan managed to lose all the money he inherited. He got lucky in Libya. Right place, right time. Otherwise, he's had a terrible track record. I'll have zero return on my investment. Ask your brother. He'll agree with me."

Sure, there were members of the Kingsley family who thoroughly loathed Ryan. Truth be told, Temple felt no fondness for Ryan, either. "He's in trouble with Sanders because he agreed to be part of our initial alliance."

"We asked Ryan to join us because Genesis was doing well until his father retired as CEO. Ryan agreed because your brother promised him money for his expansion plans. Ryan lost both his inheritance and the cash from your brother. The ambassador was not yet my father-in-law, or I'd have advised him against investing in Genesis. As I said, Ryan got lucky in Libya, or he'd have bankrupted himself *and* my father-in-law a long time ago."

A hand held up, Temple conceded. "All true. But Ryan *did* join our alliance, and now, Sanders is after him. Also, Ryan has more things to worry about. You saw what Gaddafi did to British Petroleum. Genesis Oil is small, but Gaddafi won't spare anyone. Especially not Americans."

"Barrons O & G is a business," Andrew said. "Not a charity. I don't see any reason to sink money into unprofitable ventures. Senator, we need to focus on what Sanders is going to do to *us*."

A loud honk blasted through the air. Temple jumped, nearly spilling the cold coffee he'd forgotten he was holding. The glass was slick with condensation. Temple set it on the desk and pulled out a tissue from his pocket to dry his wet fingers.

Andrew grimaced. "They're learning to drive."

"Who—oh, the kids you want to adopt."

"'Want' being the operative word. They haven't agreed."

Temple had already heard the story. He tossed the scrunched-up wad of tissue into the small trashcan to his left. "They're twins. You should've known better than to offer to adopt just one."

With a nod, Andrew said, "I made a mistake there. I didn't need her and thought it would be fine as long as both could stay with me. It made no sense for either to refuse."

Most people would've known it was at least a possibility... most except billionaires who never thought of anything beyond what *they* wanted and seldom heard the word "no."

"And the goddamned state won't let me adopt them without their consent," Andrew continued griping.

"They *are* fifteen," Temple pointed out. "Not infants. The government of New York does require their signatures on such documents."

"Unless I can prove they're mentally unstable," Andrew agreed.

Temple slitted his eyes, wondering if Andrew would really sink as low. No. An allegation of mental incapacity wasn't something he'd throw at the boy he wanted as son, and the young man clearly loved his sister enough to stop the driller from pulling such a dirty trick on *her*.

Andrew groaned. "I need to figure this out... I want Daniel as my heir. The board of directors should have no room to question it. For it to come about, I need to officially adopt him, but he won't agree unless the girl does. If they don't, I won't have an heir."

There were times when Temple wondered what he'd been trying to achieve with the alliance between the three families. Yes, Jared Sanders was a ruthless tyrant, but the businessmen who joined hands against him were not exactly angels. Here was Andrew, talking as though the son he already had didn't exist. Temple gritted his teeth. It was an old argument between them, and there was no point in once again raising the issue only to go in circles.

"I don't have any leverage where she's concerned," Andrew groused. "If I threaten to kick her out, I'll lose Daniel."

Dryly, Temple suggested, "Instead of going on about what *you* want, offer her something *she* wants. Invest in her to get the return *you* want—Daniel as your official heir."

"Don't you think I've tried?" Andrew snapped. "Clothes, jewelry, vacations... she rejects everything except food and a couple of bare necessities. I even told her I'd pay for college." The same oilman staunchly refused to finance his own son's education in retaliation for the young man's defiance. "She claims she'll manage on her own."

"Surely, her parents left her something?"

"Survivor benefits from the ambassador's government service and a few thousand in the bank. There's the house in Brooklyn and the shares in Genesis, but those are supposed to be divided equally between her and her brother *and* my wife. Delilah says she'll work to make up the difference."

Temple raised an eyebrow. As his departed mother would've said, the girl had moxie. Another loud blast sounded from the horn, followed by a string of curses in a male voice. Whoever was teaching the twins how to drive did not seem happy with their progress.

Andrew glared into the garden. "She acts as though she's doing me a favor by staying here."

Fighting a sudden urge to laugh, Temple coughed. "What does Delilah want to study in college?"

"Daniel says she wants to go to law school."

Law? Temple once knew another woman who wanted to go to law school, someone more willing to compromise her principles. Deliberately, Temple slammed a mental door on the painful memory. The past was the past. Nothing he could do to change it, just as there was nothing he could do about Andrew's problems with the orphaned twins. Besides, there were other challenges demanding their attention. "We need to talk about Sanders—"

Andrew thumped a fist on the desk. "I don't have much time left. I need to get the paperwork done in the next couple of years before Daniel turns eighteen."

"You can still adopt him as an adult," Temple said, wanting to bring the discussion to an end. "You might even have better luck persuading Daniel to agree once he and his sister are out of this home." The girl wouldn't be left feeling like a fifth wheel.

"Not possible. If he becomes an adult without being legally recognized as my son, there's a good chance the board will refuse to certify him as my heir. I need to find a way to force Delilah—"

Huffing, Temple said, "Andrew, I came here to talk about *Sanders.* As you said, he's going after Ryan and looking for a way to go after the Kingsleys. You're too big for him now, but the situation could change in a few years. I know you don't think much of Ryan, but if we stick together, there's a chance—"

"No."

"Hear me out."

"We tried it once. Because of *your* family, it didn't work. I'm not making the same mistake a second time. Also, don't take me for a fool. The only reason you're here, asking me to bail out Ryan, is you couldn't talk your brother into doing it. I've already done all I'm willing to do. I warned Ryan it's stupid to hang on in Libya. Now, I need to deal with my own problems."

Temple fell silent, contemplating options. Sanders was a problem for Temple, for the three families who once tried to go up against him, and for the nation. Hell, with the number of despots Sanders kept in his pocket, he was fast on his way to becoming emperor of the world. The only way to beat him was through collective action, and if big businesses like Barrons O & G and Kingsley Corp wouldn't do it, no one else would. Unfortunately, Andrew and the Kingsleys would not work directly with each other. Temple had hoped to get each working with Ryan and join forces through him, but there was no cooperation from any front. Neither Andrew nor the Kingsleys could see any benefit in collaborating with the Sheppards.

The ruin confronting Ryan wasn't enough to force the other two to team up. They would have to either face a catastrophe of their own or see personal profit in working together. Temple could only hope Sanders didn't succeed in destroying all of them before they came to their senses.

A shrill ring broke the silence. Picking up the phone on his desk, Andrew boomed, "Hello?" His brows drew together. He held out the receiver and pushed the phone across the desk. "For you. Your chief of staff."

Temple blinked. His office was calling him at the Barrons residence? Even before he could utter a greeting, the chief of staff's excited voice came over the line. "Senator, we have news."

"Problem?" Temple asked.

Words tripping over each other, the chief said, "Yes. Not for us, though. At least, I don't think."

Temple glanced briefly at Andrew, debating whether to have the chief hold on to the news until they could talk in private. Andrew was a contributor, but there was a limit to what Temple was willing to share with him. But then, the chief would not have called here with any information Andrew could potentially use against Temple.

"My source at *The Washington Post* called," said the chief. "They're sitting on something big."

At the pause, Temple bit back a sigh. The chief—who'd dabbled in theater back in college—liked to milk the drama in every situation. "Like?"

"Remember the break-in at the Democratic office at the Watergate complex last weekend?" asked the chief. "Well, someone called in a tip to this reporter at the *Post* saying it leads back to the White House."

Temple sat up, his heart pounding. *"What?"*

"Rumors are," the chief said, "the CIA did the job."

"My God," Temple breathed.

If the White House and the CIA were indeed involved, the crisis Temple was trying to stave off had arrived. The Middle East might not yet have erupted into flames, but the U.S. was about to. Every thought of Ryan Sheppard fled Temple's mind. Every worry about Jared Sanders slipped away.

Chapter 5

November 1972

Tripoli, Libya

In one quick move, Harry scooped up the cards from the top of the blue, thirty-six-inch crate and tucked them into the pocket of his red coveralls. "Be right there, super," he said, leaping up from the smaller box he'd been using as a stool. His steel-toed boot bumped against the metal corner protector on the crate, setting up a subdued clang. The break was over.

The rig superintendent—a fortyish Italian with a crew cut and a skinny mustache—walked from the tepid sunlight just a few feet away and joined Harry and the rest of the roustabouts in the shadow thrown by the service truck.

One of the Sudanese men sitting around the crate groaned. "Five more minutes," he grumbled in heavily accented Arabic, "and I'd have figured it out. He gets a royal flush every single time. It's like magic!"

Slapping on his hard hat, Harry grinned. Not magic. Quick counting and deft shuffling. Plus, a glib tongue to distract the other players.

"What for?" the super asked in the same language. His eyes were on the clipboard in his hands. "You're not allowed to bet more than pennies. Not on *my* watch."

Harry had been told not to bet *any* money when playing poker with the rig workers. He didn't need the warning. He showed up to work only on weekends and school holidays, but he was treated as one of the men. Yet he was not one of them. Losing even small change to the boss's son would've caused resentment.

He played because he enjoyed the camaraderie. Also, he needed *something* to take his mind off all the problems. Harry wished there was enough cash in his wallet to call Lilah every week. Just talking to her would be enough, but it wasn't possible. When he played cards with the men, he could forget the constant pressure his parents were facing from Gaddafi.

The dictator gave foreign oil companies operating in the country two options. Agree to sell 51% to the Libyans or lose their entire investment. The Sheppards couldn't afford to sell at the piddling price offered by the madman. As long as they continued to refuse, the strong-arming would go on and on. Gaddafi's goons would keep cooking up bogus issues—about licenses, about working conditions, about quality control.

Then there was Sanders and *his* insulting offer to buy Genesis for pennies to the dollar. Harry didn't get it. Jared Sanders wasn't a loony like Gaddafi. From what Harry heard, Sanders arrived in the United States as the toddler son of a Maltese immigrant. Daddy Sanders started the drilling company, but it was the son who made it into the hugely successful enterprise it was. The savvy businessman couldn't possibly think his offer would be accepted. So why did he make it? Hell, Harry didn't get what it was about Genesis which interested Jared Sanders in the first place. Sure, their rigs produced quality oil, but it would be a mere drop in the gasoline bucket for someone like Sanders. Still, it was the only explanation Harry's father came up with.

"Looks like rain," the super commented, glancing skyward. "Move your arses. It ain't no fun hauling equipment in a storm."

The sweltering heat of the summer was down to a tolerable seventy-four, but it didn't make any difference to the dust and grime and smell of diesel fumes clinging to the air around the rigs, spilling over barbed wire fence into the streets outside. Grabbing his bottle of cola from the top of the crate, Harry took a swig. Completely flat now. And sickly sweet.

"Get moving, men," barked the super.

Harry got moving. Boss's son or not, part-time worker or not, he'd get reprimanded for wasting precious minutes.

The only other part-time employee in the team was Saeed al-Obeidi, the Bedouin kid. He lived somewhere around Benghazi and came down to the rigs only when school was out, staying in the camp with the rest of the crew. He usually hung out with Harry on breaks, but this was prayer time for him.

When Harry followed the super and the Sudanese men to the pre-job meeting at the rig, Saeed was already there. Roles were quickly assigned. Harry was as usual at the taglines—ropes holding the two-ton load steady in mid-air, preventing it from oscillating or spinning. Saeed was told to help the electrician fix the generator at the campsite.

"*I* want to do the taglines," Saeed muttered. "I've been here long enough." He was planning a degree in oil engineering and was rabidly enthusiastic about every aspect of drilling. The rig supervisor very likely left out Saeed from the job because of his height. At six-feet-four, Harry matched the tall Sudanese workers. Saeed was a good eight inches shorter. Still, he was as used to hard labor as the rest of them and was as muscular. Like Harry, Saeed was a fan of Muhammad Ali, *the* greatest boxer of all time.

"Talk to the super," Harry suggested. Protective glasses and work gloves on, he jogged to his spot.

The rest of the team was already in place. The crane operator was in the cab on top of the pedestal. During the entire procedure, the only team member the operator would be able to clearly see was the signalman on the ground. He'd make sure the operator didn't damage any of the equipment or injure the roustabouts.

The main lifting hook was connected to the load. The signalman raised his arm, indicating the load was ready to be hoisted. The crane operator pushed the lever. Like the neck of the bird with the same name, the boom of the crane angled up. The crate lifted off the ground.

Even through the thick material of the glove, Harry could feel the burn of the rope. Legs apart, he held position. His quads hardened. His deltoids and biceps bunched painfully. The two-ton load *had* to be kept under firm control. If the heavy crate accidentally struck something, it would cause tens of thousands in damage.

Ten feet... twenty feet... both hands up, the signalman instructed the crane operator to move slower.

Someday, Harry wanted to be the one calling signals. Then, the man pushing the lever. He needed to know everything about drilling for oil. He wasn't crazy about the process as Saeed was. Still, if he wanted to make Genesis a badass company, he'd have to know how everything worked. Joining the navy and getting into the SEAL program was Harry's personal dream, but he wasn't about to forget Genesis. He *would* get them to the top. He *needed* to... if only for the Sheppards to finally have financial security.

"Harry," the super called. "al-Obeidi will be taking over."

Harry grinned. Saeed clearly talked the super into giving him a chance. Harry waited until Saeed got his hands firmly around the rope. Letting go, Harry jogged backward a few feet before turning around.

"The electrician still needs an assistant," said the super, glancing at his clipboard.

"Right away, Super," said Harry.

With a quick nod, the super turned his attention to the men moving the load. His eyes widened. His mouth opened, but no sounds came out. Terror. There was absolute terror on the super's face.

Harry wheeled around. There was the same frozen scream on the face of every man in the team, the same horror of watching disaster unfold. One raised an arm as though to ward off impending tragedy.

The boom of the crane had swung a few degrees clockwise. The load was now directly over Saeed's position, the spot Harry occupied only seconds ago. It was coming down. Fast. The signalman was swinging his arms out, demanding an emergency stop. Saeed was staring straight up, his hands still on the tagline. He wasn't moving. He wasn't running to safety.

Harry didn't wait to think. He sprinted, leaping at Saeed in a football tackle, hurtling with him a few feet to the other side. The rope whirred out of Saeed's hands. He and Harry tumbled to the hard ground. The world spun as they rolled.

A crash. The earth trembled. Shouts, screams. Thundering feet. Dust rising in small clouds.

"Harry," bellowed someone. "al-Obeidi."

"Call the ambulance," yelled a second person.

Heaving himself off Saeed, Harry sat up and coughed. "I'm all right." There was something in his right eye. The protective glasses had flown off his nose. He blinked furiously, trying to get the speck of grit... dust... whatever... out.

"Santa Maria," breathed the super, looking up at the heavens. "Thank you. What about you, al-Obeidi? You okay?"

With a groan, Saeed scrambled up. "My shoulder hurts." His eyes went to the spot he'd been at mere seconds ago. His face blanched. *"Ya Allah,"* he said, calling God.

The boom of the crane was bopping up and down like a murderous bird intent on pecking its prey to death. Right below it, the two-ton crate lay on its side, the ground beneath sunk in at least a couple of feet. If Saeed were there...

"al-Obeidi," said the super. "You're going to the nurse's office. I'll radio her to take a look at the shoulder. You, too, Harry. Let the nurse make sure *you're* all right." Peering up at the cab where the crane operator was, the super snapped, "Get the idiot down here."

Harry stomped a couple of times, trying to get the trembling out of his legs. At least, the speck in his eye seemed to be gone.

Walking with him toward the one-story concrete building housing the first-aid office, Saeed muttered, "I could've died."

"You didn't," Harry said matter-of-factly. He hoped like hell the accident didn't scare Saeed out of his plans to be an oil engineer. It was only chance he happened to be in the spot. *Harry* stood there moments before the crate dropped. They wound their way between boxes. The temperature hadn't changed, but under his coverall, Harry was sweating like a pig. He smelled like one, too.

"I could've," Saeed insisted. "You saved my life."

"Yeah, well..."

"I owe you."

"C'mon," Harry said, embarrassed.

They were at the office building. The nurse—her white shirtdress and frilly cap spotless—waited at the door. She led them to the first-aid room. Rolls of gauzy bandages sat neatly arranged on a long table set against the wall. A metal tray held a couple of scalpels, forceps, and a large pair of scissors. There was a small desk against the opposite wall next to a file cabinet. At the far end was the window, the rumbling air-conditioner fitted underneath it.

Harry and Saeed pulled the plastic chairs meant for patients as close as possible to the air-conditioner and sat.

"I do owe you," Saeed said. "My parents owe you. My whole family owes you."

"There's no need for so much drama," Harry mumbled.

"It's not drama. I mean it. I swear to you... you're my brother from today. My family—my entire tribe—will consider you one of us."

Harry would've rolled his eyes. Except, he knew the Bedouin kid probably meant every word. The tribes maintained a strong sense of family and clan bonds.

The nurse soon pronounced Saeed's shoulder pain a mere muscle pull. Just as she was signing them out of there, the super walked in. "I informed your father," he said, nodding at Harry. "As soon as his meeting is done, he'll be here."

"Didn't you tell him I'm fine?" Harry asked. There was already enough for the family to worry about.

"Yes, but he's going to want to hear for himself what happened. The damned fool crane operator says the lever failed. He should've had enough presence of mind to stop the job as soon as he noticed the malfunction. My God! As far as he knew, *you* were still in that spot! Even the dumbest piece of shit would've known better than to kill the boss's son."

A month later

"Belly dancing club?" Harry asked doubtfully.

"Shh," said Saeed, his eyes darting around the mobile unit which functioned as the dining hall for rig workers.

Rare winter rain pattered against the metallic walls of the unit. The few other workers in there were digging into their late lunch or chatting low key among themselves. No one appeared to be paying attention to the two teenagers at the table closest to the food counter. There was only one man at the counter, leaning against the wall, eyes drooped shut.

Elbows on the tabletop, Saeed bent toward Harry. "Not just *regular* belly dancing. It's a bit more... you know... *adult.*"

"Adu—got it." More skin. Even before the accident, Harry discovered Saeed's favorite reading. They'd debated the merits of the various topless beauties who graced the pages of the *National*

Geographic over the years. Harry took another bite from the juicy chicken sandwich. Chewing on it meditatively, he said, "I've watched belly dancing before but not... uhh... the adult kind." Actually, he'd never been to a club of any sort—for belly or any other form of dancing. "Will we need passes?"

"Here's the thing," said Saeed. "You know, the crane operator?" After the tragedy he almost caused, the man was demoted to roustabout, but Harry and Saeed still referred to him as the operator. "He says he wants to make up for what he almost did. He's the one who told me about the show. *He'll* get us the passes, but we're gonna have to come up with IDs, or the guard won't let us in."

"I already have one," Harry said.

"I do, too," Saeed said promptly. Grinning, they raised their glasses of soda.

"Clubbing's not legal," Harry mused. Gaddafi had banned even regular belly dancing, calling it contrary to the teachings of Islam. "But who's gonna find out?"

"So we're going?" Saeed asked.

An evening away from home, away from the constant discussion of the problems with the business. The near miss with the crane had only been the first in a series of accidents. Last week, it was the faulty insulation which could've electrocuted Harry if he didn't hear the crackle from the diesel generator and leap back just in time. There were also the fires and the leaks and the tanker which broke down exactly when a shipment was due. The Sudanese workers even started muttering about ill omens, but the rig supervisor put an immediate end to the nonsense. Still, no one could deny Genesis had operated at a loss for a couple of quarters, and this one was going to be worse.

"Hell, yeah," said Harry. "We're going. I'm gonna need to make a detour, though. Got some shopping to do."

Saeed flopped back in his chair. "Lotus oil? Again? No wonder you never have money to play *real* poker."

The sun had set hours ago when they got to the market. Shoppers still crowded the brightly lit stalls on either side, haggling noisily with merchants over clothes and spices and saddles strung on ropes hanging from the ceiling. The dirty water flooding the narrow street lapped at Harry's ankles. Unlike the dry interior of the country, Tripoli occasionally got rains, and when it did, many of its roads turned to canals, strewn with sewage. Like the Libyans, Harry learned to take it in stride. Also, to wear rubber boots.

Skirting a little boy and a woman with a *hijab* around her head and neck, he called, "Hurry up, Saeed. I want to get there before the old man goes home for dinner. Only he can give me a discount. His nephews won't dare cut the price when he's not around."

The smell of warm camel piss nearly drowned out the piercing odor of incense pervading the block. Harry hefted his backpack more securely over his left shoulder and tugged the edge of the black-and-white *kufiya* across his mouth and nostrils. This was the reason he'd worn the local headdress with his bellbottom jeans and cotton tee.

Saeed was dressed similarly for the same reason. He splashed through the water, trying to catch up. His shoulder caught the edge of a steel rack crammed with men's shirts and sent it rolling.

"*Ya homaar,*" shouted a man, calling the boys donkeys. He ran after the truant rack.

Not bothering to respond to the insult, Saeed said to Harry, "This time, ask for a bigger discount. If they refuse... well, there are other shops in Tripoli which sell lotus oil."

"I need the *blue* kind," Harry said, striding along. Lilah's parents used to get it for her through their contacts in the Middle East. After their passing, Harry went from store to store in this *souk*—one of the oldest bazaars in Tripoli—until he found a blend which was an exact match. He might not have enough money to make international calls more than once a month, but sending her a bottle of her favorite fragrance was something he *could* do. "Only this shop sells the blend *she* likes," he continued. "Also, if the shop doesn't make a profit, they'll have to close. Then, where will I go for the perfume? We can't sacrifice long-term benefit for short-term gains."

Saeed groaned. "Brother, you're a bloody fool. No girl is worth this much trouble."

Lilah was. Each time Harry thought of her, there was a gush of warmth in his heart. Besides, she was living with the Barronses. The coldhearted couple couldn't care less whether she felt loved. She did have Dan, but the Barronses were trying their best to steal him away. Lilah needed to know there was one person in the world who cared a helluva lot about her. Well... in her letters, she'd mentioned a couple of friends she'd made in school, but they were different, like Harry having his own buddies. He and Lilah... Harry grinned. It was a damned good thing she was nothing like his friends, especially the stocky, bearded one currently walking next to him.

When Harry and Saeed got to the perfume shop, the old merchant beamed. Wrapping up the bottle in old newspaper, he said, "Ten dinars."

Almost twenty-five dollars, which at the minimum wage Harry was paid, was a week's paycheck. He slipped the package into the backpack and zipped it shut. "One more stop before we get to the club."

As soon as the owner of the silk store spotted Harry, he shouted to someone at the back of the stall. The crimson silk scarf Harry ordered was already packed in a plastic bag. The bag was tucked carefully into Harry's backpack—between his textbooks—so the scarf wouldn't get crushed.

"Another ten dinars down the drain," Saeed grumbled.

"*This* is for a special occasion. She's turning sixteen." Harry might not be able to wish her a happy birthday in person, but he was damned well going to make sure she knew he was thinking of her. "I hope it gets there on time. It's in January."

Saeed threw his head back and laughed, sounding as hysterical as a hyena. "Man, I hope I never fall in love. I don't want to go crazy like you."

"For *my* birthday, she sent me an autographed copy of *The Day of the Jackal*." God only knew how she'd managed to get her hands on one when the author lived in Britain. "It's a best-seller."

"A *book*?"

"It was written by a former RAF pilot. Exciting plot."

"If you say so," Saeed muttered, tone doubtful.

It was hard to explain the appeal of the story to Saeed. Lilah knew Harry would love the thriller. She also knew Harry would find the author's bio fascinating. Harry didn't even bother telling Saeed about the peacock feather tucked between the pages of the book, with a note claiming Naani—Lilah's Indian granny—sent it for his protection.

Naani, my ass. Half the time, the old lady couldn't remember who *she* was. Smart, logical lawyer-to-be Lilah sent the talisman. Now that she was recovering from the tragedy of her parents' untimely deaths, she'd started to get uneasy over the problems in Libya. The gift was followed by a couple of letters insisting she didn't believe in such superstitions. Half of Harry was tickled Lilah was anxious enough about him to momentarily lose her skepticism. The other half fervently wished she didn't need to be.

He hadn't let on there were more problems than she already knew. When they talked, Harry kept discussion of the trouble in Libya to the minimum. Long-distance phone calls cost an arm and a leg, and he didn't feel like wasting money on the dumbasses hounding the Sheppards. Putting things in a letter would only alarm her without giving him the reprieve he craved.

He longed to see her in person and blurt out everything. Unfortunately, he had no idea when they'd meet again. Andrew wasn't making the trip over to Libya, and the Sheppards couldn't risk leaving the country for even a day.

A tightness coiled behind Harry's eyes, stretching his brain to the point of snapping. The pressure popped up each time he remembered their precarious situation, which he did almost every other minute.

Harry was only barely aware of the other things going on in

the world, like the political drama back home in the States with President Nixon. Normally, Harry would've gone through every article he could find about it and tried to deduce for himself what must have happened. He would've debated Lilah about it until they decided on the best course of action for the nation. But Harry hadn't been able to focus even on his personal plans—not on his schoolwork, not on his hopes of getting accepted to Maritime College.

Somehow, the family needed to put all the problems behind them so Harry could get back to what he was supposed to be doing... like preparing for college and life back in the U.S. Right now, he was only scraping through tests. He still kept up with his wrestling and boxing lessons. He *had* to, or he'd lose it.

Harry pinched the bridge of his nose and shook his head. "Next stop, the club." He needed the break.

"Where did we park?" asked Saeed, looking around.

In five minutes, Harry was on his knees before the second-hand motorbike he'd bought two years ago. "C'mon," he begged. "Don't let me down." The airman at the now-closed U.S. military base in Tripoli had warned Harry the elderly Honda Dream 305 was cantankerous, but he didn't care. He paid the fifty bucks and brought it home. His parents didn't object to the idea of their teenaged son riding a motorbike around the city. This was Libya. There was a minimum driving age somewhere on the books, but as long as your feet could touch the ground, the government wasn't bothered. His mother did tell him if he could ride the bike, he could drive his baby sister around in the family car. Harry didn't mind. It was a small price to pay. For all his efforts, the bike rewarded him by breaking down every ten minutes. "It's going to run," Harry assured Saeed. "All it needs is a little tweak."

"I don't care as long as we get there before the show starts," Saeed said quickly. As he always did, he was gawping adoringly at the scratched steel and worn leather. "Riding up on a bike is way cooler than taking the bus."

Harry glanced at the watch on his wrist, the one expensive thing he owned. His brother, Hector, gifted him the Rolex a couple of birthdays ago. Unlike the elderly bike, the watch worked very well. There wasn't much time left before the show.

With a muttered plea, Harry took another go at starting the bike. This time, it didn't stall. Crowing in triumph, he straddled it and waited until Saeed climbed on behind.

The streets they took weren't waterlogged, so they made good time. Rolling to a stop, Harry turned off the rumbling engine. The block was completely dark, but the sliver of moon in the sky revealed the large, shadowy buildings, one of them partially demolished. Debris was piled here and there. All was still and quiet. They were the only ones outside.

"Hatchoo."

Harry jumped.

"Sorry," said Saeed, wiping his nose on his sleeve. "It reeks here."

That it did... of crumbling concrete and rotting wood and dirty water which collected over weeks, becoming breeding ground for mosquitos. The whole street stank of desolation. To their back was the main road they'd left. The hum of traffic was still faintly audible, punctuated by the occasional honk. Ten minutes to the front was the port. There would be much more noise there from the boats and the cars and the crowds of shoppers. And cops. Gaddafi's cops, who'd be on the lookout for illegal activities.

For a moment, Harry contemplated turning back. No, he needed this break, or he'd soon explode.

In silence, Harry and Saeed rolled the bike toward their destination, the abandoned warehouse at the end of the street. Broken glass crunched under their rubber boots. When they got to the narrow alleyway next to the building, Saeed cursed. "No space." Bicycles and motorbikes crowded the lane. There was even a car or two.

"We'll leave it over there," Harry said, wheeling the Honda back. He leaned it against the wall of the previous building.

If the cops drove by, the vehicles in the alleyway would be out of sight, but Harry's bike was also hidden, shrouded by shadows. Besides, it wasn't as though any thief would be able to start the bike. It required skill to cajole the mechanical diva into cooperating.

Their headdresses were left in the saddlebag. His backpack slung over one shoulder, Harry followed Saeed to the warehouse. The building was fair-sized, more than a hundred feet in length. The designated entrance was the door on the far side.

At a light touch from Harry's fingertips, the steel door squeaked open. There was a muffled rumble in the distance, interrupted by a clatter not two feet away from them. In the dim light stood a bulky guard, glaring at the boys. There was an aluminum chair lying on its side on the dirty gray floor.

"We have tickets," Saeed said quickly.

The guard verified their tickets but didn't ask for identification. Harry was six-foot-four, and he always let stubble grow when he worked at the rigs. It allowed him to fit in better with the men. Saeed was a good deal shorter, but he also sported a scraggly beard.

The steel door shut behind them. Their rubber boots didn't make a single sound when they followed the guard through the musty hallway. As they approached the inner door, the subdued rumble became louder, devolving into the clamor of chatter. Blood thrummed through Harry's veins. Wiping his suddenly sweaty palms on his jeans, he entered the cavernous room.

Bright, yellow light. Concrete walls, twenty-foot ceiling with pipes running across it, corrugated asbestos sheets forming the roof. At the back of the room was a makeshift stage made of five or six low tables. There was a dark-blue curtain behind the stage. A small group of forty or so men was crowded around, waiting for whoever was behind the curtain to make an appearance. The air was warm and thick with the stench of sweat.

Keeping a firm grip on his backpack, Harry took a quick survey. "No women."

Saeed snorted. "Of course, no women. This is Tripoli, not Beirut." He laughed. "Don't tell me you're disappointed. What would your Lilah say?"

"She won't—" Frowning, Harry mulled her possible reaction to his presence in the underground club. Even if there were no women in the audience, there would be one on stage. His best friend would totally get why he was here, but would his girlfriend? "Maybe I should leave."

"C'mon, brother. I was kidding. This is just a show. Like a play or a movie. Why would she get mad at you for watching a movie?"

"When you put it that way..."

A drum roll reverberated around the room. A low roar went up from the waiting men. "It's going to start," said Saeed, voice trembling in excitement. When he jogged to the back of the group, Harry followed.

"Gentlemen," a disembodied voice boomed. "Presenting, *Malika al-Jamal*, the queen of beauty, Zaynab."

The curtain twitched, parting in the middle by a scant few inches. A foot poked out, followed by the rest of the leg. A bare leg, smooth and long.

At Harry's side, Saeed gurgled. The drum music picked up tempo. Harry's pulse pounded in rhythm.

The curtains were ripped apart. A woman spun onto the stage. Her long blonde curls whipped through the air. Her shell-shaped bra did a piss-poor job of covering her breasts. Some kind of jewel glittered in her navel. The black skirt she wore was ankle-length, but it sat so low on her hips and was so sheer, she might have as well danced onto the stage in her underwear. Plus, there was the slit which went all the way to her upper thigh.

"I heard she's Russian," Saeed said, tone almost devout. "Belly dancing is very popular there."

Was it? What the Russian dancer was doing didn't seem remotely similar to any version of belly dancing Harry saw before.

Shaking her hips in time with the drumbeat, the dancer

twirled her way to the front of the stage and bowed low. Darkness descended on the room, leaving her alone in a circle of light.

The roar of the crowd got louder, almost drowning out the drums. Saeed mumbled something, but Harry couldn't hear. If he'd heard, he probably wouldn't have understood a word. His brain was wholly occupied, dealing with the visual feast on the stage. The creamy cleavage.

The dancer whirled away from the audience, giving them a glimpse of the tattoo at the bottom of her spine. A grapevine disappeared beneath the narrow waistband of her skirt. Her buttocks quivered as though involuntarily. Arms swaying one way, and then, the other, she shimmied her tush.

Harry couldn't take his eyes off the tattoo. With each beat of the primal rhythm and each writhing movement of the vine, blood surged into his groin. *Stop,* bellowed his mind. *Think of something else.*

"What the hell are you doing?" hissed a furious voice. A heavy hand landed on Harry's shoulder, spinning him around. The backpack on his shoulder slid down to his elbow. A tall, lanky African-American waited for an answer, his hair prematurely gray. He was dressed in his customary striped shirt and dark pants. At the sight of the familiar face of Dante Maro, his father's secretary, all thoughts of the sexy Russian dancer fled Harry's mind. He was screwed. Big time. Grabbing Harry by the scruff, Dante shoved him toward the door. "We're getting out of here. You, too, al-Obeidi."

"Yes, sir, Mr. Maro." Saeed wouldn't dare object. He was an employee of Genesis Oil, and Dante had the big boss's ear.

When they exited to the hallway, the guard was waiting. "I didn't know they were underage." The music continued inside, with the door vibrating in time with the drums.

In broken Arabic, Dante snapped, "You would've if you'd checked their IDs." No, he wouldn't have, but Dante didn't need to know about the fake cards. "First of all, skin shows are illegal," he raged at the guard. "Secondly, you compounded the problem by letting minors in. If I report this to the cops, you'll be in jail."

"Sorry," whined the guard. "Don't report me, please. I have a wife and two daughters."

"You're lucky I don't have the time to deal with you," Dante said. A hand on the back of each boy, he propelled them forward.

Silently, Harry let himself be marched out into the dark night. Could he claim they'd accidentally walked in? Damn, there was nothing else on the block to validate the excuse. And Dante definitely was in no mood to be sweet-talked into overlooking Harry's little rebellion.

When they reached the shadowed alleyway being used as a parking lot, Dante said, "You're both going in my car. I'm parked on the main road."

Somewhere not too far away, an engine revved. A clunker on the main road, probably. Harry ventured, "My bike—" The rumble of the engine got louder.

"You can pick it up in the morning," Dante said, tone firm. "No thief in his right mind will steal the contraption. If someone does, tough luck. It's what you get for pulling a stunt like this." There was nothing Harry could say in response. Dante continued, "As though we don't have enough to worry about!"

They did, and Harry had needed something—*anything*—to get his mind off it all.

Twin beams of light pierced the darkness. A car drove up and went past them—white in color, with a wide, black band across the side.

"Cops," whispered Harry. Inside his chest, his heart speeded up. There was a muffled squeak from Saeed. Dante tugged on Harry's elbow, pulling him into the interior of the alleyway. The police car parked about a hundred feet from them, in front of the warehouse door. A raid? "No," muttered Harry, shrugging off Dante's hold. "We can't hide here. Everyone inside will be trying to get to their vehicles. If the cops give chase, we'll also be found."

The engine died, making further conversation impossible without risking discovery. The headlights turned off.

Danger. Every hair on Harry bristled. He inched away sideways until his shoulder bumped against the wall of the next building. The shadows were deeper here. There was less chance of being spotted. Dante and Saeed followed. Harry could hear them shuffle. He felt the air move with their every breath. He could almost smell their fear. The feeble moonlight hadn't changed any, but Harry could see everything—even the small piece of paper fluttering about in the mild breeze.

Four cops got out of the car. One of them banged on the steel door with his baton.

Flattening himself against the wall, Harry continued creeping away. He could reach sideways and touch his bike, but it wasn't as though they could use it to flee the scene.

The steel door opened. A rapid-fire argument in Arabic broke out, with the guard promising free passes to the cops for future performances.

"Shut your trap," said one of the cops. "We want to get the people who organized this event. Not you." The guard sputtered to a stop. "And your guests," the cop continued. "All Libyans are expected to obey our laws. They're all in trouble. Other than the Russian dancer, any non-Libyans inside?"

Harry stiffened.

There was only a moment's hesitation from the guard. "No."

Perhaps he never recognized Harry as a foreigner. Or it could be that Dante's threat scared the guard into keeping silent. Also, Harry was no longer there. Technically speaking, the guard was telling the absolute truth.

Pushing the guard to the side, the cop in front walked in.

Harry watched, the sweat trickling down the back of his neck making him itch.

The second cop followed.

Go in, dammit. If even one of the cops stayed behind, they wouldn't be able to make a run for it. Not without drawing attention.

The last two cops barged inside. The steel door closed behind them, cutting off the light from inside the building.

Harry heaved in a breath. "Let's go." In a couple of quick strides, he was by the Honda and kicked the stand up. At Dante's irate mutter, Harry said, "No choice. If they find it here, they're going to run the license plate." He wheeled it back in the direction of the main road. Dante and Saeed walked behind. "If they come outside, go as quickly as you can to the closest building," Harry mumbled. "Doesn't matter if we get split up. Just hide until they leave."

They walked in the shadows, glancing back every few seconds at the warehouse. No one talked, but every snap of a twig under their shoes, every crunchy leaf, seemed to echo up and down the street. They barely got to the main road when shouts boomed from behind. His hands still on the handlebars of the bike, Harry turned and watched men being shoved out. From this distance, they were only silhouettes.

"Doesn't look like they're arresting anyone," Saeed whispered.

"Keep moving," said Dante. In a few feet, they were next to his car. He'd parked in the small lot in front of an office building. "You two, follow me home on the bike."

It took two tries, but the Honda did start. Air whistled around Harry and Saeed as they followed the taillights of Dante's Toyota. Thoughts whirled around in Harry's mind. How had the cops figured out there was an illegal show in the warehouse? If they were planning a raid, why were there only four men? Why had they asked about non-Libyans? They'd specifically asked for foreigners other than the Russian dancer.

The dancer. God. Harry could still hear the drumbeat in his ears. He could still see the quivering tattoo on her lower spine, the stalk of the vine disappearing under the pretense of a skirt. Harry blinked. The woman no longer had blonde curls. Her hair was dark and thick, draped over her shoulders. Her eyes were large and a familiar hazel. Biting her lower lip in a nervous smile, the dancer ripped off her skirt and tossed it to the only man in the audience. To Harry.

"Brother," a voice shouted in his ear. "What are you doing?" A large, blurry shape whizzed past them, blowing hot, thick exhaust fumes into their faces. Harry coughed. "Speed up," yelled Saeed. "Or we'll get crushed."

Harry glanced at his speedometer. Ten miles an hour? Cursing, he twisted the throttle and sent them jerking forward.

When they got to the street where the Sheppards had their villa, all the residents appeared to have retired for the night. The windows were dark. Except for a couple of dogs barking, everything was quiet. It was the peaceful silence of a safe neighborhood, not the ominous one around the abandoned warehouses. The date palms lining the driveway swayed in the mild wind as they rode up to the short flight of steps leading to the house. Only the garage light was on.

Dante's car was already parked, and he was getting out the door. "Inside," he snapped. "Both of you."

Turning off the Honda's engine, Harry said, "I asked Saeed to go with me. Don't punish him for my mistake."

Saeed gulped. "Harry, you don't have to—" He got off the bike.

Dante raised a hand. "I already know Saeed was the one who bought the tickets."

Shit. Harry wouldn't starve even if he were fired. Saeed, on the other hand, needed the money for the engineering degree he was planning. Also, the experience on his resume.

"How do you think I found you?" Dante asked dryly. "One of the kitchen crew overheard your discussion and called me. The idiot who sold you the tickets will be terminated in the morning. As for you, al-Obeidi, I'm going to ask Mr. Sheppard to let it go. This time."

"Thank you, sir," said Saeed, relief evident in his voice.

"You can crash in Hector's old room," said Dante. "Harry, don't go to bed yet. I need to let your parents know you're home, and afterward, I want a word with you."

"I'll be right here in the garage," Harry mumbled.

Ten minutes later, Dante returned. The window on the far side of the three-car shed was large, but the miserable excuse for a moon in the sky outside did nothing to help Harry see the sheet music on the folding table. He didn't really feel like practicing saxophone or even like eating the baklava he'd brought from the kitchen. Neither was going to delay Dante by much. Sardonic look on his face, he was even now watching Harry's antics from the footstool by the back wall.

"Stupid bulb," Harry muttered, glaring at the only light fixture in the shed, the one next to the door to the main house. Father's and Dante's cars occupied that half of the garage. This side held Harry's Honda and his mother's car, a.k.a. the family van.

Dante heaved himself up from the footstool and reached for the flashlight on one of the shelves. "Here."

"Thanks, old man." Dante was only thirty-one, but his prematurely gray hair earned him the moniker from Harry when they met around two years ago.

Grabbing the flashlight, Harry settled it on the folding table and tried to direct it toward the sheet music. The table wobbled on its bad leg and sent the plate of baklava sliding off. Harry dived, but before he could catch it, the pastry fell onto the concrete floor. The fork bounced away. He stayed on his haunches on the floor, staring at the crumbled pastry.

Dante clucked. "Get more from the kitchen."

Unfortunately, it was the last piece from the package Saeed's mother sent her son's friend after she heard it was Harry's favorite snack. Scooping the bits back into the plate, he stood. "I'm good."

"Not really."

Harry decided not to respond and picked up the saxophone from where he put it—the passenger seat on the Honda. He played a few experimental notes.

"Wait," said Dante. He was using his "boss" voice.

Harry instantly stopped. It wasn't often Dante pulled rank, but when he did, he expected immediate compliance. In addition to Harry's duties as part of the rig crew, he played gofer for Dante. Plus, Dante *lived* with the family. When Harry's parents were not around, Dante was in charge.

"I'm supposed to attend an early meeting tomorrow, but I'm in this garage at—" Dante glanced at his watch "—eleven-thirty-five only to talk to you in private. I want an explanation, Harry. Why were you at the skin show?"

"Belly dancing," Harry corrected. At the look of incredulity on Dante's face, Harry grumbled, "Okay, fine. It was a skin show."

"Gaddafi has made even belly dancing illegal, and here you

are... you've had your moments, but you've never been this irresponsible. What's going on?"

"I just..." Harry put the sax on the wobbly table. "The company, the problems... we're not even making money now. All those accidents..." As though Gaddafi and the other vultures weren't enough, everything which could possibly go wrong did go wrong. Fires, spills, leakages, equipment malfunction. "I haven't been able to focus on anything else," Harry confessed. "My grades are so damned bad... at this rate, I don't know if I'll even get into college."

Any time he hit the books, all he could think of were the problems in Genesis. What business did he have selfishly worrying about his own future when the rest of his family was staring into a black hole? But if he didn't, there would be no Maritime College. No meeting Lilah in New York. No heroic career in the navy.

"I sometimes wish we could all just return to the States," Harry muttered. "There must be something else we can do."

Back home, there would be no more predators, waiting to tear Genesis apart. Free from worry, the Sheppards could start a new venture. *Harry* would be there to help his parents build financial security for the entire family. His older brother—Hector—moved to New York many years ago. He'd worked as a boxing instructor for a long time and was currently setting up his own gym. But the extended family would take a beating if Genesis closed up shop. All the investors would lose their money.

"I'm in the same boat," Dante commiserated. "I haven't seen my wife in a year. My son is ten. He's probably forgotten what I look like by now." Eyes wistful, Dante added, "Still, I have a living to earn. I took this job for the sake of all three of us."

"Can't they visit?"

"I wish. I don't have the money to bring them over just for weekends, and I don't have a place for them to stay any longer."

"When Lilah's mama and papa were alive, they used to visit all the time."

"I remember." Dante settled himself back onto the footstool. "You miss her."

Only like every day. And night. "A little."

A muscle twitched in Dante's lower jaw. "You can't simply replace one girl you like with another, Harry."

"I... uhh..." No, he wasn't about to deny Lilah. How did Dante figure it out, anyway? Harry never told anyone in his household he and Lilah went from swapping stickers to swapping spit. *She* certainly wouldn't have said anything to Dante; they'd met only a handful of times. "I wasn't trying to replace her. I needed a break is all."

"So you went to a skin show? What if she heard about it?"

"I didn't *do* anything for her to get mad," Harry argued. "It was like going to a play or a movie or something."

"Oh, yeah? Does it mean she can do the same?"

"The princess at a skin show?"

Yeah, Harry imagined her on stage, but the audience of her performance had been limited to one. If she were actually asked to dance, she'd probably shoot the spectators a look so affronted they'd shrivel into little prunes.

A tickle started in Harry's chest, spilling out of his mouth as laughter. A hand on the folding table, he nearly bent double, hooting. Tears sprouted in his eyes. "Thanks, old man. I needed that."

A smirk on his face, Dante clarified, "I meant is she allowed to ogle other boys? You know, just because she might be missing you."

Laughter coming to an abrupt stop, Harry straightened. *Shit.* She wouldn't, would she? Not after they kissed. "Lilah's not like that."

Dante slapped his thigh and howled like a hyena. His guffawing got louder each time he encountered Harry's glare. "Maybe I should have a talk with her."

"Old man," Harry ground out.

"All right, all right." Still sputtering, Dante held up both hands. "Far be it from me to get in the way of young love. I have to say, Harry, you have good taste. She's a nice girl."

Harry tossed his annoyance aside and grinned. Dante saw beneath the princess façade Lilah put up.

"Pretty, too," Dante said, his thumbs up in approval.

"Heh? I suppose..."

Dante's thumbs went down, and his eyebrows rose. "You don't agree?"

"I guess I do." People were always saying it. After hearing it for what could be the hundredth time, Harry took a photograph of her and studied it side-by-side with pictures from *Vogue.* Technically speaking, he could see Lilah in the magazine. With her figure and long legs, she could easily grace *Sports Illustrated's* swimsuit cover. But... scratching his jaw, Harry said, "I don't really know. Whenever we meet, I feel like... it's not the first thing I think of. Sometimes, I don't even remember it. She's Lilah. We've been best friends from the time we were kids. When we're together... it's great. Really great. I feel like I'm *flying.*" Hell, she made him feel like he was the king of the world.

Dante's eyebrows got higher, but he didn't say anything.

Harry continued, "Only now, I also want to... uhh... when I see her..." His heart swelled as it did each time he thought of her. So did his crotch. Nonchalantly, Harry grabbed the saxophone from the folding table and held it in front of his pants.

Dante groaned. "Teenage hormones. Well, it's more evidence you *are* only sixteen."

"What do you mean?"

"You act like a kid one minute, and the next, you're a fully grown man... like tonight, when the cops got to the warehouse. I don't know if I would've shown the same presence of mind."

The cops. "Dante, did you tell Father and Mother where I was?"

"Nope. All they know is you were out with Saeed and asked me to pick you up. But I'm gonna have to tell them."

Harry pasted on his usual grin. "Dante, you're like a big brother—"

"Don't bother," Dante said, tone wry. "I'm on to you and your little tricks."

"You *are* like a brother to me," Harry insisted. "See how you got me out of trouble today?"

"At the club. Doesn't mean I'm going to get you out of trouble with your parents."

Shifting on his feet, Harry considered options. He was in for pain. They'd probably dock his pay. He hoped like hell they didn't suspend his phone privileges.

"We don't have a choice, Harry." Dante brooded. "Ryan needs to know about the cops. I don't think they were there to raid the club. Or they'd have brought more men. They said they were looking for non-Libyans."

Harry started. Precisely the same weird idea he'd been grappling with. "You think they were... how would they know I was... c'mon, you can't seriously think Gaddafi would send his cops after *me*. I'm pretty sure he doesn't know I exist."

"I wouldn't have thought so, but what other explanation is there?"

"They were there to shake down the club owners." Any other reason was simply too bizarre to imagine.

"I hope you're right," said Dante, not at all looking convinced.

"You're crazy, old man," muttered Harry.

Chapter 6

January 1973

New Castle, New York

Sweet sixteen was not what Lilah once dreamed it would be. Savoring the rich, creamy frosting of the chocolate cake, she pictured herself at her former home in Brooklyn. She imagined the hall, all the furniture moved someplace else to make room for dancing. In the living room beyond, there would've been a buffet table. Tandoori chicken and samosas for Lilah because she loved Indian food. Pizza and Chinese for Dan. There would only be one cake, but it would be huuuge! New clothes and birthday presents. Friends and relatives. Harry. Dan. Papa and Mama.

A heavy weight settled into Lilah's rib cage. There was pressure in her throat, grief welling to her eyes as tears. Ferociously batting them back, she nodded as the maid offering coffee to the guests around the table appeared next to her chair.

She was *not* going to cry, not even in private. After moving into the Barrons mansion, she'd sobbed into her pillow for months, missing her parents. She missed her twin horribly despite living under the same roof as him. There was no time when it was just the two of them. Andrew was always around, trying to monopolize Dan's days. It was as though she lost her brother right after she lost her parents.

Only when school started did Lilah and Dan get some time by themselves. Sitting at the desk at the far end of the school library, she'd gripped her twin's hand so tightly, he winced. They both shed silent tears and told each other they needed to move on. Papa and Mama would want them to.

Sorrow eventually turned from a sharp pain in her heart to a dull throbbing, but there were days when Lilah would catch herself thinking of something to tell Mama—especially after Harry called. Mama never got the chance to hear how Lilah felt. Her parents had always adored Harry, and they'd have been happy with her choice, but she wished—oh, she *wished*—she could go back in time and tell them all about it. Sometimes, Lilah would hear Papa call and turn around, only to find herself alone in her room at the Barrons mansion. The sense of loss would be so acute it would hit like a bat slamming into the middle of her chest. The loneliness was excruciating, the feeling of being alone and lost in the crowd... like today, at this dinner to celebrate her and Dan's birthday.

"Sixteen," Andrew muttered from the head of the table. Broodingly, he eyed Dan, sitting to his right, next to Lilah. "In two years, you'll be eighteen."

Too old for Andrew to adopt. Even in the middle of her unhappy thoughts, Lilah forcibly bit back the urge to smirk. *Hold on,* she told herself. Two years, and she'd free of the suffocating Barrons home. She'd be in college, building a future for herself. So would Dan. Andrew Barrons could simply twiddle his thumbs in the huge mansion, wondering what he did wrong.

Lilah knew she was an ungrateful little twit, but she couldn't help it. The hostility in her toward her brother-in-law was so intense her hair bristled at times. If Andrew were gracious enough to offer to adopt both her and Dan in the first place, she'd have never known she was an afterthought. She *would* have known she was taken in out of responsibility, unlike Dan, who'd have been accepted out of love. But she wouldn't have felt so worthless.

Andrew's surprise when they refused was so obvious as to be almost comical. How could someone as successful as Andrew Barrons not know it would happen? Didn't the *über* rich businessman understand people at all? Didn't he realize she had self-respect? A sense of self-worth?

Lilah was very sure Andrew wouldn't have let her live in his home if he weren't still hoping to adopt Dan. She was accepted only for her brother's sake. Even this celebration dinner was planned for her twin's benefit. For Andrew, her entry into the world the same day as Dan was an unimportant coincidence.

Dan said neither he nor Lilah felt like partying. Not when they were still grieving their parents. So the Barronses decided to have a small dinner, instead. The guest list was limited to Ginger Rose, makeup heiress, and Vivian, the youngest of the nine daughters of a hotelier daddy. Oh, the excuse was the girls lived in the same neighborhood and attended the same school as Lilah and Dan. Ginger was in the same English class as the twins, and she and Vivian were best friends since elementary school. The real reason was that Dan was mad about Ginger, and Andrew was very enthusiastic about the potential connection with the equally wealthy Rose family. He was doing everything in his power to encourage the romance. Vivian, Lilah supposed, was invited to keep her occupied.

What Andrew didn't realize was Ginger met Dan through Lilah, not the other way around. Ginger's mother insisted she join the chess club, no matter how dull she found it. Her bored look vanished at the first club meeting of the school year when Lilah's win wiped the smirk off the face of the reigning champ. Said champ *was* an annoying little twit with a habit of proclaiming women the weaker sex—in their heads. To Lilah's bemusement, she immediately found herself under the collective wing of Ginger Rose, the most popular girl in school, and Vivian, her best friend.

Ginger was across the table, sandwiched between her mom and dad. On Lilah's left, Dan was trying hard not to gawk at the strawberry blonde.

At the other end of the table, Caroline was laughing away at Grandfather Rose's tall tales of his time in the military. The old man might look like Santa Claus, but he was the owner of a worldwide cosmetics empire. Caroline, for all her attempts at distancing herself from her own flesh and blood, was very much the daughter of her diplomat father. She knew exactly how to handle Andrew's associates. She was even warming up to Dan. It was only Lilah who was still invisible to the Barronses.

Lilah gritted her teeth and told herself to snap out of it. A miracle was not about to happen. Caroline was not going to suddenly change and discover a fount of affection for the half-sister who so strongly resembled the stepmother she never wanted. Besides, Lilah found friends when she wasn't even looking.

Ginger was here to celebrate Lilah's birthday with her, and so was Vivian. She and her parents were on Lilah's right. Vivian was also blonde, but her hair was buttery and cut in a short bob. Those huge, round glasses of hers kept slipping down her nose. Whenever Lilah pictured Vivian, it was with her finger pushing the glasses back up.

Mr. Rose—Ginger's daddy—cleared his throat. "What are

you planning to do after school, Dan?"

"West Point," Dan said instantly, eliciting a proud smile from Andrew.

"He's going to need to be nominated," Andrew said, shooting a dark look at Lilah. "It would be easy if he were my son."

Lilah bit her lip. Dan's college was the one thing worrying her in the tug of war with Andrew. The military academy required nomination letters from members of the congress, something Andrew could get with no trouble. Even before she voiced her fears, Dan told her he'd toss the idea of West Point altogether if she gave into their brother-in-law's plans only for his sake.

"I'll join the Junior ROTC," Dan said, tone easy. The army reserve program for high schoolers could also nominate students for admission to the military school. "I assure you I'm not worried."

Mr. Rose turned to Lilah. "And you? What are *your* plans?"

Dabbing at her mouth with a napkin, Lilah started, "I—"

"You don't have to join the ROTC," Andrew said, nodding at Dan. "I've already talked to a couple of senators about your nomination." Looking down to the far end of the table, he boomed at Old Man Rose, "Sir, I believe you have some influence with—"

Looking straight at Ginger's daddy, Dan said, "Lilah wants to go to Harvard after her undergrad degree." There were red slashes across Dan's cheeks. This was not the first time her twin spoke over Andrew, refusing to let the oilman ignore Lilah around the neighborhood social circle. "She's been planning it from when we were in grade school."

"Harvard?" asked Mr. Rose, eyebrows raised. "Ambitious."

"I'd say," Dan enthused. "She wants to be a supreme court justice."

"She's working really hard at it," said Ginger. "All those old books she reads..."

"Aristotle and such," contributed Vivian.

Lilah smiled in gratitude at the support. From the day she said she planned a law degree, her parents made sure her reading material included works which would help her achieve her goals. Not that they exempted Dan from the activity, and Harry's frequent visits to their Brooklyn home meant he was expected to know the ancient philosophers well enough to debate the ideas championed by them.

Appreciative murmurs went around the table. Andrew's face looked as dark as the night sky outside the large windows at one end of the dining hall.

"We'll see," Lilah said, trying her best to sound humble. "I want to do constitutional law. After that, I'll need to clerk for one of the current justices."

"Good game plan," contributed Vivian's father.

"Delilah," called Mrs. Rose. "Tell me, do you use spray tan?"

Okay. Startled at the odd question, it took Lilah a second to open her mouth.

Ginger chuckled and dropped her fork onto her plate, causing a mild clatter. "Mother, I told you Lilah's partly Indian. I asked her the same question when we first met."

With a brisk nod, Mrs. Rose said, "I know. Her skin seems so smooth and clear I just had to double-check. And her eyes... *gorgeous*. I see only a little liner. No mascara."

Suddenly, all their guests were squinting in Lilah's direction as though she were sitting in a petri dish. She struggled with an acute urge to hold her napkin up, concealing her face.

"You should smell her perfume," Ginger said enthusiastically. "It's a Middle Eastern blend. Lotus oil, right, Lilah?"

Mrs. Rose sat up. "Really?" The woman looked ready to walk around the table and sniff at Lilah's neck. "Where do you get it from?"

"When my parents were alive, I got it from Cairo," Lilah said. "Now, a... umm... friend buys it for me from Libya." She ignored the soft snigger from her right, where Vivian was. Both she and Ginger knew about Harry, and in Lilah's letters to him, she'd talked about the two girls. She didn't even know what Harry's friends looked like. His letters carried only bare minimum detail.

"We've been considering branching out into fragrances," boomed Old Man Rose. He could out-boom even Andrew. "Blue lotus used to be Queen Cleopatra's favorite perfume."

Lilah grinned. She'd always been tickled by the little piece of history. "That's the kind I wear. Cleopatra bathed in it. Egyptians used to melt solid fat and stir in the flowers. They'd keep adding fresh flowers until the fat was saturated with the fragrance."

"Thus making blue lotus pomade," Mrs. Rose said with an approving beam.

Old Man Rose raised his coffee mug at Lilah. "What do you plan to do *before* law school? For your undergrad degree?"

"I'm not quite sure," she admitted. "Something that can get me a job. Just in case I don't get into law school." Oh, but she had to. She simply couldn't imagine doing anything else.

"Smart," agreed Vivian's father. "Well, if you know as much about hotel keeping as you do about blue lotuses, you can have a job with us."

"I prefer roses," Andrew interjected, sounding a little impatient. "In fact, we have a couple of rare varieties in the greenhouse." Nodding at Old Man Rose, Andrew added, "One of them was created by your grandmother." It was what led the family to change its name from the German Rosenfeld to a British-sounding Rose.

"Can't believe *our* garden doesn't have that one," Ginger said, tone girlishly high. Tilting her head, she shot a meaningful glance at Lilah.

With an inward sigh, Lilah administered a good hard kick to the shin of her clueless twin.

Dan jumped. "What? Oh... would you like to see it?"

Ginger fluttered her lashes. "Are you sure? I don't want to put you to trouble—"

"No trouble at all," assured Dan.

Smoothing her peach mini, she stood and waited for Dan to walk around the table to offer an arm. Miniskirts were kind of Ginger's thing. No matter what the weather, she wore minis. Vivian donned whatever was in, like the striped shirt and bellbottoms she had on tonight.

Lilah's birthday outfit was a wine-colored shirtdress with long sleeves she bought before her parents died. Andrew's secretary had informed her there would be extra in her allowance this month for any new clothes she might wish to buy, but since she never touched a penny of it except for essentials, it didn't matter. There was the cash from her parents' survivor benefits, but every dollar she could legitimately call her own was earmarked for college. Lilah's current budget included only school essentials and the occasional gift to Harry and Dan. With a regretful sigh, she'd tossed the Sears catalog in the trash can.

Not Dan, though. His dark-blue suit was custom-made. With Ginger's hand tucked into his elbow, he walked off, looking very much the prince the kids at the old school used to call him.

Talk resumed between the adults, mostly about business and politics and the results of the presidential election. In spite of the news about President Nixon using the FBI as his reelection tool, he'd been voted back in by a huge margin. No one knew what was waiting down the line for the nation.

"I almost wish McGovern had won," Andrew brooded. "Four years, and he'd have been kicked out. But now..."

"All this uncertainty is terrible for business," agreed Vivian's father.

"Young people," Old Man Rose said indulgently.

Vivian snorted. Her dad was surely pushing fifty. So was Andrew though his wife—Caroline—happened to be only thirty-three. Lilah bit her lip to stop from laughing but encountered Mrs. Rose's unblinking gaze. Feeling a little unnerved, Lilah returned her attention to the chocolate cake. Caroline and Vivian's mother were chatting, neither paying any mind to the men.

"There's always been uncertainty," Old Man Rose continued. "Good businessmen know how to take advantage of it."

"I was talking about the stock market," Andrew said. "Last year was good, but I smell a downturn."

"Ahh." Old Man Rose shook his head. "I'm afraid it might have already started. Plus, all the trouble in the Middle East... oil prices will go up, making things worse."

"Barrons is doing fine," Andrew said. "A year or two from now... the Middle East, and now, this thing with Nixon... we're going to see some turbulence."

Lilah sat up, her heart thundering. She'd tried asking Harry what was going on with the business problems he mentioned before the plane crash, but he refused to spend precious phone time on Genesis and Libyan politics. All they talked about was their personal lives... their hopes... how much they missed each other. His mention of a couple of accidents at the rigs was so casual it didn't occur to Lilah to worry until they hung up.

At her side, Vivian groaned. She was totally uninterested in anything to do with business. Her main aim in life was to find herself a rich husband who could support her in style. But she was so open about it that it was kinda cute. Plus, Viv was fiercely loyal to those she considered friends.

"Speculators might make money," said Mrs. Rose. "Lilah, I heard about a young lady at a party the other day. Her name's Martha Stewart. She works for a brokerage firm." Lilah nodded, unsure why the comment was directed at her. "She used to work as a model," continued Mrs. Rose, staring expectantly. Okay. Ginger was a fun friend, but her mom was weird. "How about it?" Mrs. Rose asked.

"How about what?" Lilah returned, confused.

With an impatient huff, Mrs. Rose leaned forward. "I think you'd be the perfect model for our teen line."

The conversation at the table lulled. Swallowing the bit of cake in her mouth, Lilah blurted the first thing that came to her mind. "I'm only five-eight." Tall for a girl, but nowhere close enough to be a model.

Mrs. Rose waved a hand. "Height's not an issue for our products. I could put you in touch with the agency we use, but you'd be exclusive to us for a few years."

"Umm..." Lilah glanced both ways, unsure how to respond. "I... college..."

"That's why I told you about Martha Stewart," Mrs. Rose explained. "She went from being a model to a broker. You could work for us through college, then go to law school."

Awkwardly, Lilah started, "I don't know—"

The clickety-clack of high heels interrupted the discussion. Ginger appeared at the door, followed by Dan. For some reason, she was frowning. Dan looked thoroughly perplexed.

"Everything all right?" her father asked, glancing between her and Dan.

Casually flipping her hair, Ginger said, "Everything was until Dan reminded me of the book report we're supposed to do for our English lit class. It's due on Monday, and I haven't even finished reading the first half of the story."

Disapproving clucks went around the table. "We'd better get you home, young lady," said Ginger's mom. "Schoolwork first."

Lilah and Vivian eyed each other, the thought on Lilah's mind evident on Vivian's face. The book report wasn't due for two more weeks. What in the world happened in the greenhouse?

They were forced to wait until the party broke up to ask. As the adults were still in the dining room, wrapping up their chitchat, the girls congregated by the front door. "What's going on?" Vivian asked, drawing on her coat and gloves.

"Nothing," Ginger said.

"What do you mean by 'nothing'?" Lilah asked, feeling anxious. Dan wasn't the kind to do anything to annoy a girl.

"I mean, absolutely nothing happened." Ginger tugged her hat low over her ears. "He asked for permission. Can you believe it?"

Lilah huffed. The Roses were capable of driving a perfectly sane person stark raving mad. Apparently, they believed other people should be able to intuit what they were thinking. "Permission for what?"

Baring her teeth, Ginger hissed. "To kiss me."

Lilah waited a beat or two before asking, "So? I thought you wanted to... you know..."

Waving her arms about wildly, Ginger exclaimed, "Who waits for permission to kiss? What kind of a sissy does that?"

"Hey," Lilah snapped. "Dan's a gentleman."

"Oh, yeah?" Ginger growled. "I don't want a gentleman."

Doubtfully, Vivian contributed, "Did you really think Dan was a grab 'em by the neck and French 'em type?"

Lilah grimaced. *"Eww.* You're talking about my *brother.* Can you not do it in front of me?"

Tucking her hands into her coat pockets, Ginger said, "He would wait for permission before doing 'it' in private."

Double eww. No, a *hundred* times eww.

Walking back to her room later, Lilah smiled. *Harry* waited for her to say "yes" before they kissed. There was nothing sissy about it, either. It was kind of gallant, like a... a knight or something. Heroic. She'd have to tell him the story when he called to wish her a happy birthday. Lilah took a quick glance at her watch and yelped. She'd better wait in the library.

The flick of the switch sounded loud in the darkness. Light flooded the small room to one side of the library. The phone was on the end table next to the couch facing the French windows. "Hello?" said a male voice. From the couch, a lean man sat up. He'd likely been lying down, watching snowflakes drift to the ground.

Lilah jumped. "Who—" Sandy hair fell shaggily to his collar, and sideburns stretched to the middle of his cheek. Sleepy brown eyes stared back over a droopy mustache. "Shawn." Andrew's son with the first wife who'd died at childbirth—the son who'd been disinherited. Shawn was twenty-three or twenty-four. A few years ago, he'd been expelled from West Point and was now working for IBM. In the months since the twins moved in, he'd been to the mansion only a handful of times. Even before, Lilah had barely met him once or twice. "I didn't know you were home."

The sleepy look vanished. His hand went up to his neck, his fingers stroking the amber beads he habitually wore. "Home? I suppose... did you need something from here, Delilah?"

She shifted from foot to foot in her platform shoes. How was she supposed to tell him to get out so she could have privacy when *she* was the interloper in this house? "Lilah," she muttered.

"Heh?"

"I prefer 'Lilah.'"

"Andrew calls you—of course. He does what he wants, and you don't object because you need the money."

Shock surged. Shawn never said an unkind word to her before this. Actually, she couldn't remember him saying anything more than a gruff "hello." Anger flared. "I never asked for any money. Dan didn't, either. Neither of us ever wanted to live here. In case you don't remember, our parents *died*."

Shawn grimaced. Holding both hands up, he said, "I know. It's not been a good day, but I shouldn't be taking it out on you. I'm sorry."

"Shawn, man," Dan said, coming up behind Lilah.

She jumped a second time and pivoted. Her twin was at the door, holding a plate with a large piece of the birthday cake. "You knew he was here?"

"Yeah," said Dan. "He got home after lunch."

Turning back to Shawn, Lilah asked, "Why didn't you come down to dinner?"

He shrugged. "I wasn't invited."

"Not invited?" she asked, feeling confused. "It's your home."

"Andrew told me to stay away," Shawn clarified.

"But..." Lilah trailed off, unsure what to say. There was the whole getting kicked out of college thing which would be reason enough for someone like Andrew to disown Shawn. Plus, she'd heard gossip in school that Shawn, one of their former students, recently came out as gay. "Why do you keep returning? Don't you get angry with Andrew... I mean, for trying to adopt Dan... us?"

With another shrug, Shawn said, "Your brother already apologized a hundred times. I'm going to tell you the same thing I told him. I've been disinherited. Whether Andrew adopts anyone else makes no material difference to me. But like you, I don't have any other place to call home. Andrew doesn't want me airing dirty laundry in public, so he doesn't have me thrown out. As long as I don't embarrass him by showing up to any of the events, he doesn't care if I putter around in this place whenever I feel masochistic enough to return."

"Have some cake," Dan said, striding to the couch and placing the plate on the coffee table in front.

Lilah joined them, choosing the armchair to one side. She eyed the small stand at the other end of the couch and the phone on it. Right now, the phone was silent, but it would ring any minute. Harry would be calling. She needed to pick it up before anyone else in the household answered on some other extension.

Shawn dug into the cake. "Mmhmm," he said around a mouthful. "The chef outdid himself. This is really good." He glanced from Dan to Lilah. "I don't have a present... presents. I didn't know it was your birthday."

Dropping to the couch next to Shawn, Dan asked, "How could you? You don't live here."

"Where *do* you live?" Lilah asked.

"I rent a studio in Harlem," Shawn said, his voice muffled by cake.

Lilah frowned. "That's so far from your job." IBM headquarters was only a few miles from the Barrons mansion in New Castle.

"I work at their Watson Lab in Columbia. They let me take a couple of classes a semester."

Leaning forward, Lilah asked, "For free?"

"Yeah."

"Won't it take a long time to get a degree like that?" Lilah asked doubtfully.

"Very," Shawn admitted. "But I can't afford to do it any other way."

"Can't afford—" Lilah stopped before she blurted out the question about Andrew Barrons's son not being able to afford college. If Andrew could disinherit his only child for being gay, he was obviously not going to pay for the same child's education. "What about scholarships?"

"There's a lot of competition for those," Shawn explained.

"Plus, most of them cover only part of the tuition. Also, I still need to live... pay rent, buy food, watch a movie now and then... everything costs money. Including boyfr—" Coughing, he darted a worried glance at Dan.

Lilah's brother nodded. "She knows."

There were enough other things for Lilah to worry about than Shawn's sexual preferences... like the rest of the stuff he mentioned. *She* was banking on winning some kind of scholarship. Her share of the inheritance from her parents... would it last her through four years of college? Not to mention law school. "What are you studying?"

A look of relief flitted over Shawn's features. "Electrical engineering. I'm going to open my own business someday."

"Electrical business?"

Shawn laughed out loud, spraying bits of chocolate cake on his stretchy shirt and boot-cut pants. "Computers."

The phone rang. Two rings, then it stopped. Harry's signal.

Lilah scrambled out of her chair. "You need to leave. Both of you."

Fork halfway to his mouth, Shawn paused. A bit of frosting hung off the prongs. "Why?"

Dan groaned. "It's Harry. He's gonna call back in a second."

"Harry who?" Shawn asked, licking the frosting off the fork. "Wait, don't tell me. I know. Hector Sheppard's little brother? Hector's always mailing me membership forms to his gym. He doesn't seem to get I can't afford it." Shawn waggled his eyebrows at Lilah. "Something going on with you and young Harry?"

Face contorted by mirth, Dan said, "He and Lilah are keeping it a big secret. She's told a couple of her friends and me. And now, you."

"Why's it a secret?" Shawn asked.

"No reason," Lilah mumbled. They weren't really keeping things quiet. She didn't have anyone else to tell it to, and Harry's parents were not exactly chummy with their children. "Can you please leave?"

"Harry and Lilah, sitting in a tree," Shawn sang. "No, *hiding* in a tree. K-I-S-S-I-N-G."

Dan exploded into laughter.

"Are you in middle school or something?" Lilah asked. She glanced at the phone. "Get out of the room, *please*."

"Make us leave," Dan said, tone singsong.

Lilah gritted her teeth. In one quick move, she grabbed the fork from Shawn's hand. "Get out, or I'll stab you both to death."

"Okay, okay," said Shawn, laughing. "We're going. No need to get violent. Jeez."

When they were at the door, the phone rang a second time. Lilah pounced.

Instead of the customary "Did you miss me?" she heard "Happy Birthday to You" sung in Harry's rich voice.

Lilah sank into the couch, its pillows still warm from the two clowns who'd occupied it moments ago. She closed her eyes and imagined Harry's face... the grin, the mischief, the heat in his dark gaze.

She told him about the party, and he said he was eating baklava in celebration of her birthday.

"You eat baklava every day," she accused.

"So? Tonight, it's for your birthday. Did you like your present?"

The scarf was still in the middle of her bed. "Love it."

"When am I going to see you in it?" he asked, acute longing in his voice.

Laughing, she said, "I'll wear it to the airport when you come back home for college interviews."

"College," he repeated. "Yeah... umm..."

"What's wrong?"

"Nothing. It's just... there's stuff going on."

The discussion at the dinner table... the worry about oil stocks... "What's happening with Genesis? There have been so many things in the news about Gaddafi..."

"He's crazy. Completely cra—let's not talk about him. I want to know if you still miss me."

"Harry," she warned.

"I'll tell you all about it. I swear. Just not now. It's your birthday."

She huffed. "Fine. But next time, I'm not letting you slither out." At his sudden guffaw, she asked, "What?"

"I just remembered the lizard you thought was a snake."

"Argh. Don't think *I* forgot."

"How can I? You never forget *any*thing."

They argued about it for a couple of minutes.

When it was time to hang up, Harry said, "Habibti, I need to see you. I don't know how I'm supposed to hang on for another year without—"

The high-pitched dial tone told Lilah their time was up. The telephone receiver back on the cradle, Lilah contemplated the snowflakes falling outside the window. It wasn't only longing she heard in his voice. He sounded desperate. Almost on the verge of... something.

In less than a month, Lilah was again at a party she didn't particularly want to attend. The boy facing her turned a deep shade of red, almost matching the giant cardboard hearts hanging from the ceiling of the school gym. His gaze skittered over the crowd gyrating enthusiastically to the shrieks from the live band in one corner. Sweat rolled down his long sideburns. It *was* more than comfortably warm in the gym. Alarmed, Lilah placed a hand on his elbow. "Don't faint—"

"You wanna have sex with me?"

"Huh?" Lilah's jaw dropped open. She snatched her hand back. "Eww." Beady eyes almost bugging out, the boy lurched forward. The skunky smell surrounding him intensified. "No," screamed Lilah, jumping back into the crowd behind her. One of the cardboard hearts oscillated, poking her in the brow. "Argh." Her shout was drowned out by the screech of the electric guitar.

The boy heaved. Vomit splattered on the hardwood floor, and bits of slime-covered potato chips landed on Lilah's black wedges.

The couples around them stopped their enthusiastic leaps and jerks. Girlish squeals abounded, one "Hey, man," and an authoritative "Again, Preston?"

In less than two minutes, Robert Preston III was hauled off by the chaperone and told to set his skinny backside down in the school secretary's office to wait for his mother to pick him up. The janitor arrived, his bucket clanging, and mopped up the barf. The curious crowd drifted off, leaving Lilah with Ginger and Vivian. The band switched to a slow number. Couples swayed awkwardly to the dreamy voice of the female singer.

"I told you not to talk to him," said Ginger. She was dressed in a lilac sweater and a royal-blue mini tonight. "I've known Bobby since grade school. His mother's been warning him from then girls will try to have sex with him for his money. Plus, didn't you *smell* him? He's been smoking pot, and it always makes him barf."

"All I wanted was to ask him about the job at his father's bank," Lilah said, checking her mauve jumpsuit for vomit spatters. Nothing, thank God. She couldn't afford to have her clothes ruined.

"Doesn't matter," said Vivian, pushing her glasses up her nose. She was also in purple. *Everyone* was wearing purple this year. Vivian's plum-colored sweater dress was cinched at the waist with a wide belt. "You're a girl. You went to Bobby and tried to talk to him. He connected the dots."

Lilah gritted her teeth. "Creep."

She crossed the bank job off her mental list. Neither could

she take the modeling job offered by Mrs. Rose. Ivy League law schools tended to be on the conservative side, and Lilah wasn't about to let them use it as excuse to fling her application into the trash can.

Following her talk with Shawn, she'd done some rough calculations. She needed a job. Pronto. Unfortunately, there weren't many positions she was qualified for in the wealthy town. Not the kind of work which the Barronses as her legal guardians would give permission to do. She'd found *that* out over the last few months.

Bobby Preston's father owned a local bank, and they'd advertised for a weekend teller. Even the Barronses couldn't possibly find fault with the position. Lilah possessed no experience whatsoever, but she could learn. She'd always been good with numbers. It was a chance to pad her savings. With her resume blank, the only way she'd get the job was if someone recommended her. Someone not named Andrew Barrons. Since the owner's son went to the same school as her, she'd thought... Lilah certainly didn't want the job if it meant putting up with Creepy Bobby.

"I might as well go home," she muttered. "No one ever asks me to dance, anyway."

"I've been meaning to talk to you about that," said Vivian. "Forget about jobs for now. We need to discuss your social life. Do you realize all the boys are afraid of you? Even the ones in the chess club."

"Hey," snapped Lilah. "Look what happened when I *tried* to talk to a boy."

"Bobby's a weirdo," Vivian admitted. "The rest are mostly okay. But except for Ginger and me, you don't talk much to the girls, either."

Worriedly, Lilah bit her lower lip. "I'm not shy." Unlike Harry, she didn't feel the urge to make friends with the rest of the world. She was happy with the handful of friends she did have, and she didn't see the need to broadcast her thoughts to anyone else. "I'm not very chatty is all. Doesn't mean I'm snooty or anything."

"I *know* that," said Vivian, tone impatient. "I'm telling you to try being a bit friendlier to the *boys*, at least. Finding a job is well and good, but you need to keep your options open. Look for a man with earning potential."

Lilah and Ginger exchanged meaningful glances. Vivian kept an actual list of likely husbands from among the boys she knew. She was also quite willing to share said list with her friends. In fact, worried as she was about their romantic futures, she *insisted* on sharing the names with them.

Adjusting her glasses with one hand, Vivian waved the other in an arc. "I get that you already have a boyfriend, but it ain't smart to put all your eggs into one—" Her eyes arrested.

Lilah and Ginger moved in unison, following Vivian's gaze.

"What's going on?" Ginger asked, trying to peer through the crowd.

Pursing her lips, Vivian said, "Prospect number three at eleven-hundred." Before either of the other girls could object, she flounced away.

Ginger rolled her eyes. Turning to Lilah, she said, "How are you going to leave without Dan? He came with you in your car."

The 1970 Dodge Colt once belonged to Lilah's parents. She'd driven it today under the careful supervision of the Barrons chauffeur, and the man would not leave Dan at the school gym to take her back to the mansion. He'd say he needed to check with Andrew, and Lilah would have to make up an excuse... she didn't feel up to it.

Squinting at the crowd, Ginger asked, "Where *is* Dan?"

"I thought you lost interest in him," teased Lilah.

Ginger shrugged. "He's too nice. I don't do 'nice' in boyfriends." After the birthday dinner at the Barrons mansion, she'd dumped Dan. Being between boys, she opted to go to this Valentine's Day party as a girls' group with Lilah and Vivian. "If you really want to go home," Ginger offered, "you don't have to wait for your brother. I can call *our* chauffeur."

"*You're* too nice," Lilah said warmly. "Your whole family. First, your mother offers me a job. And now, this."

"The job's still yours if you want," Ginger said. "You'd be perfect for our products. Also, we pay better than Preston Bank."

Regretfully, Lilah said, "Martha Stewart might have made it, but I still can't take the chance. It's already not easy for women to get into law school. If I have 'model' on my resume, they might not believe I'm serious about becoming a lawyer."

"You could continue modeling for us after school. We'll both get chemistry degrees and be partners. I can take care of the cosmetics, and you can be in charge of the fragrances. You know your perfumes. You won't get to be a supreme court justice, but we *could* win the Nobel Prize for chemistry."

Lilah giggled. "I don't think they hand them out for perfumes."

"They should." Ginger's eyes crinkled in mirth. "Between Vivian and me, you're getting plenty of career advice."

"Actually, you've helped a lot. Until we met, I never realized you needed a chemistry degree to create makeup. Because of you, I've been thinking about doing chemical engineering for undergrad."

"Really?"

"The job prospects are good. Especially in the oil and gas business."

Frowning, Ginger asked, "You want to work for your brother-in-law? I thought he didn't like—*you* didn't—" She flushed. "Sorry. I should shut up."

Lilah hadn't shared the details of her status in the Barrons household, but it wouldn't have been too difficult to guess. The old clothes, the ordinary car, the need for a part-time job... the indifference of the Barronses was all too obvious at the birthday dinner. "I know a few other people in the business," Lilah said. "Harry's family for one."

The knot in her chest made a reappearance. The acute pleasure at the thought of Harry mingled with the pain of missing him and the worry over what was going on in his life.

This month, it was Lilah's turn to call, and she was determined to cross-examine him. She'd seen the senator from New Jersey on the evening news, talking about some kind of committee formed by the private drillers operating in the Middle East to take collective action against coercive governments. Surely, Harry already knew from his father what the committee decided to do with the Libyan dictator. Why was he hiding it from her? Also, he used to be so gung-ho about his plans for college, but now, he never mentioned it unless *she* brought it up. Then there were the random accidents he mentioned before.

Andrew's words rang in Lilah's mind. *"The situation is unstable... Genesis is not worth the risk."*

She needed to pin Harry down on this. She had to make sure he wasn't in any actual danger.

"That's *after* undergrad," Ginger said. "What will you do about tuition?"

What? Oh... Lilah dragged her mind back to the Valentine's Day party. The band was now playing Mungo Jerry's "In the Summertime." Tamping down worry, she said, "I have some money from my parents, and I'm really hoping to get a scholarship." Until her conversation with Andrew's son, Shawn, Lilah hadn't realized how much competition there was for the few scholarships which covered living expenses as well as tuition. Her grades needed to stand out— "Maybe it's a good thing I don't have a job right now. I'm taking the SATs in April."

Ginger made a moue of distaste. "Did you *have* to remind me?"

"I'm sorry. I know I've been boring you and Viv with the job talks." In the last few weeks, the only things Lilah could think about were Harry's safety and making sure she and Dan would be free of Andrew once they left for college. The survivor benefits from their parents and the small amount of cash in the bank wouldn't be enough to buy them independence.

Laughing lightly, Ginger said, "Don't be sorry. My parents think you're a good influence on me. Good grades, chess champ, planning for college... all that stuff. Mother still hasn't forgiven me for breaking up with Dan. Even my grandfather—tell you what? *He* might have a job for you. In his office, I mean."

Months later, June 1973

To Lilah's right, the typewriter practically hummed under the magical fingers of the elderly typist. Across the room, one of the accounting clerks was leaning over the desk of the executive secretary, flirting madly. It was your average morning at the corporate headquarters of Rose Cosmetics.

Setting the mug of fragrant coffee on her own tiny desk in the office suite, Lilah smoothed her black, knee-length skirt before sitting. The badge clipped onto her white shirt displayed her picture and name with her title—office assistant—written in large letters underneath. The crimson scarf—Harry's birthday gift—was tied jauntily around her neck and made the dull work outfit slightly less boring.

Lilah's summer job involved mostly filing papers and carrying messages and ordering food for conferences. She made little more than minimum wage. Ginger rolled her eyes and mouthed *model* each time she walked by.

Still, Lilah felt the thrill of pride when she got her first paycheck. Oh, she'd worked before her parents died. Her previous job stacking books in the local library supplemented her pocket money. But *this*... somehow, her spine was a tad straighter when she returned every evening to the Barrons mansion.

Plus, it was fascinating to see how much there was to running a business. It wasn't only about the right product. There was a great deal of strategizing that went into positioning yourself exactly right in the market. Old Man Rose—the CEO—kept a close eye on the finances of the vendors supplying the company. He was fond of theorizing to his secretarial staff on Wall Street's likely reaction to events. Lilah was amazed at the frequency with which his predictions came true. She was even more surprised to see how many of them matched Andrew's when he was tutoring Dan at the dinner table. Her brother-in-law was a total jerk, but it appeared he did know the stock market. If the business magazines Lilah had taken to studying were accurate, Andrew was an excellent executive. The rest of the world might be in the grip of a bear market, but Barrons O & G still showed a very healthy profit margin.

Eyeing the rolled-up newspaper on her desk, Lilah wondered if she dared apply the theories she learned to the numbers she'd seen in *The Wall Street Journal.* For fun, of course. She didn't have any money to invest.

"Delilah," called the secretary, her tone high and musical. "We're expecting a price list from one of our vendors. Run down to the telecommunication room for me, please. Bring it to the boss's office."

In fifteen minutes, Lilah was entering the executive suite, a wood-paneled room with a massive desk in the middle.

"Right on time," said Old Man Rose. He pushed his leather chair back from the desk. "Let's see the numbers."

With a vague glance at the top sheet, Lilah held out the papers. She frowned.

From the other side of the desk, the secretary asked, "Something wrong?"

Lilah handed the printouts to her. "Not at all. I was just surprised to see the name of the vendor." Sanders, Incorporated. "Isn't that an oil drilling company?"

Old Man Rose grinned. "We buy some of our ingredients from them—the petrochemicals which go into our products. But labeling Sanders an oil driller is like calling Cornelius Vanderbilt a ferry service operator. Sanders's company does a lot of things besides drill. *There's* an incredible businessman. Austrian roots... father and son used to live in Malta. As far as I know, the mother died in childbirth. When the First World War started, Jared's father asked for asylum in the U.S. to avoid getting conscripted. They had barely anything to their name when they got to Oklahoma. Now, Sanders, Incorporated, is all over the world—the Middle East, the Americas, Asia, Africa."

"Africa?" Lilah queried hesitantly. "Like Libya?"

"Among other countries," said Old Man Rose. "Why do you ask?"

"All the things in the news," Lilah mumbled. The ache in her chest returned. Harry still hadn't answered questions to her satisfaction. Out loud, she explained, "I was watching something on Watergate, and there was a senator on CBS, discussing it. The chairman of the commerce committee. There was a question about Libya."

The politician hadn't really answered it. He mouthed a couple of platitudes about the government doing everything it could to ensure the safety of American expats, and the anchor moved on to another topic.

"Temple, I'm sure," mused Old Man Rose, rocking back in his chair. "Mets fan," he added, tone suggesting the senator's support of the baseball team was a horrific error in judgment.

The secretary laughed.

Chuckling along, Old Man Rose continued explaining to Lilah, "Temple's a friend of Andrew's. Temple's family is also big in oil. Kingsley Corp."

"Kingsley?" asked Lilah, her attention caught. "As in Supreme Court Justice Godwin Kingsley?"

"The same."

She would've loved an introduction to the justice. She could work hard at paying for her own college, but hard work was not going to be enough to put her in the vicinity of Justice Godwin Kingsley. She never realized he shared a connection with Andrew Barrons. Not that she'd given Andrew any reason to help her out with her career.

Harry's face popped into her mind, laughing uproariously at her predicament. *"You should've been nice, Princess,"* he mocked. Mentally, she stuck her tongue out at him. She could make it on her own, thank you very much. She was a chess player. She could create her own winning strategies.

"You keep up with current events," remarked Old Man Rose. "I appreciate such curiosity in a youngster. Ginger tells me you did very well in your SATs. *She* hasn't even taken it yet."

Neither had Dan. He was also waiting for their senior year. He'd proudly announced Lilah's scores at the dinner table, though. Beyond a stiff nod from Caroline, there was no acknowledgment from the Barronses.

With his St. Nicholas smile lighting up his chubby cheeks, Old Man Rose added, "I'm meeting Andrew at the golf course this weekend. I'll have to tell him he's doing a fine job raising you."

Lilah forcibly stretched her lips into a smile.

"Lawyer, huh?" The old man nodded to himself. "Yes, I can see it. I don't know if you'll get to the Supreme Court, but you'll do well. Good stock. Long run."

#

September 1973

Washington, DC

"Allende Dead in Chilean Coup," screamed the headlines on the front page of *The Washington Post.* Temple dragged his eyes from the pile of newspapers on his desk to the chessboard on the coffee table. He'd been holed up in the library in his office suite, hoping for a brief reprieve from the constant barrage of bad news over the Watergate scandal. One day to call his own with some wine and the pleasant company of an old friend was all he wanted. Together, they'd mourn the current state of the New York Mets even with a baseball legend like Yogi Berra as the manager. Plus, Frank Sinatra crooning "My Way" from the turntable at the far corner of the room. The universe apparently decreed peace was not in store for Temple. Not this afternoon.

First, Andrew Barrons called, saying he was on his way to the senate office building. Then, Temple's chief of staff brought him a transcript of the dead Chilean president's last radio address to his people, one he made even as he watched the tanks rolling toward the national palace.

The man occupying the other leather chair sighed. "You can't stop thinking about it, can you?" Noah Andersen, former attorney general, was now back to running the securities law firm he'd started. Temple met Noah when they were both freshmen at Yale. With his hair dyed jet black and his eyes a startling green in the gaunt face, Noah resembled a monk from the Middle Ages. His lean physique added to his ascetic appearance.

Temple used his pawn to capture one of Noah's knights. "President Salvador Allende was a staunch believer in Marxism. He and I agreed on very little, but we both essentially wanted the same thing... a better life for all people. He knew he was about to die, and his last thought was to reassure his countrymen with: 'Other men will overcome this bitter and gray moment... great avenues will open on which free men will walk and build a better society.'"

"Powerful," agreed Noah, taking a sip from the glass of red wine in his hand.

"'These are my final words,'" Temple continued, "'knowing that my sacrifice will not be in vain.' Allende seemed certain of it."

"But you aren't?"

On the turntable, Sinatra finished his song. Not bothering to switch vinyl discs, Temple shrugged. "Allende and his gang didn't understand macroeconomics. Their policies were disastrous for Chile. General Pinochet is likely to be more market-friendly.

Better for American business interests." In fact, there was strong feeling around the world the CIA helped arrange the coup.

"Then why are you this disturbed?"

"Dammit all, Noah." Temple shoved his chair back from the coffee table and stood. Walking to the world map on the wall behind the desk, he said, "Don't you see? Allende was in it to help his people, but he had no clue how to do it. He gave up his life for nothing. Then there's the situation here. Even with everything going on, President Nixon insists he's a patriot. Like Allende. Unlike Allende, Nixon has some brilliant people advising him. He himself is an incredibly intelligent man. Still, he pulled something stupid like—"

Noah snorted. "Are *you* claiming to be above dirty tricks?"

Temple laughed. "I'll plead the Fifth." Amusement fading, he turned to face his friend. "Dirty tricks in our elections are as old as the United States itself."

"Thomas Jefferson," Noah said, tilting the glass of wine toward the bronze bust on Temple's desk. The founding father had spread rumors about his colleague, John Adams.

"JFK," Temple contributed. There was widespread suspicion the Massachusetts politician won because of ballot box stuffing in Illinois. "I won't claim to be any better than the lates and the greats. Still, I've tried to make sure I don't hurt the nation with my actions. Whenever I... strayed outside the lines, I tried to limit the damage. If I were caught, I'd like to think I'd step aside rather than cause the people I swore to serve to lose faith in their government. If Nixon were fighting to prove his innocence, I could understand his insistence on staying the course, but at this point, there's enough evidence against him. He claims to be a patriot, but he's refusing to save the country grief by stepping down. Instead, he's clinging to power. There's no willingness in him to sacrifice."

"Temple, don't you remember his so-called last press conference back in 'sixty-two? He told the media they won't have 'Nixon to kick around.' Clearly, his ego took a beating. Ego—especially a bruised one—can be a double-edged sword. It helped him fight his way back into politics, all the way up to the White House, and now, it will not let him admit mistakes. He will keep going down this dangerous path, and he will drag the nation along, purely out of ego. Incredible, all-consuming ego is capable of overpowering the capacity to reason or feel any other emotion, including compassion for his countrymen."

"I agree." Moodily, Temple eyed the world map. "With the U.S. in turmoil, the criminals around the world believe they have the upper hand."

For a few months, Libya slipped down in his list of priorities, but recent moves from the country's mad dictator pushed it back up. The lunatic completely took over one of the biggest American companies in the North African region.

"Gaddafi?" Noah asked.

"Yes. Like Allende, Gaddafi talks a lot about national pride, but he seems determined to drag the country back into Stone Age. Our presence there creates problems for him and his agenda, so he's trying to drive us out. Plus, he wants complete control of the money. He thinks he has us by our—OPEC is using oil to influence our foreign policy. Because of them and the Soviets, we can't do a single thing about the madman. Not without risking further problems within the United States."

"Gaddafi is also one of the strongmen Sanders keeps in his pocket," Noah said, tone unnaturally even. His green eyes burned brightly with anger at his own failure to get the criminal businessman during his tenure as the attorney general. He'd watched Temple fail at his attempt to form an alliance against Sanders. "He's promoting bad behavior. Writing checks to American politicians does not guarantee absolute power, so he uses thugs like Gaddafi to control our policies. Austria might've lost the world wars, but one of theirs is now the *de facto* emperor of the world."

"Maltese," corrected Temple. "Sanders has Austrian roots, but he insists he's a Maltese immigrant. We've both heard him."

"Political ploy," Noah said succinctly. "You know how it was back in the day." While Austrians in the U.S. during the global conflicts didn't suffer rigid bans as did the Germans, the civilian population remained suspicious. Claiming to be from Malta would've made life—not to mention business—smoother for the Sanderses.

Nodding vaguely in agreement, Temple said, "We need a new leader, someone capable of keeping all the rogue elements in check, including Sanders. We need someone with the intelligence and empathy to understand the concepts of morality and justice. Someone with enough steel in his spine to defend the truth. Someone ready to sacrifice in service of truth."

"Someone like you," Noah said loyally. "Run for president, Temple."

"I've been thinking about it," Temple admitted. "But presidents have a lot of constraints on them. I'm talking about someone who can operate outside such constraints."

"Sanders operates outside—" Stopping, Noah asked, "Another alliance against him?"

"It didn't work the first time. The parties concerned are not ready to cooperate a second time." Certainly, Andrew Barrons and Temple's own family—the Kingsleys—were not willing to cooperate. Neither wanted anything to do with Ryan Sheppard, who was too deep in trouble to be of any help. When Temple couldn't persuade his own family to join the alliance, the rest of the big oil companies couldn't be expected to jump in. "We need a winning chess move against our enemy... we need to find one leader under whom all of them will agree to unite."

"A *replacement* for Sanders?"

"Yes." Whimsically, Temple asked, "Tell me... where do I go to find someone capable of checkmating the emperor... dethroning him?"

"When was capability ever enough?" Noah countered. "Your leader will need opportunity, too."

"Plus, he needs to be strong-willed enough to force compliance from businesses like Barrons O & G and Kingsley Corp."

Noah whistled. "Intelligent, empathetic, brave, willing to sacrifice... *and* with the strength and opportunity to get corporate titans to fall in line. You don't ask for much, do you?"

Before Temple could retort, there was a soft knock on the door. "Mr. Temple," called a refined female voice.

"He's already expecting me," Andrew Barrons bellowed from

outside, clearly trying to bully Temple's secretary into letting him barge in.

"C'mon in," Temple called out, ignoring Noah's knowing smirk. Andrew could not be snubbed by a refusal to meet. It wasn't just about his generosity toward politicians; he was the master of a company which could, if he so chose, help Temple with his plans to wrestle control back from tyrants around the world.

The door flew open, bouncing off the wall with a dull thunk. Andrew pushed in ahead of the secretary. The oilman stopped short at the sight of Noah. "Andersen," said Andrew, tone cautious. "I didn't know you were here."

On his way to welcome Andrew with a handshake, Temple paused for a second. Noah elicited that reaction in some people—those who'd fallen prey to his innuendos. Andrew had never been a victim of the former attorney general's tricks, but a member of the Barrons board was now behind bars thanks to Noah's hints to the board member's wife how he might be transferring assets to a bank in the Caribbean so he could run off with his secretary. The wife gladly handed over to the FBI every piece of paper she found in her husband's office, realizing much later the husband's only crimes were financial. He'd never even imagined straying from his spouse of thirty-some years.

"Now, now," chided Noah, standing to greet Andrew. There was a mischievous glint in the green irises of the former attorney general. "I'm sure you didn't mean to make me feel unwelcome."

Andrew flushed. "Caught me by surprise, that's all. I came to ask Temple for help. I have a problem."

"I can leave," Noah said immediately. Eyes crinkling, he nodded at the chessboard. "I'm about three moves from losing."

"Please, stay," said Andrew, a hand up. "You might be able to help me figure out a way." Settling into the small couch on one side of the coffee table, Andrew said, "*She* plays chess."

"Who?" Temple asked, pouring red wine into a fresh glass and topping up his and Noah's glasses.

"Delilah," Andrew responded broodingly.

"Del—oh, c'mon, Andrew," Temple exploded. "Don't tell me that's your problem."

"Who's Delilah?" Noah asked.

"A child he's trying to adopt," Temple explained, snapping the cork back onto the bottle. "Only, New York State won't let him do it without her consent, and she has so far shown no intention of *giving* consent."

Fifteen minutes were all Temple would give the oilman before hustling him out. There were favors he was ready to do for a long-time supporter. Refereeing family squabbles was *not* one of them—especially when it involved disgruntled teenagers.

Andrew quaffed the wine and set the glass on the table. Desperation in his blue eyes, he said, "I don't have much time left, Temple."

"What do you mean you don't have much time?" Noah asked. "Are you... er... ill?"

Andrew threw a glance at Noah. "Heh? No, I'm not, but I have barely more than a year left before they turn eighteen."

"Stop," Noah said, holding up a finger. "I want to get this right. The *child* you're trying to adopt is seventeen?"

"Sixteen," Andrew corrected. "She'll be seventeen in January. And I don't want *her*. I want her brother."

Temple groaned. "Let me." Quickly, he gave Noah a rundown of the melodrama going on in the Barrons household.

Noah's expression went from confusion to surprise to outright mirth.

"I'm glad you're finding it funny," Andrew snarled. "But the future of the Barrons family is at stake. Without Daniel, I have no heir. Do you understand?"

"You *have* a son—" Temple ground his teeth, telling himself for the hundredth time he needed Andrew.

Andrew didn't even bother to respond to the reminder. "She's waiting it out. I *know* she is. Once she and Daniel turn eighteen, I won't be able to do a single thing to make him my son. She refuses to use the allowance I give her and goes off to work as a gofer for... she's trying to make sure I never have any kind of power over either of them."

"You have power over them now," Noah pointed out.

Slicing the air with a hand, Andrew said, "I can't use it. The minute I threaten her, I'll lose Daniel. He's quite attached to her." The driller actually sounded puzzled by the fact.

Unbelievable, Temple muttered in his mind. Andrew was no idiot, but it was incredible how blinded by wealth and privilege he was to normal human feelings.

"No matter where I try to take Daniel, he refuses to go without her," Andrew continued with his litany of complaints. "Take this week, for instance. I wanted to start introducing him to all the people he'll need to know, so I asked him to go with me to DC to meet my good friend, Senator Temple. He told me Delilah wouldn't get time off from the little part-time job of hers. Can you believe it?"

"Why didn't you simply offer to bring both of them?" Noah asked. "You've already seen their bond is strong."

Clearing his throat, Andrew said, "Yes, well... she seems to be interested in clothes and makeup... and perfume. What's she going to do while Daniel's meeting the senator? She might get bored."

"There are plenty of stores in town to keep young Miss Dilly busy," said Noah, now sounding as annoyed as Temple felt.

Andrew's gaze skittered. "Lilah," he corrected. "She prefers to be called Lilah." Yet Andrew persisted in using her full name. "Temple, I need your help."

"What do you expect *me* to do?" Temple asked, itching to tell the oilman to get the hell out.

"I don't know," Andrew muttered. "You could meet Dan quietly someplace."

So the driller arrived in DC to persuade Temple into a clandestine meeting with the boy. Temple got a sudden vision of himself skulking around the capital city, avoiding a sixteen-year-old villain in high heels and hippie beads. "No," he snapped. "There's a limit to what I'll—do what Noah said. Bring both of them."

"She'll be in the way," Andrew insisted.

"Either get her out of the way or *let* her get bored," Noah said impatiently.

"Get her out of the way?" Andrew repeated. "How?"

"You're supposed to be the businessman," said Noah. "Find her price and meet it."

"I would if I could." Andrew slumped back into the couch. "As I said, she doesn't seem to have a price tag."

Noah raised an eyebrow. Temple knew exactly what the former attorney general was thinking. There was something not quite right in the picture painted by Andrew Barrons.

Temple asked, "You know what your problem is, Andrew? You assume everyone else is like you. The price is not always money. Figure out what she wants first. Ask someone who knows her better than you what would be a good enough bribe. And for God's sake, get someone else to offer it. After the way you've pissed her off, she might not accept it even if you deed her your entire fortune."

Andrew sat up, his eyes narrowed. "Someone who knows her better..." Five minutes later, the secretary led him out. "You will like Daniel," Andrew said as he was exiting the library. "He's an impressive young man. Well-spoken, well-behaved, intelligent, good-looking... I'll call you and set up a meeting once I find something else for Delilah to do."

The secretary shut the door, leaving Temple and Noah contemplating the wood panels in silence.

"Andrew doesn't want you meeting the girl," Noah said thoughtfully. "Wonder why."

"Easy enough to answer," Temple said. "He wants the focus on his heir. But why would he think Delilah—Lilah—will draw my attention?"

"A sixteen-year-old airhead with an attitude. She's strong-willed enough to thumb her nose at Andrew's millions and smart enough to plan for an independent future. Yet she is so ditzy she can't even entertain herself for a couple of hours."

"She wants to be a lawyer." At Noah's raised eyebrow, Temple added, "Andrew mentioned it some time ago."

"More contradictions. She wants to be a lawyer but is so flaky she would get bored meeting a senator." Noah frowned. "Andrew's lying. Any idea why?"

"None, whatsoever." Temple didn't have the time or the inclination to puzzle through it all. He shook his head. "Andrew and his..." he muttered. "There are things going on in the world... dammit, I'm not a family counselor. I'm a senator. A *U.S.* senator."

"Of course, you are," Noah agreed between guffaws.

#

Two weeks later

Tripoli, Libya

Harry coughed and grabbed the napkin before he sprayed bits of eggplant and minced lamb all over the dinner table.

"Lilah and Dan are coming to visit?" squealed his ten-year-old sister, Sabrina, her green eyes wide in excitement.

"They *can't* visit," interjected Dante. His fork clattered onto his plate. "It's too dangero—Ryan, it's crazy. The whole situation with Egypt and Syria..." President Nixon had announced aid to the Israelis in their skirmish with the Arabs, and OPEC immediately followed with a retaliatory embargo. "Plus, Gaddafi and his antics with us... we're sitting on a powder keg!"

"We don't know if Dan and Lilah are coming yet," said Harry's father. "At this point, we're simply asking Harry if he wants to invite them to spend Thanksgiving with us."

Would he ever? Swallowing the garlicky moussaka, Harry said, "I haven't seen her... them in a long time. But how are they going to make it here? It's not like Andrew's going to buy them tickets."

"We'll take care of the tickets," said Harry's mother.

"Sophia," exclaimed Dante. "We barely made payroll last week. We can't afford any additional expenses at this time."

Ignoring the objection, Sophia asked, "Sabrina, what's that in your hair?"

Harry took a quick glance. There was a piece of electrical wire stuck in one of Sabrina's blonde pigtails. No surprise there. She was always taking her toys apart. She'd even shown their father an ad for something she called a personal computer. To Harry, it looked like a bigger-than-usual calculator. Eventually, Dante vetoed the idea of buying it for the business. At five-thousand bucks, it was simply too steep.

Two tickets from New York to Tripoli wouldn't be as bad, but still, in their current financial situation... Harry muttered, "Airfare's pricey around the holidays."

Waving a dismissive hand, Ryan said, "Don't worry about the

money. Some funds came through from the States."

"What funds?" asked Harry, not quite sure whether to believe it. Were they pranking him? But why would they play such a cruel trick?

"Someone I know paid us for a favor," explained Father, deftly pulling the piece of wire out of Sabrina's hair and tossing it into the trashcan.

"Really?" Dante heaved a sigh of relief. "Good. We really need to replace a couple of the generators."

"We'll get to the generators," said Harry's father. "Before we do, all of us need to relax for a day or two. Especially Harry."

Eyes puzzled, Dante objected, "But—"

"Weren't you the one who told us the pressure was getting to him?" Harry's mother asked.

"I meant for you to send Harry and Sabrina back home to live," said Dante. "Not bring Lilah and Dan *here*. With all the stuff going on? It's *insane.*"

"Can we really buy her a ticket?" Harry asked, daring to hope.

A rare grin on his face, his father said, "Well, you can't just invite *her*. It will have to be Lilah *and* Dan. We can buy tickets for both of them."

Yes! Harry was struck by an urge to jump up and down, cackling like a horny chimp. And it was going to be only one ticket. Even if Harry needed to promise Dan a kidney, Lilah's twin was going to stay back in New York. Dan wouldn't object, though. He'd know how his sister felt. Lilah would've told him. A thought occurred to Harry. How did his *father* know about him and Lilah?

Dante blabbed?

"What are you doing, Ryan?" Dante asked, voice tense. "Even if money's no problem, it's simply too dangerous. Remember what happened when Harry went to the..." Dante trailed off, shooting a glance at Sabrina.

"We already discussed the incident," Harry's father said. "You and I agreed it had to be a coincidence."

"We also agreed there was no way to be sure," Dante retorted. "It's why you wanted to send Sabrina with Harry when he left for college."

"It will be fine," soothed Harry's mother. "Lilah—and Dan—will be here for less than a week."

A half-hour later, Harry was in the shower stall, turning the tap to the extreme right. After a day spent in the hot and dusty city, a cool rinse was essential to wash off the grime. With a high-pitched hiss, needles of water sprayed from the showerhead, stinging his back. Water sluiced through his hair, soaking his scalp, falling in a curtain in front of his eyes.

He reached sideways and grabbed the piece of soap from the slit in the tiles—peach in color to match the walls. Harry tossed the soap into the air. On its way down, it slipped out of his grasp and skidded over the floor tiles. He crouched and part-blinded by the water pelting down, reached for the soap.

There it was. His fingers made contact. Once again, it slithered out. Harry guffawed. "Surrender," he commanded.

The peach enemy went still.

Harry pounced. "Got ya, soap," he shouted. "You're a

prisoner of war now."

He slathered it all over him, even on his hair. A fruity smell saturated the air. Wiping off the lump of foam from his upper lip, Harry tossed the soap back to its home in the wall slit and grabbed the showerhead from the mount. The jet rinsed the foam from his chest hair.

"Burning Love," he crooned, trying his best to mimic Elvis Presley, who used to be Harry's favorite until Led Zeppelin came along. Harry popped his hips from side to side and belted out more of the King's recent hit. Swiveling his knees in tandem, Harry wiggled to a half-crouch and back up. He whipped open the curtain and serenaded the sink on one side.

The soap was all gone from his body. Sticking the showerhead back in the mount, he shuffled in tune toward the sink and imagined Lilah's face in the mirror. Dream Lilah blushed at the sight of his naked form, but she continued to gape.

Harry waggled his eyebrows. "You like?" To his extreme disappointment, she blinked out. He curled his lip at the glass, king-of-pop style. *Hmm.* His cheeks were smooth. Too smooth. Time to put the fuzz back on his face. No shaving for a couple of days.

Wheeling around, he grabbed the dirty clothes off the floor in one quick move. In they went to the laundry hamper.

He was now all ready for a decent night's sleep. With a damp towel around his hips, he padded over the small puddles on the tiles. A bump from his shoulder opened the bathroom door. Still humming, Harry did the sideways slide into the hallway... and came face-to-face with Dante who was leaning against the opposite wall.

Harry screeched to a halt. The towel slipped down his butt, and he yelped, grabbing it in the nick of time. "Sorry, old man. Almost gave you a free show. Were you waiting long for the bathroom?"

"No, I was going to talk to you about—" Dante huffed.

"About what?"

Silently, Dante studied Harry for a couple of seconds. "Never mind," he finally said. "It's only for a few days."

Chapter 7

November 1973

Tripoli, Libya

Lilah watched the wine-dark Mediterranean through the window of the jet as they neared Tripoli. A flight attendant repeated landing information in a few languages. Ignoring her recital, passengers collected their luggage from overhead bins.

The woman in the seat next to Lilah emitted a delicate snore, her head lolling about. She'd fallen asleep the moment she sat and clicked on her seat belt. *Lilah* hadn't been able to sleep at all on the flight to Cairo or on this connecting one from Egypt to Libya. One minute, she was busy dreaming of Harry, and the next, she was obsessing over his family's invitation. They'd asked both Dan and her, but Harry was sure his parents meant the invitation mainly for her. He said they acted as though they knew something changed between him and Lilah. Harry assured her they weren't surprised in the least she chose to make the trip alone, that Dan decided to spend Thanksgiving with the Barronses.

She wasn't really *worried* about the Sheppards knowing about her and Harry. Her mama and papa had been so close to Harry's parents she'd called them uncle and aunt. They accepted her as family even when her own half-sister didn't. Still, it would be weird, meeting the Sheppards as their son's girlfriend. Or maybe not. Dan knew, and he didn't find it weird.

He wasn't happy about this trip, though. After all, he read the news, too. It took a lot of convincing on Lilah's part before he agreed not to have Andrew torpedo the plan. She swore up and down she'd stay safe before Dan agreed to remain in New York and let her go off to Libya on her own. She needed a few days alone with Harry simply to make sure he was okay. Problems from Gaddafi, the insane number of accidents on the rigs... there seemed to be no end to the troubles faced by the Sheppards. She was counting days until Harry was safely stateside for college.

Waiting in line for the plane doors to open, Lilah unzipped the tote on her shoulder and took out the scarf Harry sent for her birthday. She smiled in pleasure at the sensuous feel of the scarlet silk and wrapped it around her head and neck. Non-Muslims weren't required to wear headscarves in Tripoli, but with her light-brown complexion, Lilah was often mistaken for an Arab, and her exposed hair was likely to attract censure.

When she stepped out of the aircraft, a warm blast of dry air hit her face like a puff from bellows, and she was thankful for the scarf. Heat radiated up from the tarmac as she pulled her carry-on toward the terminal.

Lilah spotted Ryan Sheppard amid the crowd. He looked like an older version of Harry, only with mild gray at the temples and in his short beard. She waved tentatively, grimacing inwardly at the awkwardness she felt. Ryan rushed her to the car with a short greeting, and Lilah smiled at the tall black man in the driver's seat. "Hello, Dante."

Before Dante could respond, Ryan Sheppard opened the back door and hustled her in. "Let's get out of here," he said, his voice terse as he got into the passenger seat in front.

Her tote on her lap and carry-on at her feet, Lilah willed herself to relax and watched the once-familiar streets of Tripoli rush past. Traffic was crazy as usual with constant honking from the vehicles crowding the road. An old Arab in a patterned headscarf led a camel across the street as they waited at the intersection. Dark, pungent cigarette smoke drifted in through the open window and stung Lilah's nostrils. She sneezed.

A high-pitched siren sounded behind. "Cops," said Dante, shooting a panicky glance at Ryan.

Lilah wiped her nose with a tissue and studied the men. Now, they were *both* acting strangely. Police cars and sirens weren't unusual in the city.

Engine revving, the car passed them and sped away. "Thank God," muttered Ryan.

Lilah frowned. She debated asking what was going on, but the expressions on the men in front didn't welcome questions.

As soon as Dante turned their car into the street where the Sheppards made their home, she glimpsed Harry at the front door. Without even waiting for the vehicle to enter the driveway, he was jogging down the steps.

Surreptitiously, Lilah tucked all loose strands of hair under the scarf. Her jeans and the long-sleeved, yellow shirt were only mildly crumpled, but she wished like crazy she'd spent a couple of minutes in the restroom before rushing out of the plane. She did have a hairbrush and a tube of lipstick in her purse, and she could've splashed some water onto her face to make her eyes not so puffy from the lack of sleep. But she'd been so anxious to get to Harry... they'd never gone this long between visits. She did, however, remember to chew gum.

Dante stopped the car in front of the garage to the left and waited for Harry's father to open the shutters. Lilah used the delay to scramble out, dragging her purse back onto her shoulder and pulling the carry-on along.

Harry was at the bottom of the stoop and hopping from foot to foot.

The utter thrill of seeing him almost brought tears to her eyes. Lilah glanced at the car, willing the men to disappear quickly into the garage so she and Harry would be alone.

She peeped back at him and saw the same impatience in the look he was darting at the vehicle. Lilah bit her lip to stop the delighted giggle from erupting. Unfortunately, he winked, and the joy she was trying to conceal came out as an inelegant snort. A gleeful grin exploded on Harry's face, and he loped toward her. Schooling her features into what she hoped was cool dignity, Lilah raised her chin in a regal tilt. His jog broke into a smug swagger, and she lost it. Without having exchanged a single word, they both laughed hard, barely noticing it when the car eased into the garage.

She couldn't look away from him, couldn't stop drinking in the changes in her best friend. *He's taller,* she noted. At seventeen, he'd already shot past six feet, and the boxing and wrestling lessons gave him muscles to match. He looked impossibly handsome in his jeans and black tee. Light stubble matted his cheeks. His silky, dark hair was still slightly overlong, and mischief sparked in his eyes. Lilah once fancifully told him his irises were the color of Lebanese coffee grounds. Dissolving into fits of laughter, he begged her not to attempt poetry. God, she'd missed him! Even his ridiculous jokes and the peppy tunes he played on his sax.

With furtive glances in each direction, Harry wrapped his hands around her arms. Every bit as self-conscious, Lilah let go of the carry-on and placed her palms on his chest. Closer... closer... the sandalwood smell of his cologne... the warmth of his breath...

"Get inside," shouted someone. Dante. "This is not New York."

Harry stumbled back. With a small squeak, Lilah grabbed the handle of her bag to keep herself from falling.

Shooting a glare over his shoulder in the direction of the garage, Harry took her fingers in his and dropped a quick kiss on her knuckles. He didn't let go of her hand even when he hoisted her carry-on and led her inside. He didn't let go until they were at the door to the guest room.

Lilah barely got enough time to shower and change before dinner. In five minutes, she was wishing she'd claimed to be too sleepy to eat. Everyone was acting so weirdly. Talk was limited mostly to "pass the salt, please" and "thanks," all said with little to no eye contact. Even Harry seemed on edge. Lines of strain marked his face, disappearing only when he grinned at her.

Oh, Dante and Harry were talking plenty, but their conversation seemed uncharacteristically unfriendly. Lilah nibbled on her fingertip, baffled at the exchange.

"No," Dante said, mouth set in firm lines. "*I'll* drive you two."

"I've lived in this city since I was six," Harry argued. "Lilah and I *both* speak better Arabic than you. We don't need your help."

Dante wouldn't budge. "You can't take Lilah around Tripoli on your sorry excuse for a motorbike. It breaks down every ten miles. Your mother will need the family van, and you're not getting your hands on my car or your father's."

"I've fixed my bike," Harry said.

"Harry, you—" Dante broke off.

Lilah took a sip from her glass of water, wondering what was going on with Harry. He usually charmed people into doing what he wanted, never argued with them.

Dante eyed Lilah before turning back to Harry. "It's too dangerous," he said with finality. "Either I go with you, or you spend the weekend at home."

"Did you decide on a college, Lilah?" Ryan Sheppard asked as though he'd suddenly remembered her presence.

"She could go anywhere," Harry interjected, a smug note in his voice. "She did well on the SATs."

"Good," said Ryan.

She'd already mailed in applications to a number of colleges offering chemical engineering courses. "I'm hoping to get into—"

A metallic clatter. Sophia Sheppard shrieked and clapped a hand over her mouth. Her blue eyes were wide and fixed on the harmless fork next to her plate.

Lilah jumped, only just managing to hold on to the glass before it slipped from her grasp. What in God's name was going on with the family?

"Calm down," Ryan snapped. "For Chrissake, calm down, everyone."

The occupants of the table fell into tense silence, including Harry. Lilah took another sip of water and willed her pulse to stop pounding.

Asking Harry and Lilah to clear the dinner table, the rest of the family soon left. Lilah scraped leftovers into the trash can and piled the plates in the sink. "What's going on with everyo—"

"Hey," Harry exclaimed, turning the tap on full blast. "Did you watch the Watergate hearings?"

Of course. President Nixon's misdeeds... the Arab-Israeli war... the oil embargo... back home in New York, airwaves were filled with bad news. "Yes, I watched the hearings. But tell me what's—"

"The attorney general, the deputy attorney general, the special prosecutor... Nixon fired all of them. Ain't it crazy?"

"What *I* want to know is—"

Shaking an emphatic finger in her face, Harry quoted the embattled president, "'I am not a crook.'"

A droplet of foam landed on her nose. Wiping it with the back of her hand, she glared. "All right," she said, not bothering to hide her annoyance at his evasion. "Let's talk politics."

Loudly debating the scandal back home, Harry washed the dishes while she dried and stacked them in the cupboards. "'All things will be produced in superior quantity and quality and with greater ease when each man works at a single occupation in accordance with his natural gifts and at the right moment without meddling with anything else,'" he said, quoting one of the ancient Greeks. Waggling his eyebrows at her, Harry continued, "Democracy is crucial, but at the end of the day, society also needs the kind of order Plato mentions here. Or chaos will erupt; civilization will cease to exist."

"Seriously, Harry?" Lilah snapped, grabbing the last clean dish. "I have a quote for *you*. 'Beware lest in your anxiety to avoid war you obtain a master.' Demosthenes said it. Your idea will reduce the citizen to a mute observer with no power over how his representative votes because... well... he's the expert, right? Eventually, it will lead to tyranny. Chaos is small price to pay for the freedoms we enjoy."

The corner of Harry's mouth twitched. She knew—she *knew*—he was provoking her on purpose. Before their lives were turned upside down by the plane crash, they used to have noisy discussions on politics and current events with bits of philosophy thrown in thanks to Lilah's papa's sly prodding. Her parents even used to place bets on who would win. Mostly, both Harry and Lilah ended up exhilarated by the argument and could at least agree to disagree. Sometimes, he found it convenient to infuriate her into vehement responses. Like today, when he was trying to avoid explaining to her what was going on in the Sheppard residence. Harry dried his hands and returned to sample more dessert from the only plate left on the table. "Anarchist," he accused.

He pulled out a couple of the chintz-covered chairs and dropped into one. She followed suit, baring her teeth. "Give me a reasoned argument instead of making *ad hominem* attacks."

Sputtering, Harry reached for the last piece of baklava. "*Ad hominem,*" he parroted, perfectly mimicking her annoyed tone. "You, lawyer, you." Breaking the pastry into two pieces, he offered her one. "How the hell will you actually practice law if you blow up at the first hint of provocation?"

"I know how to deal with troublemakers without having myself a fit. Only *you* have this... this *talent* for driving me up the wall." She never realized how much she missed it... the crazy debating and his needling. Lilah flipped her hair and waved away the pastry. "Too sweet for me." Baklava was Harry's favorite, and he usually binged on it. "How come you're offering to share?"

"It's a sacrifice," he said solemnly. "But for *you*, anything." The heat in his gaze belied the easy tone.

For a few seconds, everything turned a little sharper. Brighter. Clearer. She couldn't look away. He studied her mouth with intense concentration, and her lips quivered under the scrutiny. Lilah's chest felt heavy, as though she'd forgotten how to breathe.

He hummed a soft tune.

"Stairway to Heaven?" she asked, images from the last time she heard him sing Led Zeppelin's song crowding in. Almost two years ago... the park by the Eiffel Tower... when they returned to the hotel where their families were staying, the news of the plane crash which killed Lilah's parents was waiting for them. The familiar ache took hold of her heart.

Breaking off, Harry said, "Habibti, I'd like us to keep the good memories from that day. Also, your mama and papa would've been happy about us."

Lilah smiled. Sadness dissipating, she said, "I hope they somehow knew I was with you."

"God," Harry muttered. "*I* hope they didn't actually know what we were doing."

Her smile dissolved into helpless laughter.

"Have you thought about it?" he murmured, his coffee-colored eyes turning even darker. "The morning, I mean."

In her mind, she heard her and Harry run up the stairs to the observation deck of the tower. She saw him, his gaze pinned on her. She saw their first kiss.

Actually, her *only* kiss. She frowned, wondering if Harry bumped lips with other girls since then. After all, they'd been apart a year and a half.

With his finger, he reached out to tickle the furrows of outrage between her brows. "What are you getting mad about?" he whispered, voice husky.

She bit her lip and debated whether to interrogate him. If Harry confessed things she didn't want to hear, what would she do? "Find myself *five* boys, that's what," she snarled.

His hand dropped. Eyes snapping wide open, he asked, "Huh?"

Yikes. Lilah clapped her fingers over her mouth. "Nothing," she mumbled.

It was Harry's turn to frown. "What five boys?" he asked.

"Stupid idea," she muttered. "If you found another girl or something..."

When the smug look returned to his face, she pummeled his shoulders with both her fists. "You got jealous, too."

"Hell, yeah."

Loud thumps sounded on the stairs to the kitchen, startling them. Ryan Sheppard's irate voice asked Dante to secure the doors. Watching Harry's face go taut, Lilah's pulse skittered. "No more messing around, Harry. You *have* to tell me what's going on."

Glowering in the direction of the adult voices, he said, "The same old stuff with Gaddafi. His council members are always starting trouble. The last couple of weeks were really bad. Some of our employees were hauled to the police station."

"For what?" Lilah exclaimed.

"I wish I knew," said Harry. "As far as we could figure out, the cops asked some really stupid questions. How many non-Libyans visit my father during business hours? Anyone from the American military? Does the pilot who sold me the Honda still live in Libya?"

"Genesis is an oil company. You're *going* to have non-Libyan visitors to the office. Also, didn't the American air base close a few years ago?"

"Yeah, but a few of the military families still live here. They visit. The pilot who sold me the Honda returned home, though."

"Still..." Lilah argued. "Why are the cops harassing you about it? Uncle Ryan should put in a complaint."

With a short laugh, Harry said, "It won't work. This is not the same Libya you used to visit... I was even thinking of asking you to cancel the trip."

"I'm glad you didn't," Lilah said immediately. "I'd have gone out of my mind."

"I was already halfway there," Harry admitted. "I think my

parents felt sorry for me, so they told me I could invite you. Mother says as long as we avoid trouble, we should be okay for a couple of days. I really wanted a chance to hang out with you... just you and me, I mean. But Dante's worried... do we have to talk about it now? I don't want to waste any of my time with you on dumbass Gaddafi."

"Are you *trying* to drive me crazy? I can't go back to New York unless I know for sure you're going to be okay."

Taking her hand in his, Harry begged, "Habibti, please. Just for tonight, let's talk about happy things. I... I need it. I swear I'll explain everything tomorrow."

The fatigue on his face... the tension in his shoulders... "Tomorrow," Lilah agreed. "I want all the details."

A quick smile brightened Harry's eyes. In a jubilant tone, he crooned, "You did miss me."

She crinkled her nose. "Not even a bit. I was too busy spending Andrew's money."

Harry ran a knuckle along her jawline. "Too bad."

"Why?"

"'Cause I missed you like hell," he murmured thickly and leaned forward.

"Whatchu doing?" an inquisitive voice asked.

Harry sprang back. Lilah's heart raced before settling down.

From the door, Sabrina—Harry's little sister—glanced between them, her bright green eyes holding deep interest. Her cotton tee and flannel shorts meant she was dressed for bed, but she held a toy stunt cycle in one hand, the front wheel partially torn loose from its white body. Whenever Lilah saw the child, she always had a semi-dismantled toy with her.

"Aren't you supposed to be in bed, Runt?" Harry asked.

In a singsong voice, the child said, "I'm telling Mama you called me 'Runt' again." Firmly, she added, "You *have* to call me Sabrina. I *am* ten."

"Okay, Miss Sabrina," Harry conceded. "Why are you here?"

"I was trying to see how it works," said the child, glancing at the toy in her hand. The motorcyclist was hanging on to the handlebars, his feet sticking straight up into the air. "I think I lost one of the screws. Can you help me fix it?"

Harry groaned. "Couldn't it wait until tomorrow morning?"

Nodding in exaggerated agreeableness, Sabrina said, "Yes, it could. 'Cause I changed my mind about fixing it. I'm gonna sit here and chat with Lilah." She pulled up a chair and settled herself comfortably in a good viewing position.

Harry slithered down in his seat, flopping his head in dramatic fashion. At his frustrated moan, Lilah giggled, and he sat back up with a reluctant grin.

Lilah lightly tugged the kid's fat braid, the same shiny gold color as her mother's.

"Sabrina." Sophia Sheppard's voice floated down the kitchen stairs. "Lilah, why are you still up? You should be getting to bed after that long flight. Plus, tomorrow's Thanksgiving. We're all going to lunch at the American Club. You don't want to be yawning through it."

"Umm... I was about to go," Lilah called back. Turning to Harry, she whispered, "I'd *better* go. We don't want them... you know..." Once again, her cheeks heated. "...checking on us or something."

The grin on his face turned to consternation. "No, we definitely don't."

"I *am* kinda sleepy. And we have almost a week to hang out."

"We do," Harry agreed.

Lilah held out a hand to Sabrina. "Come on, kiddo. We can chat while I tuck you back in."

When they were at the door, Harry called, "Sleep well."

"I will." Lilah smiled. "We're in Tripoli, not New York. It's quiet here."

The luminous hands of the wall clock in the guest room showed half-past midnight when harsh bellows sounded outside the window. She wasn't asleep, but each shout made her jump, gasps exploding through her lips. Peering out the window, she spotted a third government vehicle roar into the compound. Men in law enforcement gear rushed out. Lilah placed her sweat-slicked hand on the knob, and the guest room door flung open without warning. She staggered back as Sophia Sheppard exploded in.

Breath coming in short huffs, Sophia said, "Go! Hide!" She tugged Lilah to the hallway. "Don't get out until they've left." Lilah clung to Harry's mother and shook her head, fingers trembling. Sophia hissed, "Hurry!"

"Where's Harry?" Lilah asked.

Sophia shoved her toward the back stairs. Hammering continued at the front door. Sophia ran down the wide, curving central staircase to join her husband.

From the second-floor gallery, Lilah heard the door shatter, and black-clad men rammed into the house, screaming in Arabic. Lilah tore across the carpet and dived behind a pillar, back against the marble. She bit her lip to muffle the shriek threatening to erupt. The metallic taste of blood filled her mouth.

The kitchen stairs were only a few feet away. She clenched clammy hands on her white cotton nightgown, heart slamming against her ribs. Pushing aside the damp hair clinging to her cheek, Lilah bent double and ran to crouch next to a wall console. Eyes wide, she scanned the scene below through the railings. Almost sobbing with relief, she noted Harry wasn't there. *Be safe, be safe. Oh, God, be safe, Harry.*

One of the intruders kicked over an ottoman, sending colorful pillows sliding across the polished wood floor. The tall bronze lamp in the corner crashed down and sputtered, throwing the room into shadows. Moonlight filtered in through gauzy curtains as menacing figures escalated the argument. "*...jāsūs*!" the leader shouted.

A spy? Why were they calling Harry's father a spy? She needed to find Harry.

Keeping to the darkness, Lilah crawled on all fours toward the door to the kitchen stairs, the folds of her nightie twisting around her legs. Through the rails of the gallery, she saw Ryan shaking off the intruders' hands until one swung a lethal-looking cane at his head. He crumpled to the floor. Sophia reached to help, a choked cry coming from her throat.

Lilah gasped, protective instinct yanking her to her feet. A hand clamped over her mouth and jerked her backward.

She couldn't breathe, couldn't scream. Feet slipping under her, Lilah clawed at the fingers below her nostrils. "Quiet, please!" hissed Harry. When the hand withdrew, she spun to face him. They were inside the stairwell leading to the kitchen, hidden behind the partly open door.

In a shrieky whisper, she said, "Those men..."

He tugged her face against his shoulder, his shirt muffling her protests. "Shh," he whispered, voice trembling in anger and fear. "They'll hear you."

Shoving at his chest, Lilah turned within his hold to peer through the door crack. "Why are they calling Uncle Ryan a spy?" There was a ball of terror within her belly, confusion at Harry's refusal to intervene. "They're arresting your parents!"

The lamp downstairs was back on, and the scene there was visible from the stairwell. Sophia was pulling her husband up, urging him to cooperate.

Harry snarled. "It's probably the Gaddafi government's way of renegotiating contracts."

Wild with fright, Lilah could barely think. "We have to... don't let those men take them!" She tried to pull away, but Harry wouldn't let go.

Dante appeared behind them with a whimpering Sabrina in tow. They were all in their bedclothes.

Still holding Lilah to his chest with one arm, Harry hugged his sister close with the other. "Papa's told me what to do, Runt," he soothed, the fingers convulsing around Lilah's shoulder giving the lie to his confidence. "They'll be okay for now; Gaddafi's men can't do anything before a show trial, at least. But we need to stay out of sight before anyone thinks of hauling *us* in."

Wheezing in fear, Lilah objected, "But they—"

"We can't panic," he told her, his eyes darting toward his baby sister.

Lilah nodded jerkily.

"My God," Dante muttered. "We never thought the bastards would go this far."

When the vehicles roared out of the driveway, the group remaining in the house ran down the stairs to the living room windows. Except for Sabrina's sobs, there was only silence in the night. None of the neighbors were outside to check what happened to the Sheppards. Perhaps no one dared.

"The embassy," said Dante. "We need to get help. Fast."

They ran to Ryan Sheppard's home office. Dante pulled cards out of the Rolodex while Harry dragged the telephone closer. Sitting on the edge of the desk, Harry rotated the dial.

The first call he made was to New York. Leaving Harry's older brother who lived in Manhattan to contact the Sheppards' acquaintances back home, Dante and Harry took turns calling the government agencies. For forty-five minutes, the room rang with their desperate pleas, but there was no one willing to help. The U.S. embassy was barely staffed. State department officials in DC promised to "look into the matter," but they didn't seem very interested in the arrest of a small-time oil driller in Libya. The expat community in Tripoli pleaded helplessness. Finally, Harry went to the chair behind the desk and sat, his trembling fingers pinching the bridge of his nose. There was no one left to contact and no way of locating his parents.

On the love seat, Sabrina clung to the folds of Lilah's nightgown. Dante stood next to the window, his tall form slumped against the wall, his face unnaturally pale. A lead weight settled into Lilah's stomach when she saw Harry in his father's chair, face sweaty and eyes wide. Andrew had warned them—

Lilah frowned. "We haven't tried Andrew."

"Your sister's husband?" asked Dante.

"Barrons O & G is pretty big," Lilah said. "I'm sure he has some clout. Let me call him."

"Dunno if he'll help," Harry muttered, "but we can try."

Hoping like crazy Andrew wouldn't hold her behavior against the Sheppards, she dialed the number. He wasn't home. Neither was Dan. The housekeeper reported all of them were in DC to meet an acquaintance of Andrew's. From home to the office of a senator in DC, then to a restaurant in town, it took Lilah half an hour to track down her brother-in-law.

Andrew didn't use the opportunity to rub it in, but he didn't mince words, either. "I can't guarantee anything, but there may be someone willing to help. Temple, the senator from New Jersey. He knows Ryan Sheppard well."

"Anyone at all, Andrew." Her words ended in a small sob.

Promising to call back, he hung up.

In a couple of hours, pink sunrays dissipated the darkness of the night, ushering in Thanksgiving Day. Lilah and Sabrina stayed on the love seat. Harry paced, and Dante took the chair. Every other minute, one of them would look toward the wall clock, then at the phone.

A shrill ring rent the silence. Harry pounced, but Dante got there first. "Hello?"

Andrew was calling back with details on where Harry's parents were detained. Lilah's brother-in-law had also made arrangements to secure their freedom.

After Andrew, Dan came on the line and requested to speak to Lilah. Abruptly, he said, "I asked Andrew to book you on a flight back home tomorrow."

Lilah winced. She couldn't blame her twin; she'd have done the same in his place. "Ahh... okay."

Surely, once Harry's parents were free, they'd be planning to send *him* back as well. Sabrina, too. They wouldn't want to risk their children's lives. If they wanted, they could use Lilah's parents' old home in Brooklyn until they found a place of their own. The house was sitting empty, and Dan wasn't going to object. Caroline wouldn't care one way or the other.

In fifteen minutes, Lilah walked out of the house with her hand holding Sabrina's. She'd made sure they were both covered from head to toe in jeans and long-sleeved blouses and scarves to conceal their hair.

Dante and Harry waited for them, dressed in the oil-stained khaki shirts, pants, and work boots they typically wore to the rigs when they weren't suited up in protective gear. As usual, Harry strapped his Rolex on his wrist, but no other accessories. Libyan natives rarely dressed up while visiting government offices, and neither man thought it prudent to stick out. They'd decided to tuck small amounts of cash in their pockets in case there was any need to "incentivize" the cops as Dante put it.

Harry was not happy about having Sabrina accompany them. "I need to go with Dante, but I don't dare leave you and Runt here alone."

"I wouldn't have let you go on your own, anyway," Lilah responded, climbing into the Jeep.

The morning air already shimmered with heat. A poster of Gaddafi adorned the side of a building in the old Medina as they drove past it, the green tip of a minaret projecting over the dirty yellow wall. Next to the crumbling stone arch forming the entrance to the old town stood a solitary date palm. A turbaned man pushed a cart piled high with colorful scarves bound for the bazaar inside.

They reached the office of the People's Council in under an hour. It seemed Andrew already greased enough palms, and Harry was expected. They were told the Sheppards would be out in a few minutes and were pointed to a rickety bench in the walled yard. Save for the wooden seat and a spiny acacia tree—gnarled and twisted with a few tufts of brownish-green grass at its roots—the place was bare. Sweating under the hot sun, they waited. A few people queued up at a side door, glancing curiously at the Americans.

"That is it?" muttered Dante. "After all the trouble they took making the arrest? I'm getting a bad feeling."

"Let's see what happens," said Harry, eyes troubled.

When the Sheppards came out of the concrete single-story building, there were no guards with them. Their clothes were unkempt, but both appeared uninjured. Sabrina jumped off the bench and ran to her papa, followed by Dante.

With a mumbled prayer of thanks, Harry started forward.

Tires squealed loudly. A van roared into the yard, its blue paint chipped and scratched, churning red dust everywhere. The people standing in line jumped out of the way as it screeched to a halt, blocking Harry and Lilah from the others. Doors flung open, and four men rushed out, wielding guns and sticks.

One of them sprinted toward her with a large sheet. Frantically, Lilah willed herself to run, to get to safety, but her legs wouldn't move. Dirty white fabric descended on her. Flailing at the cloth, she gasped for air. Behind her, she heard Harry's roar and a thud. She tried to turn, but suddenly, there were rough hands around her, hauling her off her feet and throwing her to the side. An electric bolt of pain ran up her right elbow as it connected with something hard.

When she dragged the sheet off, she was inside the van in its backseat. On the facing bench seat, Harry was struggling with the three men holding him down. She screamed as loud as she could.

Harry's knee slammed into the abdomen of one of the men. A string of curses in Arabic followed, and a bottle was thrust under Harry's nose. He coughed hard, and his eyes fluttered shut. To Lilah's horror, his body went limp and slid to the floor.

The vehicle jolted, and her head slammed back into the seat. The shouts from the courtyard faded as the van drove away from the grounds at breakneck speed.

Chapter 8

The throbbing behind his eyeballs woke Harry. Through a fog, he heard someone calling his name in a hoarse, shaky voice. Memories returned in a rush, and he jerked up, heart pounding. Lilah was crouching with her hand on his chest and rocked back at his abrupt movement.

Relief swept through him. She was alive. Harry blinked to clear his vision and ran his eyes over her. Skimming his hands down her shoulders and arms, he asked, "Are you all right?"

Lilah nodded.

Bastards didn't hurt her, thank God.

She was still in the jeans and the long-sleeved, black shirt she wore on their way to get his parents. The headscarf was nowhere in sight. Dust coated the dark hair tied messily at her nape, and tears stained her pale cheeks. Fatigue showed in her large hazel eyes.

Lilah brushed gentle fingers over his temple, smoothing back matted hair. Pain shot through his head. Harry winced. "Blood." Her trembling hand dropped to her lap. "From when they hit you. All the way here, those men kept forcing something down your throat."

"Habibti." Tenderness welling, he gathered her close. "I'm awake; I'm fine."

With a squeeze to her shoulder, he looked around their prison—a shed with concrete walls. Gaddafi's doing? It had to be.

The two captives seemed to be sitting in a pool of light coming from God knew where. Shadows loomed all around. Kindling and scrap metal were thrown in heaps along with bricks and a length of what looked like a garden hose. Harry squinted, trying to locate the source of light. There... on the back wall... sunshine filtered in through a vent barely big enough for a kitten. Dust particles danced in the beam, landing on a small stack of cement blocks within Lilah's reach.

The smell of rotting wood mixed unpleasantly with the putrid stink emanating from one corner. *The latrine.* When he got to his feet, staggering from the dizziness, she stood with him, letting him place a hand on her shoulder. "Any idea where we are?" he asked.

"I think we moved east. It was dark when we got here, but I saw a house next to this shed. The men probably went there after locking us up."

Startled, Harry looked back up at the vent and the beam of sunlight. A whole day and night passed? Lilah had been in the van for hours with the criminals while Harry was unconscious. His heart quaked. "Oh, God, Lilah. I'm just glad—" He drew her into a quick hug. "You must've been scared out of your mind."

"I'm okay," she said, her words muffled against his shoulder. Pushing away, she added, "They told me they'd put me to sleep, too, if I kept screaming. But I was allowed to sit with you." Terror still shadowed her eyes. "They left us alone once we got here." She glanced toward the door near which were a dented metal bowl and a jug on the ground. "Someone threw in food and water last night."

Right on cue, his stomach rumbled. "I... umm... need to use the latrine."

The wooliness in his head having dissipated, Harry was able to shuffle without support toward the source of the stench. The light was enough to show him how filthy it was. He wondered how Lilah managed; she was picky about such things. Zipping up, Harry returned.

Lilah was holding the metal bowl and staring pensively at the contents. "Pita bread," she said. "Two pieces."

Harry tried to ignore the sharp pang of hunger in his belly. "Can't take the chance; what if they doped it?"

With a clatter, she set the dish back and picked up the jug. "The water's okay. I held out as long as I could but got too thirsty."

"It'll have to do."

They sat on the dirt floor, leaning against the back wall of the shed. She handed him the pitcher. "The men were talking in the van, Harry. They didn't care what I overheard."

A frisson of fear went through his chest. "Maybe they didn't know you speak Arabic?"

Her tongue darted out to lick chapped lips. "They knew. I was screaming at them in Arabic until they threatened me."

"What did they say?" Lifting the jug, he gulped the warm liquid.

"Jared Sanders gave them a bunch of money. He's the owner of Sanders, Incorporated, right? The Maltese man?"

"What?" Water went down the wrong way, and Harry coughed. Setting the pitcher down, he waved away her concern.

"Yeah, Sanders owns one of the biggest drilling outfits in Libya. He's the one I told you about... the dumbass Andrew was talking about in Brooklyn. Sanders has been after my father to buy Genesis, but what does he have to do with *this?*"

"I think Sanders hired these thugs to kidnap us. But why? To force Uncle Ryan to sell? If that's true, why did the *council* arrest him? Are they also working for Sanders?" Her words tripped over one another.

"The council... Sanders... why would they..." Harry pinched the bridge of his nose. "Gaddafi's been giving us lots of trouble. And Sanders's people have been calling us on a daily basis, asking to buy Genesis."

"You think they're working together?"

"I... uhh... I don't know," Harry said, thoughts whirling. "Father said Gaddafi was the one..." It wasn't adding up. "If it was Sanders all this time..."

"Gaddafi must be in on it," insisted Lilah. "At least some people from his government were involved. Or the council wouldn't have ordered your father's arrest, would they? It can't be coincidence... the arrest... the thugs showing up right when we were waiting for your parents..."

"Yeah," Harry agreed. "They have to be working together." All this time... everything was on Sanders's orders? "Maybe the arrest was to force Father to sign Genesis over to Sanders." Harry's mind raced furiously through probabilities. "It fits. When Andrew got the U.S. government involved, the Libyans had to let my parents go or admit to working for Sanders."

"Instead, they got *us*."

Harry nodded. "I guess Gaddafi's men can now claim we've been kidnapped by random criminals completely unrelated to the government. But since they have me, Father can't refuse to negotiate."

"And I'm the insurance against Andrew Barrons," she completed. "A fork... no, it's a double attack from Sanders and Gaddafi... the Maltese Attack." Lilah and Harry were merely pawns in a brutal game.

"My God, Andrew was right," Harry whispered. "Sanders *is* crazy. Genesis is nothing compared to his company." Heaving himself up, Harry bounded to the door. There was no knob on their side. He tried to pry the door open with his fingertips. It didn't budge. "Get me one of those cement blocks," he called, unable to help the tremor in his voice. They needed to get out of there. Sanders was certifiably nuts... had to be to do this to a couple of teenagers only to get his hands on a two-bit company... but he wasn't even making a pretense of not being behind it. Not before his victims, anyway. The kidnappers felt free to spill the identity of their boss. Nope, there wasn't much time.

"I tried it last night," Lilah said, bringing him one of the oversized cement bricks.

With the block, he battered the hinges, hoping the dull thunks wouldn't be heard by the kidnappers. Gray dust rose in small clouds, and he coughed. Rough concrete scraped his fingers. Other than the minor dents left on the steel plates, the door repelled his assault. "Bastards rigged it," he huffed, dropping the brick.

He cursed and punched the wall. A sharp pain ran across his

knuckles, then his fingers lost feeling. Shaking away the numbness in his hand, he turned to face Lilah. "I wish... if it hadn't been for me, you'd have been safe back in New York."

"Yes, and going crazy." Her eyelids trembled. "I'm sure Dan's going out of his mind. Especially, if Andrew's been talking about... you know... the things he said to your father about Sanders... rivals disappearing and all that. Why does he want Genesis so badly?"

"I wish I knew," Harry muttered. "Could be the low sulfur content in our wells in Sirtica. It makes the oil sweet." At her puzzled look, he clarified, "The quality's high, and sweet crude is in demand. Plus, transport to Europe's easier because of the location."

"That's it?" Lilah exclaimed. "He kidnapped us for a few wells? This is truly insane."

"Yeah." It didn't look like she realized yet what was in store for them, but she would soon. *God.* She wouldn't even be here if Harry didn't drag her into this mess.

"What do you think will happen?" she asked. "Will your father have to sell?"

"Most likely." His parents were for sure worried sick. Sabrina... she was only ten... she would be terrified.

Arms across her chest, her hands massaging her shoulders, Lilah looked around the shed. "Those thugs are not going to let us live, are they? Or they wouldn't have said anything about Sanders."

Harry wanted to lie if only to make her feel better, but she'd always preferred brutal honesty to pointless reassurances. Taking a sharp breath, he admitted, "Once the thugs get what they want, we're dead."

The dread in her eyes solidified. A small, gray mouse scurried across the floor, squeaking as it ran over Harry's boot. Lilah jumped, yelping. The rodent disappeared under a pile of rubble next to the latrine. Cobwebs hung from the roof and walls. November weather in the desert nation was usually tolerable, but the closed room was stuffy and warm. Her skin glistened with sweat. After a few seconds, though, she tilted her chin up. "No, we're *not* dead. They can try, but they're not going to kill us."

Harry clenched his fists. "We *are* going to get out of here. Let's wait and see. They need us alive until Father signs the papers, so someone will come in with food. Then, we'll figure something out."

Over the next couple of hours, they heard voices outside but at a distance. No horns or sounds of engines. Unable to sit still, Harry paced the shed. Every now and then, he dropped down next to Lilah's spot against the back wall, and they gulped one mouthful of water each from the pitcher, only enough to keep thirst at bay.

When footsteps finally approached the door, Harry moved to lie in a lax position, eyes almost closed. Lilah sat next to him with legs crossed.

Through slitted eyes, he watched the steel door open. A woman appeared clad in a black *niqab*, the veil concealing her entire face except for the eyes. She waited a few moments, blinking furiously as though to adjust her vision from the bright sunlight outside to the shadowed shed. A man in fatigues covered her with a Colt Single Action Army. Placing a deep dish and a glass pitcher holding milk on the floor, the woman scurried back.

When the door closed, Harry cursed and sat up. "If they continue doing this, we won't get a chance to escape."

He scratched his neck, perspiration annoying him. His throat was parched. Eyeing the new pitcher, he scooted over to pick it up. A drop of the white liquid splashed over the spout and onto his hand.

Lilah was right behind, her tongue moistening dry, cracked lips. Exhaustion marked her eyes.

"Here," he said, handing her the vessel. There would be enough left once she took a drink. Harry wiped the sweat from his stubble with his knuckles, the drop of milk smearing his upper lip. A faint smell reached his nostrils. Harry sniffed.

Lips parted, Lilah was ready to guzzle the milk.

"No," he shouted and sprang, knocking the pitcher from her hands.

With a short scream, she jumped. Milk spilled across the dirt floor as the vessel tumbled on its side.

"Smells weird," he gasped. "Kinda like tobacco. There's something in it."

"We don't have anything else to drink," she said, her wide eyes fixed on the milk which was now vanishing fast into the dirt floor. The water jug was almost empty.

They hadn't eaten any of the food, but they wouldn't be able to survive long in this heat without fluids. "Sanders's thugs are trying to make sure we take whatever's been mixed into the milk," Harry said grimly. "Could be something just to dope us, but once he gets what he wants..."

"Harry," she whispered, voice trembling. "Even if we don't touch anything they give us, they could simply lock us here and leave." That is if the criminals didn't opt for more rapid methods to kill, like a knife or a rope or a gun.

Panic mounting, Harry and Lilah stared at each other. "Enough with this," he said. "We need to get out the next time someone opens the door." *If* they opened the door.

He turned a three-sixty and scanned the room, thinking furiously. Rummaging through the rubble in the shed to check for better weapons than the bricks, he came upon the length of hosepipe he'd noticed before.

He eyed the roof and flung the hose high to loop it around a beam. When he tugged with all his weight, it held. "Good enough." He sat again on the dirt floor and pulled her down to his side, going over the crude plan he had in mind. "I knock down the guard, and you grab his weapon. Got it?"

"Got it," she said.

"You can't freeze," he warned. "Not even for a second."

"I won't." Lilah wasn't a girl used to rough stuff, but he did trust her intent. Also, they needed to take this chance, or the likelihood of them getting out alive would drop to zero.

As morning turned to noon, the heat continued to climb. Hunger spasmed Harry's gut. His throat hurt with thirst. The same exhaustion was in Lilah's eyes, but she didn't say anything.

When footsteps sounded again, she was dozing. Shaking her awake, Harry nodded, finger to his lips.

The veiled woman opened the door as quietly as she did the last time. Lilah sat in her line of vision. The woman shifted, looking around the shadowed shed and at the open door of the latrine. She said something to the man behind her. He laughed, slamming the steel door to the side, apparently expecting Harry to be hiding there. When it clanged on the wall, the laughter cut off.

He took two steps inside—which was all Harry needed. The guard's back was exposed to the teen swinging on the length of hose hung from the roof on the latch side. Harry's hard boots connected with the guard's spine, and the man fell forward with a grunt. Lilah bashed his head with a brick and snatched the weapon from his loose fingers.

Harry dived, seizing the woman's wrist and pulling her to the side. Before she could scream, he moved behind her and wrapped his other arm around her neck, intending to keep up the chokehold until she fainted. It was easier than the holds he placed on his wrestling partners. The woman hardly put up a fight. When she dropped to the floor with a gurgle, he wiped his upper lip with his sleeve and stood breathing heavily, staring at her limp form. The foul odor of evacuated stool permeated the air.

"Harry, why's she...?" Lilah asked, tone shrill.

The guard was recovering from the shock of the attack and the blow to his head. With a weak yell, he lunged at Lilah. Grabbing the Colt from her hands, Harry brained the man with the grip, knocking him out.

Lilah scrambled to the woman, placing fingers on her neck.

What's Lilah doing—no way. The woman couldn't be dead. Dreading the answer, Harry asked, "She's alive, right?"

Lilah looked up, her whole body trembling.

"Impossible." He glared, daring her to contradict him. The woman *couldn't* be dead. He'd done headlocks a thousand times before. "It was only a few seconds." Harry dropped to his knees and shoved Lilah's hand aside to check the woman's neck. No pulse. The head lolled. "Oh, my God," Harry said, panting. "Oh, my God. She's... she's... Oh, my God." A violent quaking started within. "We need to... what do I do? What do I *do?*"

Outside the shed, voices came from a building not too far away. Harry jerked his head between the corpse and the source of the noise, the main house. If someone decided to check on the prisoners...

Lilah's voice shook. "They're going to kill us."

Sweat plastered the khaki shirt to Harry's chest. "We have to go." He lifted the woman's flaccid neck and unwrapped the black scarf. His stomach heaved. Sour fluid filled his mouth. He swallowed hard, trying not to retch. "*She* tried to drug us."

When he tossed her the piece of cloth, Lilah stuffed it into her pocket with a hysterical nod. "I know."

Shutting the door behind them, they scurried around the corner of the shed and plastered themselves to the sidewall. The concrete structure was blistering hot against Harry's back.

He scanned the compound and cursed under his breath. Except for the shed and the main house—another squat concrete building—the property was bare. It was also walled with a single gate directly in front of the house. Making a run for it was out of the question. They would easily be spotted.

There were no sand dunes to be seen over the walls, no rock formations, no date palms. They heard no sounds of traffic or animal noises. Nothing except the cloudless sky and the hum of insects and scorching air.

Lilah had said the kidnappers drove east. From the direction and duration of the drive, they were likely in the lowlands... one of the small Libyan villages not far from the Mediterranean, ruled by criminal overlords like the thugs who kidnapped Harry and Lilah. Even if they somehow managed to escape the compound, the locals would march them back to their prison.

The Colt stolen from the unconscious guard in his grip, Harry gestured at the house. "We can hide there until dark. Hope they forget to search under their noses."

"Risky," muttered Lilah.

"No other option," Harry murmured back.

They hurried across the compound to the back of the main house. The voices from the front were only faintly audible.

The door was locked. Harry peered through the frameless window, noting the rusting motor on the floor, the metal pipes, and the cables thrown in careless piles. A junk room. There was another door on the far side, leading to the inside of the house. Harry noted a third door in one corner, rotting oranges scattered in front. *Pantry?* Judging by the decomposing fruit, no one had entered the storage space in recent times.

Vaulting across the window, Harry helped Lilah in.

A surprised yelp sounded from the shadows. They froze. A thin, sand-colored cat padded out and glared at the unwelcome visitors, one malformed ear flat against its head. Harry started to breathe again. In a few seconds, the cat turned to grooming itself, hind leg stuck straight up, meowing softly in displeasure.

"This way," Harry whispered, tugging Lilah toward the pantry.

The room was unlit, and it was small... merely enough space for them to stand. Leaving only a crack to let sunlight in, he shut the door. A squelching sound came from under his boot. The smell of rotten flesh exploded, making him gag. In the darkness, he could just make out the carcass of a rat.

When shouts sounded outside, Harry tightened his grip on the gun, praying no one would check the house itself. He could feel Lilah trembling, hear her trying to mute her breathing. Neither dared whisper a word. The Colt held ready in one hand, he gripped Lilah's arm with the other, fingers slick with perspiration.

Through the door crack, he watched a man enter the junk room. The fellow shouted over his shoulder, informing the person behind their missing comrades were not there. The sand cat got to its feet and glowered in the direction of the pantry, whiskers twitching. Silently, Harry pleaded with it not to give them away.

With an angry grunt, the man left, the wood door swinging shut. The cat settled down, chin on its paws, and continued to keep an eye on the intruders.

Bellows and thuds continued, the fury in the sounds cresting when the criminals discovered what happened to their colleagues. Squeaks came from one corner of the pantry. More rats, probably. The stench of the dead one under Harry's boot mixed with the stink of their sweat, adding to his queasiness. His throat was so parched, it hurt to swallow.

Minutes crawled by, turning into hours. Men stomped through the junk room a time or two and shouted instructions to each other on the ongoing search for the missing prisoners. No one checked the pantry for the captives. Beyond twitching an ear, the cat said nothing.

Sunlight had long faded into gloomy dusk and black night before the voices died. Harry stole out of the pantry and unlatched the door leading to the compound. As they hurried into the shadows, the cat peeked out, its greenish-yellow eyes glowing eerily in the dark.

Chapter 9

There wasn't much of a moon, but Harry could see the yard quite well... the twigs on the ground, the lock on the gate. He could hear the jitteriness in Lilah's breaths. Even with no wind, it was as though he could feel the air molecules shift with their every step. *Adrenaline,* he thought, dazedly glancing between the shadowed house and the shed which served as their prison.

Pulse thundering painfully behind one eye, he led the way to the wall and heaved himself up to straddle it. Leaning down toward Lilah, he gripped her upper arms and hoisted her next to him. "Hurry," she mumbled.

He jumped, landing with a thud. Lilah was already scrambling down, her fingers clinging to the top of the wall and her feet dangling above the ground.

The dirt paths were shrouded in darkness, with mud-brick houses in clusters on either side. A village, as he'd guessed. Harry and Lilah hurried along at a brutal pace under the cover of shadows. They had no idea of the direction they took, their only aim to get far away from the kidnappers before daylight.

At every shout from one of the houses, at every distant rumble of an engine, they dived for whatever cover they could find—the gaps between huts, behind a pile of tires, and once crouched next to a chicken coop which reeked of bird shit. Heart racing in panic, Harry shoved Lilah behind him and scanned the path they just traversed. But there was no one chasing them, no headlights to expose their hiding place.

They couldn't have been walking long when the huts got farther and farther apart. They were nearing the boundaries of the village. Once they left the settlement behind... water... who knew when they'd find some? Harry's throat was burning dry by now. Not to mention the dizziness. He could only imagine how Lilah felt. But they couldn't ask any of the villagers for help. They needed to put as much distance as they possibly could between them and the kidnapper's stronghold.

"Keep moving," he said hoarsely. "At some point, we'll get to the next village. We can get water there." He fervently hoped so.

They'd been on the move for hours when they came to a small house on its own. Harry crept around the clay building, checking the windows. No panes. Some of the poorer homes in the region barely had basic amenities. *This* home did have a water tank on the roof, and there was surely an outlet inside.

Someone snored from one corner of the darkened room. Hearing a voice curse in Arabic, Harry froze. The snoring stopped, and the house turned silent. Harry let out his breath.

He moved to the next window. At the third one, he found the kitchen and nodded to Lilah. She quickly joined him and stood with her back to the wall, keeping watch as Harry clambered over.

There were canteens right next to the sink. Opening the tap to a mere trickle, Harry first took a gulp directly from it. His throat spasmed. With a shaky hand on the pipe, he stood, trying to breathe quietly through the tightness around his chest.

Eyes frequently darting to the room outside where the occupants of the house were sleeping, Harry filled the canteens. His pulse pounded with every sound. It seemed to take eons for the containers to fill. Handing them through the window to Lilah, Harry stuffed his pockets with dates and a few pieces of flatbread he'd found. On a small table, an envelope lay torn open. It would have given him a clue as to where they were, but in the darkness, he couldn't read the address.

Harry slipped it into his shirt and brought out a few crumpled *dinar* notes from his pocket. Thank God, the kidnappers hadn't bothered with robbery, probably figuring there would be plenty of time to strip their victims of anything valuable once they were killed. He stared at the cash in his hand and with a mumbled apology to the family whose food he was stealing, stuffed the notes back into his pocket. He and Lilah would need the money to escape. Plus, it would be insanely dumb to leave a clue for the kidnappers.

Climbing out through the window, he gestured at Lilah to follow him. There were no more houses along the path, but they kept moving in the same direction, hoping it would get them to a city where they could get help. The night remained dark and silent, with not even a chirp from a stray cricket.

They guzzled water while walking. Harry handed part of the stolen food to Lilah and tore into a piece of bread, but it was nowhere near enough to ease the pain of hunger in his belly. Lilah slowed enough to wrap a couple of dates in bread and tuck it into her pocket.

It was close to dawn before they took a break. Sitting on the side of the road, Lilah took the food from where she saved it. Bits of lint stuck to the bread. Brushing it off carefully, she handed it to Harry.

At his questioning look, Lilah shrugged. "Not hungry."

In two mouthfuls, Harry finished what remained of their rations. He eyed Lilah in worry, hoping he could get them both to safety.

The niqab from the dead woman was in Lilah's back pocket, with its frayed end hanging out. Harry fought a losing battle to shove the image of the corpse away. The protruding eyes, the foul smell of expelled stool. His stomach clenched. Harry scrambled to a tuft of grass and lost the scraps he'd put in his belly moments ago. Breathing hard, he turned to find Lilah watching him with wide eyes. "I'm okay," he said.

They both knew it was a lie. Her fingers trembled when she handed him the canteen.

Wiping his mouth with the back of his hand, Harry studied the barren countryside. A few shrubs dotted the landscape. The bush next to them rustled, and a small fox with oversized ears darted out, barking softly. When the first orange-red rays of the morning sun appeared, he took the envelope from his shirt. Lilah scooted to him. Squinting, they read the Arabic writing.

"Suluq," he said. "So we're close to Benghazi. We can find our way to our wells in Sirtica from there." Once they got to the wells, they'd be in friendly territory. They'd be safe.

He reached to Lilah's side and tugged the niqab from her pocket.

Fingertips to her lips, Lilah said in a thick voice, "I don't want..." Sickly pallor marked her face. "The woman..."

"I know, but we don't want to be spotted. It's just a piece of cloth."

She nodded, a fast and jerky movement. "Right. Only cloth." A few deep breaths later, she wrapped it around her head, leaving her eyes uncovered.

"Let's get going; it's almost daylight."

"Hold on," she said. Reaching up, she brushed a few strands of Harry's hair down over his temple. "The bruise."

Right. They didn't want any obvious identifying features.

They continued to walk in the shadows. There were more houses in clusters, followed by another stretch of road with only a few scattered shacks.

Not much later, Harry spotted a glint a few feet ahead. The rays of the morning sun bounced off the chrome fittings on a motorcycle. He did a quick visual scan of the terrain, observing a couple of huts but no one outside. All was quiet.

Motioning Lilah to follow, he jogged to the bike. No keys, obviously.

"We're going to steal?" Lilah whispered, tone troubled.

"Borrowing," he whispered back. "When we get to Sirtica, we can have one of the workers drop it off at the police station."

He kicked off the stand and wheeled it quietly for some distance. With Lilah watching wide-eyed, he followed the ignition wiring to the socket, tugging the wires loose and twisting two of them together. The bike clicked on. Luckily, the tank was still half-full.

"You did it," Lilah exclaimed.

"Thanks to my Honda." With his experience working on it,

Harry knew enough to *build* his own bike.

In slightly over an hour, they made it to Benghazi. Standing in the arched doorway of Old Town Hall, they gulped more water. Whitewash peeled off the pillars of the once-grand Italianate building, and a board with Arabic lettering in green hung over the large balcony. When the plaintive tones of *adhaan*—the call to prayer—sounded from the minaret to the north, they slipped behind the arches, waiting while those in the street fell to their knees in supplication. Wiping the sweat off the back of his neck, Harry muttered a prayer of his own.

Afterward, he spent ten minutes asking about pawnshops before they were pointed in the direction of Al-Funduq market.

Driving the bike through the crowd was tough. With the ground uneven, water puddled on the roads, and the wheels of the motorcycle churned dirt, spraying pedestrians with red mud. Soon, they found themselves outside a stall in one of the narrow side streets. They parked in front, taking up the sliver of space between two cars.

From an ancient radio on the shelf behind the counter, a contralto voice crooned a love ballad while Harry haggled with the pawnbroker over his one expensive possession, the Rolex.

In a dish next to the wireless set, *bakhoor* burned, the pleasantly spicy fragrance of the incense driving out the smell of raw meat from the butcher shop next door. Lilah poked the pile of old maps on the table next to the counter, sending a scroll sliding off to roll over the carpet. Clouds of dust wafted up, and she sneezed. "Don't touch," yelled the shopkeeper.

"*Ana asfah*," she apologized.

When Harry bent to help her pick up the map, she gestured toward the door with her eyes. A frowning man was outside on the street, asking for the owner of the motorbike blocking his car.

Lilah hissed, "Not a good time to try sweet-talking. Let's take the offer and go."

As Harry stood, the pawnbroker took a hard puff from his hookah, raising his eyebrows in question. "You're a damned thief," Harry said in Arabic and took the watch off his wrist. "This is worth ten times more, and you know it." The old man cackled and counted out cash, deftly removing a couple of notes from the pile as payment for the road map Harry asked for. The folded sheet displayed the same four projections of the country in four quadrants, and only the main routes were sketched. The poor excuse for a map would have to do until he and Lilah got to a tourist store or something without being spotted.

They couldn't very well hot-wire the bike under the irate eye of the car owner, so they wheeled it out of the market. Stopping next to a street vendor selling shawarma, they bought the chicken and cucumber wraps. Warm, crisp, delicious. "I want another one," Lilah mumbled, mouth full of food.

"I thought you weren't hungry?"

"That was this morning."

"Yeah, right," he muttered, annoyed at his own thoughtlessness.

Harry got a couple more wraps to go. Stalking to the bike, he twisted the wires back together and gestured at her to climb on.

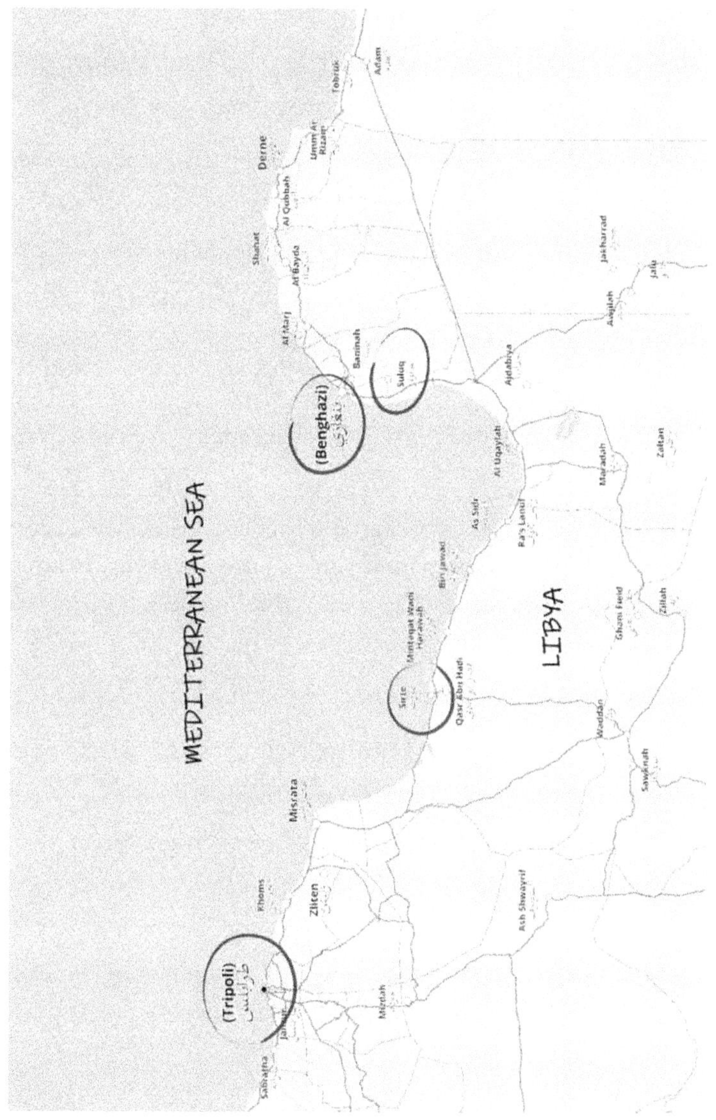

1. Harry's markings on the map, showing their journey thus far.

Barely on their way out of town, they were forced to stop at a long line of vehicles in front.

"What's going on?" Lilah asked, paper rustling as she folded the road map they bought from the pawnshop.

"Checkpoint," he said tersely. "Dammit. The police moved fast."

"You think it's for us?" she asked, doubt in her voice.

"The cops probably know—" The image of the dead woman returned. The grotesque face of death. He swallowed. "They know I killed the woman."

"She was trying to kill *us,*" Lilah whispered. "We can explain what happened."

"Gaddafi's men are working with Sanders, remember?" Harry muttered. Now, the Libyan police did not need an excuse to arrest Harry. There was a good chance even the American government would not be able to save him.

"I guess we can't take the risk," agreed Lilah.

"They know Genesis has wells in Sirtica," Harry said. "They've probably figured out which way we're headed."

"If that's the case, won't they check *every* route to Sirtica? And I'm sure they're going to tell everyone in town to watch out for us."

"Damn it," Harry bit out. "We need to get out, checkpoint or not..." Thinking fast, he said, "If they're expecting us to go to Sirtica, we'll go someplace else. I know someone who might be able to help. My friend, Saeed."

Security was stopping every vehicle bound westward and demanding identification. The line was long, and several cars pulled out to head back rather than wait, so no one noticed the bike turning around.

Harry went northeast, opposite of where Sirtica would be on a map. He'd joined the al-Obeidis in their home in Benghazi district for both *Eidh al-Adha* and *Eidh al-Fitr* this year, both major Islamic holidays. In less than half an hour, he eased the bike into a parking spot next to a mosque in Kuwayfiyah, a neighborhood on the outskirts of the district.

"We'd better walk from here," Harry said, climbing off after Lilah. "If the cops somehow know Saeed and I are friends, they might be watching his house. We'll be easily spotted if we ride up." She glanced questioningly at the vehicle. "It will still be here," Harry said. He sounded way more confident than he felt. "The cops are not going to know *we* borrowed it."

A gentle breeze drifted around them as they walked down the street. A couple of men passed Harry and curiously peered at him. Lilah was wearing jeans, but the black niqab concealed her face. Harry was still in his khaki shirt and pants. His hair and eyes were dark, but without a beard, he was more easily identified as a non-Arab. Plus, there was the bruise on his temple. It was a telltale mark.

Harry casually brushed at his hair, making sure some of it fell over the bruise. Studiously ignoring the passers-by, he started a monolog in Arabic, instructing Lilah on the proper way to cook *yabrak*—stuffed vine leaves. There was a muffled snort from inside the niqab, but Lilah didn't say anything to give away his desperate attempt at camouflage.

In the twenty minutes it took them to walk to their destination, sweat glued Harry's shirt to his chest and back. Lilah was probably baking inside her veil.

He gestured at her to follow him into an alleyway where a couple of young boys in local robes were rolling a car tire around. Concrete buildings lined up on both sides of the narrow lane, blocking the mild comfort of the Mediterranean wind. The screams and laughter of the kids mingled with the honks from the main road.

Harry stopped before a small door sandwiched between two other equally small doors, all with faded and chipped paint. When he knocked, the wrinkled brown face of a Libyan woman poked out—Saeed's *ummih*, his mom. Her eyes widened. She grabbed Harry by the sleeve and dragged him into the kitchen, wildly gesticulating at Lilah to follow.

In rapid-fire Arabic, they were told it was good they didn't try the front door. The cops *had* been to the house to check if Saeed al-Obeidi's friend showed up at his doorstep.

Saeed's mom glanced behind Harry toward Lilah. Her eyeballs almost bugged out. Harry wheeled around. There was no one except Lilah, unwrapping the niqab from her face. '*Masha'Allah,*" Saeed's mom breathed in appreciation. Scurrying up, she snatched the scarf from Lilah's hands and draped it back around her face, scolding her all the while to keep herself covered and safe.

Before she finished wrapping, Saeed was in the kitchen, followed closely by a girl around the same age. He was dressed casually in jeans and a cotton tee, but the girl was wearing the traditional floor-length dress of the Bedouins, just like Saeed's mom.

Harry introduced Saeed to Lilah. "He works with me at the oil field when school's out."

In the living area, Harry updated Saeed, wolfing down spicy lamb and chickpea stew from a chipped bowl. The girl they'd seen in the kitchen returned to offer Harry a plate of sweets.

He smiled. "Baklava. My favorite."

"She's my cousin," Saeed informed them. There was a thread of annoyance in his voice. At Harry's raised eyebrow, Saeed mouthed, "Later."

Breaking off a small piece of the flaky pastry, Harry waved away the rest. "I gotta let my father know we escaped before he sells Genesis to Sanders. I'm gonna call the house in Tripoli, but in case I can't get hold of anyone... if they contact you, tell them we're headed for Egypt."

"Too dangerous," Saeed said. "Call your father and wait here for him."

Harry shook his head. "Thanks for the offer, brother. But you know it's impossible. Even if the cops don't return here, Sanders knew enough about my family to have me and Lilah kidnapped. We were watched; I'm sure of it. If Father comes here to pick us up, Sanders's men could be right behind. I can't put *your* family in danger." When Saeed started to object, Harry held up a hand. "No," he said firmly.

"Can't you call your embassy?" Saeed asked.

"There's almost no one left there," Harry said. They'd

discovered the absence of officials when they called for help after his parents were arrested. The remaining staff proved more interested in not ruffling feathers than in helping fellow Americans. There was no predicting their reaction, especially once they realized Harry had killed a local.

Saeed scratched his chin. "Go to Musaid and take Halfaya Pass," he suggested. "It's safer than crossing the desert. Also, our tribe camps in Musaid. I can somehow send a message you're on the way there. They'll help. Gaddafi's also a Bedouin, but there are many of us who don't like him."

Which was exactly what Harry hoped for. "Thank you," he said with heartfelt gratitude. Saeed meant it when he called Harry his brother, and his Bedouin parents considered such bonds divinely ordained.

Harry and Lilah were told to ditch or cover up their Western attire. She was given Saeed's mother's clothes to wear, navy blue with red embroidery, and a matching veil to cover her hair. "Safer to you to wear married robe," the cousin said. "Girl with boy not husband..." She waved her hand in Harry's direction. "...not right in Libya."

Harry took a minute to wash the bruise on his temple before tugging off his shirt. He donned a long white robe over his khaki pants, and the stolen gun went into the pocket of the robe. A sleeveless mantle and a kufiya—the black-and-white checkered scarf often worn by Bedouin men—completed his disguise.

The cousin pressed into Lilah's hands what must surely have been much-needed cash for Saeed's family.

"Thank you," Lilah murmured.

Saeed's home didn't have a telephone line, but even if it did, Harry couldn't take the chance of using it. If the family were accused of helping the fugitives... no way. Harry didn't even dare risk making the call to his parents from the same town.

Once they retrieved their stolen bike, Harry and Lilah headed eastward and stopped at a phone booth near the Roman ruins in the town of Daryanah. He dialed a number. It was picked up within a couple of rings.

The line crackled with static before it settled into a faint hum. "Hello?"

"Dante?"

More crackles. "Yes?"

In a mechanically cheerful voice, Harry said, "Delivering message for Mr. Dante Maro. You're expected in Alexandria."

Stepping outside the booth, Harry said, "The line sounded bugged. Hope Dante figures out that's where we're going." If someone were indeed listening, they would also know where Harry and Lilah were headed. Somehow, they needed to make it to Egypt without being captured.

They headed out farther eastward and northward, reaching Ad Dirsiyah before running into another long line of stalled vehicles. There were men standing outside their cars, cursing at the cops. Women walked to and fro, soothing crying toddlers. Not deigning to respond to any of it, officials were making their way down the line.

Behind Harry, Lilah shifted. "This road doesn't go to Sirtica. So why are they—"

"Either the phone line or the owner of the bike." Or someone spotted them in the act of hot-wiring the stolen vehicle.

Harry turned the bike around.

"You there," shouted a voice. "Stop."

"Hold on tight," said Harry. After the two long seconds it took Lilah to fling her arms around his waist, he twisted the throttle, sending them gunning.

"There's a Jeep behind us," Lilah shouted above the racket created by the old engine. "Cops."

They needed to lose the Jeep. With Lilah clinging to his back, Harry took the motorcycle twisting and turning through the narrow streets of the town. Both his robe and the headscarf billowed in the wind, flapping noisily. Pedestrians leaped back in shock; vendors shoved their carts out of the way. Captive birds screeched in rickety cages. Screams, shouts, and curses abounded.

"They're still behind us," Lilah bellowed, fear and frustration in her voice.

Two carts loomed in front, blocking the bike. There was no space on the sides to squeeze through. It was as though the carts were monsters, zooming toward Harry and Lilah, not the other way around. The Jeep was behind them.

"Stay low," he shouted. "We're gonna have to—" He rammed into the space between the carts, sending them flying.

A sharp pain ripped across his left shoulder. Pieces of wood flew. Harry slitted his eyes against the debris and felt Lilah bury her face against his back. With every breath, he inhaled gritty sand and gasoline fumes. But there was no way the larger police vehicle could follow without mowing down the vendors.

Within seconds, the bike was on a highway. Wind slapped his face, rushing past his ears in a hissy whistle. Only a couple of vehicles were going up and down. Shrubs dotted both sides of the road, along with a few warehouses and parked trucks. Squawking birds flew overhead, sitting on swaying electric lines. Harry swore. Not only did he have no clue where they were, they were very visible. "Trees," Lilah shouted above the wind, waving her left arm.

He drove into a dirt path leading to what looked like a small grove guarded by a couple of headless marble statues. There was a white tour bus parked in the small clearing beyond the grove. He screeched into the clearing, coming to a stop next to the tour bus. "Hurry," he said, turning off the bike.

On the other side of the clearing, a tall post loomed as well as two pillars made of large concrete blocks. Beyond the structures were the Roman ruins ubiquitous to Libya. Columns tumbled all around, and yellow bricks were piled on one side, the remains of what must have once been a circular building. All of it sat on uneven land sparsely covered by tufts of greenish-brown grass.

Furry goats gamboled among the ancient structures, nibbling at the dry grass and bleating intermittently. The smell of goat shit pervaded the air. Tourists—a dozen, at the most—were wandering around and clicking pictures.

Harry pointed to the tumbled-down circular building. "Over there." Concealed by the walls which were still standing, they tried to catch their breath. Lilah's eyes went to his left arm, but she didn't say anything. Harry put his hand to his shoulder. Pain. Blood. He wiped off the wetness on his pants and keeping himself hidden by the wall, tried to saunter as casually as he could manage to the entrance of the building to peer out. No cops yet. The tour bus and the bike were still there. A few other cars were parked in the clearing. "We need to get out of here," he muttered, studying the vehicles.

"The cars?" Lilah asked.

"Hmm." But to hot-wire one of those automobiles in full view of anyone who might care to look... whichever group owned the car or the van or whatever would descend on Harry and Lilah. Even if they somehow managed to get away with it, the vehicle would immediately be reported stolen. They wouldn't get far before being spotted.

Harry's eyes got to the last vehicle parked at the other end of the clearing about a hundred feet from where they were hiding. A hoodless Jeep, beige paint marked by dents and scratches, stood unattended. Arabic and English lettering marked one side. Harry started. His heart thundered. A *police* Jeep?

There was a mountain of a figure some distance away dressed in uniform. His back to the vehicle, he was grunting as he peed against one of the crumbling columns. A cop, but there was no partner in sight, unlike the tourists who likely arrived there in groups. *One-on-one,* Harry mumbled in his mind, hoping like hell he could manage it.

He didn't allow himself more time to think, much less debate options. Grabbing Lilah's arm, he tugged her toward the Jeep, keeping close enough to the parked cars to duck for cover should the cop turn around. When they got to the police vehicle, Harry eyed the ignition. As expected, there was no key. He helped Lilah into the cargo area of the two-seater and scrambled in behind.

When he yanked at the edge of her veil, she untied it and handed it to him. She didn't say a word, didn't utter as much as a questioning squeak. He tucked the scarf into his pocket.

They crouched in silence and waited for the policeman to approach his vehicle. There was furious muttering in Arabic as the man cursed his boss and his mother-in-law. Something thudded. Keys clanked against each other.

Harry pressed the muzzle of his Colt into the cop's nape.

"Don't move," he said in Arabic. Sweating like a pig, Harry willed the weapon to stay in his hand and not slip from his slick grip. One second passed. Then, the next.

The cop's fingers inched toward the rifle on the passenger seat.

Harry thrust the gun harder against the beefy neck.

The man grunted. His hand stilled.

"I'll shoot," Harry said. A red haze clouded his vision. *Could* he shoot? In cold blood? He didn't know if he had the stomach. Cursing profusely in his mind, he wished he'd pointed the gun someplace else on the cop's body. *Don't show fear,* Harry ordered himself. Swallowing hard to stop the quaking, he called in English, "Lilah, get the rifle."

He felt her scramble out of the cargo area... saw her from the corner of his eye as she got to the passenger side and took the rifle. He counted seconds until he felt her clamber back beside him.

"Keep the rifle trained on him," Harry commanded. Now,

there were two weapons aimed at the officer. In the rearview mirror, Harry could see the man's bloodshot eyes angrily watching him. "Slide over to the passenger seat, buddy," Harry ordered the cop. "Slowly."

Inch by damned inch, the man sidled right on the bench seat to the passenger side. Behind him, Harry kept up, still with the Colt pressed on the neck. Perspiration trickled down his body, gluing the robe to his chest hair. Under the khaki pants, his thighs itched.

As soon the cop was completely out of the driver's seat, Harry flung his left arm around the enemy's neck in a rear choke. The officer's hands came up, clawing at Harry's arm. The man's mouth opened. His feet kicked out. Harry tightened the hold, not allowing a single sound to escape.

He dropped the Colt to the floor and tugged Lilah's scarf from his pocket. Harry smashed the scarf against the enemy's nose. He snarled, feeling every one of the victim's gasping breaths against his chest. Sweat soaked the cop's hair, rubbing off on Harry's face.

The officer's hands left Harry's arm, leaving blood spurting along the scratches. The man flailed, reaching for the steering wheel. Harry jerked his arm back as hard he could. The scarf was suddenly sopping wet. The sharp smell of vomit reached his nostrils.

The head lolled. The body became limp. Keeping the scarf over the man's mouth, Harry loosened his chokehold.

"Is he—" Lilah asked, voice trembling.

"No," Harry said. Not this time. "Gag him." Once Lilah

secured the foul-smelling scarf around the enemy's mouth, he said, "Get in the driver's seat and go in the opposite direction of where we came from."

The cop stirred. Harry tightened his hold once more. Once again, the head lolled.

With a tiny whimper, Lilah scrambled off the cargo area and walked around to the driver's side. The key turned in the ignition. The engine revved. She eased them out of the parking lot and onto the highway.

It couldn't have taken them more than ten or fifteen minutes to find a deserted warehouse, but the cop showed signs of waking up at least a dozen times. At each instance, Harry tightened his hold, sending the enemy sliding back into unconsciousness. As Lilah drove in next to the squat building, Harry was soaking wet with sweat.

He directed her to take the vehicle all the way to the back. It wasn't easy to roll the giant cop out of the Jeep, but they managed. Lilah's veil stayed as the gag, and the headscarf Harry borrowed from Saeed went around the unconscious man's wrists. Tugging off the belt from his khakis, Harry tied the cop's ankles. There was a hemp rope wrapped around the front bumper of the Jeep, much like the pictures Harry had seen of the old Willys trucks used by the U.S. Army in WWII. For good measure, he unwrapped the rope and used it to secure the man's wrists to the bars of one of the windows of the warehouse.

With Lilah still in the driver's seat, they roared out. At a muffled rumble, Harry glanced back. The cop was awake. What was visible of the giant man's face under the gag was contorted with fury.

"Sounds like a monster," Lilah said, her eyes ahead.

"Looks like a bull," Harry muttered.

She continued driving all the way into Al Marj while Harry rested.

#

They both needed at least a short nap. Lilah hadn't slept in three days, starting with her flight from New York, and after all he did to get them out of Gaddafi's clutches, Harry was certain to be exhausted. She parked near the ruins of the old city to avoid prying eyes. As the engine died, she sank back, relishing the cool wind ruffling her hair. The temperature had dropped, thank God. The headlights dimmed, then completely went out, leaving them with nothing but the faint light from the starry sky.

Harry had been uncharacteristically silent throughout the drive, buried in his thoughts. She'd thrown quick sideways glances at him, but he didn't respond. Now, when she turned to look at him, his profile was directed straight at the crumbling stone columns before them. Outside, a frog croaked a few times before settling down for the night.

She watched in the gloom as he ran a hand through his hair, fidgeting in his seat to drum the dashboard with his knuckles. A few seconds later, he uttered an angry grunt and slammed his fist hard into the steel console.

Lilah scooted across the bench seat of the vehicle and took his abused hand. Stroking the bruised knuckles, she tried to find the words to soothe his hurt.

He said abruptly to her bent head, "Damn it, I was only trying to knock her out." Breathing heavily, he turned to look at the ruins outside. "The *cop* didn't die... my coach says chokes can kill people with heart problems. She must've been sick or something." He pleaded, "Right?"

Lilah nodded, quiet tears running down her cheeks.

"Aren't you shocked?" he challenged.

"They put poison in the milk they gave us," she reminded him, voice shaking. "The woman was one of them. *She* gave it to us." The toxic assassin.

Harry's head fell against Lilah's, and he took in deep, rasping breaths. She wrapped an arm around his shoulders. Between them, their entwined fingers held on tightly.

Later, when she shifted a little, he begged, "Don't let go."

"I won't," she promised.

As they sat there, his body slumped against hers, her eyes drifted shut.

Wake up, she ordered herself. They couldn't sleep. They needed to keep moving. So far, they'd escaped scrutiny *because* they were driving a police Jeep. The second the tied-up cop was found, the risk of discovery would skyrocket. *Just a small nap*, she promised herself. And they'd be moving again.

Lilah dreamed vague, disquieting dreams of being chased. She dreamed of Dan, standing on the other side of a busy highway, hysterically screaming at her to wake up and run to him. The terror in his eyes... she wanted to do as he asked. She needed to get to her twin and tell him there was no reason to be scared. She was okay. Harry was okay. But she couldn't move.

There was something heavy on her chest, weighing her down—a dampness on one side of her neck. Slowly, she opened her eyes.

Where... the bench seat of a car with Harry sprawled across her. His face was buried in the crook of her neck. All she could see was the back of his head. His body was pressing hers into the seat.

Her pulse went crazy. *What? Did we... no.* The Sheppards, the arrest, the kidnapping... they needed to escape.

She glanced at the sky outside. The horizon was a light pink.

"Oh, my God." The night was already gone. "Harry? Wake up."

His eyes flew open, and he bolted upright, his head hitting the roof of the vehicle.

"I fell asleep," she wailed, scrambling up.

"We were both tired." Harry flexed his shoulders and winced. His hand went to his left arm.

"You're hurt." She'd seen the rip in his sleeve and the blood coating the edges but in the exhaustion of the night, forgot about the injury.

"Yeah, the carts yesterday."

In a couple of minutes, Lilah pulled out the third splinter from the scrape. "That's it, I think," she announced. "We need to get it cleaned."

"Next place we stop."

They stood outside the vehicle, spreading the map they bought at the pawnshop on the hood to review the routes to Egypt. "How long do we have before the cop is found?" Lilah asked worriedly. "Yesterday was Friday, so no one would've gone to the warehouse." It was the official weekend break for the Islamic country.

"Some of the businesses open on Saturdays," Harry said. If the warehouse were one of those, it wouldn't be long before news of the stolen vehicle was radioed to every cop in the nation. "We need to get rid of the Jeep, but we also have to get some kind of transportation."

"Bus?"

"No chance of escape if we're spotted," he said. "We have to keep the Jeep for now."

"So the coastal roads are out. Too open."

Harry mused, "As Saeed said, the Sahara is dangerous. Riskier than Sanders's goons. The mountains are our best bet." Their *only* option. Across the mountains through Halfaya Pass, they'd escape to Egypt. "We'll see if we can trade the Jeep for something else in one of the towns."

They patted some dirt onto the number plate, trying to obscure it without making it seem too obvious. Getting back into the vehicle, Lilah eyed the rifle on the floor, lying next to Harry's shoe. At her papa's insistence, she'd learned which end of a gun did what, but being any good at using a firearm... forget good, she could barely aim straight. *This* rifle was one ugly weapon which looked like it meant business. "When did you learn how to use such things?"

"Hmm? Oh, the rifle? First time I ever saw one." He'd still decided to take on the giant cop, armed only with the Colt and his wits.

Her mouth opened and closed a few times before she could speak. "Thank God, nothing happened."

"You had a better idea?" Harry asked.

It took her a few seconds to say, "No." Her grudging admission made him laugh, and she noted with relief that the turbulence in him was dimming somewhat.

Lilah waited for a chance to swing the Jeep onto the road. A truck was roaring along the highway, tilting alarmingly to one side as it took a curve. There were a few vehicles straggling.

Leaning back, Harry closed his eyes. "AK-47."

"What?" she asked, tucking a stray strand of hair behind her ear. She sneezed from the dust churned up by the truck.

"The bad boy on the floor—selective fire Soviet assault rifle," Harry explained, chortling.

Lilah turned off the engine to pummel him. "You've never seen one before?" she asked in between blows, torn between outrage and laughter.

Sobering, he said, "Actually, I *wasn't* sure I could use it. I mean, I know how... I learned at the shooting range... but it's different to shoot an actual person." He swallowed.

Lilah nodded, watching the shadows return to his eyes. The memory of the woman who'd died at his hands.

Chapter 10

In companionable silence, they drove across the lush green Jabal Akhdar mountains in the direction of Shahhat. Wispy clouds floated around them as they got higher and higher. Through the dust-streaked windshield, Harry could barely make out a vineyard in the distance. The sun climbed in the sky, and soon, even the breeze turned warm. By noon, they reached Qasr Libya.

"Peace be with you, brother," Harry called to the shopkeeper selling curios and souvenirs. He chatted with the man as Lilah sat in the Jeep. "Your son?" Harry asked, pointing to a black-and-white photograph hanging on the wall. The shopkeeper brought the picture down and told Harry about the bespectacled young man in the dark suit who was studying to be a doctor.

The shopkeeper was soon joking and laughing with Harry. They talked about the beauty of the sand dunes of the Sahara and commiserated over the horrible traffic in Tripoli. When Harry guided their conversation into a discussion of used cars, the man didn't seem to find it odd. Not many people in the small town owned cars, he said, but most of the foreigners living in the area did, and he told Harry where to find Americans.

At the end of twenty minutes, Harry jogged back, grinning in triumph. He tossed the package containing the hand-painted Virgin Mary icon he'd bought into Lilah's hands. "We're in luck. Seems there are a few American soldiers and their families in town. But first..."

They used the latrine in the back of the shop to clean up before driving to the address they were given.

Easing the Jeep through the path, Harry strained to glimpse the Byzantine fort between the trees. The shopkeeper had said it housed a museum, and a church still functioned within the structure. There was an extensive meadow around the brick fort, with yellow flowers clustering in patches on the green grass. Combined with the blue sky above, the effect was postcard-like. The few tourists walking around were clicking pictures.

As he'd been directed, Harry got to the street behind the fort and its grounds. No tourists were here, no one sauntering along the road. Except for a couple of buildings, no one was around to enjoy the beautiful view.

Spotting their destination, Harry swore in relief. The one-story brick structure with bars on the windows was the American Club. He drove straight through the gates into the walled yard. The road might have been empty of people, but he didn't want to risk leaving the Jeep outside to be IDed. The rifle was safely concealed under the passenger seat, and the Colt stayed in the pocket of his robe.

The front door, painted bright red, was open, but when they walked in, the reception area was deserted. Through the side window, they saw a man stroll into the bare yard, whistling. He stopped next to the Jeep and peered at it, inclining his head to read the lettering on the side of the vehicle.

"Excuse me, sir," called Harry.

The man turned, looking surprised. When he came in the door, Harry presented himself and Lilah as cousins, faking a story about running into trouble with local authorities during a picnic trip and needing to return to Egypt.

"I'm Ryan," Harry said, using his middle name.

Taking the cue, Lilah introduced herself as Harriet. When Lilah and Dan were born a few months after Harry, their mothers thought it cute to stick Lilah with the feminine version of Harry for a middle name. She avoided using it unless absolutely necessary.

"Colonel Sheffield Parker," the man said. "U.S. Army, retired." His stance alone would've revealed him as a soldier. There was some gray in the brown hair, a few wrinkles around the stony eyes... fortyish if Harry hazarded a guess.

When Harry asked the colonel for some help with transportation, he looked at them speculatively, raising an eyebrow at the police vehicle parked outside. "We got it a used car sale," Harry lied in response to the unasked question. "But the engine's acting up. We can pay for a used car or bike."

"Sure. I can call a couple of people who may be willing to sell." The colonel went inside, presumably to make the calls.

Harry and Lilah waited in the reception area near a desk with a chair behind it. A small floral sofa sat right next to the inner door. Narrow windows overlooked the fort and its grounds. A ceiling fan twirled lazily, the droning of its motor hypnotic. Harry stood under the blades and let the sweat dry on his skin, relishing the coolness of the breeze.

"Why didn't you tell him the truth?" Lilah demanded, keeping her voice low. "He's American."

"He's not going to simply take our word for it," Harry said. "If he calls anyone for verification—even my father—Gaddafi's men and Sanders could figure out where we are." They would be back in custody by the end of the day.

Returning from inside, Colonel Parker handed Harry an address. "There have been wires about a couple of American teenagers wanted for vandalism and destruction of property. In case it's you, I suggest you go on your own, Ryan. Chances are no one will suspect a boy wandering around the country by himself. And the seller's a council member, so be careful."

Harry thanked the colonel, making rapid calculations in his mind. He turned to Lilah. "Harriet, I hate to leave you alone—"

Lilah interjected, "No."

"She can wait here." The colonel gestured at the sofa.

Lilah flicked a glance at the colonel and pulled Harry by his arm to the front door. "You just said we couldn't trust him," she whispered. "And what if *you* get caught?"

"I know," Harry muttered. "But seems like he's already figured things out. He's still trying to help us. Also, he's right; there's less chance of getting caught if I'm by myself." If Harry *were* caught, Lilah would be safe at the American Club. Harry was Sanders's main target, not Lilah. Since *she* hadn't killed anyone, the Libyan police wouldn't bother arresting her. She could get home with the colonel's help.

A woman appeared at the inner door and asked Lilah if she wanted some food. With a wary look, Lilah squinted at the room behind the woman.

"Eat and get some rest while I'm gone," Harry suggested. "Then, you can drive the rest of the way."

Lilah glanced between Harry and the woman. "All right," she

finally said. "But hurry, please."

Still whispering, Harry said, "Don't say anything to the colonel yet. When I get back with the car, we'll talk to him." She nodded. "I won't be long," he promised, adding with a wink, "Harriet... Harry."

He was about to climb into the Jeep when she called him. "Ryan?" He turned back. She shook her head. "Be careful, please?"

He smiled at her and drove away.

In less than an hour, Harry tore up the address in disgust. *What a waste of time.* None of his usual tricks had worked. The old man quoted an absurd price. So high, it would've left Harry and Lilah with no money for the rest of the trip. He tried to bargain it down, but the wily Arab quoted an even higher amount, ostensibly for the sin of arguing with an elder. In desperation, Harry agreed but demanded to inspect the vehicle before he handed over as much as a penny. When the promised car finally huffed its way to the council building, Harry stared at it with incredulity. The dilapidated old thing wouldn't even get them halfway to the next town through these mountains. Blistering the man with a curse, Harry stalked back to his Jeep and drove to the club.

Parking in the walled yard of the club, Harry walked in. He didn't see Lilah in the reception area. "Harriet?" he called at the inner door. No answer. He returned to the outer door to peer into the street. The fort across the road glowed like a reddish-orange jewel. The sun was still shining, but autumn chill was already starting to take hold of the afternoon air. *Where did she* go? They needed to leave this town as soon as possible. There was a slight sound from inside. Wheeling around, he returned to the inner door. "Harriet?" he called again.

There it was. The sound of someone walking on creaking floorboards. A moan, almost inaudible. As though someone were calling his name.

His hair stood on end. Dread. Stomach-churning dread.

Harry strode through the door to check inside. There was a bar with some dining tables but no people around. The door behind the bar was open, and through it, he saw a woman, the same one who'd offered food to Lilah. The woman sat at the kitchen table, sobbing quietly and wiping her eyes with the hem of her long sleeve.

"Where's the young lady?" Harry asked in Arabic.

The woman looked up and stood in alacrity, one hand stifling a scream. She turned to run. Harry sprinted, catching up at the back door and roughly jerking her around. "Where's Lilah?" he shouted, voice harsh.

The woman blabbered, clutching at the hems of her sleeves and gesturing her helplessness. "The colonel," she kept repeating. She finally pointed behind him, and Harry dragged her in the direction.

The room leading off the dining area was bare except for the Persian carpet and the naked form of a girl on it, her eyes closed, lips moving without sound.

Lil— Blood rushed into Harry's head. He ran to kneel beside her. *God, God, God, what—oh, my God. No.*

Her left eye was swollen shut. Finger marks were already turning blue on the delicate skin of her neck. Scratches marred her breasts and abdomen. Blood stained the rug beneath her thighs. She moaned.

Breath stopped in Harry's throat. "Lilah?" he pleaded. "Lilah?" He grabbed her left hand in his. Wildly, he looked around for help, but none was coming.

He stood and yanked off his mantle. Wrapping it gently around her, he picked her up.

She opened her eyes a crack and spoke through bruised lips. "I knew you'd come for me."

A force slammed into his chest, threatening to crush it in.

Harry carried Lilah, now frighteningly limp, to the Jeep. The woman from the kitchen followed. "Church," she babbled, pointing at the fort. "Get help."

He stared into the cargo area of the vehicle, not knowing how else to transport Lilah to the church. The woman from the club climbed into the passenger seat and gestured in turn at her lap and Lilah's unconscious form. The woman cradling the injured girl, Harry drove them out.

There couldn't have been more than a few feet between the club and the church, but the trip seemed to take an eternity with Lilah's life seeping out minute by terrifying minute. "Hurry," he said though he was the one driving.

The churchyard was deserted. As soon as Harry scooped up Lilah in his arms, the woman ran in and returned with a bearded old man in priest's robes. Muttering in distressed tones and crossing himself, the priest led them into what looked like his residence.

Harry lay Lilah on a narrow pallet on the stone floor and searched her body for the source of bleeding. He couldn't find any hemorrhaging wounds. The blood on her thighs slowed to a trickle. The woman offered to wash Lilah, but Harry wouldn't allow it. He couldn't let go; he needed to hold his girl, keep her safe.

With the wet cloth provided by the woman, he wiped his beloved clean. When he dabbed at a deep scratch on her thigh, she flinched. Tears streaming down his cheeks, he leaned forward to whisper, "I'm here, habibti."

Her only jewelry, the thin silver chain she wore, swung to the side when he shifted her head to dab at her face. The cheap trinket he bought for her in Paris... holding her close to his chest, Harry wept.

The priest returned with clean clothes. Harry dressed her himself. Through the haze of anguish and burgeoning rage, he heard the priest saying the Jeep was now hidden.

After tucking Lilah into the pallet, Harry went to the next room. The woman from the club was at a dining table, weeping while the priest consoled her. They looked up when Harry walked in. "The colonel?" he snarled, asking for confirmation.

The woman nodded.

"You *saw* him do it?" he asked in Arabic. He was unable to understand how she could remain unmarked and uninjured if she tried to help. "You did *nothing*?" His hands curled into fists.

The priest mumbled something about surviving in the town.

Harry couldn't breathe. He couldn't fathom how the woman

could've let it happen. "You left her on the carpet," Harry accused, voice shaking. Lilah, naked and bleeding, was left to die as though she were worthless.

The woman shriveled.

A dark fog descended on him. "Where did Parker go?" he growled. He'd tear the bastard apart, burn the building down.

Wringing her hands, the woman muttered, "The council."

"Listen, young man," the priest said, knocking his chair back in his hurry to stand. "The council leaders work with Colonel Parker. If you want to get out of town alive, forget him. You can hide here while the poor girl gets better. Don't get out of your room until you're ready to leave and don't tell a single person we helped."

Harry needed to beat Parker until the bastard fell unconscious. He would bleed as Lilah was bleeding. He'd be left to die as Lilah was left. Harry took a step toward the woman. "Where's Parker?" he roared, unable to see anything beyond Lilah's broken body, her blood on the carpet.

"Please," the woman begged, tears flowing. "I have a family."

The priest placed himself in front of the woman. "It's not just us who'll be in danger. The council won't let you live if you attack Parker." Harry spat a foul curse at the cleric, who didn't flinch. "Think of the *girl's* safety," he said. "Do you want to risk the council getting anywhere near her?"

The words penetrated the dark storm raging in Harry's mind. Lilah. He needed to keep her safe. No one, *no one,* could be allowed to get near Lilah. Harry wouldn't allow anyone else to hurt her. They had to escape. He pivoted and ran back to Lilah's side.

"What are you doing?" shouted the priest.

Kneeling next to the pallet, Harry gathered Lilah into his arms, blanket slipping off. The priest and the woman were right behind when Harry stood. "I have to get her out of here," Harry said, breath coming in spurts. "Where's my Jeep?"

"Don't be an idiot," exclaimed the priest.

"You said... the council... Parker... where's my *Jeep?*"

The priest crossed himself. "Young man, you were lucky you got to the building right when Parker left to get his cronies. You can bet they're searching for the two of you. Parker's not going to let you live to accuse him of rape. Also, *she's* in no shape to travel."

"We're *not* going to get caught," Harry said.

"What if you do?" the priest asked. "How far will you get if you run?" The bundle in Harry's arms shifted, mewling weakly. Lilah's eyes were scrunched as though she were in the throes of a nightmare. "Hide here for a few days and wait for Parker to stop looking," advised the priest.

The woman offered, "I can tell Parker you took her and drove off. He won't be looking for you in town."

"Stay with me until the girls get better," the priest said. "Then, you can leave. Then, you *must* leave."

They didn't have another option. Lilah was so pale... sweaty even while she was shivering. "She needs a doctor," Harry said abruptly.

The priest shook his head. "I can't."

"Call someone, *please*," Harry begged, voice breaking.

"Don't you understand?" the priest asked. "The council controls everything. Even getting a doctor will be dangerous. *You'll* be in danger, not just us. We'll help you with food and clothes. But you have to stay hidden."

"She'll *die*," Harry pleaded, tears flowing.

"I don't think so," the woman from the club offered, her voice timid.

"If Parker and the council get to her, she *will* die," the priest said. He gestured at the woman. "Fatimah can help. She takes care of her sick sister-in-law. She knows how woman things work."

"No," Harry exploded. "Not her."

The priest sighed. "At least let her tell you what to do."

Harry returned Lilah to the pallet. Sitting on the floor mattress with his back to the wall, he rocked her on his lap and listened to the instructions rattled off by the woman.

The priest ventured, "Er... there was a rifle in your Jeep. Will you feel safer here if I bring it to you?"

Shock surged. The rifle... the Colt... he'd taken both with him when he went to find a new vehicle, leaving Lilah alone and completely defenseless. He let his guard down at the American Club, and she suffered for his stupidity. Harry eyed the back of the cleric as the old man departed to get the weapon from the Jeep. *No.* No one—*no one*—could be trusted.

When the priest returned with the rifle, the Colt was in Harry's hands. Until the rifle was placed on the floor, he kept the revolver aimed at the old man. There were no recriminations from him, only a sympathetic nod.

The weapons stayed on the floor, next to Harry's hip. He didn't move from his spot on the pallet all night, his back against the wall, Lilah held close to his chest. When she shivered in the cold mountain air, he pulled the thin blanket over both of them. There wasn't enough space for another bed in any case. The stone room was small. Other than the pallet, the only furniture was the desk on the opposite side, a stool tucked under it.

Before dawn, Lilah became conscious. "Harry?" her puzzled voice croaked. Her face showed the exact moment when memory came rushing back. Eyes widening in horror, her throat worked as she tried to scream. Her arms flailed.

"Shh." Harry hugged her close as she took great gasping breaths, and shudders racked her frame. Praying wildly to every god he knew, begging to make her pain his own, he held her. When the sun came up and the bustle of daily activity started in the church proper, her dry sobs finally slowed to a stop.

The priest entered the room with what looked like porridge. Lilah's gaze went to the dish and followed the hand holding it to the face of the priest. With a scream, she scrambled deeper into Harry's chest, her entire body shaking. She wouldn't touch any of the food. She barely drank water all day. Lilah stayed mute in Harry's arms, terrified gaze darting to the door every few seconds.

Next to their room, services went on in the church with prayers chanted in Greek and Arabic. The scent of burning incense drifted in.

The rapidly darkening circles around Lilah's eyes scared Harry. "Habibti," he begged, "Please, eat. We need to get you better so we can leave this place." Finally, just before nightfall, she took a few spoons of salty lamb soup.

She needed Harry to carry her to the latrine. He took the bloodstained clothes from her and brought her new robes to wear, the ones offered by the woman from the club. Limping back to the room on his arm, Lilah muttered, her eyes feverishly bright, "Everyone's sleeping; let's go."

"We can't," he said in a broken murmur. "You're in bad shape, girl."

"I don't care," she whispered, violently shaking his shoulder. Her knees buckled. When he carried her back to the pallet, she sobbed. "Take me away," she pleaded, voice hoarse. He said nothing to her demands, and she beat at him with her fists, accusing him of being in cahoots with the monster who attacked her. The punches were weak, but her nails left scratches on his face. "You... you left me alone," she raged. "On purpose." Escape... she could flee the place if only she were strong enough to overcome the monster's accomplice, Harry.

He took every one of her feeble blows, chanting "I'm sorry" with every breath.

Even when her fury petered to a stop, Lilah didn't sleep. She started at every small sound outside, gaze fixed on the door to their room. Harry didn't know when he dozed off, but when he woke, Lilah's back was burrowed against his chest, and she was clutching his arms, wrapping them tightly around her torso. He thought it was because of the cold until he saw she was still staring hard at the door. The revolver was now on the floor on her side of the pallet.

The same pattern ran in an endless loop. The days and nights took on the surreal quality of a bad dream. During waking hours, Lilah ate little, staying silent and vigilant, holding the Colt and a fork she saved from one of the wasted dinners as weapons. The priest offered prayers in the church, praises to the Almighty. Fragrant smoke clung to the walls, to their clothes, to their hair.

When night fell in the mountains, Lilah begged Harry to take her away. When he failed to comply, she alternated between pleas and recriminations, attacking him however she could, with words, with fists, with her nails. She even staggered to the door once, falling to the stone floor in tears as she realized she wouldn't make it. When she tired, Harry returned her to the pallet, only to have her sleeping in fits within his embrace, trembling awake at the slightest sound.

Every now and then, she would mutter to herself, rocking back and forth. She whispered pleas to the Almighty for reprieve from this nightmare. She begged for rescue, for someone to take her away from this hell.

In a couple of days, Harry stopped seeing bloodstains on her clothes. But Lilah was still pale, still couldn't walk without support. He didn't dare take the risk of her not being able to run from potential pursuers.

Toward the end of the second week, Lilah sat on the floor, knees drawn up and back to the wall. Harry was lying next to her, lost in thoughts. Without a trace of emotion, she announced, "I'm not pregnant."

Willing into her every ounce of love he felt, Harry held her, the sweat on her body soaking into his clothes. When she curled up in pain from menstrual cramps, he rubbed her back, uncertain how else to help. She remained silent and stiff in his arms.

Before dawn, Harry went to the faintly lit altar. The church formed only a small part of the fort, the rest of the structure housing a museum. The wooden pews were dark and empty and silent, and the dusty smell of frankincense permeated the air. The stone walls were cold. There was no heat at night, no air-conditioning during the day.

Staring at the mosaic figures on the dome above the altar, Harry silently mocked Him for the one mercy. The brutality visited on Lilah had not created a new life. The mute deity did not retaliate, His kindly eyes telling Harry to find his own answers.

"Harry," called a terrified voice. *"Harry."*

Wheeling, he sprinted toward the door.

Lilah stumbled into the church. *"Harr—"*

Skidding to a stop, he reached out and tugged her into an embrace. "I'm right here."

Between violent trembles, she pleaded, "Don't go anywhere without me."

Harry flinched and turned her to the door to guide them back to their room. Before she'd taken two steps, she glanced at the altar and halted. She shrugged out of his arms and staggered to the pews.

They spent what was left of the night on one of the wooden benches, clinging to each other in complete silence.

Afterward, Lilah stopped her daily tirade, even murmuring "I'm sorry," stroking one of the many scratches she'd left on Harry's cheek. Her eyes filled with remorseful tears.

At the apology, he caught her hand in his. "One more week, and we're out of here," he promised. He needed to make sure Lilah could run if she had to. From Parker, from Sanders, from the Gaddafi government, from all the enemies chasing them.

It took a few days longer than a week. Fatimah brought news the colonel would take off for parts unknown to celebrate Christmas, and for his cronies in the local council, *Dhu'l-Hijjah* was about to start—the twelfth month of the Islamic calendar when many prepared to travel to the holy place of Mecca in Saudi Arabia. With the town empty of its villains, Harry and Lilah stood a better chance of escaping.

Still, they didn't dare bring the Jeep out from the priest's garage until late at night. Thanks to the cleric, Harry wore a new beige robe and another headscarf. The priest drew a cross in the air and muttered a short blessing over Harry while Lilah waited in the Jeep, clad in the black burka Fatimah scrounged up. Not a single part of Lilah was visible. Even her eyes were hidden behind the mesh screen of the veil. One spare set of clothes each lay stuffed into a fabric bag in the cargo area.

Lilah didn't acknowledge Fatimah for the donations. Nor did she say a word to the elderly priest, shrinking away when he got close to the vehicle to tuck some money into Harry's hands.

After they drove off, Harry remained behind the wheel the entire time as Lilah couldn't seem to stop glancing back for anyone who might be chasing them. They kept to the forests, sleeping in the Jeep and entering towns only for gas and rations. It was slow going as they were forced to hide the stolen vehicle and walk to the stores. They didn't dare rent a hotel room even to use the latrine. By the time they got to the coastal town of Derna on Christmas Eve, both smelled rank.

Harry parked behind a two-story building, taking care to keep the Jeep out of sight of anyone shopping in the market along the main street. He pinched the bridge of his nose with his thumb and forefinger. They needed to clean up, they needed food, and they desperately needed rest. He couldn't keep driving without at least a couple of hours' shut-eye. But with the cover provided by the sparse forests gone, they couldn't sleep in the Jeep any longer. They needed to find a quiet place somewhere. A safe place. He eyed the building with its peeling paint and garbage bags piled next to the back door.

Chapter 11

2. Harry's map, showing their journey thus far.

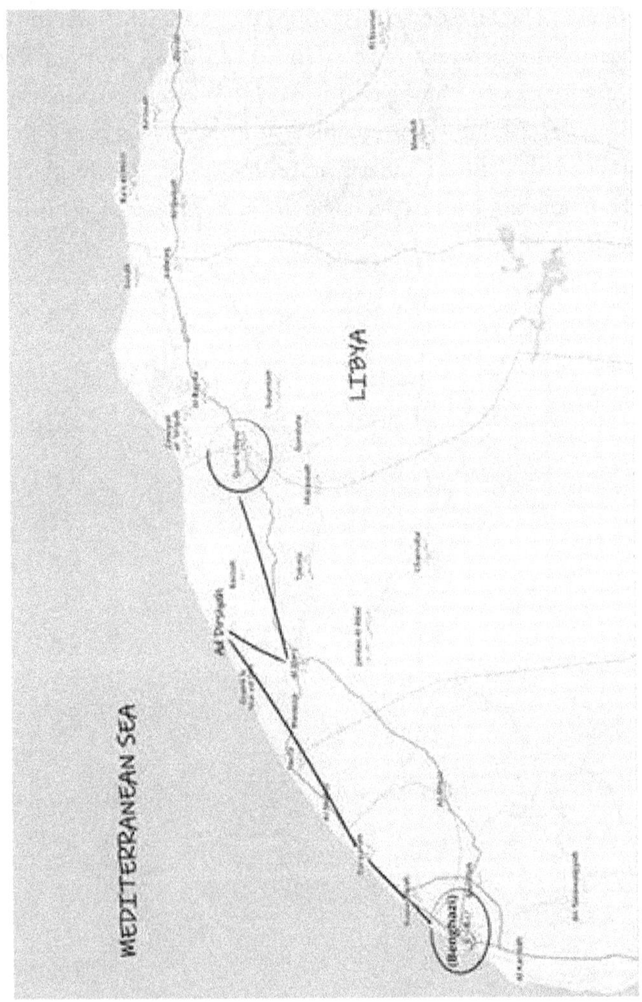

"No!" Lilah tried to scream, but her throat spasmed, killing the cry. In the middle of a vast desert, the monster stalked her. Her feet slipping in the sliding sheets of sand, she turned to run, but she collapsed to her knees. The demon kept getting closer. She knew it was going to kill her. She would die that day.

Lilah woke, gasping for air, her body drenched in sweat. Loud voices argued outside the windows of the budget hotel, and evening light filtered in through the dusty panes.

Stumbling over the hem of her robe, she ran to the door to make sure it was locked. The slide bolt was still in place, and the desk she dragged across before her nap still barred the door. The black burka lay discarded on the heavy iron chair in front of the desk. She wheeled toward the side table. On it was the AK-47 they stole from the cop.

She was okay. Still safe. But her arms and legs wouldn't stop trembling. Nor would her insides. Tongue licking dry lips, she reassured herself, *Only a nightmare.*

Harry might have gone to buy food, but she was safe in the locked room... safe in the prison she constructed. Lilah rubbed her chest, wanting the pressure inside to go away. This feeling of weakness in her limbs... she hated it. She longed to sleep without—

Lilah glanced at the cheap alarm clock on the side table. *Fifteen minutes.* It was the longest she'd been able to sleep staying still. In the Jeep, she couldn't close her eyes unless Harry kept driving. It was the only thing which made her feel safe enough. He stopped only when he was too tired to continue. Held tightly in his arms while he fell into an exhausted slumber, she'd stay wide awake, trying not to jump at every sound outside.

As soon as they got to the hotel room, she and Harry used the tiny shower to clean up. Then came the thought of hunger, but she didn't want to brave the crowds. She told him she would barricade herself in the room for the time he was out. He showed her how to use the rifle and kept the Colt with him. Thanks to her papa, Lilah learned the basics of using a firearm. She wasn't great at it, and the revolver would've been easier for her, but Harry couldn't possibly carry a rifle while shopping for food.

How much time did it take to run to the market and buy something, anyway? Surely, he'd been away too long.

"Lilah!" a feminine voice bellowed from outside the hotel.

She started.

There was an alcove to her right with a single window and a bench seat beneath. With a pounding heart, she scurried, plastering herself against the wall. Taking care to stand to the side, Lilah peeked into the street but didn't see anyone she recognized. A middle-aged woman called out to her maid, harshly ordering the servant to hurry up. Lilah grimaced and laughed mildly, relieved to be wrong. *Leila, not Lilah.* The maid was called Leila. It was a popular name in the Arab world.

She was about to return to bed when the sweet, zesty smell of nutmeg wafted to her nostrils. Curiosity caught, she inched closer to the window, peering at the old souq outside. The marketplace was busy. People thronged the street, haggling over prices with equally enthused vendors. Piles of fresh fruit and baskets of spices made the displays colorful and fragrant. Children darted around with harried mothers chasing them.

There were two girls calling their little brother to play hide-

and-seek amid the baskets, but the boy clearly wasn't interested. The enterprising cherub was in the process of climbing the boxes stacked haphazardly at the street corner.

Lilah grinned. Brothers were great fun, but it was difficult to get them to—Dan used to—

"Get down, or else!" yelled one of the women on the street, standing at the bottom of the pile of boxes. The boy's mother?

He turned to glance at her, and the boxes tottered dangerously. When he fell, landing on his bottom, he only guffawed before scampering back up the pile.

His spirit, his resilience... Lilah watched, open-mouthed. *I want to be* him—*fearless. My God, look at that! He's already forgotten he ever fell.*

She took a deep breath and turned to eye the desk blocking the door. Did she dare? The rifle was on the side table, but the employees at the hotel... Harry had lied and claimed he and Lilah were a married couple on their way to visit her family for Eidh al-Adha, the Islamic festival of sacrifice. Teen marriages were not uncommon in the country, and no one asked for proof. Still, the front desk staff might have seen him leave after check-in. They'd know she was alone. What if—

Another knock. Lilah jumped. Gasping, she scooted backward toward the side table where the weapon was.

"It's me," said Harry, voice low. When she opened the door, he carried in a few packages and placed them on the table. Unable to shave these last few weeks, dark hair matted his jaw. Between the bristles and the clothes, he now looked like any young man of Arab descent.

The melancholy in his eyes... Lilah hated it. She didn't want it there, reminding her of what happened. He needed to forget. *She* needed to forget. It was crucial to scour away the horror from both their memories. She wanted to be the same Lilah who flew out of New York City. She wanted him to remember her as that girl, not this weepy weakling.

Desperately, she grinned at him, silently begging him to respond in kind. He smiled back, but she didn't see the familiar flash of mischief across his face.

Sitting at the window, they ate *batata mubattana*—fried potatoes and spiced meat—and watched the market. When a brave rock pigeon plucked a date off a basket, the shopkeeper chased it off, threatening to make pigeon soup for Christmas lunch. A tickle started in Lilah's chest. Covering her mouth with a hand, she giggled and couldn't stop. "Did you hear that?" she gasped.

Lilah knew there was a hysterical quality to her laughter. Harry let her titter away, and he laughed with her. After a minute, when she ran out of breath, she said in a hard tone, "I'm no victim, Harry. Don't act like it."

He took her hand. "I wouldn't dare."

"I *will* get through this."

"'Course you will. You're Delilah. You can do anything." This time, her giggle was genuine, though slightly watery. He pointed. "Look. The dumb bird is back again."

"How can you tell it's the same one?"

"I have a good memory for faces." She twisted around, lips

pursed. He poked at her cheek with a finger. "It wasn't *that* bad; gimme at least a tiny smile." They both sputtered. For now, they were content in this cocoon, pretending all was well with their world.

The vendors soon closed for the day, and the shoppers went home, but Harry and Lilah continued to sit there. *Could I do anything?* Could she fight through this nightmare? Could they escape to safety? The men who held this part of the world in their cruel grip did not plan to let their prisoners live. The ones who'd offered help could barely help themselves.

Lilah was resting her head on Harry's left shoulder when the call to prayer rang through the streets. As the city offered *salāt* to God under the black velvet sky, she asked, "Harry, if I were in charge of the world, what do you think I'd do?"

"What?"

"The people who run things don't care about the rest of us. The U.S. government doesn't have time for ordinary citizens, but when Andrew Barrons gets involved, they make time. Jared Sanders buys off an entire government to kidnap two teenagers. A former soldier from the U.S. Army—" she broke off, closing her eyes against horrific memories.

Wrapping an arm around her, Harry drew her closer. "If you were in charge, I'd want to live forever."

Later still, she asked, "What do you think is going on with your parents?"

"Dunno. I've been too scared to call. Gotta feeling the line was bugged the last time we tried. I just hope they've figured out we're on our way to Egypt." Harry rested his cheek on top of her head. Almost to himself, he muttered, "If they did, they would've left Tripoli. If they stayed... God... I hope not. Gaddafi and Sanders..."

"What about Genesis?"

"If the company's been sold, it would have been in the news. I know it's small, but the Gaddafi government makes sure their victories get published in every local paper. The priest at the church was keeping an eye out."

"But your father would've offered, right?"

"Yeah." Harry shrugged. "Don't know what's happening."

"So Sanders and Gaddafi's men are still after us? I mean, if they haven't gotten Genesis..."

"Guess so."

"Dan must be worried sick," she murmured. A pain squeezed Lilah's heart. Her twin had to be terrified, begging the universe to return his sister to him, not to leave him utterly alone in this world.

"Runt," Harry mumbled. "She saw them take us." Harry's sister was only ten. She'd witnessed the arrest of her parents, followed by the abduction of her brother. "All of them. My mother, my father, Hector... Dante..."

Lilah closed her eyes, bringing to mind the face of her twin. It was the first time in days she'd thought of him. The first time she'd thought of anything beyond the horrible, horrible dream she was trapped in. Harry had been the only thing she recognized in that realm. His embrace was her safe place.

His arm was still around her shoulders. She settled her head on his chest, counting the reassuring thudding of his heart.

When the bells from the only church in the old city announced Christmas, Harry murmured, "We should go to bed. Long day tomorrow."

"Yes... we need to... have to... we *will* get back home." Home, where her twin was. Where Harry's family was. Where they were safe. Where she could go back to being the strong, smart Lilah she used to be.

"We will," he agreed, tone firm.

She lay awake into the night, darkness bringing back frightening memories and the feeling of powerlessness. "Harry?" she called.

"Hmm?"

"Those children in the street?" she whispered. "They were so sweet. Innocent." As she turned her face, she saw his shadowy form, very still, watching her. "So easy to break," she continued. "Fragile." An oppressive heaviness settled into her chest. Suddenly, her throat tightened. She couldn't breathe. "Harry? I..." Her hands curled into fists, scrunching up the thin sheet. "He... that man..."

Harry was instantly at her side, holding her close.

A muffled sob escaped her. Tears rolled down her cheeks. "I couldn't fight back. I thought I was going to die." She'd been too afraid to close her eyes, worried the monster would walk through the door. "I don't want to die. I want... but I... I was so weak. I couldn't do *any*thing."

Shoving Harry away, she vaulted from the bed and ran to the

small plastic trash can next to the window. She knelt on the floor and heaved into it. Harry dropped to his knees, his hand on her upper back. The acidic smell of vomit filled the room. When she was done, she leaned back against his chest. The room was silent except for her raspy breathing.

Finally, she said, "I never want to be weak again."

He gathered her into his arms. "You're the strongest person I know."

"Don't let go," she begged, clinging.

"I won't." Harry pulled her closer and turned his face into her hair. He kissed her temple. Hot tears dropped from his lashes, scalding his cheeks, staining her skin. Wrapped in each other's arms, they wept for the children they used to be.

Chapter 12

The Mediterranean sparkled a brilliant turquoise as they drove alongside it. There were no forests to hide in, so they'd again muddied the license plate as best as they could without making it too obvious. They couldn't do anything about the police markings on the side, but unless they were stopped, no one would know it wasn't a cop out for a ride, his wife in tow.

Perspiring under the heavy burka, Lilah peered through the mesh screen concealing her eyes and tried to read the road signs. With a loud honk, a truck whizzed past, making her veil billow in the wind.

Harry maintained a steady speed, alert eyes on the road. When they passed a mile marker, he muttered, "Two hundred miles to the border. Four or five hours, depending on how many stops. Let me know when you need to eat."

"Keep going," Lilah said. "No breaks."

"Drink some water," Harry suggested.

They carried a couple of bottles with them. Passing one back and forth, they continued. They managed to get to Bardiyah, less than an hour from Egypt, before they needed gas.

Stopped at the pump, she waited in the Jeep, her hand on the Colt next to her thigh. When Harry returned from the cashier's office, his face was pale and sweaty under all the hair. He handed her a crumpled flyer, cursing foully under his breath while she smoothed it out. Lilah gasped. Pictures of her and Harry... there was a blurry shot of the Jeep, too, with the license number at the bottom in large print.

Sirens blared.

She looked up, watching the black-and-white Fiats flying through the streets. "Harry... are they... did someone spot us?"

"Don't know," Harry said, voice shaking. "The Jeep, maybe. They don't know we're *here,* at the gas station."

The AK-47 went under Lilah's burka. The Colt and the old map they bought at the pawnshop in Benghazi were tucked into Harry's robe. Abandoning the vehicle, they strolled along the sidewalk as though they were tourists. Lilah held her veil down against the Mediterranean wind as Harry hailed a cab. Just as they exited the vehicle at the bus station, patrol cars barreled in.

"The docks," Lilah whispered.

Another cab, another dead end. Policemen blocked the pier, gesturing wildly at the person manning the boat rental booth. All the ways out of town were blocked.

Harry swore. "This way," he muttered to Lilah.

Stores catering to tourists lined the street leading to the marina. Keeping their demeanor casual, they sauntered into one. Harry's shopping list was short—diving suits, plastic bags, tape, a few bars of chocolate, and a couple of bottles of water. For some reason, he bought a waterproof compass which ate up a good chunk of the money they carried. At the counter, he asked the cashier for directions to the nearest hardware store. Soon, they owned a set of screwdrivers.

Lilah didn't dare ask questions with so many people around. Even in the street, they kept talking to a minimum.

Hailing another cab, Harry instructed the driver to take them to Al Burdi Castle. Outside the castle gates was a tunnel with a sign prohibiting entry and an iron fence to keep out trespassers. The number of visitors to Libya having dwindled after the most recent skirmish between the Arabs and the Israelis, the place appeared deserted.

Harry paid the cab driver and waited until the vehicle disappeared down the road. "I've been here before. School trip, so I know how to get to the docks from here. They have mostly cruise boats and trawlers, but there should also be smaller boats *we* can handle." They'd again steal as they stole the bike and the Jeep. "We *have* to get out of here," Harry added. Escape... at any cost.

"Which way do we go?"

"The tunnel," he said, pointing to the "No Entry" sign. "It leads to the sea." *Of course,* he'd figured it out. Harry would've found the forbidden passageway impossible to resist.

He scaled the iron fence and helped her across. Lilah followed him into the pitch-black interior. Groping the wall for balance, her fingers slid on slime, and she stumbled against him.

"Careful." His voice echoed eerily.

Water dripped somewhere to the side. The tunnel was muggy, the odor of stale urine attacking her nostrils with each breath.

A few minutes later, a beam of sunlight pierced the darkness. Changing into diving suits in the faint glow, they taped the sealed plastic bags with their robes inside to their chests and backs. Their weapons, the compass, the map, and the screwdrivers were also in the bags. Except for two bars of milk chocolate, so was their food. Lilah ate her share of the chocolate and licked her fingers clean.

"Man," Harry muttered. "I'm thirsty."

"We have water."

He shook his head. "Not until we absolutely have to. Water's more important than food. Who knows how long it's going to be before we find more that's safe to drink?"

They went to the opening and stood looking out for a moment, Lilah inhaling deep lungfuls of fresh air. The mountain dropped off into a steep precipice, and the blue-green sea lapped at its rocky base. It was a glorious day.

It was also the perfect spot to escape into the sea, separated from the docks by the cliffs.

"Ready?" he asked.

She looked down the vertical drop and gulped. She'd dived from boards before, but this was different. The world tilted as she stared at sharp rocks protruding from the water on one side.

Harry's hand took hers. "I'm with you," he told her.

I will not be afraid, she vowed. "We could hit the rocks..." It would mean death. *Painful* death, but not that of a weak, helpless victim. "Sanders is *not* going to win," she muttered. "His tactics will not work. *We're* in control of this thing. We may go down fighting, but we're not going to admit defeat. We will *not* let them take us alive."

"No, we won't."

Her arms went up, hands linked and palms facing the sky. Her biceps tightened. She fixed her eyes on a potential landing spot and nodded. "Over there." It looked like enough space for both her and Harry.

"Jump," he said.

Taking as deep a breath as she could, she leaped. One second, two—her open palms hit the surface of the ocean, ripping a hole in it. Her body slid in. Water gurgled all around. Warmth. Wet warmth... in her nose, in her ears, in her eyes.

Lilah splashed up and with a loud cough, gulped air. She wiped her eyes to find Harry next to her. They trod water for a few minutes, grinning at each other in unexpected elation.

Something glided under the blue surface. Lilah craned to see. Without a sound, a *thing* rose, a humongous creature straight out of a horror movie. Reddish-brown and yellow, it eyed the back of Harry's head with a teary gaze. Lilah tried to speak, but only a croak came out. Mouth open, she wheezed.

"What?" Harry asked, whirling around. "Gak," he yelped, coming eye-to-eye with the weeping monster. He splashed back and to Lilah's shock, started laughing.

"Turtle," he gasped between chortles.

It took her a few seconds to get her breath back. Covering her face in embarrassment, she, too, sputtered. "Why's it crying?" she asked.

"Not crying," he explained. "We talked about it in science class. Something about drinking salt water... I'm not sure."

"Maybe her best friend gave her a snake for her birthday," Lilah suggested.

He threw his hands in the air. "Oh, God, not the same old story." Sputters turned into full-throated laughter. The mirth was cathartic, and when it died, he said, "Let's go."

Swimming in the direction of the pier, they heaved to the shore not too far from where the fishing boats were tied for the night.

Concealed by a jutting rock, they waited in silence for the fishermen to leave for the day. Squawking seagulls circled their hiding spot. The heat and the breeze dried their wetsuits as they sat on the narrow strip of sand, waves lapping gently at their feet. They took little sips of the water they hoarded, telling each other it wouldn't be long before they found a boat to take themselves to safety.

"Pick one which looks simple enough for us," whispered Lilah.

"Something I can hot-wire," Harry agreed.

She'd guessed as much. "Do you know how to do it with boats?" They'd both been sailing in the Mediterranean—anyone who ever visited the area would have—but it was always with someone experienced. Harry was successful with the bike, but he couldn't have much idea about watercrafts.

"An engine is an engine," Harry said, tone steady. "Once I get the motor started, it's a matter of steering the boat in the right direction." His warm touch landed on the back of her hand lying on the sand. "We *will* get out of here."

Mud squishing between her fingers, Lilah turned her hand up to grip his. Defeat was not an option. She would not be a victim. Nor would Harry.

He glanced toward the sea. "Egypt is thataway."

Alexandria was where they hoped his family would be waiting... his parents, his brother, his sister. Dan would be with them, praying anxiously for his twin's safety.

"Soon," Lilah murmured.

Sunset arrived. With the fishing boats returning, the noise level at the pier peaked. It seemed like eons before the voices died down.

When the only light left in the sky was the deep orange at the horizon, Harry and Lilah waded to one of the motorized dinghies and untied it. There wasn't anyone around, but they didn't want to take chances by making noises with the engine, so they both took the rope and swam hard. With every splash they made, they looked around to check, but it was only them and the boat gliding silently behind. Even the raucous seagulls returned home for the night.

Back under the cover of the rocks, they climbed in. It took Harry three tries and more than a couple of dozen muffled curses, but he managed to find whatever wires he was looking for. The engine rumbled to life.

As they started eastward, Harry glanced down at the dashboard, now lit an eerie green. "I wish we could just sail across," he muttered. "But we can't. The coastguard will shoot first and ask questions later."

"Best we can do is get within a mile or two of the border," Lilah agreed, shivering in the suddenly cool breeze. "Do we have enough gas?"

"I don't think we're going to get quite so close. If I'm

calculating this right, we're going to have to walk a few miles."

"After that, we still have to get past the guards at the crossing."

Harry grimaced. "Let's see what the situation is like. Bedouin tribes go back and forth all the time. I'm hoping we can slip across with them."

The last rays of the sinking sun vanished. Cloaked by the night, they took the boat along the coastline, keeping as far away from the rocks as they could without risking getting spotted by the coastguard.

Harry needed to use the faint glow from the dashboard to see the compass and steer the boat where he wanted it to go. "Damn it. I forgot about a flashlight."

There was not even any moon in the heavens to light their way. Not a single star could be seen. Even when her vision adjusted to the darkness, Lilah felt rather than saw Harry sitting at her side. Thankfully, no one else seemed to have had the idea of sailing the Mediterranean at night. Except for the phut-phut of the engine, the only sounds were those of the waves crashing against the rocky shore.

When the fuel gauge turned red, Harry guided the boat into an inlet. The craft jolted to a halt. Lilah jerked back, grabbing the edge of the seat before she fell off.

Harry swore. "Rocks."

Abandoning the boat, they slipped into the cold water. Lilah's teeth chattered and with two quick strokes toward the shore, a sharp pain shot down her elbow, all the way to her fingers. She screamed, muffling the sound in the next breath.

"What's wrong?" Harry asked.

"Same thing," she said, gritting her teeth against the searing pain. "Rock."

In two minutes, it was Harry's turn to grunt. His knee.

They lost count of the number of times they encountered something sharp or hard. Bruised and scraped, they made it to the shadowed beach. Breathing raspy, they lay on the strip of sand and finished the chocolate. After their hard swim, the gentle wind was comforting, almost stroking Lilah's eyelids into slumber.

A harsh curse.

Her eyes snapped open.

Harry was sitting up, staring at the bottle of water in his hand. "It's *empty?* How—dammit, there's a tear in it. The rocks." With a muffled roar, he flung it away. "I need to drink *some*thing." He stood and strode toward the sea.

"No." Lilah hauled herself up and gave chase. She grabbed his elbow with both hands, pulling him back. "Harry, don't be stupid. It's salt water. It will dehydrate you. You're going to feel worse after you drink it."

He tugged against her hold and stomped ahead, but she refused to let go. Her bare feet sank into the wet sand.

"Stop," she snapped.

He halted. It took him a couple of seconds, but his body became marginally less tense.

"We still have one bottle," Lilah said.

It wasn't enough. Not nearly.

Harry helped her clamber over the rocks separating the beach from the rest of the terrain. Once they got to flatter land, they pulled on their robes over the diving suits. The compass guided them to the coastal highway. Except for the occasional headlights zooming down, the road was empty and dark. Each time they heard an engine, they threw themselves face down on the ground, hoping to go unnoticed.

It could've been minutes; it could've been hours. Lilah didn't know. Her thighs burning in fatigue, stomach tearing in hunger, and throat spasming in thirst, she trudged alongside Harry. She couldn't see his face, but in his heavier steps, she heard the same exhaustion. Neither mentioned stopping to rest. They kept trekking toward the border crossing. Toward Alexandria. Toward safety.

Chapter 13

Musaid, the last town they needed to pass before getting to Egypt, didn't look like a big place. There was no lighting on the streets, not many people out at this time of the night... except when they got to the border crossing. A long line of vehicles waited along the unlit road. There were police cars and uniformed cops inspecting each one with the aid of flashlights.

Watching from the shadows at the tail end of the line, Harry cursed. There was no way they could simply walk through.

"Oh, God," Lilah said, her voice muffled by the burka. "We're so close. Can't we just cross a mile or two from here?"

"We would be asking to be shot at," whispered Harry. "Saeed's tribe camps in town. We can ask them for help."

"Saeed—your friend?"

"Yeah. He's Bedouin." Lilah surely heard Saeed mentioning the tribe, but it was weeks ago, and many things happened since then.

"Harry, I..." She gulped. The last time they went looking for help... Lilah was going to have a hard time trusting anyone.

Not daring to draw attention by taking her hand in public, Harry brushed his knuckles against her sleeve. "Remember, the cops were already at Saeed's house, looking for us. He still helped. He's not going to hurt us."

"I know, I know. Saeed was even willing to risk having us stay in his home. But this is his tribe, not him. Also, if we go to the

Bedouin camp, they'll have their rules. What are the chances they'll let us stay together?"

"None," Harry admitted. "Not if we're there a couple of days. If Saeed has talked to them, they'll know we're not related." Unrelated men and women were not allowed to mingle, let alone stay in the same room. It was very likely they wouldn't even be allowed to have a private conversation. "I'll find a way... I swear I'll be around. Plus, you'll have the Colt."

With a sound somewhere between a laugh and a sob, she said, "You can't always be around me. I can't live that way, Harry. I don't *want* to live that way. I have to forget—" An impatient snarl came from inside the veil. "I'm in control. I can take care of myself. I... *we're* not going to let anyone take us."

"No, we're not." Harry doubted Saeed would've so easily suggested approaching his tribe for help if he thought there was the slightest risk from them, but in case he turned out to be wrong, the Bedouins were going to find both Harry and Lilah prepared to fight to their last breaths. "You're Delilah; you can do anything."

Her chest heaved in a deep sigh. "Will the tribe *agree* to help?"

"Saeed said his family's not too fond of Gaddafi. They have a feud going on with him. Even if they're not willing to help, they might give us food and water."

"Okay," Lilah mumbled.

They crept back to the town. Vehicles were still coming up the road—cars, bikes, trucks. More than a couple of camels.

"*Ibn shaytan,*" yelled an irate voice, calling someone the son of the devil. A boy about Harry's age was tugging a donkey toward the pass. A very reluctant donkey.

"Excuse me," Harry called out in Arabic.

The boy swiveled toward them, his hands still gripping the harness. The beast snorted and reared. The boy lost his hold and fell on his bottom. The donkey hee-hawed almost fiendishly. It trotted forward a few feet, tossing a smirking glance over its shoulder.

Harry dived for the reins. A kick landed on his thigh, perilously close to his plumbing. Electric pain shot up his nuts. He stumbled, wondering if future generations of Sheppards had just died ignominious deaths. He could see Lilah as a dark blur running around him and reaching for the donkey's harness.

With another curse, the boy heaved himself off the ground and snatched the reins back from Harry. "Thanks, but you didn't have to do that. The demon doesn't run away. It simply doesn't like being told what to do." He nodded at Harry. "What did you want?"

"The Obeidat camp," Harry wheezed.

The encampment was in a fenced-in clearing less than a mile from the border. At the entrance, they were confronted by a couple of hefty men carrying kerosene lanterns and rifles, no trace of welcome on their faces. When Harry asked for the chief, the guards escorted them in, weapons ready to fire at the first sign of trouble.

The tents dotting the dark landscape glowed from lamps within, guiding their steps as they weaved their way through sounds of squalling babies, quarreling couples, and sniggering young men. The smell of smoke and goat meat cooked on open fire drifted through the air.

Harry shook his head, willing away the sudden lightheadedness. They needed to get to safety before worrying about food.

A wizened old man in beige robes and patterned headscarf sat on the ground by the door flap of the largest tent—the sheik. Fire crackled in a pit in front.

"*As-salāmu alaykum, Sheik*," Harry said, respectfully wishing peace on the man. Lilah stayed a few steps behind, the burka hiding her identity.

"*Wa alaykum as-salām,*" the chief returned. He continued in Arabic, "What can I do for you, young man?"

"We've been stranded and need some help, sir. Saeed al-Obeidi of Kuwayfiyah is my friend. He belongs to your tribe and can vouch for me."

The Obeidat chief straightened. His shoulders suddenly stiff, he contemplated Harry for a few seconds and flicked a quick glance at Lilah. "Saeed doesn't merely 'belong' to this tribe; he's my grandson."

Harry started. He hadn't known. Saeed never said anything about...

"He's a good boy," continued the old man. "Says he wants to be an oil engineer."

"Yes, he's smart," Harry acknowledged, his heart thundering. Were they about to catch a break? Finally?

"Is he? I'm happy to hear it. Our culture's different, but the old ways are dying out. We're going to need new blood, new ways of thinking." The sheik turned and called to someone behind him. "My granddaughter has just returned from visiting them."

As a girl stepped through the door flap of the tent and into the pool of light thrown by the fire, Harry and Lilah came face-to-face with Saeed's cousin, the same one they met in his house.

Inclining his head in the direction of the arrivals, the sheik asked the girl, "Is this Harry?"

The flames from the firepit threw flickering shadows on the girl's face as she squinted at him. "He didn't have this much hair on his cheeks when I saw him, but yes, it's Harry."

"Good." The sheik nodded. "Saeed's been sending message after message, checking if we heard from you and your friend. Where have you been for the last one month?"

Lilah stiffened.

"We... uhh... got into some trouble," Harry said. "I got assaulted. Robbed. I couldn't walk, so we had to hide."

"All this time?" the sheik exclaimed. "You have powerful people hunting you, young man. You're lucky to have escaped."

Harry inclined his head in acknowledgment. "We got *this* far, but we won't be able to cross the border without help."

"Lilah?" asked the cousin, peering at the burka-clad figure. When Lilah nodded, the girl caught her hand and led her to the side of the tent.

Carefully keeping the girls in sight, Harry addressed the sheik. "I'm hoping *you* can get us across."

"My brother and I against my cousin. My cousin and I against a stranger. Such is our way. What loyalty do we owe *you*?"

"Saeed calls me 'brother,'" Harry said, stomach knotting.

"True," said the old man. "Ahh, who am I kidding? The Gaddafi government wants you arrested, so it will be my *pleasure* to help you escape." He turned and shouted to his granddaughter to get her "*sitto*"—her grandmother.

Nauseous with relief, Harry thanked the sheik. "There's... uhh... one more thing. We need some food. And water."

He followed the sheik into the large goat-hair tent. Lilah was already walking in with Saeed's cousin.

It was the smell which hit Harry first, the piercingly sweet odors of cinnamon and ginger. Kerosene lanterns hung from the poles, their yellow glow lighting the interior. The ground inside was covered by patterned carpets. A couple of steel trunks were lined up on the left, with a few books on top. There were only two wooden stools, one of them supporting a wide bowl overflowing with dates. Scattered around the tent were dozens of pillows of all colors and sizes.

Harry kept an eye on Lilah's back until she disappeared behind the thick, colorful rugs hanging from the roof. She'd be eating in the *mahram*—the women's section—with the ladies of the sheik's family.

With the three other men asked to the meeting, Harry settled on the pillows arranged around the large platter on the central rug. "*Bismillah, al-Rahman, al-Rahim,*" he chanted in unison with the rest, thanking God, the most gracious, the most merciful. Afterward, he got busy, gulping water and stuffing his face with pita bread and juicy meatballs. It was close to midnight, long past dinnertime, and he didn't know if the others were merely giving him company while they discussed the matter at hand. Thankfully, no one seemed taken aback at the near barbaric way he pounced on the food.

The sheik appeared content to make small talk about the one time he traveled to Tripoli. Only when coffee was brought around did he introduce the topic of their guests' predicament. "In three weeks, the Awlad Ali tribe will be here. Your best bet will be to go over the border with them when they return."

Three weeks? Every day they stayed in Libya, they were risking capture.

"It's Dhu'l-Hijjah," explained one of the other men. "The holy month. A number of our people are in Saudi Arabia for the *Hajj*." It was the pilgrimage to Mecca undertaken by Muslims all over the world.

The sheik nodded. "We don't have enough men to provide you cover. The next big group to cross the border will be the Awlad Ali clan. When they return, they can take you with them."

Come the morning, Gaddafi and gang could very well notice a boat was missing from the docks in Bardiyah. When their quarry wasn't found in town, the cops might deduce what happened. They already knew about Saeed. They would know his tribe camped near the border. "What if the cops come here?" Harry asked, wiping his mouth with the back of his hand.

The sheik shot a glance at Harry. "You see only this little camp, young man. This is just one of the many subtribes. The Obeidats constitute the largest tribe in East Libya. Hasn't Saeed told you anything about our history?"

Saeed never did, but Harry heard a lot about the noble clans of Libya from the men who came to work at the oil wells. "You're one of the nine main tribes," Harry recited. "Your homeland covers a large part of Libya. But Gaddafi... he could still..."

A murmur went around the group. "Not *any* large part," the sheik said, tone smug. "Our *watan*—our homeland—includes Tobruk."

"The port?" asked Harry, sitting up.

Someone brought a hookah to the sheik's side. The old man puffed hard, creating gurgling sounds. Small clouds of sweet-smelling white vapor floated around. "Yes. Because of where the port is, it's almost impossible to destroy it with bombs. If Gaddafi ever gets into a conflict with the Westerners, he's going to need Tobruk. He's going to need the Obeidats... which is why he's trying to control us."

"Until he gets the control he wants," Harry said slowly, "he can't afford to piss you off too much."

The sheik set the hose of the hookah down close to Harry. "Mint flavor."

"Thank you," Harry said, raising a hand to decline. "It doesn't agree with me."

A superior smile flitted in and out of the old man's face. "We may not have much money, but we do have clout. And for every Bedouin, it's God, tribe, and country, in that order. When Saeed first contacted me about the cops going to his house, looking for you, I sent word to the other subtribes. Gaddafi and his cronies have been tiptoeing around the Obeidats, trying to explain their behavior toward one of us. It's going to continue for the next few weeks. The government won't dare send men into this camp until the issue gets settled."

Feeling profoundly grateful, Harry nodded. "Thank you."

"Saeed calls you 'brother,'" the sheik repeated his words from before. "We'll still need to take some precautions."

The sheik offered Harry a spot in the tent of his youngest son. Respectfully declining, Harry chose the hard earth not too far from the back of the sheik's tent where the women of his family slept. The sheik's chief wife and his granddaughter—Saeed's cousin—graciously agreed to share their living quarters with Lilah. If she needed help, if she called Harry's name, he'd be close enough to hear. Neither the old chief nor his wife objected to what was most certainly odd behavior even for an American like Harry.

In the morning, he found out what "precautions" meant. Breakfasting on tangy camel milk yogurt, he'd been trying to think up an excuse for needing to talk Lilah in private when there was a metallic jangle. The rug separating the women's section was pushed to the side, and Saeed's cousin walked out. There was another girl right behind.

A colorfully patterned caftan hung on her body, and a white veil framed her deeply bronzed face. Under incredibly thick eyebrows were a pair of familiar hazel eyes.

The yogurt got caught in Harry's throat, making him cough. He grabbed the coffee mug and took a healthy gulp. *Lilah?* What the hell had they done to her? Even her eyelashes seemed different. Short, stubby.

"You already have a beard," mused the sheik. "A tan, too, but you're still pale-skinned. Not like *her.* We need to fix the problem."

Apparently, there were some kind of stones the Bedouin ladies rubbed together to make their own face powder. Harry was told to apply it all over his body if he were to ever venture outside the camp.

He was also told there was no way they could get a message across to anyone on the other side of the border without alerting the authorities. If the Sheppards were waiting in Alexandria, they wouldn't know Harry and Lilah were only minutes away.

Harry heartily agreed with all of it. The delay and the disguises were small prices to pay for their safety and the security of the Bedouins who were risking their necks to help two strangers.

He tried to thank the tribe by doing little jobs for them. He helped clean the interior of the goat-hair tents, beating out the carpets covering the ground. He fed the camels, for which the alpha of the flock rewarded him with a squirt of foul-smelling spit straight to the eye. Wiping off the saliva with his sleeve, Harry spat right back, surprising the grinning beast and his harem.

The tribe maintained its own well, but the contraption rigged to pull the pail was broken, and it was hard drawing enough water for all the families in the camp. As an unrelated male, Harry wasn't allowed to converse with the women, but they found him every morning at the well, hauling heavy bucketsful. They would leave their pots next to the crumbling walls for him to fill up—which he did, careful not to acknowledge their presence.

Once, he caught a group of girls gawking at his shirtless torso.

Lilah was with them. As though unaware of his audience, he set the pail down and stretched, flexing his biceps in the process. There were a couple of feminine murmurs, which stuttered to a stop when he turned to face the group. Slashes of red blooming on her cheeks, Lilah glared at him, then at her companions. Maybe a better man than Harry wouldn't have enjoyed provoking her quite so much. Before he realized what he was doing, he shot her a wink. Giggles rose. When the sheik's chief wife shooed off the ogling girls, Harry smothered a grin and returned to his labors.

As Harry expected, he and Lilah weren't allowed private time. Genders were kept strictly segregated, and the rules of the tribe could not be broken even for guests of the sheik. The sheik's granddaughter—Khadeeja—brought Lilah along every day when she visited her grandfather. Harry would look at Lilah with a silent question, and she'd nod, indicating all was okay. They had to be content with as much. But somehow, he managed to remain within hearing distance of her always, no farther than an arm's reach if she needed him. Harry knew his peculiar behavior couldn't have gone unnoticed by the sheik, but the old man asked no questions.

Khadeeja was determined to use Lilah's presence to improve her English and gave Lilah a pair of throwing knives in return. When the Bedouin girl's blade hit the target dead center, Lilah's mouth dropped open. Her newly heavy eyebrows drawn together in fierce resolve, she took lessons. More often than not, her throws went off the mark, once ripping a hole in a robe on the clothesline ten feet away, and even the goats in the camp soon learned to stay at a safe distance. But she kept at it day after day. The women of the tribe giggled over the American girl's inept weapons practice and gossiped as they painted henna on each other's hands. Seeing Harry walk by, they would elbow Lilah in the ribs, making her laugh. And every morning, the shadows in her eyes receded further.

Shortly after the arrival of the new year, the kid goats of the camp joined Harry one night at his usual spot behind the sheik's tent. Bleating softly, one of them butted its head against Harry's arm. With a gentle hand, he pushed it away. It was an unusually warm winter night even for the desert nation, and the black coats sported by the animals were sweat-slicked. Sweaty goats smelled much like Harry's wrestling shoes after a bout.

Lilah drew the flap back from the window of the tent as she did every night. With a grin, he turned his head in her direction, twisting around and raising himself on an elbow. Her lips curved up in a soft, sweet smile. When she mouthed at him to go back to sleep, he shook his head and laughed. The strains of a simple song drifted to him, accompanied by twangs from lute strings, as the men of the tribe gathered around the campfire, entertaining themselves with music and tall tales.

"Lilah," an imperious voice called from inside the tent. The sheik's wife. Lilah grimaced and closed the flap.

Harry lay back, and suddenly, inexplicably happy, he fell asleep.

#

Lilah fluffed the pillows and curled up on her side on the rough carpet, pulling the thick, scratchy blanket up to her shoulder. A hand on the Colt next to her pillow, she took a couple of deep breaths. Her sleeping spot was right beneath the window. Harry was on the other side of the flap, only a few feet away. The thought of him spending the night in the open air just so he could be close to her sent warmth gushing through her heart, but she *could* take care of herself. She *would* forget everything. She refused to cower, refused to cling to Harry merely out of fear.

No one in the tribe batted an eyelid at her weapon. They were used to the harsh facts of life, to the idea that women needed to know how to protect themselves. Or at least, this particular tribe made sure its girls could use a gun. In addition to knowing how to throw a knife, Khadeeja was an excellent shot.

She and her grandmother were kneeling on the thick mat in front of the wooden chest at the far end, chattering furiously in high-pitched Arabic. Their jewelry and good clothes were in the box. A cousin was getting married in a month's time, and they wanted to make sure they had things ready for the celebration. With Khadeeja's mother dying soon after she was born and her father—one of the sheik's many sons—enlisting in the Libyan army, she was raised by her grandparents and really close to them.

It was a long time before she slipped off her shoes and collapsed onto the pillows next to Lilah's. "Sorry," mumbled the Bedouin girl. "You probably couldn't sleep with all the noise we were making."

The sheik's wife was walking around, turning off the kerosene lanterns. Soon, the only light came from the moon rays filtering in through the sliver of space around the window flap.

Lilah turned to lie on her back. "Please... don't apologize," she said, keeping her voice low. At the other end of the mahram, the sheik's wife was settling down on her mat. "You're letting us stay here."

"Saeed has made it very clear Harry is family."

Which meant he was family for everyone else in the tribe. "The bond you have is just incredible. Within the clan, I mean."

"It's not just about clan bonds," Khadeeja admitted. "Saeed is important to us."

"Oh?"

"My grandfather values traditions," Khadeeja said in a whisper. "But he's also a realist. So far, we've been able to hold off Gaddafi, but at some point, brute force will win out. We need an exit strategy. Saeed is it."

"What do you mean?"

"He is, by far, the most ambitious of the whole tribe. Of all of us, he has the best chance of getting a foothold in the wider world. If it becomes necessary, he could get the rest of us out. My grandfather offered to supplement his parents' income so they could live in town and send him to school there. If Saeed has a chance to study in Europe, Grandfather will help pay for that, too. Somehow."

It wouldn't be cheap. College in Europe was likely to cost as much as back home in the U.S.

"It won't be cheap," Khadeeja said, startling Lilah by echoing her thought. "But it will be an investment in the future. Saeed will have to pay us back by taking responsibility for the whole tribe."

"He is *lucky* to have all of you."

Khadeeja laughed softly. "Tell that to him."

In the darkness, Lilah frowned. "He doesn't agree with the

plan?"

"It's not about the plan. He knows what's expected of him, and he's fine with it. Thing is, when his parents visit the camp, Grandfather sometimes sends me back with them to stay in town for a week or two. Just so I can see that kind of life. Saeed thinks they're trying to marry me to him."

Lilah bit her tongue, stopping the thought that Saeed and Khadeeja were first cousins. Their fathers were brothers. But cousin marriages were not uncommon in this part of the world. "Do *you* want to marry him?"

"Meh. I have to marry *some*one."

"What enthusiasm," Lilah teased.

"If Grandfather says I have to marry Saeed, I'll agree. He will, too. He might not want to, but he'll still agree. It's for the good of the tribe."

Lilah turned on her side to face the other girl. "If he doesn't want... how can you be so calm about it?"

Khadeeja sighed. "Don't get me wrong. I want a nice, loving husband. But when there are so many things going on, none of us has the luxury of dreaming of love. Our *existence* is at stake. My pride can't be bigger than the survival of my family. It's a matter of priorities."

Her heart aching for Khadeeja, Lilah said, "I understand."

"You don't have to feel too sorry for me," Khadeeja said, laughing once more. "Saeed's not a bad choice. Only, his mother says he has a thing for Russian women."

"Really?"

"Yeah." Khadeeja nodded toward the window flap. "Not like your sultan out there. Most of the girls in the camp think he's really cute, but *he* has eyes only for you."

Lilah had to giggle at that, her soft laugh devolving into a yawn. "Sorry."

"It's late. Go to sleep."

As she did every night since her arrival at the camp, Lilah closed her eyes and brought her brother's face to mind. She remembered the cemetery where their parents were buried. Her friends in school... the Sheppards... so many people were waiting for Harry and Lilah to return. They *were* going to make it back. They *were* going to make it home.

Slowly, she drifted off. Also as she did the last few weeks, she woke almost every hour. Each time, she imagined herself at the edge of the cliff in Bardiyah, ready to leap into rock-strewn waters. For the first time in days—no, in the *months* since her parents' deaths—she'd felt in control of her own destiny. She survived the jump. She could survive whatever else life chose to throw at her. When she sank back into sleep's embrace toward dawn, there were no monsters around to chase her through the desert.

In the realm of her dreams, she saw Harry. He was lounging royally against a seated camel, dressed in the colorful robes of a potentate from *Arabian Nights*. Kid goats and simpering girls scampered around. A saxophone appeared in his hands. Putting it to his mouth, he seduced the girls with his song. They danced around him in a circle, and with heaving bosoms and twitching hips, each tried to tempt him to her side. Declining all their overtures, he kept calling out melodramatically for his "habibti."

The next day, Lilah was called into a tent the sheik called his war room. Harry was there, reclining on pillows, talking to two men dressed in camouflage.

Flanked by the sheik and his wife, she knelt on the rug and lowered herself to a sitting position.

"Drug smugglers," Harry said, his eyes on the two strangers.

Before Lilah could even open her mouth to ask what on earth was happening, one of the men threw open a large roll of paper. "You need to study this," said the man. "This is a map of the landmine locations in these cliffs."

Lilah gawked.

"World War II leftovers," Harry explained.

"Every child in the tribe is taught the locations," said the sheik. "If they wander off, we don't want them losing their limbs. *You're* going to need to memorize all of it in the next few days. The gentlemen here—" The sheik nodded at the smugglers. "—will also go over with you some essential survival tactics. And they've kindly agreed to sell you a couple of weapons which might come in handy."

"We do have a gun and a rifle," Harry said. "But—"

The sheik nodded in understanding. "*Those* weapons are not going to be of much use against the entire border patrol."

The smugglers dragged a steel trunk to the center of the small gathering. When they opened the lid, Harry scrambled over to examine the contents.

"Smoke bombs," said one of the men. They looked like toy grenades. As the smugglers explained, the grenades *were* toys.

Only, they'd been doctored to create enough smoke on detonation to hinder visibility for a crucial few minutes.

The sheik paid for it all.

Another couple of weeks went by when all they could do was prepare for their departure. It was well into January when a group of Awlad Ali traders came with goods from Sollum, the town on the other side of the border. The Obeidat chief negotiated passage for Harry and Lilah, taking heavy losses in trade in return. The sheik waved away Harry's gratitude, warning him for the millionth time to be careful. Security was bound to be tight on this side of the border crossing.

Chapter 14

3. The final leg of Harry and Lilah's journey.

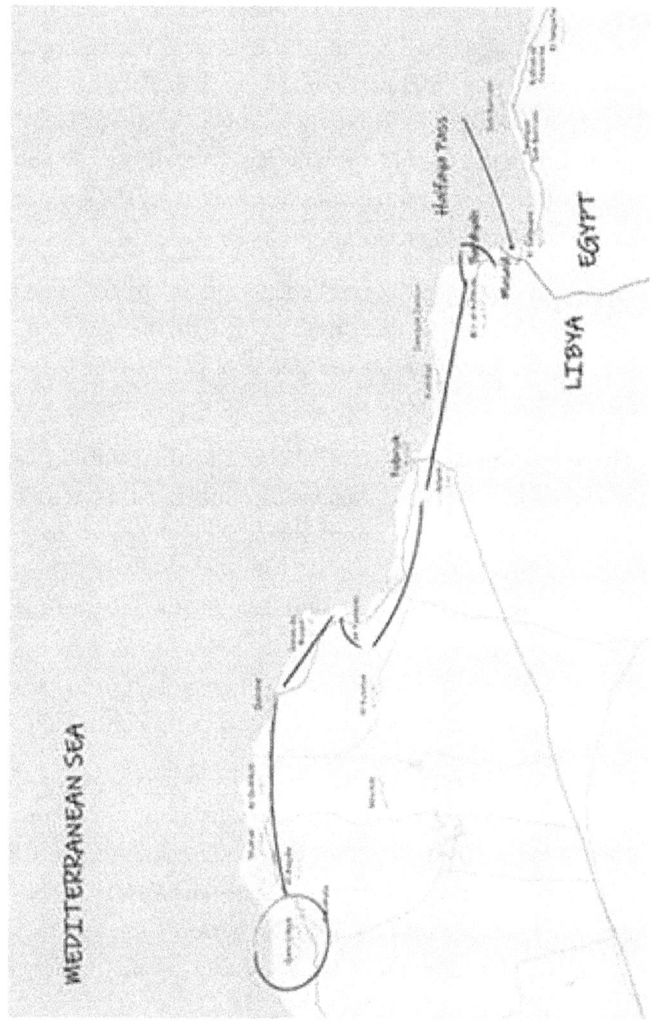

January 1974

Halfaya Pass

Libya-Egypt border

Lilah held on to the edge of the bench seat in the back of the Toyota pickup. With each bump of the truck at each pothole on the road across the cliff, her stomach rattled. Around her, the women of the Awlad Ali tribe chattered. Like them, Lilah was dressed in bright colors, and a yellow veil covered her hair and the lower half of her face, secured with bobby pins. If she'd worn her black burka, she would've stood out.

Harry kept his beige robe and checkered headscarf. He was in the cab, seated next to the driver. Through the streaked rear window, Lilah focused on his bearded profile. His face looked as tense as her knotted insides.

The revolver and rifle stayed behind in the Bedouin camp. The sheik strongly advised against carrying firearms across the pass. If the border patrol found them, they wouldn't need any other excuse to take Harry and Lilah into custody. The only weapons they possessed were the smoke grenades camouflaged as toys, now in the trunk resting at Harry's feet. The bombs nestled amid the dolls and the race cars and the tiny guitars meant for the children of the Bedouin traders waiting on the Egyptian side.

Clearing the security check at the mouth of the pass, the caravan headed deeper into the escarpment. Limestone boulders rose on one side of the road. Scattered on the other side were large rusting pieces of metal, debris from destroyed WWII tanks. The caravan was probably making good time, but it seemed to Lilah they were crawling along, inch by nerve-racking inch. She wiped sweaty palms on her yellow robe and squinted into the distance, hoping to glimpse the gate at the other end. The brakes squealed, throwing the women against each other. She strained to listen over the excited chatter.

Harry appeared at the back of the truck and motioned for her to come. As she stepped out, he said in a low voice, "There are more officers up front. They'll separate men and women before the inspection. Be careful."

Lilah lined up with the rest of the ladies. A sandy gust blew into her face, making her veil snap in the wind. Swatting the covering down, she waited with downcast eyes.

"Mr. Melanthios," the security chief said to his associate. "Women have to be checked by female officers. Colonel Gaddafi has specifically said we're not to start trouble with the Bedouins."

"Mr. Sanders trusts only his own employees to do this," insisted the man called Melanthios.

Sanders? Knowing the way Gaddafi's government moved for the American driller, Lilah and Harry fully expected to find men stationed at the border to watch specifically for them. The disguises, the smoke bombs, the hours they spent learning the terrain... it was all to escape Sanders, but her heart still quaked in fear at the sound of the name.

The chief shook a finger. "This is your first time here, Mr. Melanthios, so I'll give you some advice. We are *not* going to mess with the Bedouins. Moreover, *these* Bedouins are Egyptian citizens, not Libyan. Don't start an international incident, please."

Melanthios swore. "Your lady officers can check the women, but I'm going to keep an eye on things."

With a huff, the chief said, "We haven't had the same problem with other employees of Mr. Sanders. I'm going to make sure Colonel Gaddafi hears about this." He pivoted and left to check the men, muttering irritably about uncooperative Greeks—Melanthios, presumably.

Melanthios stayed, keeping a distance but monitoring the inspection.

Lips dry and stiff, Lilah complied with the instructions of the lady officer to move the veil aside and show her face. The officer nodded, apparently satisfied with Lilah's bronzed skin and thickly lined eyes, and gestured at her to drape the veil back. Lilah was almost faint with relief.

She needed to pass Melanthios as she returned to the truck. Even though the veil was now back on her head, she kept her face averted from his hard stare.

"Hold on," he said.

Her skin prickled in fear.

One of the older men standing next to Harry fell onto an officer, toppling him. "Watch what you're doing, clumsy fool," yelled the officer.

"I beg your pardon, sir," the old man wailed. "Someone pushed me."

Everyone's attention turned. Lilah didn't dare look toward Harry. With the crowd focused on the bawling old man, she darted forward, chest hurting from the effort to mute her breathing. She got to the pickup and hesitated for a second. What if Melanthios... edging by the side of the truck, she squeezed herself into the space between two rocks.

Not too far away, Melanthios said to the chief, "One of them looks like... I'm going to check."

The chief rumbled something, not sounding happy. From her position, she saw Melanthios walk around the truck to stare intently in the direction of her hiding place. Silently, Lilah moved, seeking refuge behind another boulder. Sweating under the hot sun, she watched as Melanthios jogged toward her previous hiding place, the wedge between the two rocks.

Lilah trembled, frantically wondering how to rejoin the caravan. Somehow, she *had* to evade Melanthios and make it back to the truck on time. Harry would give her until the last minute as they planned, and then, he would use the smoke bombs to distract the border patrol. But with so many officers around, there was a good chance *he'd* get caught.

She eyed the terrain. The mines... the map... *nothing* looked familiar. Although... the rocks... something about the arrangement... the clearing in the center... but how could she be sure? What if she tripped over a mine? She'd been warned these were the kind which could kill, not just maim.

Finding the space between the rocks empty, Melanthios halted and turned a half circle, taking a sweeping look across the landscape.

Lilah didn't give herself another chance to think. She whirled and ran toward another rock. The wind gusted. Her yellow veil billowed.

"Stop!" he hollered.

She dived behind a different rock, frantically swiping at the fluttering veil. Tucking it close to her body, she watched Melanthios. At the shout from the Greek, the border security chief came jogging to the edge of the road.

"I saw the girl," Melanthios shouted, flapping his arms in excitement.

The chief scanned the area. "There's nobody here," he snapped.

"I saw her," Melanthios insisted.

The chief swore in Arabic. "Stop chasing mirages and stay with the patrol like you're supposed to."

Lilah bit her lip hard. She had to—*had* to—get back before Harry used the smoke bombs. He'd know he'd get caught, but he'd still do it. He wouldn't leave her there to make her way across by herself. *She* couldn't simply watch him get arrested and escape to safety under cover of the distraction he provided. She gritted her teeth. No way was she going to be a victim a second time. No way was she letting Harry become one.

With the back of her hand, Lilah wiped off the perspiration from her upper lip and studied the terrain. She was trapped. The only way to evade Melanthios was to go on the attack... to take the pawn out of the game.

Waving his arms about, the chief continued his tirade, "This area is off-limits—"

The phut-phut of a helicopter sounded above, drowning out the rest of the chief's warning. Lilah looked up for a second, frantically hoping the pilot wouldn't spot her.

The chief wheeled around and marched off in the direction

of the caravan. Face angry, Melanthios glanced between the back of the departing chief and the rock concealing his quarry.

Lilah loosened her grip on her veil. The yellow cloth rose with the wind, one edge remaining secured to her hair with bobby pins. Letting it fly high, she ran in the direction she hoped was correct. She hid behind another boulder, an open area now between her and Melanthios.

"Stop," he shouted, striding forward.

Yes! Lilah curled her hands into fists.

A blast tore through the ground. Melanthios looked down in surprise as his body was ripped apart. An arm flew high and fell at Lilah's feet, fingers twitching. Blood and gore spattered over the hem of her robe. Her stomach heaved. A hand clapped to her mouth, she turned her eyes firmly away.

Screams, shouts, thundering feet. Officers came running at the sound of the explosion. A few men from the caravan also arrived, and there were a couple of women trying to peer through the crowd.

One of the officers held a hand up. "The stupid Greek got himself killed."

Keeping carefully out of sight and off the minefield, Lilah slipped behind the boulders. The pickup was still where it had been. Carefully, she eased around the side of the truck to its back. Two or three of the female passengers were milling about outside, chanting hysterical prayers. To the left was the clamoring throng of border patrol officers and travelers, peering at the minefield in morbid curiosity.

Lilah scanned the crowd for Harry. There... at the back of the group next to the minefield... he'd spotted her. Seeing her alive and in one piece, the silent terror drained out of his face. She gave him a tiny nod and climbed into the pickup, seating herself in her prior spot amid the Bedouin women. Prattling to each other in panicked tones, they paid no mind to Lilah.

The danger was almost over. An unlucky pawn was sacrificed. A hard weight settled into her belly. A chess move was all it was. She'd simply taken out a piece from the enemy's army.

The shock on the face of the man... the realization he'd be dead in seconds... the twitching arm... the blood spatters on the hem of her robe... Lilah crossed her ankles, tucking the soiled part of the hem behind her legs and out of sight. She willed herself to remember Melanthios would've handed her and Harry over to Sanders.

The border patrol herded the travelers back to their vehicles. As Harry was climbing into the cab of the pickup, the border security chief strode past, talking to someone on the radio. Lilah listened intently as a curt voice came through loud and clear, "Mel had to have seen something. Hold everyone there. I'm on my way."

The man at this end was having none of it. "Mr. Sanders, the inspection is over. The Greeks are, for sure, going to start trouble because of Melanthios, and I don't want to add to the problem by pissing off the Egyptians, as well. Plus, these are Egyptian *Bedouins.* We already have enough issues with our own tribes. I'm letting the caravan pass."

Lilah almost whimpered in terror. She didn't know what Sanders looked like. She'd never seen even a picture of the man.

His voice—it was so normal with nothing to suggest he was a criminal who'd ordered the cold-blooded murder of two teenagers. There was nothing to warn the universe it was the voice of a brutal tyrant willing to kill merely to get his hands on a couple of oil wells.

This was the man Melanthios worked for. No, she didn't do anything wrong. The Greek needed to die. But now, Sanders was on his way to the border.

Lilah peeked into the cab. Harry was staring straight ahead, his shoulders tense. Had *he* ever met Sanders? Harry never said so in all the weeks he and Lilah spent running across Libya. Like her, he was surely praying this wouldn't be the day they came face-to-face with their foe.

An engine vroomed somewhere ahead. Right in front of them, a donkey brayed, pulling its cart forward. The caravan inched toward Egypt. The breeze from the sea blew against her back, but Lilah continued to sweat. With every jolt of the pickup, with every honk and shout, she glanced back at the path they'd already covered, silently urging the line of vehicles to move faster, to let them escape before the enemy arrived. "Almost there," said one of the women in the truck, craning her neck. "I see the gate."

Lilah peered at the lower end of the escarpment. The donkey cart was ahead of them, and there seemed to be a truck and a Jeep farther in front. Then, there was the gate, beyond which the vehicles and the animals were dispersing into Egypt.

"I'm never making this trip, again," continued the same woman, tone at once aggrieved and fearful. "Not in my lifetime. My husband can handle—"

The beat of chopper blades sounded once more. A black shape appeared in the sky, casting a humongous shadow over the caravan. A malevolent whirlwind swirled around them.

Even before Lilah realized this had to be Sanders, the boulder on the right side of the road exploded, sharp pieces of stone rocketing in every direction. Dust and gravel erupted all around. A plume of fire shot to the sky right in front of the truck, accompanied by a deafening boom.

Bomb, Lilah thought, dazed. Sanders was bombing the caravan.

The truck swerved to the left. The vehicle whirled. The world spun. Then, it came to an abrupt halt. Body jerking forward in the momentum, Lilah scrambled to hold on to the bench. A bulky form pushed her aside. Lilah lost her balance and slid to the floor. The truck shook as the women in the back thundered out, shrieking loudly. A heavy weight landed on Lilah's hand. Yelping, she scooted to avoid being trampled.

There was a sudden tug on her scalp as someone stepped on her veil. The covering slid off, ripping a few of the hair follicles by the roots. The yellow cloth glided away with someone's shoe... foot...

Explosion followed explosion. Brown sand and rock pellets swirled in a storm. Lilah couldn't see anything, the women running from the truck reduced to screaming shadows. The smell of burning plastic diffused through the air. There was heat, intense heat.

When she managed to get out of the truck, thick smoke stung her eyes. "Harry!" she screamed over and over.

The gate loomed in front of her. Waving a hand in front of her face to swat away the smoke, she peered at the other side. Egypt. Safety.

"Harry," she shouted.

They needed to get out. The flames were fast approaching the gate. If they didn't run across now, there would be no escape.

Harry didn't answer her shout. He didn't jog out of the shadows.

Lilah pivoted, ready to run back into the cliffs.

A roar cut through the tumult. "*Lilah.*"

Even through the smoke and flames, she recognized him. Harry was on top of a rock facing Egypt, and behind him were soldiers, scaling the cliff.

"Run!" he yelled. Then, Harry jumped.

Bellowing in anger, soldiers clambered to the edge of the rock. One of them pointed in her direction.

Lilah whirled toward the gate. Where was it? She couldn't see it any longer. She couldn't see *anything* in front except fire. A sudden gust blew, and the flames rose in a giant wall, enveloping her. The soldiers disappeared. The world vanished. The red blaze was everywhere. Heat. Unbearable heat. Her lungs burned with every breath. Her body was going to explode any moment.

Then, she heard another shout. An unexpected voice screamed her name. *Daniel?* Her brother came crashing through the fire. Grabbing her hand, Dan charged through the inferno. Lilah stumbled behind, flames licking at her hair.

Chapter 15

April 1974

New York, New York

Escaping the hands waiting to pull her and Dan out of the fire, Lilah had run to the bottom of the rock where Harry was. She pushed through the small crowd and fell to the ground where his body lay broken and bleeding, his life leaching out as she shrieked for help.

The ambulance ride... frantic prayers... blood... there was so much blood. Lilah refused to budge from the chair outside the operating theater. When the hospital attendant placed his wrinkled hand on her shoulder, she screamed, threatening murder. In minutes, the commander of the search-and-rescue team strode to Lilah and ordered her to go with the nurse for an examination of her own. Sitting on the edge of the exam table, Lilah rocked back and forth. The sudden prick on her arm barely registered.

When she woke up, she was in a wheelchair at the airport, waiting for her flight back home. Harry was already airlifted to the U.S. naval base in Greece. The hours it took to cross the Atlantic were a blur. She clung to Dan's arm and took in harsh, raspy breaths, sobbing silently. In the Bedouin camp, she'd prayed every day to get back to her twin, but now, her mind was far, far away, with Harry.

"You're okay," Dan murmured, patting her head as though making sure she really was in the seat next to him. He kept doing that throughout the flight.

Her chest... it was getting so hard to breathe. She tried to take in a big gulp of air, stopping when she heard a whistling sound.

"Shh," Dan soothed. "It's 'cause you won't stop crying."

Lilah nodded jerkily. She managed to get through the next couple of hours and somehow stumbled out of the plane into the terminal.

At one of the counters, her chest tightened as though her ribs were in the grip of a vise. Frantically, she opened her mouth. Air. She needed air. Everything dimmed.

Light... dark... light... dark...

"What's going on?" Dan's agitated voice echoed strangely around her.

"Get the boy out," yelled someone. "Where's the oxygen?"

Beep... beep...

Darkness... almost never-ending... drifting in and out of memories. "I taught you how to play chess," said Mama, a worried frown on her face. Lilah laughed, her chest sore when she did. Was Mama demanding a rematch? How could she since she was dead?

Beep... beep... beep...

"Harry," Lilah croaked, but there was something stuck in her throat. Sounds wouldn't come out. Her head hurt.

"Give her some diazepam."

Beep... beep...

People talked all around. Someone sobbed, telling her she couldn't—she simply couldn't—leave him. Dan? Why on earth would she leave him?

Beep... beep... beep...

"'The price of being misunderstood, he thought,'" Dan recited. "'They call you devil, or they call you God.'"

He was reading from Jonathan Livingston Seagull? *Lilah smiled. She'd watched the movie. Some of the reviews were terrible, but she'd totally loved it.*

Beep... beep...

"She will come through," someone said. She'd heard the same voice a few times in the darkness. He was usually talking to Dan. "Think positive."

Lilah frowned. Who was he?

"She got herself out of Libya," agreed Dan, tone encouraged. "She will get herself out of this. Shawn, I need a favor."

Shawn? Andrew's son? *It was nice of him to visit her in the—where was she?*

She tried to open her eyes. It was so hard... as though something was hanging on her lashes, weighing them down. She gritted her teeth and tried again. Almost... almost... *a bright light slammed painfully into her eyes. She instantly screwed them back shut. "Dan," she called. It came out garbled, nothing like her brother's name. The voice didn't even sound like hers.*

A sudden silence. Thundering feet. A familiar hand took her fingers. "Are you awake?" Dan asked.

"Are you sleeping any better?" The warm voice of the psychiatrist broke the train of Lilah's thoughts. He'd been seeing her regularly since she woke in the hospital room three months ago.

Handing her a paper cup, the shrink settled into his chair. The midtown office was bright, sun pouring in through horizontal blinds. Plastic daisies in a crystal vase on the doctor's desk completed the picture of cheer and optimism.

She took a sip of the water, letting the coolness soothe her dry throat. "I'm not coughing as much," she said, grimacing at the husky sound.

"Your family physician says the pneumonia is all gone. Dangerous thing, smoke damage. You were lucky you'd already landed in New York by the time your airway completely closed up. However, you didn't answer my question."

The oversized chair was cozy, but Lilah was too agitated to be comfortable. "You haven't answered mine, either," she croaked, chin raised. "Why can't I visit Harry? No one will even let me *call* him."

Even Dan pleaded ignorance when she asked him to get her Harry's phone number. She knew her twin wouldn't lie to her. For whatever reason, the Barronses were keeping *him* in the dark, too. Andrew would only say Harry spent a few days in the sickbay at the U.S. naval base in Greece before being flown to New York. He'd been under the care of the surgeons at Presbyterian Hospital since. She'd read a copy of his statement to military authorities about their abduction and subsequent escape. Harry had left out the part about the assault, leaving it to her to fill in the blanks if she so wished. Which she didn't. Not at this time. Right now, her priority was finding out how he was doing. Whenever she asked Andrew for more information, he invariably hurried out, claiming he'd already wasted too much of his valuable time in the hospital.

It left Lilah wondering how she could possibly have imagined the Barronses' efforts to rescue her from Libya came out of familial affection. They'd never hidden their abject disinterest in her. Andrew at least showed up a few times in the hospital when Lilah was still admitted. Caroline, Lilah's *half-sister,* never visited even once. The Barrons couple helped her for Dan, nothing else. In fact, they frequently demanded he leave her side to attend whatever events they arranged for him. Dan wouldn't budge, of course. Except to return to school or when she had her doctor's appointments, he rarely left Lilah's sight. Neither was she about to encourage him to go with Andrew when she'd been begging God for weeks to let her get back home to her brother.

Nor would the Barronses let Lilah contact the one other person who loved her. When the hospital finally sent her home, she found not a single employee in the Barrons household would help her. Even the psychiatrist seemed to be in their pay.

"Lilah, it took you six weeks to even start talking," the doctor said, his tone irritatingly patient.

"My voice is not yet back to normal," she allowed.

"And it may never get there," the doctor warned. "Like your insomnia. We may need help getting our mind to relax."

Our? Annoyed, she said, "Look, I don't know about your mind, but *I* managed four hours of sleep last night *without* those pills you tried to push on me. When I can't sleep, I read." When dark images rose, she closed her eyes and imagined herself at the edge of the precipice in Libya, diving into the blue waters of the Mediterranean. *She* was in control of her destiny. If the cliffs couldn't beat her, nothing could. "Even my eyelashes grew back. My voice will be fine; *everything* will be fine."

"I'm sure it will," the shrink soothed. "You're a resilient young lady. Going back to school, I hear."

"Next week."

There were only a few weeks left until high school was done, but she *wanted* to return. Dan already received his acceptance letter from West Point, but like the rest of their schoolmates, Lilah would spend the time remaining anxiously waiting to hear back from colleges. Prom, graduation... she wanted it all. She even dug into the money she'd saved from her time working for Rose Cosmetics to buy herself a couple of new outfits. Nothing very expensive, but still, she felt good having them.

Everything would return to the way it had been before she flew out of JFK International Airport when her major goals in life were escaping the Barrons mansion and making sure Harry was okay. Not eluding monsters hiding in the shadows. Moving on would be easier than she expected since no one in school knew about the abduction, not even her friends.

News of problems in the Barrons family could cause more ripples in the already-battered stock market, and the feds instructed all concerned not to speak about the matter to anyone not directly related. The Barronses put about word Lilah was already on her way back from her Thanksgiving trip when the problems in Libya happened. The explanation for her absence from school was she caught some kind of illness and was quarantined.

Not so for Harry. *His* parents were small-timers. Lilah spent most of her convalescence reading, and she saw a para or two in the papers about the abduction and one when they were rescued. Correction: she saw one para describing *Harry's* rescue. There was nothing about her.

Nothing showed up in the media about Sanders, either. Once

again, the government warned everyone concerned not to start trouble without solid proof. Accusations of kidnapping slung at the owner of a billion-dollar enterprise by another large corporation wouldn't simply cause troubles in the market. It carried the potential to bring an already struggling economy to its knees. As far as the public knew, Gaddafi was the only one responsible for the crime. Even the Egyptian government was persuaded to dismiss the bombing of Halfaya Pass as the handiwork of some imaginary terrorist group. Still, according to what Dan said, there were rumors aplenty about Sanders and Genesis.

Bitterness welled each time Lilah remembered the trauma she and Harry suffered because of Jared Sanders. Everything resulted from... no, she was *not* going to dwell on it. She needed to get her life back on track.

She *would* get where she wanted to go—college on her own terms. In a few months, she'd be eighteen and free of the suffocating presence of the Barronses in her life. She simply needed to make sure Harry was fine before she could focus on her future.

"Your brother was saying you want to enroll in self-defense classes?" the shrink asked.

"Kickboxing," Lilah said. "And shooting. Something wrong with that?" She was also looking into joining a climbing club or something. The mountains would help her keep the nightmares at bay. *She* was in charge, not the monsters hunting them.

Lilah took her brown duffel from the carpet and settled it on her lap. Her gym clothes were in the bag. When she started out for this appointment, she entertained the idea of going to Harry's brother's gym to sign up for a membership. Only, it wouldn't be just for kickboxing lessons. If no one in the Barrons mansion would give her Harry's phone number, she'd go to someone who would definitely know where he was, like his brother. Unfortunately, the Barrons chauffeur who drove her to this appointment stated he was under strict orders to stick to schedule and allow no detours. Not that anyone was worried Sanders would go after her within the borders of the United States. Apparently, she needed clearance from her doctors before being allowed out on her own.

There was one other option left. She was going to ask Shawn to track down Harry. Even if Shawn and Andrew were not on good terms with each other, it would still be awkward asking the son to go behind the father's back. But the Barronses left her with no other choice.

"Kickboxing is an excellent idea," the doctor said. "I would've suggested you wait until you recover some more, but it *will* give you a sense of control over things, so—"

"Over what things?" she asked, hiding her trembling fingers under the gym bag. She hadn't said a word about the assault, not even to her twin. Harry wouldn't have divulged anything without checking with her. Not to the government, not to the doctor.

"Lilah," the shrink exclaimed. "You just escaped a damned—" Coughing, he said, "Most people would consider an abduction significant trauma. It's the reason you haven't been able to sleep well. Stop pretending it never happened, or you'll find it hard to recover."

Lilah let out the breath she'd been holding. The doctor was

talking about the kidnapping. "I'm not pretending," she said. "Only trying to put things behind me. As you said, I'm resilient. Strong. So strong that I'm not answering another question until you tell me about Harry."

The psychiatrist scribbled in his notebook. "Harry broke both his legs and a shoulder, but he's on the mend."

"Is he still admitted?" she asked, anxiety tightening her throat. From what she was told, he'd been stable when the medics at the U.S. naval base in Greece allowed him to be flown to the Presbyterian Hospital in New York. But leg fractures took a long time to heal, didn't they?

"He was sent home," said the doctor.

"So why can't I see him? Why hasn't *he* called?"

"Delilah," someone chided from behind. "Don't be selfish."

Startled, Lilah dropped the duffel bag on the floor and twisted around, grimacing inwardly when she saw her brother-in-law, Andrew Barrons, at the door. Of course, Andrew didn't think twice about barging in anywhere, doctor's office included. The shrink wasn't objecting, though.

There was another man behind Andrew. Height a little below six feet, salt-and-pepper hair, blue eyes... Lilah had seen him on television a few times. Still, she might not have recognized him were she not told about the part Temple, the senator from New Jersey, played in their rescue. He and his pilot were in the helicopter she saw right before Melanthios... Lilah gritted her teeth. She did what was needed to stay alive. Nothing more, nothing less.

The senator shot an exasperated glance at Andrew.

Not that Andrew ever gave two hoots about anyone's censure. He continued, "Harry was injured. The Sheppards lost everything, almost to the last penny. They have many things to worry about, not just you."

Lilah flushed. "I was only—" Unexpected tears pricked her eyes, and she batted them back, reminding herself she wouldn't have to put up with her brother-in-law for much longer. She'd already be counting down to the first day of college if she weren't so anxious about Harry.

"Let me," the senator said to Andrew.

The politician took a couple of steps toward her. Hands tucked in his pockets, he scrutinized her. There was a look on his face... bemusement and something else... as though he were tallying numbers in his mind. At the moment, Lilah didn't care. She needed to know what was going on with Harry.

Tone kind, Temple explained, "Harry's parents took him home a couple of weeks ago, but he's not fully mobile." At her restless shifting, he held a hand up. "I wouldn't worry. He's expected to completely recover. Only, he's not quite there yet. Also, Andrew is correct about the finances. I don't know if the family can afford a phone line in their house. They're barely holding things together."

"They can't afford..." Lilah stood. Her knees were suddenly weak. "But... they..." Surely, the Sheppards had some savings. Then there was Hector, their oldest son with his own business—the gym.

"Please, sit," said Temple. "We don't want you falling."

She wasn't going to. The days on the ventilator left her limbs weak and uncoordinated, but she'd gotten over it. It was only the news about the Sheppards—

The shrink's hand suddenly appeared at her elbow, urging her back to the chair. Lilah swatted it away. "Will you stop that?" she snapped at the doctor. The man had an obligation to protect her privacy, but he tossed professional ethics out the window the minute Andrew Barrons appeared at the door. Now, here he was, shamelessly pretending concern for her well-being. "I'm *not* going to fall."

With a sudden laugh, Temple said, "You want answers, and you're not going to stop until you get them. All right, I'll tell you what I know." He nodded at the doctor and added, "We can wait outside while you finish up."

"We've gotten as far as I think we ever will like this," said the shrink. "Same with the young man. I want to try a joint session. We're going to need the families involved, too."

Lilah started. She hadn't known Harry was seeing the same doctor. That meant he was at least well enough to travel between his family's new home and the medical office.

Eyes crinkling in a paternal smile, Temple asked, "In which case, why don't we sit someplace where we can talk?" He crooked his elbow at her. "The ambassador—your father—was almost the same age as me. Humor this old man and hold on, will ya?"

She inclined her head in agreement and wrapped her fingers lightly around the senator's arm. Harry was physically all right. Even if he and his family lost all their money, they'd somehow get back on their feet. She knew Harry. Somehow, he'd still find a way to make Genesis the "biggest, most badass" oil company in the whole world as he once vowed.

Her chin tilted up, she ignored Andrew and the yes-man shrink to sail out of the room. She'd soon be done with all of them. College waited for her and Dan. Once they turned eighteen, they'd be free of the Barronses. There was nothing Andrew could do to keep them in his clutches.

#

Fire, ferocious monster, raged, setting alight scant vegetation among the rocky hills bordering Egypt. Dry winds twisted the flames into tall spirals, and in the middle of the blazing column stood Lilah, as though being forged by the giant tongues of destructive energy surrounding her. Dan Barrons sprinted out of the inferno, dragging his twin sister with him. Sparks followed, reluctant to let the girl leave the scorching womb. In charred yellow robes and with flames and smoke trailing, Lilah seemed an incarnation of the fiery deity.

A gust blew, plastering the burnt rags to her figure. The poet in Temple noted the girl was so exquisite the gods surely sculpted her themselves, but the father in him wanted to shield her from the gaping men around... the travelers, the border force, even the rescue team. Her long, dark hair floated behind like ocean waves, the singed ends curling. Heat heightened the reddish hue in her cheeks, her mouth slightly open in the effort of breathing. Her eyes were the color of autumn leaves, the pools of liquid fire reflecting the glow without.

"Here's your tea," announced the waiter, snapping Temple out of his reverie.

More waiters deftly maneuvered their way between the crowded tables in the enclosed garden room at Lutecé, the four-star French restaurant in midtown Manhattan. Around them, cutlery clinked, and chatter hummed. The green slate floor, the whitewood trim, the hut-like roof... everything added to the ambiance of airy cheer.

Enjoying the warmth and the tangy sweetness of the tea, Temple eyed the young woman across the table. With a regal nod, she accepted her dessert—raspberry soufflé. The employees at Lutecé were trained to be efficient—almost invisible—but there was still a dazed look on the waiter's face when he moved on to Andrew.

Incredible, Temple mused. The names "Andrew Barrons" and "Senator Temple" got them a table even without a reservation, but the staff were responding more to the presence of the seventeen-year-old princess—"girl" was too mild a word for Lilah—than to the billionaire businessman or the politician.

She was stunning enough to startle most people into second and third glances. If the princess who emerged from the fire were merely lovely, the one in the restaurant was eye ravishing with no crude makeup to mask the God-given beauty. In the four months since her escape, burnt hair had been trimmed so the blue-black waves perfectly framed her face. Her cut lashes grew back, forming silky fringes around large hazel orbs. The floral midi and boots were common enough on the streets of the city, but on Lilah, they looked breathtakingly dramatic. Plus, there was the fragrance. Something exotic. She was wearing enough of it to trigger asthma attacks within a two-mile radius.

The only incongruent feature was her speech. Amid all the regal loveliness, her voice was husky and rough, a result of smoke inhalation as per her family physician.

The restaurant staff didn't seem to notice the hoarse tones, and their reaction couldn't merely be in response to Lilah's looks. Her entire demeanor was that of someone born to rule. The straight back, the firm gaze, the confident—almost haughty—set of her chin... everyone around responded to it from the *maître d'* to the waiters. Even the famed chef came by, presumably to greet the senator and the businessman, but he seemed very keen to know what Lilah thought of the dishes.

Temple was already aware of her beauty from the encounter in Egypt, and he was prepared to meet a headstrong girl at the doctor's office, albeit one with a soft corner for the younger son of the Sheppard family. The conversations with Andrew Barrons left the senator with the distinct impression of a girl more intelligent than the driller let on. Ambitious, too. According to her brother, Lilah's sights were set on Harvard Law. There was also her resourcefulness, her nerves of steel. Temple hadn't said a word to the military investigators about his firm belief the death of Melanthios wasn't merely a lucky break for her. She intentionally led the man to the landmines. All in all, Temple expected to be introduced to an exceptionally gifted and courageous young lady.

The aristocratic manner was what caught him by surprise, more so since he was aware of Lilah's middle-class upbringing. Didn't she realize almost all her money was now gone? With the loss of Genesis, most of her already meager inheritance was wiped out. The survivor benefits from her parents' jobs wouldn't last forever. But somehow, Temple knew the lack of funds wouldn't make a difference. Even penniless and homeless, Lilah would remain a proud princess.

"Lunch is done," she said, dabbing her lips with the pristine white napkin. "You said we'd talk after food."

"What do you want to know?" Temple asked.

"Harry," she stated. "You said he's going to recover. What about money and all that? How are they—"

Temple smiled. "Why don't we start at the beginning?" Idly, he stirred the miniature spoon in the teacup, watching the golden-brown liquid swirling. "I knew Sanders was creating problems."

Lilah glanced at her brother-in-law. "Looks like lots of people knew."

"I warned Ryan," interjected Andrew. "I'm sure you heard me at the funeral."

Unfortunately, Andrew hadn't been willing to extend any sort of financial help to the Sheppards. Temple discussed the oilman's intransigence with Noah, former attorney general. They knew Sanders needed to be dethroned, replaced by someone with a deep understanding of the issues at hand. The new leader would have the courage and the will to defend the truth with his last breath. Noah pointed out wisdom and pluck were never enough. The would-be usurper needed an opening as well. Right place, right time. Neither Temple nor Noah realized that day how far the enemy had gone in his malevolence. They didn't recognize the urgent need for action.

Meditatively, Temple continued, "We also knew about Gaddafi's little tricks. He'd been pulling the same stunts with the other companies in the country, so we didn't connect the two."

"Neither did the Sheppards," Lilah said promptly. "I heard the kidnappers talking about it. That's how Harry and I figured out what happened."

"We—Andrew and I—still didn't realize. Not until..." Temple pushed his teacup to the side and shot a glance at Andrew. The driller shifted uncomfortably in his seat and looked away. Forcibly stopping his fingers from curling into a fist, Temple said to Lilah, "When you called Andrew about the arrest, I was with him."

They'd been at another pricey restaurant, meeting Daniel—Lilah's brother—over dinner. When Andrew hung up from the call and briefed Temple on the arrest of the Sheppard parents, Dan leaped from his chair. *"Lilah,"* he exclaimed, face pale and body shaking. *"Oh, my God. Lilah."*

It took Temple only moments to deduce Andrew indeed took the advice the senator once casually flung out. The driller found a bribe to induce Lilah into getting out of the way, and the desperate Sheppards cooperated, all of them uncaring of the danger they placed the girl in. As far they knew at the time, Gaddafi was the current problem, but Sanders was still an issue. He might not have dared attack Andrew Barrons's family when they were safe in the U.S., but outside, Lilah was fair game.

Temple's hands had itched to thrash Andrew. For the first time in his self-centered life, there was trepidation on Andrew's face. No, not worry over *Temple's* reaction. Andrew was scared Lilah's brother would find out what he did. He'd lose the boy.

Reminding himself he'd played an important role in the mess the Sheppards found themselves in, Temple agreed to help. It never occurred to any of them the enemy already had a counterattack planned—Harry. None of them imagined Lilah would get caught in the trap with the Sheppards' son.

Within a couple of hours of the kidnapping, Sanders contacted Temple. Jared Sanders was too shrewd to taunt his enemies with obvious hints of his involvement in the crime. A note was brought to Temple's office by Sanders's secretary, stating he heard what happened, and if there was anything he could do to help... etc. etc. There was a follow-up call from the same secretary, offering to put up ransom money in return for the deed to Genesis. All very supportive and above board.

Lilah nodded. "Dan told me some of it."

"They gave us one week," Temple went on. "The Gaddafi government said they'd nationalize Genesis in a week unless the Sheppards were able to make alternate arrangements. Oh, everyone insisted the pressure had nothing to do with the abduction."

Andrew snorted. "Unfortunate timing was what Sanders called it." Desperate to keep the teens from harm, Ryan promised Sanders he could have Genesis for next to nothing.

"Everything changed after you escaped," Temple continued. "Sanders stopped pretending to help, and Gaddafi's officials took over Genesis." With his bargaining chips gone, Sanders urged the Libyan government to annex the business in violation of preexisting agreements, and as soon as the deed was done, he obtained the contract to run it.

Lilah objected, "We were looking out for news on Genesis. We figured there would've been *something* in the papers."

"It took them some time," Temple explained. "Gaddafi administration needed to maintain the pretense to escape international condemnation. Also, Sanders was very careful to avoid leaving direct evidence of his involvement."

"I understand," Lilah said. "Because the Libyan government

already claimed they played no part in the kidnapping or Sanders's offer. If they handed Genesis over to him right away, everyone in the world would know they'd been lying. What I don't get is this. Those men—the thugs—never meant to let us live. Not just that. Even after he got what he wanted, Sanders was still after us. Why?"

Because of my *failure,* Temple acknowledged in his mind. He'd seen the danger posed by the criminal driller decades ago. It was *his* strategy to form the alliance between the three companies. The egos involved led to the collapse of the alliance even before it began. Sanders recognized the threat to his control and bided his time. He waited for the perfect revenge, payback his enemies would never forget. Anyone who dared oppose him would know they were risking the lives of their families.

Desperation and greed ensured Ryan Sheppard stayed put in Libya, unknowingly waiting for the ax to fall on his younger son, Harry. The self-absorption of Andrew Barrons and the unthinking advice tossed out by the politician sent Lilah into harm's way. *Temple's* mistake put this young woman in danger. She was forced to kill a man to escape. All of them shared the blame for the trauma suffered by Harry and Lilah.

Out loud, Temple said, "Sanders is vindictive. His plan had been to kill Harry in response to Ryan's refusal to sell Genesis. Harry escaped. Sanders couldn't stand the idea."

Jared Sanders *did* suffer a minor defeat at the hands of a seventeen-year-old boy, and he'd never forget it. It wasn't simply about ego. Harry's escape might prompt other would-be usurpers to rise in revolt.

The truth... only, not the *complete* truth. None of them dared admit the past. Not Andrew, for fear of losing Dan if the boy ever deduced how his sister ended up in Libya at the worst possible moment. Not Ryan, for fear of angering Andrew. Not Temple, either, because, dammit, he still needed Andrew.

"As soon as Dante got the call from Harry, all of us headed to Egypt," Temple continued.

Andrew huffed. "Temple got the American military involved. None of us knew what to think when you didn't show. But we couldn't give up."

As each day passed with no news of Harry or Lilah, their families told themselves Sanders wouldn't resist the urge to parade them as trophies if indeed he'd captured them. Somehow, he'd make sure the senseless deaths of the young people remained indelibly imprinted on the minds of their loved ones. Clinging to this idea, Dan, Andrew, and Ryan took turns flying with the search team over the border crossing closest to Alexandria.

Lilah barely glanced at her brother-in-law before looking away. The cynicism in her eyes... she knew damned well he'd done it for Dan. Temple wondered what she thought of *his* involvement. Helpful statesman or politician obligated to a campaign donor?

"We ran into trouble," she said, explaining the delay in their appearance. "There was a robbery... Harry already gave his statement."

She'd been on a ventilator for weeks and afterward couldn't speak for some time, so it was Harry who talked to the government officials. Even after she regained use of her vocal cords, she'd refused to add to the information, insisting Harry already said all there was to say, including about the delay between their escape from the kidnappers and their run across the border crossing.

"Right," Temple said, carefully watching her reaction. "The robbery... I read the report."

A few weeks ago

As soon as the surgeons in Crete took Harry off heavy-duty sedation, military officials interviewed him. The young man refused to discuss anything until being given the latest update on Lilah. The only info divulged to him was that the girl was being treated for smoke inhalation and couldn't talk on the phone. The truth... only, not the entirety of it. When Harry eventually gave his statement, he admitted to quite a lot—from the death of a woman at his hands to his theft of a bike, followed by his appropriation of a police Jeep. He handed a map he bought in Benghazi to the authorities, marking on it all the places he and Lilah traversed.

There was a remarkable lack of detail in the part of the lad's statement where he claimed to have been attacked by a former colonel in the U.S. Army who stole everything the teens carried on them. Harry and Lilah had taken refuge in a church while he recovered from the assault. He maintained to military authorities he didn't have more information on the robbery. They'd have to ask Lilah if she wanted to add her thoughts about it. Yet Harry was insistent the investigators find the colonel and punish him for his crime.

When Temple later read through the document... no, it didn't ring true. He'd lived far too long not to recognize it when a teenager was lying through his teeth. Temple was waiting to hear back from his contacts in the military about this colonel.

Still, Harry Sheppard was a remarkable young man... almost preternaturally astute and quick-thinking with willingness to do what it took. A gifted linguist with fluency in many languages spoken in the Mediterranean region and then some. In the time he'd been on the run, he gained quite a bit of insight into the internal politics of Libya. From what Temple heard, the boy possessed an uncanny knack for making connections with strangers.

The day after being given the green light by Harry's doctors, Military Airlift Command arranged one of their specialized transport aircraft to fly him to New York City. He was sedated throughout.

Outside the entrance to Presbyterian Hospital, Temple waited for the medical personnel to unload the ambulance and transport the sleeping patient to his room. It was early in the morning, but there were already crowds of people going in and out. As was common to all hospitals, the air reeked of disinfectant. Cup of hot coffee in his hand, Temple followed the Sheppards to the private room arranged for Harry. He was too groggy to be of any use, but it was Ryan whom Temple needed to see. A couple of minutes later, he got consent from Harry's father for the seventeen-year-old to be interviewed again by the military brass. It took half an hour more to discuss Andrew Barrons's surprising offer of financial help.

When Temple returned with the defense secretary the next week, the CIA director joined the party. Oh, yeah. Harry Sheppard certainly lit up radar screens in certain quarters of the U.S. government.

The matronly nurse who opened the door asked them to wait

until she finished giving her patient his sponge bath. When the three men entered the white-painted room, everything was clean and sweet-smelling. In the middle of the hospital bed was Harry, dressed in a crisp hospital gown. His cheeks were now smoothly shaven and slightly sunken, and his dark hair was cut to a reasonable length. The dark eyes were slightly puffy. His left arm was in a cast, and both his legs were immobilized, but he still managed a small grin. "I didn't get a chance to thank you, sir," Harry said, looking straight at Temple. "You kept the reconnaissance flights going on all these weeks."

Temple returned the smile almost involuntarily, recognizing rule number one of politics—making the other person feel good about supporting you. Harry and Lilah engineered the escape all on their own. If it hadn't been the American military, the Egyptian border service would've surely attended to the injured young man. Temple did little to aid the teenagers' near-miraculous feats, but here was Harry, giving the senator credit. Whether the boy knew it or not, he had the makings of a politician.

"Have you been to see Lilah?" Harry asked, tone eager. "How's she doing?" He was told of her fight for life only moments before he was flown to New York. By then, she'd started recovering.

"I haven't visited," Temple admitted. He'd seen no reason to intrude until recently. Not when no one could say with any degree of certainty she'd make it. "Her doctors say she's on the mend, but it's going to be a while before she starts speaking."

"I wish—" With his free hand, Harry punched the bed. "I'm stuck here."

Reassuringly, Temple said, "Lilah will be fine. *You* have

months of therapy ahead."

"I know." Gritting his teeth, Harry sucked in a breath. "My father tells me the Pentagon is picking up the tab for everything." He turned his head on the pillow and glanced around the private room. With a slight nod at the secretary and the CIA director, Harry asked, "It's not as if I'm not grateful, but why?"

"A seventeen-year-old who defeated the Gaddafi regime?" asked the defense secretary, smilingly. "The American government considers you a hero."

"It was me *and* Lilah. We were trying to stay alive, not be heroes."

"A healthy survival instinct is essential to heroism," agreed the secretary. The will to live was strong in both the kids.

"Perhaps," Harry said, inclining his head. "And the Gaddafi administration was only the tool. It was Sand—"

The secretary held up a hand. "We've already discussed Mr. Sanders's possible involvement in the case."

Harry hoisted himself up on his right elbow. "'Possible involvement'?"

"Let me," said the CIA director. Drawing up a chair, he sat next to the bed. "I understand you have plans to join the navy?"

"Once I'm done with the Maritime College," Harry said. A grim look passed across his face. "I missed my SATs. But what does it have to do with—"

The director waved a hand. "Don't worry too much about it. After what you managed to accomplish, the navy will be happy to have you, SAT scores be damned. I'm an army man, myself."

"I know," Harry said. "World War II vet. I read an article on you some time ago."

Amused surprise lit up the director's eyes. "I didn't realize my fame had spread... well, I was trying to say I completely understand your feelings about the government's stance on Mr. Sanders. The civilian side doesn't quite operate on the same wavelength as us. Your word is not enough to convict Mr. Sanders of anything or even to charge him. At the same time, if we make noises, it will have repercussions as far as the economy is concerned. Do you understand what I'm saying?"

Hesitantly, Harry nodded.

"If we did have solid evidence," the director continued, "the government could take measures to prevent Sanders, Incorporated, from being impacted by the arrest of its president and chief executive officer. We have nothing on him at the moment. Without proof, Jared Sanders will escape, but the economy will tank."

"So he gets away with everything?" Harry asked bitterly.

"Son," called Temple. Grabbing the second chair, he also sat close to the bed. "It's not just about the economy. You already know Sanders is as criminal as he can get. You already know many of Gaddafi's men were in Sanders's pay. What you might not know is he has a great number of *our* officials in his pocket."

Harry's eyes widened.

"Yes." Temple inclined his head. "They're the ones who could've put a stop to Sanders. If they did so before you and Lilah were... you wouldn't have... what's done is done. Even now, some are too greedy to make a move against Sanders. Some are indifferent... they simply don't care what happens in the wider world as long as they can stay safe in their little bubbles. Some fear what he might do to them. The only way to force all these people to take action against Sanders is by providing evidence so clear-cut they'd have to do it to save their own skins. Unfortunately, evidence is what we don't have... not against Sanders... not even against Gaddafi except what you overheard from the kidnappers. The Libyans have more on *you* than the other way around." At Harry's sudden shifting, Temple held up a hand. "The American government supports you. There are witnesses to the kidnapping. The rest of what happened... everyone understands you were in a difficult situation."

Once again, Harry glanced around the room. "What's all *this* supposed to be? A bribe to keep me quiet about Sanders?"

Resting his back on the wall, the defense secretary laughed. "Bribe? I suppose... *we* prefer to call it recruitment bonus."

"Recruitment for what?" Harry asked.

"You're signing up to join the navy," the CIA director repeated, not elaborating further. The elaborations could come later. Right now, Temple wanted to discuss other matters with Harry. "We have to get going."

When the director and the secretary left, Harry flopped back down on the bed and stared unblinkingly at the men's disappearing backs. Temple smiled. The young man already figured it out. After all, there could only be so many reasons the CIA director would offer someone a recruitment bonus. He and the defense secretary would give Harry time to think things over before pressing for a decision.

"Harry," Temple called, needing the boy's full attention. "I asked your father if I might speak with you about something."

Harry glanced between the closing door and Temple.

"No, not about the secretary's suggestion," Temple said. "Did Ryan tell you where he was going today?"

A shadow ran across Harry's face. "Something about a loan."

Temple nodded. "He's hoping to work things out with Andrew."

"Andr—Andrew Barrons? Are you kidding me?" Once again, Harry tried to sit up, but his elbow slid out, causing him to collapse onto the pillows. "Father knows damned well Andrew doesn't help anyone."

"Ryan has no choice. He has to knock on every door. There isn't enough money even to carry your family through the next couple of months. He must have told you."

"We'll survive. Hector already has his gym, and I can start working as soon as I'm out of here. I'm sure my parents can find something to do in some oil company. They both have years of experience."

"Is survival enough?" Temple asked. "I've known Ryan a long time. Before you were born. Before Hector was born. I've met your grandfather. Genesis used to be a profitable company. Do you believe your father will be happy with a clerical job in a dingy office somewhere in Manhattan, living paycheck to paycheck? Your sister's ten, isn't she? Are you okay with her living in poverty, not knowing if there will be food on the table next week?"

"But—"

"What about the rest of the Sheppards?" Temple pressed. "Don't they deserve a chance at getting their investment back? How about your employees?" Relentlessly, Temple went on, "Ryan's secretary... what's his name? Dante Maro? Doesn't he deserve more than survival?"

"Yeah, we all do. And we'll make it. We'll be back, better than before." Jaw clenched, Harry added, "Better than even Jared Sanders. Once we are, he'll pay for what he did. I'm going to make sure of it. Give me some time."

"Time is what you don't have. Sanders will finish you off long before then."

"What do you mean? I'm in the U.S. now. There's nothing he can—"

"Harry," said Temple, keeping his tone firm. "You're a shrewd young man. You saw for yourself how his money was able to buy him support in Libya. I told you how he does the same in this country. Now, there are limits to what he can do within our borders, but do you imagine for a moment any of his supporters will revolt if he does something to the son of a bankrupt driller? Do you imagine he will refrain from doing anything to you and let his enemies hear how a seventeen-year-old boy thwarted his plans?"

Awareness dawned in Harry's dark eyes.

Deliberately, Temple said, "Deaths happen every day to the rich *and* the poor. Sometimes, violent deaths. But guess what? Any killer would think twice before daring to attack someone with money and support. Your friend, Lilah? She's safe... Jared Sanders would not dare attack the Barrons family within the borders of the United States. You, on the other hand... and it might not be just you. What happens if Sanders goes after the rest of your family? Your sister, for instance?" All color leached out of Harry's face, leaving him paper white. "You need all the support you can get," said Temple. "And right now. Which is why your father is in Andrew's office, asking for a loan."

Thoughts flitted across Harry's face in quick succession. With his right hand, he pinched the bridge of his nose. "But Andrew Barrons? What's the point in going to him for help? Andrew doesn't help anyone."

"Not unless he sees something in it for himself," Temple agreed.

"What does he see for himself in helping *us*?"

Temple heaved himself to his feet. "Perhaps something only *you* can make happen. Do it for him, and he'll help you with your plans. What was it you said? You're going to be back, better than Sanders? Without Andrew Barrons, your dreams for your future are going to remain mere fantasies. Keep the fact in mind when you decide what to do with his request."

"What request? What can we do for Andrew? He's a billionaire. He already has everything he wants."

Without answering directly, Temple walked to the door. "Something else to remember... pride, self-respect... it might get injured, but time heals such wounds. A *life* once lost will not return. Not yours, not your family's."

The boy would figure things out. After all, he knew very well there was one thing in the world Andrew wanted he didn't have yet. The one person whose self-respect he wasn't able to buy.

The billionaire businessman bribed the Sheppards to get Lilah out of the way while her brother was introduced to Senator Temple. A small reward for a small return. But Andrew was there at the border when she appeared behind the burning gate. He'd seen her wait until she saw Harry before making a run for it. He'd seen her ready to risk her life rather than leave Harry behind. Andrew finally understood Lilah's price.

Temple only got the chance to put one foot out of the room when an angry curse of comprehension erupted from Harry. Without turning around, Temple shut the door behind him and left.

From that morning, Harry Sheppard never said another word about Lilah. Silently, he listened to everything his family said. Even after the unsavory deal between Andrew and the Sheppards was in place, Temple continued to visit Harry. He still flashed the same cheery grin. He bantered with Dante Maro, the secretary, cracking silly jokes with the man's eleven-year-old son. When the CIA director returned, Harry peppered him with questions about his service during WWII and in Vietnam. With his parents and his brother, he looked over blueprints for their new business and made suggestions.

But day by day, Harry's grin became more tainted with guilt. Fear and desperation lurked behind the laughter in his eyes. Strangely, none of the Sheppards seemed to see it. None of them found it extraordinary he didn't ask about Lilah even once. Not in the hospital, not after he was discharged.

Back in the present

Temple had lied to Lilah. There *was* a telephone line in the three-bedroom apartment rented by the Sheppards. Harry was warned by everyone Andrew Barrons wanted all the paperwork ready before making any sort of announcement. The oil driller was adamant about not giving Lilah any time to devise escape routes. Ryan Sheppard forbade Harry from calling Lilah even to say "hello," but the family still kept a watchful eye on its younger son, worried he might rebel.

They needn't have. Harry didn't go near the phone. He heard her name mentioned plenty of times in connection with Andrew's deal, and each time, Harry walked away as though he couldn't bear the sound of it. He'd known Temple would be meeting her today but gave no message to carry to her.

In the airy garden room at the French restaurant, the lunch crowd continued to chatter. Temple took another sip of his lemon tea. It was lukewarm by now. Over the rim of his cup, he glanced across the table at Andrew Barrons and slightly shook his head. If they broke the news here, there was a high chance the furious princess would stage a regal exit. She needed to see for herself what she'd be risking—*who* she'd be risking—by clinging to her pride.

"You still haven't told me about Harry," Lilah accused, sliding the plate of raspberry soufflé a couple of inches to the side.

"Because I don't need to." Temple smiled. "You'll be meeting Harry today. *He'll* answer all your questions."

Lilah's hazel eyes snapped wide open.

Andrew waved a hand. "The Sheppards will be at my office this afternoon. We have to discuss what's going to happen to their business... er... the investments and so on... you'll need to be there as well."

Temple waited until later in the day when he was alone in one of the rooms at the offices of Barrons O & G to make the call to his friend. "The final test," he said into the phone.

"The intelligence is obvious in both of them," Noah said, speaking from Connecticut. The board of trustees at Yale was trying to talk the former attorney general into deanship of the law school. "Plus, *we'll* be there to make sure things are done the way they should be. Courage and strength of will have been amply proven. They both refused to admit defeat. All marks of a strong leader."

"But only one is in any position to do something with all of it," Temple said. "There have been other shrewd leaders. Brilliant thinkers with equally sharp advisers. Many have fought and died for their beliefs. It's only a few who've had a chance in hell of actually making a difference."

"Opportunity," agreed Noah. "It doesn't come around often. In this case..."

It was extraordinary how everything aligned perfectly to get all the parties to the negotiating table. The Sheppards and the Barronses harbored their own reasons to acquiesce to Temple's demands and agreed to take a subordinate role to the Kingsleys to get *them* to cooperate. Temple's stepbrother—Supreme Court Justice Godwin Kingsley—was apprised of the new developments, and he was cautiously watching to see where it would all go. They were all waiting to see if they would have the leader under whom the three businesses would unite in only a few years to take down Sanders. Guided by the elders who ran the companies, the young ruler would challenge the *de facto* emperor of the oil sector. Jared Sanders would finally be checkmated.

Shaking his head, Temple warned, "We still don't know if we have the willingness to sacrifice."

"A ruler unwilling to relinquish self-interest will inevitably become another tyrant," stated Noah. "Well... we'll find out today if the one we chose makes the right choice."

They'd see which one was ready to sacrifice their dreams for the other.

Chapter 16

The Flatiron Building was where Barrons O & G established its main office. *Bizarre,* Lilah thought, staring up at the... well... flatiron-shaped edifice from the back seat of the Barrons Cadillac, which was currently parked quite illegally in front of a fire hydrant. There hadn't been a day in her life she didn't know Harry, but she was completely jittery from the second she heard they'd be meeting this afternoon. After lunch, she kept her second doctor's appointment—a follow-up visit with the family physician—but right now, she couldn't tell what they discussed. Her mind was full of Harry. What he'd look like, what they'd talk about...

Loud honking intruded on her thoughts. Lilah jumped.

"Bus behind us," said the chauffeur, flicking an impatient glance at the side mirror. "Why don't you get out here and let me find decent parking? Call me on the car phone when you're ready to leave."

"Yes, of course." There were open parking lots in the area. Andrew undoubtedly had reserved spaces for his vehicles, but if there were a meeting to discuss business, all the spots would be taken by VIPs like the senator.

Fleetingly, her thoughts went to the politician. She supposed he'd been involved in the rescue attempts because of his connection to Andrew, but there was a kindness in his eyes—

Another honk blasted through the air.

"Miss?" reminded the chauffeur.

Lilah murmured an apology and exited the metallic-blue Cadillac, the brown duffel with her gym clothes slung over her right shoulder. Cool spring wind blew, rustling her dress and shaking loose pink flowers from the trees lining the street. Men and women in suits hurried along in all directions, tourists clicked pictures from the sidewalk, cars waited for the lights to change, engines rumbled, and gasoline fumes mingled with cigarette smoke. A few blocks up would be Times Square... all neon lights and strip joints and desperate young prostitutes negotiating terms with customers. Farther down south on Manhattan Island were the homeless and the drug addicts of Bowery.

As the offspring of a retired diplomat and a lawyer, Lilah once lived a comfortable life far from the horrific truths of those who made the streets of New York their home. After her parents' deaths, she moved to the mind-bogglingly wealthy New Castle. Still, the city should've felt familiar. It kind of did... so why couldn't she shake this strange feeling of seeing it all for the first time? She was a child of this place, but after the weeks spent on the run across the mountains and coastal towns of Libya, walking the streets of Manhattan felt akin to hiking along the bottom of a canyon. Skyscrapers towered on either side, their tops seemingly touching the heavens.

Lilah gritted her teeth. This was home. The people she was going to meet in a few minutes were family. The Sheppards might not be related to her by blood, but she was one of them. Her emotional recovery would go a lot faster once she knew they were okay. Once she knew *Harry* was okay.

Before that... smiling widely, Lilah waved at the man waiting at the entrance to the building. On a whim, she'd called Shawn Barrons from a payphone at the family physician's office building right before going in for the appointment. She no longer needed Shawn to contact Harry's brother, but she wanted to thank him for being there for Dan through the ordeal.

Shawn's roommate told her he was actually at the Barrons mansion. Laughing to herself at the absurdity of tracking him down to the house she'd driven out of that morning, Lilah made the second phone call. Shawn was terribly excited to hear her. He asked her to wait for him before she went into the meeting.

Wooden benches lined up along one side of the curved asphalt road in the park less than a block from the Flatiron Building. "I'm not supposed to go anyplace by myself," Lilah muttered, settling onto one of the benches. "The shrink has to give the okay before I'm allowed out on my own."

A rust-colored dog galloped across the green grass on the other side of the path, its joyful barks mingling with the belly laughter of the preteen boys tossing a Frisbee for it to catch.

"Really?" Shawn asked, tone teasing. "I didn't realize you were the kind to worry much about rules." He collapsed next to her, his hand tucked inside the light-yellow spring jacket. The color almost matched his sandy hair. The droopy mustache was gone, and he looked *much* better without it. He still wore the string of amber beads around his neck. Shawn never seemed to go anywhere without it.

Lilah stuck out her tongue. "The chauffeur, Shawn. I don't want him getting into trouble for leaving me alone. The poor man thinks I'm walking straight into the Barrons office while he's parking."

"You're not alone. You're with me. But I'm not going into

Andrew's office even for you. We'll talk in the park."

Funny. In spite of being disinherited, Shawn returned time and time again to the Barrons mansion. He returned to the father who sought to replace him with an adopted son just for being gay. Once, she'd asked why, and he said he didn't have any other place to call home. It seemed his sense of belonging didn't extend to the Barrons offices.

"Why did you want to meet here, then?" Lilah asked, thinking what an idiot Andrew was to disown kind, wonderful Shawn. He'd shown no resentment even toward the twins brought in to replace him.

"Not me," Shawn said. "Since I was on my way back to the city, Dan wanted me to bring you something. Right away."

"Huh? I thought he was going to be—Andrew said we're meeting Harry's family about the stock in Genesis. Dan needs to be there, too. It's supposed to be equally divided between Caroline and us."

Actually, it was the first Lilah realized there was anything left of the stock to discuss. She was trying not to worry overmuch about it. Dan got into West Point where everything was paid for by the army, and while she was still waiting to hear from colleges, Lilah was hopeful she'd win at least a partial scholarship. She could work to make up the difference even if she no longer owned the stock in Genesis as a cushion. Like Shawn, she was going to do it all on her own even if it took her more time than expected.

Shawn shrugged. "Dunno. Dan didn't say anything about a meeting. I guess he figured it involved only you." From the inside of his jacket, Shawn drew something. "Forget all the business stuff. This came in the mail for you. Dan wanted you to have it right away."

Envelopes. Two of them. Both with block letters proclaiming the messages to be from the Massachusetts Institute of Technology.

Her heart speeded. The park—the trees, the green lawn, the boys, and the dog playing on the grass—everything blurred. She stared at the addresses, unable to even blink.

"Read it," Shawn suggested, holding them practically under her nose.

Lilah opened her mouth to speak, but the words she wanted didn't come to her. With shaking fingers, she reached for the covers. One from the office of admissions. The second one, from the office of financial aid.

"C'mon," Shawn begged. "I'm dying here. Don't keep me in suspense."

"You do it," she said, abruptly shoving the envelopes back at him. "I'm too scared."

"Scared?" he scoffed, pushing her hand away. "Not you."

Lilah bit her lip and muttered a plea at the universe. Gritting her teeth in preparation for the worst possible outcome, she tore open the covers and pulled out the letters.

Dear Delilah,

On behalf of the Admissions Committee, it is my pleasure to offer you...

A half sob exploded from Lilah. She glanced at the second letter.

"What?" asked Shawn. "You have *got* to tell me."

"I got in," Lilah said, her tone trembling. "Full scholarship."

"Yes!" Shawn let out a war whoop, startling the dog on the lawn. It howled in perfect harmony, prompting more laughter from its human companions.

Lilah held the letters to her face and part-laughed, part-sobbed into the sheets. "I got in. Oh, God. Thank you, thank you, thank you. I can't believe I got in."

"Believe it," Shawn said, his brown eyes crinkling in generous happiness.

Practically hyperventilating with joy, Lilah waved the letters about. "This is my ticket out of the house. My... my *declaration of independence.*"

Shawn sputtered.

"'That these united colonies are,'" Lilah paraphrased loftily. She stopped to glance at the letters. In her mind, the words morphed into the script font of the eighteenth-century document. "That this seventeen-year-old person is, and of right ought to be, a free and independent citizen, that she is absolved from all allegiance to the Barrons Crown—I mean, family—and that all political connection between her and the Barronses, is and ought to be totally dissolved; and that as a free and independent citizen, she has the full power to levy war, conclude peace, contract alliances, establish commerce, and to do all other acts and things which independent citizens may of right do."

With each word, Shawn's eyes became more and more rounded. At the end of her little speech, he clapped. "*Brava.*"

"Wow," said one of the boys who'd been playing on the grass. The Frisbee was tucked under his arm. His brother was crouched next to the bushes on the other side of the lawn, examining something on the ground. Belly up and tongue out, the dog was wriggling around on his back and panting. "Are you in a play or something?"

"Heh?" she asked.

Shawn burst out laughing.

"No," said Lilah. "I was... umm..."

"She just won a small lottery," Shawn said.

"Oh." Look of disinterest on his face, the boy called to his brother and their canine friend. The group soon wandered off.

"I did win the lottery. This..." Lilah held the papers—one in each hand—mere inches from Shawn's face. "God, I've been waiting so long. Dan *knew* I wouldn't want to wait a minute more. Thank you for bringing these to me. Thank you so much. You're the best big brother—"

With bemusement, Lilah realized Shawn really was a big brother to both her and Dan. Shawn befriended the same twins brought in by his father to replace him. According to Dan, Shawn served as a rock during the months Lilah was missing. He never got help from any quarter with his education, but here he was, as excited as Dan at Lilah's success.

She grinned. "Tell you what... Dan and I will be out of that house in a couple of months, but we're keeping you as our brother."

Five minutes later, Lilah charged into the lobby of the Flatiron Building, needing to talk to Harry that very second.

"Whoa," said the white-haired woman in a hot pink business suit, jumping out Lilah's way. "Slow down, young lady."

"Sorry," Lilah called over her shoulder, almost flying to the stairwell. She didn't want to wait for the elevator. She was so excited she'd jump up and down inside it and scare the other passengers.

Life had taken her through some dark detours the last few weeks, but she was finally where she wanted to be. Freedom was within reach. She might have needed to live with the Barronses for two years, but she managed to hold on to her sense of self-worth. Except for the loss of the wells, Harry and his family were perfectly fine. They would rebuild what they lost.

She was going to see him in a few minutes. She couldn't wait to tell him about the letters. He, too, would have lots to share with her, his plans for the years ahead. The future might not have come about exactly the way they envisioned it, but it was still theirs for the taking. They'd both get what they wanted.

The smell of coffee greeted Lilah a few feet before she got to the conference room in the Barrons offices. The hum of conversation got louder as she approached the door. With a great deal of effort, she muted her excitement and stood at the entrance, scanning the small crowd inside for Harry.

There he was, sitting at the far end of the table, only his profile visible from the door. His dark hair looked trimmed and brushed to a shine, and his face was now clean-shaven. The navy-blue business suit and power tie suited him well. There was a metallic brace of some kind extending from his left knee to the ankle, but otherwise, Harry seemed much the same as the boy from a few months ago.

Relief welled, joining the euphoria in her heart. *Look up,* she whispered in her mind. *Smile at me.*

His attention was focused on the person in the chair next to him. Someone else walked across the room, blocking her view. Lilah craned her neck, trying to see to whom Harry was talking.

Senator Temple... the politician looked up, turning to the door as though he'd become aware of her scrutiny. The same strange mix of bemusement and calculation she saw at the shrink's office flitted across Temple's face. He nodded.

Tossing him a fleeting smile, Lilah waited for Harry to turn around.

His shoulders stiffened, but he didn't glance back.

Lilah frowned. Didn't he see the senator look toward the door?

From the sideboard behind Temple where the coffee was percolating, Ryan Sheppard protested, "I don't understand what people mean by 'no proof.' If Sanders is bribing those dictators, isn't it proof enough for the U.S. government?"

"It's not straight up bribery, Father," Harry said, his voice as rich and deep as it had been when Lilah last heard it. "The direct—Mr. Temple's friend says it was probably the C130 aircraft."

Twisting to face Ryan, Temple said, "Our government refused to let Lockheed release the aircraft to Libya in spite of Gaddafi already having paid for it. National security concerns, etc. Those seven planes are still sitting in a field at the air force base in Georgia. Sanders has his fingers in many pies, including military contracts. I'm sure he promised to use his influence. It's not against the law. Ryan, all of us know how shrewd Sanders is. Believe me, he hasn't left *any* evidence."

Andrew was also by the coffee maker, grimacing into his mug before setting it back down.

On the far side of the conference table, Harry's mother and older brother were seated, silently listening to the conversation. Dante was on the opposite side, closer to the door, his back to it. He was a couple of chairs down from Harry. There were all in business suits.

Self-consciously, Lilah glanced down at her red floral midi with the brown suede belt and matching knee-high boots. Well... she didn't know she'd be at a business meeting.

She did another quick scan of the room. Not only Dan, Caroline seemed to be missing, too. Vaguely, Lilah wondered why. Andrew said they were going to discuss investments. Dan and Caroline enjoyed equal say on their parents' stock in Genesis. Or did Andrew assume his wife and the boy he wanted to adopt would simply fall in line with whatever he demanded? Not that it mattered any longer. Caroline never cared, and Lilah and Dan were finally free from the clutches of Andrew Barrons. The letters from MIT which were in her duffel bag said so.

"Why are you even bothering to meet him, Senator?" Ryan asked, tone angry.

Lilah started. Meeting who? Sanders? Whatever for?

"We have to see if we can get him to agree to a truce," Andrew said, drawing up a chair next to Temple.

The senator inclined his head. "Even if Sanders does agree to a truce, we cannot trust him, but we have to at least make an effort to satisfy the people in the government. Still, no matter what he says, Harry has to be careful."

Lilah's stomach cramped in sudden fear. She fought the urge to fly to Harry, to grab his fingers and run for cover. Shifting her duffel bag to the other hand, she wiped her sweaty palm on the dress.

Temple continued musing, "It won't be easy for Sanders to get away with crimes within the U.S. borders, but he won't be able to stand the idea Harry escaped. Also, Sanders is not going to want anyone else thinking they might also get away."

"He has a lot of supporters in the U.S. government, too," Andrew muttered. "I've tightened up security both at home and all the offices."

"*You* don't have anything to worry about," Temple said, shaking his head. "Sanders knows very well even his buddies in the government would have something to say if he tries to attack the Barrons family within our borders. But Ryan..." The senator flicked a glance toward Lilah before turning back to Andrew. "Sanders has already shown us he considers the Sheppards easy prey. Out of them, his focus is now on Harry."

"We lost all our money," agreed Ryan, sounding bitter. "No one's going to bother if Sanders goes after one of *my* children."

Biting down on a worried mewl, Lilah took a step into the room. There was surely some way of stopping Sand—

Hands on the table, Harry hauled himself to his feet. "Old man," he called. "Can you pass me my crutches?"

Dante bent down, retrieving the crutches from under the table.

"Thanks," said Harry, his eyes fixed on the windows at the far end even as he took the crutches from Dante's hand. Hobbling over to the windows, Harry stood staring at the gleaming towers of the World Trade Center.

Frowning again, Lilah contemplated his back. Didn't he know she was going to be at the meeting? If it were her, she'd be glancing at the door every two minutes.

"Here, let me help you," said Dante, materializing next to her. He took the duffel from her hands.

"Dante," she laughed mildly. "I'm all right."

"Humor me," he insisted, dragging a chair out.

She settled in, the duffel at her feet, and puzzled over the concern on Dante's face. After all, she hadn't broken anything, unlike Harry.

Through her lashes, Lilah peeped at Harry's tense form. No way did he miss hearing her talk to Dante. So why wasn't he stumbling around, grinning at her with his usual mischief? Why wasn't he tugging her into a hug, sending them both tumbling to the carpet, brace and crutches and all?

You'd better not be pranking me, Harry, she warned. Not after the radio silence of the last few months. And now, all this talk about more danger from Sanders. She was getting so jittery even the smallest joke from Harry was likely to set her off. She'd knock him to the ground and pummel him mercilessly in front of everyone.

"Lilah, dear," called someone. With a coffee mug in his hand, Ryan Sheppard walked to her and cleared his throat. "We were waiting for you."

She'd been waiting to see *them.* They might not have any money as Ryan said, but they were all alive and unharmed. Thank God. Somehow, they were going to get Sanders to stop. Even if the FBI claimed there was no proof, the senator was on their side, and he certainly possessed clout. The Sheppards might have lost the wells to Sanders, but Harry wouldn't give up on his dream of making Genesis a powerhouse company.

"I don't see any point in delaying telling you," Ryan muttered. "Andrew has promised to advance us a substantial amount of cash to restart our business."

It took a couple of seconds to sink in. Then, Lilah bit her lip to stop herself from blurting, "Say what?"

Occupying the chair vacated by Harry, Ryan continued, "We're going into brokerage and oil trading. Maybe retail, too. Someday. We already registered the name—Gateway, Incorporated. In fact, Harry has been helping Hector draw up the plans."

"He... umm... plans?" A splinter of hurt lodged itself in Lilah's heart. Harry felt well enough to talk business with all these people, but he didn't call her even once? Or write her one measly little letter?

Her brother-in-law was on the other side of the table, next to Senator Temple. "A lot of it will depend on you," boomed Andrew.

"On me?" she parroted. None of it was making any sense.

Bluntly, Andrew said, "The loan is contingent on the adoption."

Puzzled, Lilah asked, "Adopti—what do you—*Dan?*" What did he have to do with—

Andrew continued, "You already know Daniel won't agree to an adoption unless *you* do. As soon as you agree to it, I will give Ryan the cash he needs."

What? Her head swiveled between the two men. "Blackmail?" she asked, unable to believe what she was hearing.

"Bribery," Andrew corrected. "I'm a desperate man."

Lilah shook her head, feeling slightly dizzy. Surreal—that was the word she was looking for. Did Andrew just offer millions of dollars to the Sheppards so he could adopt her? So he could adopt *Dan.*

Andrew's face... there was no desperation there, only smug certainty. He was positive she would cave. He thought she was cornered, forced to choose between herself and the family she considered her own.

Fury. Every nerve ending bristled. "Dan wouldn't have let you do this. That's why you didn't ask him to this meeting."

Andrew huffed. "Your brother loves you, obviously. You haven't shown him the same affection. The adoption won't be good only for the Sheppards. As my son, Daniel's future will be different. You're smart enough to know it, so why are you standing in his way?"

"Lilah," Ryan interjected, fawning eagerness in his voice. "The entire family is counting on this going through."

"Stop being self-centered, Delilah," her brother-in-law chided. "The Sheppards are asking for your help. Besides, you and Daniel are already staying with us; we just need to formalize things."

Again, Lilah glanced between Ryan and Andrew. *Opportunist,* she mentally spat at her brother-in-law. But *he* was only taking the chance he saw. *You,* she snarled at Ryan Sheppard. *You were Papa's friend.* Until now, she'd imagined Harry's parents thought of her as one of their own. Couldn't the Sheppards find any way of supporting themselves other than selling her and Dan to Andrew Barrons?

She glared at Harry's back, willing him to turn around and look her in the eye. He was still determinedly studying the brand-new buildings of the World Trade Center. He didn't move an inch. He didn't utter a single sound. He wouldn't dare. He'd known exactly what was going on. He'd let them ambush her.

Pain ripped through her heart. There was a pressure behind her eyelids. *How could you?* she screamed silently. *You... you...* traitor.

Lilah turned back to the people at the table, eyeing them one by one.

Andrew never gave a damn about her except as a tool to get Dan for his son. He'd already tried waving his billions under her nose, imagining she'd be tempted on behalf of her brother. It didn't work the first time, and it wouldn't work now. Dan didn't care if he didn't get as much as a penny of the Barrons money.

Andrew didn't know about the scholarship letter. He hadn't yet realized Lilah and Dan could make it on their own. The old home in Brooklyn was still theirs. They could survive on part-time jobs until college started, and then, their expenses would be covered either by scholarships or the army. Nothing would happen to them if she threw the offer back in their brother-in-law's face. Andrew could either accept his biological son or die without an heir.

The Sheppards could take their problems and... Harry could... *Harry... oh, God. Sanders will...*

Next to Andrew, Senator Temple was silent, considering her with a steady look. *"Sanders has already shown us he considers the Sheppards easy prey,"* he'd said.

Bitterness coating his words, Ryan agreed, *"We lost all our money."*

A muffled roar echoed in Lilah's mind. She and Dan were all right, but the Sheppards had lost their livelihood. Without money, without influence, they'd be helpless to defend themselves. They were all in danger. *Harry* was in danger.

His mother and brother were anxiously watching from across the table. The youngest Sheppard wasn't around, ten-year-old Sabrina. The mischievous little tyke's favorite activities included taking apart electronics and bugging her brother when he was trying to romance Lilah.

Harry... her best friend and the boy she loved... together, they'd been to hell and back. When she was too scared to jump off the cliff, he said he'd be with her. Even in the safety of the

Bedouin camp, he refused to leave her alone. *He* needed her now. His family needed her. If she refused to help, she'd have the freedom she craved, but the Sheppards would lose Andrew's support. Maybe even the senator's support. Harry could die.

Her hand went to the duffel bag at her feet. Dragging it onto her lap, her fingers flexed over the zipper. The letters... the escape she'd been dreaming of for the last two years... her freedom... Harry's life... the survival of his family... the price of their safety was Lilah's capitulation, the sacrifice of her pride.

Her fingers curled into fists. Briefly, she closed her eyes, seeing the letters from MIT in her mind. The print on the sheets of paper morphed back into mundane words and numbers and not the proclamation of her liberation. Lilah set the duffel back on the floor. "All right," she heard herself say.

A collective sigh of relief went around the table.

"Good," said Senator Temple, immense satisfaction and a strange elation in the one word.

Harry still didn't turn around, but his shoulders slumped in obvious relief.

As a flurry of congratulations broke out, Senator Temple said, "It will work out well for all of you. Harry's taking my advice to skip college and enlist directly in the SEAL program. I'll make sure his paperwork moves fast. He has things to do."

What?

Ryan Sheppard beamed proudly at his son. "He's started back on his training."

Harry finally hobbled around to face them, nodding in the

senator's direction. The tip of one crutch slid on the carpet, and it fell with a muffled thud. Harry gripped the edge of the window to steady himself.

Paying no mind to any of it, Andrew started talking to the Sheppards and Dante, Senator Temple looking on. Papers were distributed. Boisterous laughter and exuberant conversation ricocheted around the conference hall.

Harry didn't move from his spot by the window. His eyes were on the fallen crutch. The rest of the group didn't seem to notice he was missing from the celebrations. No one talked to Lilah, either.

A familiar heaviness settled in her chest, the same frightening loneliness which enveloped her after her parents' deaths. *Papa,* she whispered. *I did what* you *would've done. I hope you and Mama are proud of me.* They would be. Papa gave over his life's savings to Ryan Sheppard, a virtual stranger at the time. Mama had loved Harry just as much as she loved her own children.

He was still there next to the window. His brother walked by, gulping soda, and casually smacked him on his shoulder before returning to the excited crowd at the table. Harry's gaze didn't waver from the crutch on the floor.

Look at me, Lilah demanded.

A muscle clenched near his jaw, and he finally raised his eyes to glance in her direction. The grief in his face pleaded guilty to every charge. Wordlessly, Harry begged for clemency.

The lighting in the hall threw the angles of his face into sharp relief. Hollows showed in his cheeks, shadows around his eyes. She saw the weeks of dread he endured, knowing he'd have to face her. She saw the dilemma he confronted... the hope she'd understand and the terror she wouldn't.

Lilah stood and took a couple of steps forward. Going down on her haunches, she picked up the crutch. A shadow fell across the carpet, making her crane her neck up. The senator. She used the crutch to haul herself upright.

"You made the right decision," Temple said, his tone jubilant. "The linchpin, holding together the Sheppards and the Barronses. We still need the Kingsleys—" He broke off with a small laugh, almost sounding surprised at himself.

Linchpin? What on earth was the man going on about? She didn't have time for this. She needed to talk to Harry.

Jabbing at the air with a finger, Temple said, "Your brother says you want to be a lawyer. Someday, I'm going to introduce you to my stepbrother. You might've heard of him."

Supreme Court Justice Godwin Kingsley? Of course, she'd heard. Any other time, Lilah would've grabbed the chance, but right now, she needed the politician to go away. She needed to get to Harry.

"The family is large," continued Temple. "Seven grandsons. They're all around your age. Fine young men. The Kingsleys have a tradition of the men going into the service, so all of them..."

He went on and on. Lilah was looking at the politician but not really seeing him. His mouth was moving, and she heard the words, but she didn't have a clue what they meant. She wanted him to shut up. "Okay," she said, not caring if her response were appropriate or not.

Temple's brows drew together. He turned slightly to one side and glanced from her to Harry. "Right. You want to talk to him." Temple melted away from her field of vision.

Without wasting another second, Lilah took two more steps toward the window and handed the crutch to Harry. He still didn't say a word and took the thing from her. His dark gaze was anxious, almost as though he were too afraid to hope.

"Did you think I wouldn't agree?" she asked.

His eyes widened. "No. I knew you would... but I hated having to ask you... I didn't want to put you in the position."

"You remember Khadeeja?" Lilah asked.

Puzzlement mixed in with misery on his face. "Saeed's cousin? Sure."

"She said something to me about priorities." The Bedouin girl knew she would be asked to marry Saeed to ensure the safety of their tribe. She didn't even consider declining. *I did,* Lilah remembered guiltily. Even if only for a few seconds, she'd been prepared to walk out on the Sheppards. When she was reminded of the danger they faced, she simply couldn't do it. She could never abandon Harry. "My ego, your survival," she said, holding her palms up and seesawing them as though they were scales. "Never ever put not wanting to hurt my feelings above your life, okay? I'll kill you myself if you do."

Relief and gratitude flickered across Harry's features, followed by the ghost of a smile.

"Also, no college?" she asked, narrowing her gaze.

"Yeah, I'm taking the GED—"

"Are you *crazy?"* she asked, poking at his chest with her finger. "You can't skip college. You're going to mess up your entire future."

Adjusting the crutches under his arms, he straightened. "Go somewhere with me? I'll tell you why."

#

The old-fashioned elevator with golden fittings in the lower half and dark metal grille forming its upper part resembled more a gilded cage than the hydraulic device it was. Hissing and grunting, it headed up, jostling Harry and Lilah and the other couple of passengers—a frail old man in a wheelchair and his gum-chewing nurse.

Harry rested his butt against the back wall and transferred the crutches to his right hand. The brown duffel slung on her shoulder, Lilah was between him and the other passengers. He couldn't look anyplace but her face. Except for the raspy voice, she was the same girl he'd always known, all vivid colors and sweet smells and sparkles in her eyes. His best friend. His beloved. She was here with him. This was not one of his hopeless dreams where she ran into his arms and refused to let go—but only until she heard of his betrayal and shoved him away.

Thoughts of her had kept him alive during the weeks he spent in the sickbay at the naval base. Harry remembered the pain. Overwhelming agony was in every bone, as though he were being crushed under an eighteen-wheeler. Sobbing like a child, he'd called for Lilah. In the long, dark gaps when narcotics reduced the physical pain to a distant echo, his mind wandered the path they traversed from Benghazi to Alexandria. The moment he opened his eyes to the whitewashed walls of the sickbay, he demanded to know what happened to Lilah. He even tried to get out of bed to go look for her. It took the staff fifteen long minutes to locate his father at a payphone.

Harry had counted days until he'd be transferred to New York. After Senator Temple visited, all Harry's family wanted was for him not to advise Lilah against the plan. He found himself almost grateful to them for having taken the decision out of his hands, damned glad he was forbidden to call Lilah. When Andrew finally announced his lawyers had the adoption documents ready for the twins' signatures, Harry's insides quaked in a terrifying mixture of dread and anticipation. With shaky fingers, he checked off the days on the calendar until the meeting.

He'd known she was there the moment she appeared at the conference room door. A shift in the air... the faint smell of her perfume... his heart changed tempo. When she spoke, Harry started. Her voice... it sounded dry and gravelly, not at all the sweet, light tones he was used to hearing. *The fire*, he realized.

When his father and Andrew bluntly told Lilah what they wanted, Harry tried to steel himself against her pain and anger. If she'd actually tossed him out of her life... instead, she looked like she was about to erupt into a lecture on his decision to skip college. If it weren't for the other passengers in the elevator—the old man in the wheelchair and his nurse—Lilah would've already started. With the hydraulic contraption, there was a chance it would be a good ten minutes before she could commence her nagging.

"This thing takes forever, so most people take the stairs." Harry glanced down at his brace. "I'm not supposed to yet."

"You've been here before?" Lilah asked, a tinge of hurt returning to her voice. Her grip tightened on the straps of the brown duffel slung over her shoulder.

"Only for the last week," he said quickly. "Andrew rents three floors in the building, and he's letting us use a couple of rooms to get the preliminary work done. We didn't want to rent a place of our own until—" Guiltily, Harry stopped.

"Until I agreed to the trade," she finished. "You were here all this time, and you couldn't call me even once? You couldn't have told me about—I mean, I might have been mad for a minute or two, but after that—"

"I'm sorry." His parents and older brother might have barred him from calling her, but if he'd wanted to... he *had* wanted to; he'd known she'd eventually agree and would even forgive him. Still... Harry grimaced. "I was hoping we'd find a solution before it got to this point."

"What solution?"

Airily, he said, "Oh, I don't know... maybe I could've gone to Vegas and tried my luck."

Lilah looked toward the roof with an exaggerated sigh as though begging for divine help in dealing with her exasperating boyfriend.

"Careful," Harry said. "If you roll your eyes that far, they're going to roll all the way into your brain."

The old man in the wheelchair cackled and pushed himself backward with his feet. His elbow brushed against Lilah's hip.

She whirled, swinging her duffel like a weapon. The bag was

already grazing the armrest of the wheelchair when she lurched back.

"Lilah," called Harry, reaching for her shoulder.

There was a startled squeak from the old man.

"Hey," snapped the nurse.

Before Harry's fingers made contact with her upper arm, Lilah stumbled against the back wall. "Sorry. Lost my balance."

Frowning heavily, the old man said, "Be more careful, young lady. And graceful. In my day..." His tone lowered to an incoherent mumble, he continued griping.

Harry curled his extended fingers into a fist and gritted his teeth. If he still needed a brace on his leg, *she* was still healing from the wound to her psyche. Each time he remembered it, he wanted to find the colonel and rip his limbs off. Someday, Harry would literally do it. He'd bulldoze the whole damned building. In Libya, escape dominated Lilah's thoughts. His, too. Afterward, he faked a story for the men who interviewed him, knowing only *she* had the right to go public about the assault. Lilah clearly never breathed a word about it to anyone, or there would have been some kind of official reprimand directed at Harry for the lies he fed the military. The Lilah he knew *would* eventually want justice. She wouldn't let the crime go unpunished. And Harry was there to make sure punishment happened.

Shuddering violently, the ancient box screeched to a halt. Harry's crutches made muffled thuds on the royal-blue carpet as they proceeded slowly to the room at the pointy end of the floor in the flatiron-shaped building. "Since I'm not very mobile right now, Dante has me doing a bunch of reports... shipping routes, port fees, and the like. The rest of them are always moving around, meeting Andrew and Mr. Temple and another investor who's interested... a William Luce from Connecticut. Anyway, I have a room to myself for all the paperwork." He grinned. "I had to use *this* room. Men's latrines are only on even-numbered floors, and since I couldn't use the stairs, I'd have to spend ten minutes in the elevator each time I needed to take a piss."

"Seriously?" Lilah asked. "What's wrong with Andrew? Making idiotic rules!"

"Heh?" Harry laughed. "No, it's not Andrew. It's the design of the building."

"Why?"

"No idea. Maybe the builders wanted the tenants to exercise."

Lilah groaned.

"Hey," he said, taking mock-offense. "It wasn't that bad."

"Was, too."

He'd say it again and again if it made her laugh. He was ready to make a complete fool of himself if it would take away the shadows behind her smile.

At the far end of the room were three sash windows looking out on the city—one at the point of the triangle and the two on either side angled inward. The Venetian blinds were up, letting bright sunlight in. Blue sky, puffy, white clouds, and the Empire State Building were perfectly framed by the middle window.

Low benches lined up against the wall below each window with folders arranged on top. The small desk was flush against the wall on the right, keeping the view unimpeded. The only chair was currently tucked as far under the desk as it would go. A file cabinet sat between the desk and door, and the jar of potpourri on top kept everything smelling flowery fresh.

"This is lovely," Lilah said.

"The corner office," Harry agreed grandly. "Let's sit."

The folders on the middle bench were deposited on top of the desk. Leaning the crutches against the edge of the table, Harry grabbed the jar of roasted cashews and limped back to the bench. Lilah was already there, pensively staring out, her elbow resting on the windowsill.

He collapsed onto the bench and opened the jar, setting it on the sill. When they were both chewing on the salted nuts, he pointed toward the Empire State Building. "Know what's in there?"

She flicked a glance at him but didn't say anything.

"Go on," he said, keeping his tone casual. "I'm sure you've looked it up."

"The New York office of Sanders, Incorporated," Lilah said. "Did you choose this room on purpose, Harry?"

"Even if I didn't, it's not like I could've avoided seeing it."

"Not when you live in this city," she agreed.

"Everyone's worried Sanders won't forget about me," Harry murmured.

"*You're* not?"

"No. I want Jared Sanders to *remember* me." Dusting the salt from the cashews on the seat of his pants, Harry added, "Because I'm never going to forget what happened to us—to *you*—because of him. None of it would've—"

"I don't want to discuss it," Lilah snapped, her voice jerky.

"No one seems to know where the sonuvabitch colonel—" Beads of sweat sprouted on her upper lip, her breathing rapid and shallow. Tamping down the insane fury striking him each time he remembered the colonel, Harry stopped. "Okay, we won't talk about it. I didn't mean to—"

"I *will* get over it." She nodded, her jittery gaze wandering over the buildings outside. "When I do, I'm going to hunt him down. I *will* get justice."

"You will," Harry swore, struggling to maintain an even tone. "In the meantime, there's—"

"There's Sanders," Lilah completed his thought. "He was quite willing to have us killed by the kidnappers. He bombed the border just to get us. He *is* morally responsible for all the things. Unfortunately, there's no evidence."

"We're not the first company he's destroyed. There have been people he's driven to suicide." The dossier brought by the CIA director had been thick. "Political blackmail, overthrowing governments, murders... his name pops up in a lot of different stories."

"Still, no proof," Lilah argued, her tone more composed. She shifted on the bench, turning to face Harry.

"Not yet," he acknowledged. "We need to find some fast. Habibti, I don't have the luxury of time. If I spend four years in college, it's four years Sanders is going to stay in power. I need to get into the SEAL program now. They have teams working in some of the countries Sanders has meddled in—"

Her eyelids flickered. "Priorities, Harry. You're telling me your future is less important to you than someone else's destruction. I don't like it. That's revenge, not justice."

Shaking his head, Harry said, "You don't understand. Someone needs to make him pay for all his crimes, not just for Genesis and what happened to you and me. He has to answer for everything he's done to all those victims. There are so many of them he might not remember their names."

"Ahh," Lilah said, nodding in unhappy comprehension. "You're going to make sure he remembers yours."

"Yours, too." Staring hard at the building, Harry said, "Neither of us is going to end up as one of his nameless victims. I'm not gonna lie to you. A big part of me wants to get back at him for what he did to us, but the ones who *are* nameless need us to speak for them, don't you think? Also, every day Sanders gets to walk around free is a day he has to claim more victims. Someone needs to put an end to his criminal enterprise *now*." At her prolonged silence, he quirked an eyebrow. "Nothing else to say?"

With a sigh, she took one of his hands in hers. "Do you remember the cliff we jumped off?"

"Into the sea? Of course."

"Rocks, the boats, the cops... we could've been killed."

"We *had* to, or—"

"Yes, we had to. We took control of the situation. *We* decided we'd rather go down fighting than let Gaddafi and Sanders take us. If you're telling me your decision will help you take control, I will believe it. You're not going to lie to me. I just want to make sure you're not lying to yourself."

"I swear I'm not," Harry said instantly. "I've been thinking about this." All the weeks he spent in the hospital bed had given him plenty of time to reflect on the situation. "If someone stopped Sanders before, we wouldn't have... he tried to kill us, but we escaped. Others might not be as lucky... others who don't have the access to resources *we* did. If we let Sanders continue, people are going to keep getting hurt. What if someone does die? Another Harry or another Lilah? *Our* indifference will have turned them into victims. I won't be able to live with myself if I let it happen. *You* won't be able to, either. We cannot let innocent blood be shed because of our apathy. Nor can we ask others to stand up for the common man if we're not willing to do so ourselves."

"True," she said. "But—"

"What's the point of simply knowing the truth if we don't show the courage to defend it? According to Aristotle, 'courage is the first of human qualities because it is the quality which guarantees the others.' How can it be real courage if we lose it the moment we are asked to sacrifice something? Truth without valor is useless, and valor without sacrifice is meaningless."

"You really have been thinking about this." For a few seconds, she fell silent, studying his face. Finally, she said, "All right, Harry. If you're a hundred percent certain your sacrifice is for the right reasons, I'll jump off the cliff with you. Because you're correct. Sanders does need to be stopped. One more victim is one too many."

Harry huffed out a breath. He so badly needed her to believe in him... he looked down at their linked hands, needing equally as badly to graze her knuckles with his mouth. Her reaction to the accidental touch in the elevator... the panic in her demeanor when reminded of the assault... she needed to come to him. Harry contented himself with a light squeeze to her fingers.

Together, they looked out the window... at the sheer drop of more than two hundred feet, the towering buildings of the concrete jungle, the crisscrossing grid of streets and avenues. Cars and buses and people swarmed the island. Shouts, honks, the rumble of trains... life went on in New York City.

"Your family was forced to give up the oil wells," Lilah said, tone flinty, "but Sanders didn't get you *or* me. Let him think his attack on us won the day, but the game is still on. We're going to play it through. We will stop him."

"Jared Sanders *will* be checkmated," agreed Harry, hard certainty in his mind. "Soon."

The Beginning

A Sneak Peek at *The Manhattan Swindle*, Book 2 of the One Hundred Years of War series

June 1974

Washington, DC

In the quiet wood-paneled room on the second floor of the Supreme Court Building, Senator Temple waited for his stepbrother, the judge, to arrive. Shelves lined the walls, books on law and the constitution arranged according to topic, but Temple's attention was on the leather-bound journal in his hands. So many things to jot down, incidents to record... there was an entire collection of such diaries in his library at home, all safely locked in a vault. The secrets contained in those pages were not for another set of eyes... at least not until the people involved were long dead and gone. Still, the tales needed to be recorded for posterity. Then there were those secrets he didn't dare write down, truths which could destroy entire families and alter the existing power structure.

There was a barely audible squeak behind. Someone was at the glass door to the judge's office, pushing it open. Without turning to check the person's identity, Temple tucked the journal inside his blazer and picked up the thick tome from the desk. Casually, he leafed through *Arthashastra,* the discourse on statecraft written centuries ago in India. The author paid gold coins to be granted custody of an impoverished boy and installed him on the throne of an empire. Rumor had it the mentor did the ruling from behind the throne. Temple inhaled the sweet, musky smell of the old pages and smiled on the thought he shared a few traits with the author.

Arrayed in black robes, Supreme Court Justice Godwin Kingsley strode to the desk and settled into his chair before uttering a crisp "good morning." Like the rest of the Kingsley men, he was tall. The silvery hair drawn back into a low ponytail should've brought comments in a supreme court justice. There was also the white beard, neatly trimmed. Such was his stature in the country's judicial system, no one ever dreamed of castigating him for the eccentricities. Not to mention the powerful position he occupied as president of Kingsley Corp, one of the foremost oil services businesses in the nation. Gray eyes steely, Godwin demanded, "Tell me more about Delilah."

"Lilah," Temple corrected. "Most people call her Lilah. You read the papers I sent over. All the info you need is in the folder. Wait until your grandsons meet her. They'll be fighting—more than they do now—for an introduction."

Blood flowed blue in the veins of the Kingsleys, but they weren't exactly known for their classy conduct or their kindness toward each other. Godwin's grandsons were only in their twenties, but they were already butting heads over eventual control of the family business. The young men were likely to tear each other to pieces over the stunning seventeen-year-old girl Temple would soon introduce to them. Their crude behavior was not going to endear them to Lilah. Plus, there was Harry, the boy she grew up with. Every piece on the chessboard needed to be moved into place. "Beauty's fine," Godwin stated, "but blood and background are more important."

"Which century are you living in?" Temple asked, not bothering to hide his amusement. "My mother came from common stock, and your father had no problem marrying her." Besides, the young lady under discussion might not be aristocracy, but her father was an ambassador. Her mother—an Indian woman—was a United Nations lawyer who met and married the widowed American diplomat in Bombay. Ambassador Sheppard had been retired for a few years by the time he and Lilah's mother died in a plane crash. "You know the Sheppards well, and Lilah's Indian cousins are all in respectable positions. Military officers, bankers, civil servants... professionals."

"Upper middle class," brooded Godwin. "The same as her father."

"Yes, but she was adopted by Andrew Barrons. Not too many men more pedigreed than him." The Barronses were not merely oil-rich; they could trace their ancestry back to the Normans who conquered England. Class hadn't mattered to Andrew when he married the ambassador's daughter with his first wife. In Andrew's rarefied position, anything out of the ordinary such as marrying a few rungs below would merely be thought of as an allowable indulgence. When Ambassador Sheppard and his second wife were killed, their then-fifteen-year-old twins—Lilah and Dan—were adopted by their half-sister and her husband. "Godwin, Lilah is now Delilah Sheppard Barrons. As Andrew's daughter, she *is* aristocracy."

Tugging open a drawer, Godwin brought out a thin folder and flipped it open. "She's also smart... and ambitious." He tossed the folder onto the table and rocked back in the chair, raising an appreciative eyebrow.

Lilah was headed to MIT in the fall for chemical engineering. Her sights were set on law school after undergrad. The senator nodded. "There you go—intelligence and drive along with the Barrons money and lineage."

Godwin appeared slightly mollified, but Temple didn't give a damn about the nobility of Lilah's blood. He'd picked the right person as the intended ruler of their corporate empire. She was the right choice to dethrone the current tyrant ruling the oil and gas business.

Temple's eyes went to the book on his lap, the ancient treatise on politics and governance. Godwin had finally located a copy in the original language and called Temple. This volume completed Temple's collection. It would occupy the empty spot in his library next to *The Art of War* and *The Prince*. There was another work, the meditations of an ancient philosopher-king. He once mused the rise and fall of past empires could foretell the future. Temple could not let the mistakes of those who went before be repeated. The new leaders would rule wisely and not let power corrupt them.

"The girl does present us with an extraordinary opportunity," Godwin murmured. Through her and one of his grandsons, the Kingsleys, the Barronses, and the Sheppards would once again be allied against a common enemy. They would defeat the criminal emperor of the energy sector. "Have you mentioned anything to her?"

"No," said Temple, immediately. "We have to give her some time before bringing it up. She needs a couple of years to mature a bit." The delay would give Lilah the break she needed to recover from the trauma of recent events. She would also get a chance to see the world beyond her youthful dreams, to understand what was at stake.

"Not just her." Godwin again tugged open a drawer and took out a small chessboard. "My grandsons, too. You, me... every piece has to be in its place."

Temple wasn't even slightly startled at Godwin echoing his own previous thoughts. When they met as stepbrothers, both were in their teens and bonded over chess. "Lilah likes to decide her own place," Temple mused.

"The arrogance of youth," Godwin said brusquely. "Look at my grandsons. I'm hoping four years in college will be enough to whip them into shape. Even then, we're going to have work to do."

The young men were all at the United States Military Academy in West Point as per family tradition. "Money and arrogance usually go hand in hand," Temple pointed out, laughing. "The army will take care of them. Lilah is... she's unique." She required a different approach. Then there was Harry.

Lilah's biological father—the deceased ambassador—and Harry's were business partners and shared the same last name. The blood connection between the families was extremely remote... an ancestor back in the sixteen-hundreds from what Temple heard. Despite the tenuousness of the link, the men were close, and their kids grew up together. That Harry and Lilah saw a future with each other was clear to anyone who cared to look. Not long after the deaths of Lilah's parents, Harry's family lost the business to the criminal who took over the oil sector, and they were chased out of Libya, where they'd lived for nearly two decades. The seventeen-year-old boy was targeted by the enemy as punishment for his father. Lilah suffered horribly merely for being at Harry's side when he was snatched by hired thugs. The way he and Lilah engineered their escape was nothing short of miraculous.

Two determined young people... it wouldn't be easy to persuade either into cooperating with Temple's plans, but it was the only way to defeat the enemy. The Sheppards wanted payback, but the man responsible for their torments was shrewd, his power and cunning helping him stay beyond the reach of the law. Temple swore he would see justice done. So did the Kingsleys and the Barronses, who finally put greed and old grudges aside, acknowledging the plain fact they wouldn't be too far behind on the criminal's list. Individually, all three clans were sure to lose, but together, they could win the war.

Soon, Harry and Lilah would be told an alliance brought about through Delilah Sheppard Barrons and one of the Kingsley grandsons was needed to take on their common adversary. With the survival of the companies at stake, Lilah's feelings or Harry's couldn't matter.

Godwin pushed the chessboard to the middle of the desk. "Game?"

Temple nodded to himself. It wouldn't be easy, but he knew exactly what moves to make. Oh, yes. Both Harry and Lilah would comply with Temple's instructions. They would help him usher in a new beginning for the world, a new life, a new empire.

Want to know what happens next to Harry and Lilah? Order *The Manhattan Swindle* today to continue with this exciting tale!

Afterword

Dear Reader,

Thank you for staying with the story thus far, and I hope it interested you enough to continue with Harry and Lilah as they stumble through the dark secrets in their families. There are many, many secrets... tales of illicit romances, of vicious enmities, of brutal revenge. Political conspiracies extend across the planet... from the Americas and Europe to the Middle East, to India and China.

I'd like to take credit for the complicated plot which will follow, but it's not entirely my doing. The world of our ancestors is rich with tales of such heroism that the men and women in the stories came to be called gods. You'll be familiar with *Iliad, Odyssey,* and the Arthurian legends. There are stories from Asia... the Indian epic poem called the *Mahabharata* being one. The Monkey King from China captivates readers even today. Central and South American mythologies rival Greek counterparts in dizzying the reader with complicated love affairs, crossbred monsters, and supernatural beings.

I believe most of these stories have a kernel of truth to them. Perhaps there was a shepherd-prince who rescued a woman from a marriage she didn't want, and their romance needed to be explained away as the work of an insulted goddess. Perhaps the outraged husband was merely an excuse for rivaling clans to go to war. Perhaps there were gods/mightier kings who kept the lesser mortals fighting and thus too busy to challenge them. Perhaps the common people who were losing life and limb in the war needed to be given a noble reason so they'd continue to fight. Perhaps plagues were explained away as a curse brought on them by the hated enemy. Or perhaps the poet simply wanted to add color to his creation, mistakenly believing his audience would understand literary devices.

These tales were taken to distant lands in oral form. Bards sang of wondrous deeds, of beautiful enchantresses, of magic. Battle scenes were described with great relish. Listeners wept over tragic heroes, applauded the downfall of adulterous wives.

Over centuries, metaphors and similes came to be thought of as literal facts. Ancient man's attempt to understand evolution was interpreted as creation in a seven-day period. Tribes which lived off trees—perhaps built houses in them—were reimagined as actual monkeys. Also, when culture changed, the myths transformed to fit the norms of the society. The status of women in ancient India went from having an empress who ruled over the subcontinent to being told they were always to be under the command of a male relative. The heroines of the stories morphed into meek and devoted wives, illicit liaisons explained away as demons taking forms of legal husbands and tricking the ladies. Even the food habits weren't spared. Perhaps some ancient physician's worry about unsanitary meat led to the idea that pork was forbidden by God.

I would love to know exactly what happened in the stories which fascinate me. This cannot mean the layers which formed around the core aren't important. Like tree rings, each of these layers represents the changes undergone by society. These are records of humanity's evolution into its current form. Plus, there is literary value in the versions thus created.

Unfortunately, without knowing the central story, it is difficult to understand the changes wrought by time.

This brings me to what I was trying to say in this afterword: wading through one such tale with many versions, I realized I would never be able to get even a vague idea of what might have happened unless I knew something of the political and emotional landscape in which the characters lived. Obsessive research followed. It took me six years or so to gather enough information to reconstruct the plot, and I knew by then I wanted to put it in book form. Unfortunately, my findings weren't sufficient to write a decent story. I didn't—and still don't—know what the world was really like. If I time-traveled to the Iron Age and took in a deep breath, how would it smell? I'm aware hunting for game was a common sport, but what did old deer meat taste like? You get the gist.

Yet something inside compelled me to share with the universe what I found. Shorn of the fantasy element, some of these characters are astounding examples of what mankind could be if it so chose, and I wanted to tell their stories. Well... I had the plot, and human emotions haven't changed at all since the myths were created. Love, hate, envy, greed, grief... these things inform our actions. What I could do was translocate the saga I was working on to a world I did know. From this compulsion was born One Hundred Years of War.

So that's it. I hope I managed to tell an entertaining tale with *The Maltese Attack*. You've already met Harry, the boy who would become God, and Lilah, the embodiment of knowledge. Temple is the chronicler of their story. I'm excited to introduce you to the Kingsley grandsons in *The Manhattan Swindle,* especially Alex... soldier, prince, the best of men.

Some points with reference to *The Maltese Attack:*

Desflurane is an inhaled anesthetic which acts fast. This is what the kidnappers used on Harry.

Mandrake berries smell like fresh tobacco. Its root can act both as narcotic and as hallucinogen. This is what was mixed in the milk offered to Harry and Lilah.

A tribe named Obeidat does exist, but the particular clan mentioned in the book is strictly fictional. Obeidat characters in this story have nothing to do with the actual tribe or its members.

If I may throw a challenge to the reader... let me know if you can tell which mythology this series is based on.

Sincerely,

Jay Perin

P.S. Special thanks to the critique partners and beta readers as well as friends and family without whose help this book would never have happened.

P.P.S. If you liked the story, do tell others about it. Also, writers thrive on reviews. They help us figure out what worked and what fell flat. They help other readers make up their minds. Please do leave a comment on any of the sites.

Visit www.EastRiverBooks.com for a bunch of interesting stuff.

CPSIA information can be obtained
at www.ICGtesting.com
Printed in the USA
LVHW091507230122
709158LV00016B/87

9 781736 468012